WHAT PEOPLE ARE SAYING ABOUT

SAXON

There are several levels to crime thriller reading that resonate with the reader. One that is often overlooked is the companionship, or the bond that develops between the author and the reader as the narrative unfolds. The intercourse between the two is ever new, exciting and immediate as the reader embarks on the literary journey. The reader knows that the author has sacrificed lifestyle gratifications that immediately surround him so that he might commune with distant and unknown minds through his words. The extremely multi-talented Stuart Davies in his debut novel *Saxon* is one such author. He has begun a formidable legacy for his primary character Paul Saxon that absolutely enthralls. With an impressive and enviable mastery of detail the gory bits are dark, chilling and psychologically thrilling. He straddles the line between the police procedural and the killer's twisted mind-set expertly. While reading it, the tempo was rapid but I wanted to slow it down, I wanted to make it last longer, to envelop fully the experience of discovering the brilliant mind of the author. In short *Saxon* is genius. From the start you know where the author/reader relationship is taking you and when the climax arrives – it does not disappoint – you will reap the rewards. So read it and reap.

Tom Reilly, author of, *Cromwell at Drogheda. Cromwell – An Honourable Enemy: The Untold Story of the Cromwellian Invasion of Ireland. Hollow Be Thy Name. Life of Reilly. Joe Stanley – Printer to the Rising, Tracing Drogheda's Medieval Walls, The Story of Drogheda, Drogheda United – The Story So Far* and *Cromwell Was Framed (Ireland 1649)*

A gripping and atmospheric crime novel that won't leave your finger-nails intact.

Nigel Farndale, bestselling author of *The Blasphemer*

Commander Paul Saxon, leader of a specialist serial killer detection squad, is called upon to investigate an ever-growing number of seemingly random killings which might, or might not, be the work of a single perpetrator. With emotional troubles of his own, Saxon could be forgiven for losing his grip on the gruesome twists and turns he encounters, but his love of the job and the support of his assistant, Detective Sergeant Parker, sees him through to a satisfying finale. This book has a cinematic quality, the camera shifting from one vivid scene to another as the story unfolds. Add to this a strong plot and a broad cast of characters, and you have a suspenseful page-turner with more than a touch of class.
Carolyn Mathews, author of *Transforming Pandora and Squaring Circles*

Commander Paul Saxon – A new name in crime detection hits the blood stained murder scene, running. The new author Stuart Davies has created a multi-facetted, out of the box thinking detective who is driven by a boyhood personal tragedy to become an officer of the law.

Inventive murders punctuate the narrative which is slickly written with a nice balance of slick storyline movement and attention to detail. The writer's sense of humour adds an extra layer, often lacking in modern crime novels. The sub-title hints at a series and I for one will be pleased to see the return of *Saxon*. Recommended reading.
John McGinn, author of *Unusually Hot* and *Chilli Birds*

"Understanding the victim is …crucial if we are to understand the perpetrator." These are the words of Stuart Davies' chief investigator, Saxon in 'Book one of the Saxon Chronicles.' As to be expected from a painter, the scenes of his story are cleverly crafted; his strokes serving to both cast the shadows of the dark tale and highlight it with moments of sardonic humour. His eye for detail is evident throughout the unfolding canvas. Its pace is designed to reveal just enough to keep you watching in wait for the next plot twist in this curious sequence of mysterious murders.
Helen Noble, author of *Tears of a Phoenix*

SAXON

Book 1 of the Saxon Chronicles

SAXON

Book 1 of the Saxon Chronicles

Stuart Davies

Winchester, UK
Washington, USA

First published by Roundfire Books, 2014
Roundfire Books is an imprint of John Hunt Publishing Ltd., Laurel House, Station Approach, Alresford, Hants, SO24 9JH, UK
office1@jhpbooks.net
www.johnhuntpublishing.com
www.roundfire-books.com

For distributor details and how to order please visit the 'Ordering' section on our website.

ISBN: 978 1 78279 688 6

A CIP catalogue record for this book is available from the British Library.

Printed and bound by CPI Group (UK) Ltd, Croydon, CR0 4YY

Dedicated to the people who investigate
and catch serial killers

Enjoy

Chapter 1

Sunday, May 5, 2002, The Green Dragon Pub, Sewel Mill, 11.45PM

Christopher Janson sat on a bar stool, sipping a gin and tonic and chatting to Ralph, the landlord of the Green Dragon pub. Ralph, although well-trained in being pleasant to his customers, found Janson to be easy company – perhaps a bit over pleasant and agreeable, but overall, at least not a complainer like some of his regulars. Always well turned out – never scruffy, Janson was sixty-three years old; he had a full head of snow-white hair, which was always kept swept back, with just a hint of gel to keep it under control. A single man, he had gone for early retirement ten years ago, but had lived in the same village for most of his life. Everyone knew him and generally viewed him as harmless and pleasant.

Janson downed the last drops of his third drink of the evening. He never had more than three – walking was a slight problem after three. To have four would be just plain silly. Last orders had been called long ago but that was just a formality in the Green Dragon, the passing trade drinkers would leave promptly. However, the locals stayed on well into the night or until Ralph made it plainly obvious that he would like to get some sleep before they all came back the next day for more alcohol.

Janson heaved himself off the stool and slowly made his way to the door. He waved in the general direction of the drinkers and a few of them muttered 'goodnight,' then he set off down the High Street towards home. He always thought that he lived in the right spot in the village. Uphill to the pub, and downhill home. Downhill is good when you have been drinking.

His cottage was only a few hundred yards from the pub and, as usual, he lit a small cigar and looked up through the clear country air in awe at the millions of stars that peppered the sky.

As he reached his gate, he finished his cigar and dropped it down a drain. The key and the lock had a bit of a problem finding each other, but after a minor struggle they were forced to function as intended. He walked through the hallway into the kitchen and picked up the kettle to make himself a cup of hot chocolate. As he reached for the tap, a shudder ran down his back and the hair on the back of his neck prickled. He hadn't seen or heard a thing. For that split second, he knew he was not alone in his cottage. The instinctive feeling of danger from our primeval past flooded through him. Quickly, he turned and caught a glimpse of a figure as it moved towards him – tall and covered in what appeared to be rough pale-coloured skin. He dropped the kettle in the sink as the figure grabbed his head and twisted it firmly to his left. Janson dropped like a stone to the floor and was dead before his knees buckled.

Fifteen minutes later, Christopher Janson was tucked up in bed, his clothes neatly piled up on a chair. Within ten minutes, the man's work was almost done. Just a spot of tidying up to do, maybe a quick rub with a duster on the doorknobs. Dry fingerprints could be so stubborn – not that there would be any, but just to be sure he wiped them anyway. He was pleased; the whole process was simpler when there was no blood – less work to do. He allowed himself a slight smile as he surveyed the results of his efforts. Everything, as usual, was going to be perfect. It always was. God, he was good. Even the weather was on his side, although he could hardly take total credit for that. Although he had willed it to be so. The forecast had been for an overcast day ahead, with a slight breeze and the possibility of light rain later. This suited his plans perfectly, and later it would help in the final disposal of evidence.

He brought himself firmly back to the present, *mustn't lose concentration*. He left the bedroom, and as he walked along the narrow corridor that led to the stairs, he straightened the pictures that had been dislodged as he brushed past them whilst carrying the body up from the sitting room.

A glance at the clock at the foot of the stairs confirmed he was on schedule. He had of course allowed time for a final check. To do it properly you must eliminate the need to rush. Retracing exactly all of his movements around the cottage, he carefully studied everything he had come into contact with, checking and double-checking that all was in order.

He knew very well, that it is impossible to enter a room without leaving forensic evidence. Or it was until now. He knew that no trace of his presence would remain in the cottage.

He had weighed the risks. In his line of work he had to be precise to the point of obsession, so this kind of thoroughness was not only a part of his character, it was also in some ways an extension of his professional life. By nature, he was a fastidious person. It came easily to him.

Satisfied that nothing in the cottage showed any signs of having been disturbed, he allowed himself to relax a little. There had been no struggle, no dramatic fight; everything had gone smoothly, exactly as he had expected and as it had done on the other occasions. The old man probably was not even aware that anyone was in the house. Death had come quickly to him and there had probably been no pain.

The victim was intended to die, not to suffer, that was not part of the exercise. No weapon had been used. In fact, there was nothing to trace back to anyone, or anywhere.

It was a satisfying thought. Later, when the police were poring over every square inch of the cottage, as they undoubtedly would; there would be nothing else to cause suspicion either, apart from the dead body, tucked up in bed, of course. He looked down. No shoe prints. You needed shoes for that. No footprints, because there were no feet – nothing that would be recognized as feet anyway.

He imagined their confusion and their frustration.

Quietly, he opened the front door. He could not feel the chill of the night on his face.

Monday, May 6, Marylebone High Street, London, 1.15AM

Far away from Sussex, the inhabitants of Brentwood Mansions were all asleep, apart from Emma Saxon, who was sitting up in bed wondering whether or not to phone home.

She guessed her husband would be asleep by now but she also knew he wouldn't mind at all if she phoned and woke him. However, even if she called him and woke him, what would she say? He may not even be at home. When they were together, he often didn't come home. Work always seemed to take priority. His work was so important.

Monday, May 6, Angel Cottage, Sewel Mill, 1.20AM

A quick glance up and down the street to ensure no one was early-morning dog walking, or out and about for some other reason, and the killer slipped out from the cottage into the shelter of the hedge. Looking back, he checked that there were no lights on to cause suspicion. Nothing was out of the ordinary. He allowed himself a moment's irritation at the pretty "Angel Cottage" sign, with its flowers and its pastel colours, but the irritation passed. It was no longer relevant.

Though, perhaps it was now more relevant than it had ever been, if the occupant was no longer in the land of the living.

The sheer brilliance of his approach still thrilled him, but he was never complacent, never careless. It was half a mile across a field to his car and the walk was tedious, necessarily so. He maintained a constant watch on his surroundings, carefully ensuring that he only walked on solid ground – not that it would matter too much if he accidentally left one or two footprints. Soon, those feet would cease to exist anyway. His car, when he reached it, was small, boring, and grey, and he had taken pains to park it where there would be no tyre marks.

There were several reasons why there was very little chance that a policeman would have seen it or noted the number-plate. He ticked them off in his mind.

First, it was near other cars of the same ilk: not that old but definitely not new, certainly nothing flashy.

Secondly, the area was almost devoid of street lighting, so a smallish, slightly shabby grey car just blended into the shadows.

Thirdly, and perhaps most significantly, there were no police to take notice of who parked what car where. They had all been rounded up from the rural areas, and let loose to play cops and robbers in the towns and cities.

While he deplored the principle, he was aware that the lack of rural policing suited him just fine. It meant there was less chance of interference by some local bobby. He had his priorities. He did occasionally wonder, briefly, if he were mad, or maybe in the process of going mad. Nevertheless, if he were, surely the possibility of his own madness would not occur to him, would it? *The fact that I even ask myself the question is evidence enough that I am far from mad.* It was not a question that lingered in his thoughts for long.

No, on the contrary, what he was doing qualified as both eminently sane and essential. The situation in the country was out of hand. The future was looking increasingly tainted. However, nobody else seemed to have noticed, let alone cared. Every day circumstances reconfirmed his feeling that people were too stupid or too frightened to understand what was going on right in front of them. In the press, on TV, it was everywhere.

But he knew. Thank God. And he had to show the way ahead, albeit without revealing his identity, because he did not intend to be a martyr for the cause. In addition, he knew no good purpose would be served by his identity becoming public knowledge. Not yet, anyway. No, he knew where his best interests lay.

Being in touch with reality was surely another clear sign of a sane mind!

He crossed the field next to the lane where he had left his vehicle, and was about to climb over a five-bar gate when he heard the sound of a car approaching. Quickly he crouched down behind the hedge, expecting it to pass by. It didn't – the driver brought it to a rapid halt. The killer remained still, and to his dismay, through the hedge he clearly saw a blue light. The police. *Why are the police stopping near my car?* He heard their car door open and close, followed by the sound of footsteps on the tarmac. Quickly, the footsteps came closer until the driver was standing the other side of the hedge. Then silence for a few seconds, which was broken by the unmistakable sound of a zipper being unfastened. The killer knew that he could kill the man in a second, but there would surely be two of them. He closed his eyes and endured the warm stream of urine as it splattered through the hawthorn hedge and onto his face. When the police car had disappeared from sight, the killer climbed into his car. It started first time.

Monday, May 6, Brookhouse Bottom Woods, Near Sewel Mill, 2.00AM

He had driven five miles into the dark countryside before turning down a lonely single-track lane. Stopping the engine and turning off the lights, he left his car. He took with him a pint-sized plastic bottle, containing surgical spirit, a carrier bag and a garden trowel.

Although he was confident that he would meet nobody, he used only the small light on his key ring to show the way in the darkness. After a while, even that was not necessary as his eyes became more accustomed to the moonlight. He walked some three hundred yards or so into the woods, crouched down, and dug a small hole. He heard a noise off to his left and froze for a moment. The source of the sound scurried away into the undergrowth. Probably just a fox.

Straightening himself, he worked his fingers into the skin around his eyes. The pain of peeling off his temporary outer skin was very short-lived and he hardly noticed it. Any discomfort – and that's really all it could be described as – was quickly overwhelmed by the warm satisfaction flooding every cell of his body as a result of the night's work. His movements were quick and efficient.

Practice makes perfect. He was panting slightly from the effort.

His tightly cropped hair made it easier to peel the skin away from his head. He kept it short for that purpose. The latex solution he had used on his head was more diluted, in a further effort to make it less painful to remove. In spite of this apparent kindness to himself, he was confident that the latex was still firm enough to keep what little hair he had securely anchored to his head, and to glue down every flake of skin and dandruff. He wasn't taking any chances.

He removed the rest of the latex sheath rather like a snake shedding its skin, and it came off almost in one piece. The feet he had moulded for himself came off last. If a footprint were found – though highly unlikely, it would never be matched to any shoe on the planet.

Using the spirit, he set alight to the latex and dropped it into the hole. The little burst of heat it afforded was welcome while he put on his jeans and a sweatshirt.

When the fire finally died away, he covered the remains with the earth he had dug up and scattered the area with twigs, grass and leaves. Even in the relative darkness he was sure it was as though no one had ever been there. At least, not recently. As he walked back to the car and opened the door, it started to rain. 'Great,' he said to himself as he drove away.

Chapter 2

Monday, May 6, Rue Boissy d'Anglas, Paris, 5.00AM

One hour ahead of the UK, Fabio Gerard stirred as the alarm sounded. Now he was sorry, as he'd known all along he would be, for the extra hour across the road at the Buddha Bar the night before. He forced himself out of bed.

Fabio did an hour every morning in the gym and then thirty minutes in the pool. He was very motivated. His thirty-fifth birthday was coming up next month. Fabio was anticipating a chorus of 'No, you can't possibly be!' and 'Oh, I would never have guessed!' from the guests at the surprise party Kris would no doubt be throwing for him over in London. He was going to be gorgeous. Failure was not an option.

By 7.00AM, in this city of late risers, he was ready for his breakfast and the early-morning news. Fabio liked to get a good start on the day.

Monday, May 6, 29 St Nicholas Lane, Sewel Mill, 8.55AM

Nothing much happened in Sewel Mill, not on the surface anyway. It was the quintessential English village, perhaps slightly prettier than most. With its picturesque streets and very long history, Sewel Mill enjoyed quite a good tourist business, so people went to some trouble with their hanging baskets and window boxes. There was unspoken – but very strong – peer pressure to ensure that even the folk without particularly green fingers didn't let the side down.

As you would expect with these bastions of rural tradition, village life could be relied on. The summer would guarantee a fete, including the usual flower show, and maybe a cricket match every weekend. Autumn and spring would be occasions for jumble sales in the village hall. Bonfire Night in particular was an occasion not to be missed in Sewel Mill. And all year round there would be a host of activities organised by the WI for the non-working wives, retired ladies and, occasionally, any surviving husbands, unless the latter could get out of it somehow.

People went about their business and were pleasant to each other in an English sort of way. Outwardly, at least, they kept themselves to themselves. But not much happened in the neighbourhood without it being noticed by someone or other, who in turn felt duty bound to pass it on to another someone. Inferences were made and characters defined, based on the slightest information. Memories were long; grudges were nursed – embellished even – for decades. If you lived there for at least forty years and you were liked, you might begin to be accepted as a local. Maybe.

One of the oldest residents of Sewel Mill, Mrs Edie Hayward, was just stepping out of her little house. She was one of those locals who did the accepting. Or not, as the case may be. One of her favourite tactics was to be deceptively helpful. If Mrs Hayward judged a new arrival to have acceptance potential, she would offer her services as a cleaner.

She could turn her hand to bit of light vacuuming and a quick whip round with a duster. Not because she needed the money, you understand. What better way to know what was going on in the village than to wander freely around people's homes – and be paid for your trouble?

Mrs Hayward was no fool. She never had been. She had decided as a young girl that if she wanted to lead a comfortable life, she needed to be a reasonably large fish in a relatively small village pond.

Edie Coomber married Cecil Hayward a week after her eighteenth birthday, when he was twenty-one. He had found her girlish charm and naivety irresistible, just as she had intended he should. He couldn't wait to look after her. Even when she had chosen the date, rehearsed him in what he had to say to her father, and made all the other decisions, he just put this down to romantic enthusiasm.

Just as a politician might salivate over a safe seat, Edie was certain that Cecil would deliver the goods. She was confident from the outset that he would be a success as a small local businessman. And she had been proved right. He had done well.

Another factor in her decision-making, when selecting a mate, was that she felt secure in the knowledge that she would never lose him to another woman, and that he would be around to provide for her forever. In the charisma queue of life, Cecil had been way back with the stragglers. Edie had no problem with that. It wasn't on her list of criteria and she could live without charisma. Who needed it? Whereas a steady income and an obedient spouse were right up there at numbers one and two.

Mr Hayward was already pottering about in his shed as his wife left the house. He had relinquished the trousers quite soon after their wedding nuptials. Actually, the wedding cake was still crumbling moistly on a plate at the wedding feast when the realisation hit him that some battles are best not fought. Cecil knew that even if he had thought he might win from time to time, victory might come at too great a cost. Why not just go with the flow?

When he had worked, he put in long hours, mainly for a bit of peace and quiet. Then, when retirement finally ambushed him, he spent most of his time either in the garden or tinkering away at one of his many hobbies. Preferably in the shed, and well out of range. He knew she never went into the shed – there he could do just as he pleased.

Mrs Hayward had a very busy day ahead. First in her diary were a couple of hours shampooing Christopher Janson's sitting-room carpet. Janson was another of the elder mafia of Sewel Mill and the two usually found time to exchange a little news over a cup of coffee during the course of the morning. Mrs Hayward was looking forward to it.

Then she was due at the WI for lunch and had promised Babs

Jenner a couple of hours ironing at 3.00PM or thereabouts.

She looked up at the sky. It was going to be a fine day. The walk to Janson's cottage from her house lasted less than ten minutes, but it was like a journey back in time through a medieval village. The main street had barely changed in the last five hundred years and some properties were even older than that. Film production companies occasionally used it. All they had to do to create a bygone era was to paint over the yellow lines and spread a little straw and horse muck on the road and – cue the action.

Monday, May 6, Kemp Town, Brighton, 8.55AM

Steve Tucker turned over in bed. He farted. He looked at the clock through narrowed eyes. With flexitime, he could afford another five minutes and still be on time for work, provided he put off his shower for another day. No contest.

Monday, May 6, Angel Cottage, Sewel Mill, 9.00AM

No cameras and lights today. Some of the pavements were brick and it had rained a bit the night before, making them very slippery, so Mrs Hayward had taken her time, treading carefully. The stories she had heard (and often repeated herself) of people of her age falling and fracturing a hip, and never leaving hospital again – except in a wooden box – made her cautious. The church clock struck nine as Mrs Hayward knocked on Janson's front door. No response. She waited. She knocked again, harder. Maybe he was in the bath or still asleep, but that would be out of character. He was always up and about early, always ready when she arrived. She decided to try the back door. It too was locked.

'Christopher, it's Edie,' she called up to his bedroom window. Mrs Hayward was not a patient woman; she had things to do. If Janson were still in bed, it would be the first time. But she would work around him unless he sent her away. She knew that the spare key was in the lean-to shed at the side of the cottage.

Within a minute of finding it, she was filling a bucket with steaming hot water in the kitchen sink. She read the instructions on the plastic bottle of carpet cleaner, just to make sure nothing had changed from the last time she used it. Satisfied that it hadn't, she turned the water to cold. Mustn't have it too hot.

Monday, May 6, 47 Chudleigh Drive, Cheltenham, 8.55AM

Anna Janson thought of her husband. Today was their wedding anniversary, but the thought no longer made her weep. They had been married forty years ago, but it hadn't taken her long to realise that he was, as she subsequently put it to a close friend, 'Flying with a different squadron.'

'The signs had always been there, Emily,' she had sighed, over thirty years ago, as the two of them put Anna's belongings into packing cases at Angel Cottage, 'but I suppose I ignored them.'

Emily had nodded sympathetically. 'Well, he might've grown out of it, you know. Some chaps do,' she had offered.

'That's what I thought,' Anna had said, with relief.

But she had been wrong to think that, as had Emily, because he never did grow out of it. The marriage eventually ended after eight years with relief on both sides.

Anna had moved up to Cheltenham, to be near her sister, glad to be out of the village where everyone had known of the circumstances of her sad little divorce. While they were kind to her, she certainly didn't need to be reminded daily of the failed marriage. And she couldn't quite escape the feeling that there were those in the village who thought she hadn't come up to scratch as a wife, and that it was at least in part her fault that Janson was the way he was.

She didn't miss Sewel Mill at all.

Monday, May 6, Angel Cottage, Sewel Mill, 9.10AM

Mrs Hayward was aware of Janson's marriage in the dim and distant past. These days most people in Sewel Mill either didn't notice anything odd about Janson's behaviour or didn't care. His walk had a very slight mince, and the male-to-male eye contact lingered just that bit too long for the comfort of some of his acquaintances. None of this mattered a jot to Mrs Hayward – she liked him. He was undemanding and easy to look after. In addition, she thoroughly enjoyed their little chats. Some might have called it gossip but she and Janson never thought of it that way.

While the bucket filled, she put her head out into the hall. Still no sound of life. She stopped by the mirror and glanced at her reflection. Being less than five feet tall, she had to stand on tiptoe to get a quick look at her head and shoulders. Her blue rinse and snug perm were old-fashioned in these days of highlights and natural cuts, but they suited her idea of a respectable appearance. She nodded at herself and then listened again for the man of the house.

'Christopher, are you there?' she stage-whispered up the stairs. She herself, hated being woken up too quickly and she extended that consideration to other people. She thought that maybe he would appreciate a gentle rousing from sleep, rather than a sudden shocking awakening. The silence was intense and she began to feel the first shivers of concern. He had specifically said he wouldn't go out until she got there so that they could talk about the carpet, and so that he could give her a hand moving the armchairs. A long-case clock at the bottom of the stairs next to her chimed nine-fifteen and her heart nearly stopped.

'Bloody, sodding thing,' Mrs Hayward muttered to herself with an inward breath, her nerves allowing her to use vocabulary she would never normally give voice to. With her hand on her chest to coax her heart back to something like its normal rate, she stood for a few moments.

Telling herself to be sensible, she began to climb the stairs, checking for dust on the banister as she went. She took her responsibilities as a cleaner seriously. This was in spite of the fact that she didn't regard herself as a professional cleaner, not as such. She would never, in a million years, have contemplated signing up with one of these cleaning agencies, like Happy House or Mrs Mop, who went in every week, carrying their vacuum cleaners with them.

She was halfway up the stairs by now and she paused.

'Christopher? Are you all right? It's gone nine, you know,' she said. It was as much to quell her nerves as to get an answer. Total silence enveloped the cottage; she had never experienced this before. Always there had been bustle and noise: maybe a radio or the television, the sound of the toaster popping, or even just the pages of a newspaper being turned. This heavy, intense silence was new and uncomfortable.

At the top of the stairs she turned left along the picture-lined corridor. She no longer noticed the paintings. But the gilt-framed awards he displayed there always impressed her. Janson had been an art director in the magazine industry for most of his working life.

Mrs Hayward knocked on his bedroom door. No reply. She went in and saw Janson was still tucked up in bed, but she could tell immediately something was wrong. He was as white as chalk. She had no tray to drop – but her hands flew up anyway and she screamed.

Chapter 3

Monday, May 6, Larkshall Lane, Croydon, 9.20AM

Lynne Parker closed the front door behind her and breathed a sigh of relief. She had the house to herself for the first time in more than forty-eight hours. Her husband was up in London, where he worked at New Scotland Yard, and both the boys had been safely dropped off at school.

She adored all three of them, but right now she didn't miss them one little bit. She had a list of things to do, a mile long, but for the moment she savoured the peace and quiet. Not only did she have time to sigh, but also she could actually hear herself do it.

Monday, May 6, Angel Cottage, Sewel Mill, 9.30AM

By the time Dr Clive Marks arrived, Mrs Hayward had calmed herself down surprisingly well. She was in the kitchen, making tea. Ten minutes later, when he came back downstairs and found her with the pot brewed and the cups out ready, they sat for a few seconds, sipping in silence.

'Poor chap, he must've popped off in his sleep. Then again, I wouldn't have expected it,' sighed Marks, thoughtfully. 'After all, he was in remarkably sound health.'

Mrs Hayward had started to tremble again and had to put her cup down. Marks prescribed her a mild sedative and told her to pick it up at the chemist, then go home and rest.

'I can't possibly do that,' she snapped, irritation clearly showing. 'I have work to do around the village, people will be expecting me.'

'Well, at least take it easy, you've had quite a shock, no point killing yourself...' Realising what he had said, he allowed the sentence to tail off. 'Well,' he added, apologetically, 'you know what I mean.'

'Don't you go worrying about me, Dr Marks,' she answered, pushing her chair back from the table and carrying her cup across to the sink. No rush to wash it up now. 'I'll be fine once I've gathered my wits.' Mrs Hayward grabbed her short beige mac from the hall and hurriedly collected the rest of her belongings. She left by the back door.

Upset by what had happened, she was, and sorry for poor old Mr Janson, yes genuinely, but neither of those emotions outweighed her excitement. She could barely stop herself from running, but had to make do with a brisk walk. She relished the fact that nobody else could have the news before she parted with it. She was, after all, the one who had experienced it first-hand.

She waved to Gloria Tufnell, who was watering plants in the window box at the front of her shop in the high street. She didn't stop to chat.

She was still working out her itinerary for the rest of the morning when she got to Mrs Newbould's door. Emily Newbould was obviously the first person to call on. As Anna Janson's closest friend in Sewel Mill, she could be relied on for an enjoyable exchange of views on the subject. Mrs Hayward tried to get her smile under control and replace it with a more respectable expression of grief. It wasn't easy.

Monday, May 6, Brentwood Mansions, 9.40AM

Kate Brown looked in on Emma before she left. Being the boss meant that Kate could choose her hours. *And us creative types don't tend to get moving too early in the day do we? That wouldn't be coo-wal, would it?* Kate had a healthy sense of humour about the world she lived and worked in. Her office was only down the road in Saint Christopher's Place anyway. It was two minutes away, if you walked fast, which Kate did.

Both type-A people, she and Emma were old friends from college days, and when she had said, 'Stay as long as you like,' that was exactly what she'd meant. Kate was rich, meaning seriously rich. So much so that she didn't think about how much she had and whether or not she could afford it.

She wasn't dizzy though, far from it. She just knew she was okay financially and had never known anything else. The family was old money, her father owned large tracts of forest in north Wales, mainly for paper production, and this had been left to his father and his before him. Not being prolific breeders, but bearing enough children to carry on the line, the Brown family was well-provisioned.

She looked down at her friend. Emma seemed to be sleeping peacefully enough now, but she had been restless in the night. Kate had heard her pacing around a little before she herself dropped off.

She was looking forward to her day at work, as she always did, but she would've much preferred to wait for Emma to wake up so that they could have a good chat. She had been reluctant to press her friend too much the night before for an explanation of why she'd needed somewhere to stay at such relatively short notice. She was just delighted to have her around and happy to provide a refuge in a time of trouble.

They'd enjoyed an excellent meal, not to mention significantly more than their allotted one unit per night of wine. This was turning the clock back big-time; this was going to be fun.

Monday, May 6, Angel Cottage, Sewel Mill, 9.45AM

Dr Marks went back up to Janson's bedroom. Something was nagging at the back of his mind. Something wasn't right. He pulled the duvet from Janson's face. The angles were all wrong; the head position just didn't seem to sit right. Granted, this was the head of a corpse and you would expect it to be in a relaxed position. However, this was all wrong, relaxed but not relaxed fully.

Marks held Janson's head with both hands and moved it gently, and then he felt what he had half-suspected – a click. The realisation hit him almost like a punch in the stomach: a man with a broken neck doesn't put himself to bed.

By mid-morning, the local police were joined by a couple of specialists. Commander Paul Saxon and DS Guy Parker from New Scotland Yard.

The local police had been on the scene quickly bearing in mind there was no police station in the village. The local officers had in fact come up from Brighton this morning. Sewel Mill had lost its police presence ten years ago and Brighton was the nearest big centre that could offer assistance when a crime was committed, as it clearly had been here.

Introducing themselves to the local officers, Saxon mentioned that he himself lived on their patch, in Brighton, and had just reached the office in London when the call came to return to Sussex. He left them to continue their routine.

'You see, Parker,' he said, 'they call it cutbacks, that's how they explain it. In the old days, there would've been a local bobby, who would know everyone in the village. He would've been a mine of useful information.' Saxon shook his head in frustration. 'A couple of lads up from Brighton aren't much use to me.'

Parker had heard it before. In common with many of his colleagues, Saxon regarded the cutbacks as more of a retreat, which allowed the crooks to run amok in the countryside. He was all for value-added work practices and efficient use of people and resources, but this was daft. It meant more police were required to solve the extra crimes, which of course cancelled out any possible savings resulting from the cutbacks.

However, that was another subject, for another time, probably over a pint or two. He didn't allow himself to get distracted from the business in hand by the questions of policy and politics.

Saxon was looking around the cottage, reviewing the information he had so far. The victim was still upstairs in his bed. Downstairs, where they were now, DS Parker was making notes, which they would later go over together, comparing facts and impressions, knowledge and question marks. The first thing Saxon did on arrival at a crime scene was to fit the things he'd been told, usually by phone, into what he could see around him. He and Parker made a good team.

Joining the police force after university, Saxon had progressed swiftly through the ranks, experiencing most aspects of police work, from drug squad to vice. Now thirty-five years old, he felt he'd found his niche at this comparatively young age. He had in fact been selected from considerable competition to lead a specialist serial killer detection squad. Real life might not be too much like TV, but it was true that murders came in a reasonably steady flow, most of them proving quite easy to solve. The usual scenario was sadly predictable: the jealous lover, the deceived spouse, or a close relative who couldn't take any more.

Harder to solve were stranger killings, where the victim and the killer were never acquainted. These were much less common. A good thing, when you considered that the lack of motive often gave the police very little to go on. Serial killings, on the other hand, were something else altogether. Saxon and Parker were here in Sewel Mill because their unit assessed every murder case in the UK, with a view to establishing whether or not any connections could be found to link one or more of them in any way.

Monday, May 6, 12 Pavilion Square, Brighton, Flat 3, 10.30AM

Francesca Lewis was unpacking her equipment. She'd been commissioned to get some pictures over at Beachy Head, for a story in one of the local papers on the problems of coastal erosion.

She enjoyed that kind of assignment, particularly on a bright, sunny day. She'd been there at first light and was confident that the pictures would be good. There might be some decent library shots in among them too. Everyone seemed to be interested in the environment again this year. Good news for the world and good news for photographers and journalists. Long may it continue.

Monday, May 6, Angel Cottage, Sewel Mill, 11AM

As Saxon finished his tour of the ground floor, Dr Marks came back in through the front door. He was a tall man. Saxon guessed him to be in his early forties. Marks was slightly foppish in appearance, his forehead covered by a mass of dark hair.

'Marks,' he announced, stretching out a hand with the longest bony fingers Saxon had ever seen. 'Clive Marks. I'm one of the GPs from the Health Centre at the other end of the village. And you are?' After Saxon introduced himself, and explained that they were from the Serial Crimes Unit, Marks briefed him on exactly what it was that puzzled him sufficiently to cry murder. He explained at some length and a tad repetitively how Mrs Hayward had discovered the body and called him, thinking that Janson had died in his sleep, and how he had quickly deduced that this was not the case. In addition, that he had noticed immediately the similarities between the other two murders and "his" murder.

'Strange thing is, and I am of course no detective, you understand,' he smirked, brushing his hair back with a well-practiced gesture, 'but there is absolutely no sign of a struggle. Not as far as I can see. Nothing is out of place.'

Dr Marks was the proud owner of a pompous manner that quickly irritated people and was starting to annoy Saxon in what was possibly record time. "His neck is broken" would have sufficed.

Saxon took a pair of rubber gloves from his pocket, slipped them on with a loud thwack, and interrupted Marks as he was about to go into some detail about the position of the head.

'Yes, thank you, Doctor.' Saxon looked around the room and peered through the window. 'Tell me, where is the person who found the body?'

There was a slight pause.

'Well er, she, er, Mrs Hayward, that is, has gone off to work.' Marks paused again. 'I let her go because I didn't think that there was anything suspicious at the time.' Marks was immediately on the defensive, his voice less authoritative as his confidence waned slightly.

Saxon paused before responding. 'That wasn't very clever, was it? Tell my DS over there and he'll take her details so that we can get in touch with her.' Parker looked across and nodded, acknowledging that he had heard the conversation.

'Would you please show me where the body is, and I trust you haven't touched anything?'

'No, not a thing, Commander, it is all as I found it.' Marks was clearly offended. 'We may not get many murders down here in Sewel Mill, but I do know…'

'Yes, thank you, Doctor.' Saxon asked Marks to leave the cottage and wait outside for the scene-of-crime officers to arrive. Marks seemed slightly put out at being dismissed in such a cursory fashion. He had expected to accompany the commander upstairs so that the latter could benefit from expert medical advice. Marks was even more aggrieved that Saxon had given him such a minor role to play. How many times was he going to have to give his story? Somewhat reluctantly, he complied.

Saxon went back to his car and rummaged around in the glove compartment for a pair of plastic covers for his shoes. Properly clad for the task, he started his examination.

The doormat was clinically clean and it didn't take him long to realise that inside the cottage all of the surfaces, painted, brass or glass were also spotless. Too clean. Mrs Hayward hadn't even started to tidy up, but the place was as clean as an operating theatre. The only signs of human habitation were the teacups waiting to be washed up on the draining board, from Mrs Hayward's tea break with Marks, and the teapot still on the table.

This looked far from promising.

Monday, May 6, Conquest Hospital Mortuary, Brighton, 11.30AM

Jake Dalton was on automatic. He knew what he was doing and he mostly worked with good people, people he could trust. Much as he enjoyed his work, he was a million miles away right now, reliving the flights at the weekend. The weather had been brilliant and he'd clocked up four hours of gliding time.

Melanie Jones interrupted his reverie. 'Jake,' she said, apparently for the second or third time, judging by the tone of her voice. 'It's got to be you or Dr Clarke.' She paused expectantly. When he looked at her blankly, she went on. 'One of you is going to have to say something to him.' She sounded exasperated.

'Sorry, Mel,' he answered. 'Who are we talking about? What's the problem?'

'He stinks.' She was disgusted.

'Not Steve again,' Jake said, despondently. Steve Tucker was the fly in the ointment, the bane of his life. His working life anyway. They all hated working with him.

'I'll swear he hasn't been near soap and hot water for weeks, and we just can't stand it anymore.'

Most of the female staff, particularly the younger ones, found his presence uncomfortable. There was an unspoken pact not to leave each other alone with him, if it could possibly be avoided.

Melanie was particularly anti-Steve. It was because he never seemed to have enough room to pass her by. The gaps were always too tight – he always had to squeeze past, rubbing against her as he went. Sometimes he stood right up against her when making tea in the little kitchen. Of course, she moved away immediately. She verbalised her annoyance often, telling him to go fuck himself, but Steve, thinking that he was being witty and clever, merely grinned and suggested that she loved it, and waggled his tongue up and down suggestively.

Complaints were frequently made about his behaviour, but they were overlooked by the powers that be, since finding people prepared to do that kind of job was not an easy task, and the candidates weren't exactly queuing up at the door. Therefore, Steve kept his job, although Melanie and the others knew he should have been sacked. They knew their rights. They knew what constituted gross misconduct, and he was a frequent offender.

'Okay, okay,' Jake nodded. 'Don't worry. I'll have a word.' The clouds and the sunshine were far away already.

Monday, May 6, Angel Cottage, Sewel Mill, 11.40AM

'Thank you, Mr Killer, sir, for being so thorough. Fucking waste of time this is turning out to be,' Saxon muttered under his breath. 'But we're going to keep looking anyway, you bastard, because maybe you weren't as thorough as you thought you were.' Saxon was prone to talking to himself when he was truly focused. Even when people could overhear what he was saying. 'So you know what you're doing, do you? You know how to cover your tracks, eh? You're good, but how good? I wonder. How good are you?'

He was thinking about the two other murders that Marks had referred to. Both had taken place recently and within fifteen miles of Sewel Mill. The other two also involved single men, living on their own, who had been murdered in their homes.

David Crowley, a retired headmaster, had been found on March 12, when a neighbour raised the alarm. He was discovered sitting in his armchair, as if watching television. His neck had been broken.

Rupert Hall was a male nurse, who was reported missing on April 10 by his personnel manager at the Conquest Hospital. He had failed to turn up for work for three days in a row and nobody could reach him at home. He was found stretched out on his sofa, with headphones still on. His neck had also been broken.

When news of Janson's death came in earlier that morning to New Scotland Yard, with the preliminary report of a broken neck, Saxon decided to look at this one personally. Hence, the drive back down to Sussex. This was looking very much like a serial killer. There were other similarities too. All three bodies had been positioned to appear as natural deaths. The only difference was that Christopher Janson was in bed, Rupert Hall was on his sofa, and David Crowley was in his armchair. All were over fifty.

The other two were homosexuals. Hall was well and truly out of the closet and was something of a character around the hospital during shifts he worked. He was also a leading light in the social whirl of Brighton's thriving gay nightlife.

Crowley, on the other hand, was still firmly tucked away in his closet. They found plenty of evidence at home of his sexual preferences. It was something they would have to look into as far as Janson was concerned. God forbid that they should have a killer of gay men on the loose. The tabloids would have a field day.

In both the other cases, there was no forensic evidence of the killer and little or no evidence even of the killer's presence, apart from the body of the deceased, that is. As for motive, they were still looking for links between the two men, and now they would add Janson to the equation.

Monday, May 6, Anvil Wood House, Sewel Mill, 12.15PM

Babs Jenner was sitting down to an early lunch. She'd had a busy morning, but it had all been paperwork, which she didn't mind at all. She enjoyed being organised. *One of us has to be!* She smiled as she tucked into home-made soup.

They had been almost fully booked over the weekend. No classes were scheduled until the late afternoon on Mondays though, thank goodness. She liked children well enough, but the noise they made was extraordinary. The horses were well used to it though and patiently endured the endless circuits. Babs was thinking of getting one of the stable girls to do more of the lessons. Her various business ventures were doing well and she was sure they could afford it.

Monday, May 6, Angel Cottage, Sewel Mill, 12.15PM

'Boss, you up there?' Detective Sergeant Guy Parker called from the bottom of the stairs.

'Yes, come up carefully, Parker, don't touch anything or you'll be checking parking tickets...forever...without overtime, and certainly with no chance of parole.'

Parker was also moved to talk to himself from time to time.

'And that, my friends, was from chapter one of the Ladybird guide to "Instructions for Behaviour Appropriate to a Crime Scene" and we are very grateful indeed for the refresher course, aren't we boys and girls?' he muttered beneath his breath, as he started climbing the stairs.

As he did so, he glanced out of the window next to the front door and saw Dr Marks, and realised immediately that Saxon's remark had been made as much for the education of Dr Marks, as much as for Parker himself. He smiled to himself. That doctor was a pain in the arse, far too precious for Parker's liking.

Parker was a beanpole. He was fair-haired, twenty-eight years old and balding rapidly, with a big nose that pointed up and out at the same time. He resembled someone who was continually being led around with a meat hook up his nose. This didn't go unnoticed among his colleagues, and canteen-ridicule culture in the police force is not only without mercy but relentless. Consequently, Parker was frequently referred to as "Nosy Parker". No one would say this directly to his face though. He was known to have a temper, and a bit of rank, which he was more than happy to use when required.

Saxon handed him a plastic bag containing an address book. 'When that has been checked for prints and DNA, I want you to get it photocopied, then get the team to phone everyone in it.'

'Little black book, eh? Full of girlfriends is it?' Parker asked.

'Well, that's what I want you to check out for me, Sergeant, so maybe you'll get lucky.' Saxon pointed at the bag. 'Just get on with it and have some respect for the recently deceased.'

'Sorry, boss. Anything else?'

'Yes, you can make a note of all the framed awards on the landing. I want to know where and when Mr Janson was employed for the last umpteen years. Not only that, I also want to know who he worked with and for – could be a jealousy thing, could be an old vendetta. Long shot though, I doubt it will lead us anywhere. And check out for a will. Some of those paintings are not bad at all. Perhaps he has other stuff to pass on to a relative or friend. Maybe someone couldn't wait.

'Also, get on to traffic and check if they were in the area taking random number plates.' Saxon paused for breath.

'I've already checked that out, boss, there was a squad car in the area, but they weren't checking plates.'

'Shit, you're kidding – bring back the old days. What do they do all night – sit in side streets and stuff their faces with pizza? At least it might have given us something useful, rather than fuck all. And where is sodding SOCO?'

Monday, May 6, Conquest Hospital Bus Stop, Brighton, 12.35PM

Tucker was livid as he approached the bus stop at some speed. Two people were waiting and they both looked up in surprise as he strode up, muttering to himself loudly. 'Fuckin' bastard! Who's he think he is? Fuckin' arsehole, that's what.' He glared at his prospective fellow passengers, an elderly man and a middle-aged woman. They both recoiled. His face was almost purple with rage.

'What right does he 'ave to go on at me about me personal high jeans an' stuff?' He was still marching back and forth. The elderly man looked at the middle-aged woman and they both backed away from Tucker and towards each other.

'Go 'ome and fuckin' wash 'e said!' Tucker pointed his armpit indignantly at the couple. They withdrew further.

Monday, May 6, Angel Cottage, Sewel Mill, 12.45PM

Guy Parker was on his hands and knees on the top landing, painstakingly listing the details of each of the awards on display. He was fervently wishing that Janson hadn't been quite as successful.

Saxon glanced at him as he went back to the bedroom. He considered Parker to be an excellent police officer and, when necessary, reliable and tough. He was streetwise in a way that Saxon knew he himself wasn't, or not to the same extent. If a situation got a bit heavy, Parker was definitely one to have on your side. Not only did he have the height, he was also fit and wiry. Not many people could've gotten close enough to Parker to land a punch, even if they'd had the bad sense to try in the first place. Saxon once pictured him as a gibbon on steroids, an image that had stuck in his mind subsequently. But he'd never mentioned this to him.

Parker wasn't one to seek out trouble though. The vibes he gave off were sufficient. His appearance meant that he very rarely had to use the physical prowess people just assumed he had. He was married with two children, a fact that often played on his mind. When a police officer died in the line of duty, the newspapers always described the deceased as "married with two children". Never three, or one, it always seemed to be two.

Parker smiled, as always, at the thought of his kids. This case would mean more time away from home, while he stayed at a police house in Brighton rather than commuting daily back to South London. He didn't mind. Working sixteen-hour days meant that he would hardly have seen them anyway, so it made sense to be close by. He'd make a point of calling home in the early evening, when they were home from school and just after they'd had their tea.

He and Lynne had a routine that worked well. He talked to both boys about their day, and had a few minutes with her on the phone afterwards. She accepted the lot of a detective's wife without complaint. That was a rare thing, in Parker's experience, and something for which he was eternally grateful. The call home, though brief, was the highlight of his day, followed closely by their exchange of emails.

He went back to a thorough inspection of the upstairs of Janson's cottage, continuing with detailed notes of each of the framed awards. At this stage, he wasn't trying to infer much from the contents, just to get the details down in his notebook. They would go over them together later and see what avenues needed further exploration. Right now, the important thing was to gather the information, accurately and completely. The challenge of putting it all together came later.

Monday, May 6, Conquest Hospital Mortuary, Brighton, 12.50PM

Jake didn't want to delay anyone for long but he wanted to say something about Steve Tucker. He had called a brief staff meeting.

He was well aware that Tucker was an unpleasant individual and probably always had been. Not attractive, even to his mother, would be Jake's guess. Twenty-six years old but with a mental age of around thirteen, and that was on a good day. Five feet three inches of rampant body odour, he had the habit of fondling his genitals. In public, or private, it made no difference. Well, not to him, anyway.

His skin had the texture of someone who has dedicated their life to smoking as much as possible during their waking hours. It followed of course that with such dedication to nicotine came a certain amount of phlegm, so spitting was another facet of

Tucker's charm. This was usually done with the same rules as the genital gymnastics…anywhere that took his fancy, and with little or no regard to the comfort or safety of anyone in the vicinity. Although if there was a handy wall within range, it was more entertaining to half of his brain cells to watch it dribble the way gravity dictates. The other brain cell was occupied with breathing, noisily through a permanently open mouth.

With his round face and pop eyes, heavy eyelids and bags to match, he looked like an overgrown bug with blackheads.

Jake could well understand why the women Tucker worked alongside were disgusted by him. But Jake was also touched by a feeling of "There but for the grace of God".

'You have to reinforce the message,' he explained to Angie, Mel and Clare, hoping that if he could get them onside, the other women would at least give Tucker another chance.

'What? Rewarding good behaviour? Is that what we're talking about?' Clare asked.

Jake nodded. 'If he thinks there is a good reason for having a shower every day, then he might do it without me having to nag him about it, that's all.'

'So you want us to praise him for making an effort to clean himself up?' asked Melanie. 'Right?'

'Bit like a puppy, when you're trying to toilet train it?' Clare was an expert in such matters.

Angie could be relied on to see the funny side of any situation.

'So, can I smack him on the nose with a rolled-up newspaper whenever he gets out of line?' she asked, innocently. 'That's okay with you?' The other two girls were instantly convulsed with laughter.

Jake couldn't help but laugh himself. 'Well, if all else fails, maybe we'll try that,' he answered.

The meeting was over. Jake was pleased to have taken some action but not at all convinced that his words with Tucker would have any lasting effect. Neither were the girls.

They all liked Jake very much but thought he was too nice about Tucker. They all wondered why.

'Maybe misplaced guilt,' said Angie, when they discussed it over sandwiches in their usual spot outside the hospital.

Melanie frowned.

Angie went on. 'It's obvious. If you're tall, blond, gorgeous and very, very fit, not to mention…'

Clare interrupted. 'Angie, you're drooling again. Stop it!'

The three of them laughed. Jake was not bad-looking by anyone's standards and he seemed to be a pretty decent bloke.

'So you think he's kind to Steve because Steve's ugly and stupid and disgusting…' Melanie began, clearly not convinced.

'Yeah, because Jake's gorgeous and good enough to eat…' Angie was off again.

'Mmm. Not to mention funny. And kind. And very clean,' Clare put in, laughing.

'And healthy.' Angie was not to be stopped.

'Good teeth?' Melanie offered.

Angie hooted. 'Great teeth.'

They fell about giggling over their sandwiches and Melanie had to grab her Evian bottle to stop it falling over. People walking past them turned to look and smiled to themselves at the sight of three attractive young women, laughing together in the sunshine.

Chapter 4

Monday, May 6, Brighton Police Station, 4.00PM

The office that Saxon was to share with Parker back at police headquarters in Brighton was old but very functional, with an atmosphere of having been lived and worked in for many years. It exuded authority, formality, and even a certain menace. Saxon had used it before. He liked to think that the slight atmosphere of menace had been brought about by years of clenched buttocks involuntarily polishing the seats. Sharing the thought with Parker had induced roars of laughter, almost to the point of tears.

In Saxon's experience, just being in a police station often made people feel tense and uneasy. Even when they had little or nothing to feel guilty about, the effect was still the same.

But it had to be said that this particular room did have a certain resonance about it. One of the clerks at the station had once remarked to Parker that the room had the right feng shui for its purpose. Parker had been non-committal.

Brighton had its fair share of New-Age enthusiasts. Some might say more than its fair share. While he didn't know too much about geomancy, and cared even less, Parker was of the opinion that it wasn't just the surroundings that made people nervous, it was the tactics Saxon used when interviewing.

One such tactic was to stare at the person being questioned and not blink, sometimes for minutes at a time. Saxon could live with the silence and the hard eye contact, but not all the interviewees could. He was already well-known at Brighton Police Station, as he used their facilities from time to time. Some of the police constables had once joked that if the military ever got hold of him, Saxon could be used as a secret weapon.

The walls of the office were oak-panelled; some of the furniture was 1930s, not particularly attractive, but long-lasting. The building could not be said to be on the cutting-edge of office design and technology, but it did well enough for them.

DS Parker was given a corner to himself and he was relieved to see that he was already on line. Parker loved computers. For Guy Parker, computers held the answer to almost everything. If the solution couldn't be found in the police computer, then it was because some stupid bastard in records wasn't doing his or her job properly.

Computers were important in his personal life too. He helped his kids with their homework whenever possible, supervising their searches on the Internet very carefully. He took his parental responsibilities seriously.

When he was away from home, as he knew he would be this week, he made a point of sending an email home to each of the boys every day. Hotmail was still the best invention yet on the Internet, as far as he was concerned. They'd had great fun choosing their email addresses and he knew that "you can check your email from Dad when you..." was a powerful inducement to an ever-growing number of things, including: "finish your dinner", "pick up your clothes", "clean your teeth", "pack up your dinosaurs", and so on. The possibilities were endless. And Lynne was expert at making the most of it.

Parker was the first to volunteer to go to Starbucks so that he could check his Hotmail and send his daily messages.

The two men made themselves at home.

Monday, May 6, Conquest Hospital Mortuary, Brighton, 4.15PM

The traumas of the morning were already fading into Tucker's distant past. Melanie had just smiled at him. She'd even spoken to him. His skin came up in goose pimples at the thought.

'You look nice this afternoon, Steve,' she'd said.

And that git, Dalton, had passed some comment too but Tucker couldn't remember what it was now. Something about a big improvement and something about him, Tucker, taking things well and in a positive manner.

'Tosser,' muttered Tucker under his breath. 'Total fuckin' tosser, s'wot 'e is.'

No matter what anyone else had said to him, Melanie's words were engraved on his soul. Little did he know the effort it had cost her to say the words. Nor could he have guessed that her entire being revolted at the thought of saying them.

No, Tucker was totally unaware of Melanie's feelings as his fingers strayed to his trouser pocket.

Monday, May 6, Brighton Police Station, 4.15PM

Saxon read the pathologist's report on Janson. Depressingly sparse would be an understatement. Cause of death: Mr Janson died from a broken neck. There were no marks on the body. No bruising on the head or neck. Nothing. His general health was good. In fact, for a man of his age, he was in remarkably good shape, apart from his being dead.

There were two obvious possibilities. Saxon figured that either Janson knew the killer and let him or her in, or maybe the killer was a hit man, possibly an ex-soldier. In which case, Janson would have not known he was dead until he saw the tunnel with the beckoning white light.

The clues amounted to precisely zero, the same as in the two previous cases, and so far it seemed that none of the victims knew each other. For Rupert Hall and David Crowley, all their phone books and diaries had been thoroughly probed and, unless they were using a cipher on a par with the Enigma code, there was, as far as Saxon could tell, absolutely nothing to connect them at all – apart from their sexual preferences, their age, the fact that they were both male, over 50 and living alone.

Janson might well turn out to share the same sexual preferences. He certainly fit the other points. Overall, they didn't add up to much. Certainly, there was nothing to point the investigation in any one clear direction. Saxon sighed and stretched.

He jumped when the telephone buzzed on his desk. He moved forward again and reached for the phone. It was Superintendent Alex Mitchell, the station's commanding officer.

'Commander Saxon, good morning to you, sir.' The voice was hearty. 'It's Mitchell here. Would you mind if I pop up and have a chat with you? I know you're busy, so I'll keep it brief,' he said, sounding apologetic. The public school charm oozed through the phone line.

Saxon wasn't pleased. 'No problem,' he answered. 'Come when you're ready.' He hung up the phone quickly. He was exasperated. Saxon didn't need interruptions from Mitchell. He had more important things on his mind, than to talk about rising crime figures and detection rates. Wasting his time listening to that creep Alex Mitchell, explaining how good he was at his job, was not on his agenda – nor would it ever be if he had his way.

To Saxon, who didn't care for him at all, Mitchell was your typical fast-track cop: university, then one year on the beat. Saxon tried to avoid sweeping generalisations as far as possible, but Mitchell just invited it. In the past, Saxon had found that Mitchell was good at giving the impression of listening and paying attention. However, he soon realised that all Mitchell was doing was rehearsing his next pronouncement either to the press or the chief constable. Conversations with Mitchell were often a frustrating business.

To make things worse, his "okay yah" accent irritated people even when what he was saying made sense.

A few minutes later Mitchell knocked and entered Saxon's office.

'Superintendent Mitchell, come in, sit down,' Saxon said in a hurried manner.

'Thank you, Commander.' Mitchell looked around the room. 'Everything okay here? You have everything you need?' Parker pushed his chair back noisily and left the office.

'I just wanted to drop in and say that if there's anything, absolutely anything, I or my staff can do to make your time here more, shall I say, productive, then don't hesitate to call me at any time.'

Saxon said nothing.

'I should mention that the chief constable has asked me to personally keep him briefed on any developments regarding these cases, you know how much he likes to be on top of things, so to speak,' Mitchell went on.

This time Saxon was quick to reply.

'Fine,' he said. 'But let's not keep him too informed. He's too press-friendly for my liking. There are some details I like to keep back. If the public know too much, we'll have the usual confessors stacked up all along the seafront, waiting to admit to everything from masterminding the Great Train Robbery to the Kennedy assassination just to get their bit of the limelight.' He paused briefly.

'It would be a great shame if something were to be inadvertently leaked, wouldn't it. Particularly if the leak were to be traced back to here.' He raised his eyebrows.

Mitchell nodded slowly in agreement. 'Indeed, Commander, I do understand. Only what you agree to release, of course.'

This assurance was accompanied by a confident smile, with significant baring of teeth, and a slight bow of the head. Saxon thought that for once Mitchell seemed genuine. That thought was quickly replaced by the suspicion that it was more than likely just another example of Superintendent Mitchell's desperate ambition. The entire station knew he was obsessed with promotion and fully capable of achieving heights – or depths even – of brown-nosing that were previously unknown among the population at large.

Mitchell was unaware of the thoughts going through Saxon's mind. Just as he seemed to be oblivious to the negative vibes he provoked among his own staff. Mitchell had no doubt been on more than one personal development course, where he'd learnt some, but not all, of the pointers on body language, Saxon thought to himself. That made him smile and Mitchell was in turn sufficiently comforted that his offer had been well-perceived that he ended the conversation, repeating a slight nod of the head as he left the room.

Monday, May 6, Victoria Station, 6.00PM

Penelope Field, or Poppy, as her friends inevitably knew her, stopped at WH Smith on the station forecourt. She bought the evening paper and a copy of *Marie Claire*.

Thank God today was over. Four more days to go before the weekend. She wished, as she did every day, at least once, that she were self-employed and that she didn't have to do this awful commute every day to a job she no longer enjoyed.

She couldn't wait to get home to Sewel Mill.

Monday, May 6, 12 Pavilion Square, Brighton, 11.00PM

Saxon parked his car. Would he ever get used to coming home to an empty flat? *Will I ever have to get used to it?*

In some ways, he was already coming to terms with it. He no longer expected to see food in the fridge unless he'd bought it himself. He knew that the bedding wasn't changed unless he did it. He'd been married for six years but he had never become dependent on having someone around to do all that for him, so the transition back to a quasi-bachelor state was not difficult for him, at least not from a practical point of view. Emotionally, it was a different thing.

To his eyes, the separation had come so quickly he hardly had time to draw breath. He'd arrived home at his usual time last night, way past midnight, and she was gone. The note she left for him told him not to worry about her, and that she would phone him in a few days.

It had to be said that apart from the shock of Emma's sudden departure, and his ongoing, albeit suppressed, concern that she might not come back, Saxon was a contented man.

This was the place he had always wanted to be. He loved his job. He thrived on the combination of analysis and action, of thinking and hunting. The challenge was to spot the mistakes that all murderers make. The police macho types could keep their dark, smelly alleyways, where they waited for drug deals to go down, or their car chases with lights flashing and sirens blaring, while they belted around narrow streets. Saxon was one of those rare people who enjoyed what they did and were good at it. There had never been any other career for him.

Paul Saxon was just seven years old when his father Richard Saxon was murdered. Even now, the flashbacks still haunted him like scenes from a black and white movie. That was the point in his life, almost to the minute, when he decided to be a policeman. His desire to get the bad guys came from a very strong personal conviction that nobody should have to suffer the way he did. When confronted with a new case the thought always raced through his mind – *how dare people kill, and think that they can get away with it?*

In the kitchen, Saxon reached for the Black Label and poured himself a generous two fingers over a couple of ice cubes. Emma would not have been pleased to see the Scotch kept in the kitchen, but she wasn't there, was she.

Chapter 5

Thursday, May 9, Brighton Police Station, 2.00PM

Parker was satisfied that he had unearthed every scrap of information about Christopher Janson, but disappointed that none of it led to any real breakthroughs at all, apart from the further link with the other two cases, once it was established that Janson, too, was gay.

Although he was well-liked in the village where he lived, it seemed that Janson's former colleagues and contacts in London's magazine world were less enthusiastic about their recently departed acquaintance. The generally held view was that talent had played little or no part in the acquisition of the majority of the awards that had so impressed Edie Hayward and so exhausted Guy Parker.

Unless, that is, someone was giving out prizes for being two-faced and highly manipulative. Or perhaps a little statuette in recognition of almost total disregard for ethics and morals if they stood between him and something he wanted. The consensus was that Janson was a creep.

The village was unaware of this persona, knowing him only as a long-term resident, who had worked up in London for many years but who now lived permanently in Sewel Mill. The village viewed him as a charming gentleman, a warm and obliging neighbour. How could they know that Janson had made many enemies throughout his career? Parker was amused at the huge disparity between the two pictures he was given.

Janson was known in the industry as someone who would happily slither past anyone in his way, and then stab them firmly between the shoulder blades if a suitable opportunity presented itself. Having two faces was a minimum requirement in his view, particularly with regard to the editors he'd worked under. Behind their backs, they were morons. To their faces – they were anything he knew they wanted to be. One old colleague often referred to him as the editor's lapdog. As the editors came and went, Janson merely changed laps, usually a few weeks before the changeover. He had survived in the industry through mediocre ability combined with stealth and cunning. Not to mention a formidable talent for internal politics. His own best interests took priority, and if someone else suffered in the process, it was hardly his concern.

But while Parker had found any number of people who heartily disliked Janson, none of them looked to have the makings of a murderer and none of them could be linked to either of the other crimes. Parker had a talent for spotting guilt, but not one of the people he interviewed had any effect on his inbuilt guiltometer.

Friday, May 10, Brighton Police Station, 7.00PM

By the end of the week, Saxon admitted reluctantly – but only to himself – that they'd hit something of a wall. A dead-end. He'd suspected they would. Frankly, there was nothing to get a handle on. With no forensic evidence, there was little anyone could do but look and look again for similarities and differences between the cases and just hope for a breakthrough of some kind. He had been over the details so often, the frustration was starting to make his head throb. There had to be something that may give him a lead. No matter how many times he turned it all over in his mind, there was nothing to see. Saxon was well aware that the first forty-eight crucial hours had long passed. His chance of solving this crime was now halved.

He remained convinced that there was a serial killer at work, but he had nothing new to show from their investigations. Saxon had reached the point where he was thinking the unthinkable: the only way forward would be for the killer to strike again and next time, make a mistake. A bloody great big one.

But that was the nature of serial killers; they don't do it once because there's a problem that needs sorting: like a straying wife or girlfriend; or a hopelessly senile but otherwise relentlessly healthy live-in relative; or a sudden panic situation when some poor bloody innocent bystander was just in the wrong place at the wrong time.

His father had been just such a victim. Even twenty-eight years after it had happened, Saxon could still remember so many details of the dreadful day. The police arriving suddenly at the front door of the house in Glynde. The muffled conversation, too indistinct to comprehend, and the sudden terrifying cries of his mother. Saxon was taken to his bedroom by a WPC, on the pretence that he could show her his toys. But he was a bright child, and knew something wasn't right. Why would a police-woman want to see some boring old toys, when clearly something far more important was going on elsewhere in the house?

His father, Richard, had been a quiet, hard-working man, who described himself at dinner parties in their comfortable suburban world as a plain, boring office clerk. He was actually a highly successful accountant, working in the finance department of one of the local government offices in Westminster. He commuted between Glynde and London every day, a true slave to the British Railway system. He had his own seat, not officially of course, just an unspoken reservation. Along with his travelling companions, Richard would finish the *Daily Telegraph* crossword as the train slowly hauled itself into Victoria Station.

One day – his last – Richard Saxon's destiny was changed by one tiny action. It was so trivial that at the time no one even acknowledged it as the factor that had cost him his life. Looking back and with the undoubted benefit of hindsight, Saxon was convinced that the police, always looking for motives and intrigue, overlooked the fact that it was a simple case of wrong time, wrong place.

Under normal circumstances, Saxon senior avoided public

toilets. The character of those places dedicated to strange glances and unpleasant odours made him uncomfortable. On that day, the last one, he'd broken this habit because, quite simply, he had to. He knew he wouldn't make it home without finding a toilet and if he used the one on the train, he would run the risk of losing his seat to another anxious commuter. Besides, he had a good ten minutes before the train would even arrive, so there was time. As it turned out, those ten minutes were far from good.

Nobody saw or heard a thing, as is usual in London when a crime is committed. It was the blood. Copious amounts of the stuff, seeping out from under the cubicle door, slowly progressing over the tiles, until it reached the urinal at the far end, where it then ran faster than most of the trains, down into the sewer. The poor man, who spotted it first, apart from pissing down his leg, also emptied the contents of his stomach into the Technicolor nightmare that had well and truly fouled up his evening.

No arrest was ever made, and the file gathered dust. And more dust. Nobody ever knew what had happened. It was never established whose path had crossed Saxon's so dramatically that fateful evening. The fact that his briefcase was never found indicated that the motive was robbery. Eventually – even though the police hated to admit it, the file was put on the "probably will not be solved" pile. Although, as in all unsolved murder cases, it was never officially closed.

Saxon junior dragged himself back to the present. Serial killers were not like that. They played a completely different game. And there was precious little chance involved in most cases.

So on this Friday night, just five days after Janson had met his end at Sewel Mill, Saxon found himself in a situation that was not one he relished. By now, he normally had advanced to a more positive stage in a murder inquiry. At least, he usually had a suspect, someone to visit now and again and lean on, or even just to watch. This time he had nothing. He put the files away and checked that it was all tidy. Parker had gone back up to Croydon an hour or so ago, for a ferocious welcome from his kids. Saxon envied him and yet he didn't. He left for home.

Friday, May 10, 12 Pavilion Square, Flat 4, Brighton, 9.00PM

Saxon's apartment was in one of the Regency squares just up from the Brighton seafront. His mother had moved the family down to the coast from Glynde within a year of her husband's death, in a desperate effort to get away from the memories. Saxon had since always lived by the sea, enjoying the sense of freedom and freshness.

He often walked along the coast, no matter what the weather threw at it or him. He liked to think that the wind seemed to blow away the trivia attached to a case he was working on and leave the relevant facts neatly filed in the right part of his mind. When thinking, serious thinking, was required, there was no better place as far as he was concerned.

Closing the door behind him and locking it, he picked up the post on the mat and glanced through it. There was nothing there that wouldn't wait, at least until Saturday morning, and he spotted a few things that would go straight in the bin without even being opened. How on earth did some of these people come by his name and address?

Dropping the unopened post with his keys on the hall table, he took off his jacket as he walked through to the sitting room. The apartment was extensive and bright, chosen by Emma at least in part for its light.

Saxon had trusted her judgment on this, since he couldn't quite see much difference between the five places they had eventually whittled the choice down to. The short list, for him, was clear: transport and access to the sea-front. Once they were met, Emma had his blessing to make all the final decisions.

Fortunately, the ones she liked had met his requirements too, so there had been no disagreement on that score. They'd lived there about two years now.

Everything in the apartment was white and minimalist, but right now, it had to be admitted, it was somewhat untidy, certainly more so than usual. For a start, there were dirty clothes slung across some of the chairs. And Saxon paused to admire the tottering, but interesting, dish and plate sculpture growing in and around the kitchen sink.

Must stack that lot in the dishwasher. It wasn't the first time the thought had crossed his mind.

Saxon didn't cook much, at least not while Emma was around and even less when she was away. There didn't seem to be much point. So why rush to wash up every five minutes? They had plenty of china and enough forks. The dishes only greased up again next time you used them. He survived as much as he could on instant meals and the odd takeaway. Anything, in fact, except police canteen food. Unless of course, it was fried eggs and bacon on the menu – it was difficult to get that wrong. Any other delicacies were fed to the criminals in an effort to make them talk. He had grinned to himself, enjoying the traditional humour.

Emma was an interior designer and the flat was a prime example of her talent. He winced slightly at the thought of her reaction to its current state. He got himself a Scotch and water and stopped worrying. She and Kate were very successful at what they did. Emma's ideas were much sought after.

Money was not a problem to either of them. Her income outstripped his considerably though he didn't let it bother him. On the contrary, Emma's success was something he admired about her and always had. He'd been drawn to her in the first place by her energy and her determination.

He thought about her now, thought about what she might be doing as he sat and sipped his drink. He loosened his tie and put his feet up. Looking straight ahead, he faced the sea; it had been a pleasant day weather-wise and there were still some yachts racing back and forth between the two piers. The majority of them, however, headed back to the marina, as they were amateur sailors who didn't want to sail after sunset.

The sounds of traffic were muted because they were four floors up. Another one of the benefits of living in the top apartment. He recalled Kate's flat in Marylebone High Street. He liked the area, although he wouldn't have wanted to live there himself. They had been there for drinks and dinners on more than one occasion. He imagined the two of them coming home from work. No, they'd probably be going out to dinner somewhere, maybe after a brief drink in some wine bar with a friend or business acquaintance.

So, Emma was with Kate for the foreseeable future.

Paul Saxon settled down for a night of channel flicking and Scotch. He wasn't hungry.

Friday, May 10, Kemp Town, Brighton, 9.15PM

Across town, at chez Tucker, an altogether different kind of evening was kicking off.

Steve Tucker had earned the nickname "Fucker Tucker" during his limited time at school. Schoolboy humour being what it was, and is, there was no great mystery about the origins of the name.

Tucker had hated school with a passion. He didn't want to be there and never had. In Tucker's view, a good enough reason for not being there, but not particularly persuasive to the authorities. Sadly, nobody else wanted him at school either. Not the other kids and not the teachers either. One or two of his teachers had gone so far as to tell him that he would never amount to much, if anything.

It was hardly surprising then, that he had concluded at a relatively early age that for some strange reason he would never attain his full share of what life freely gave to others. Sometimes he thought that maybe it was his teachers' fault that his life was so clearly substandard compared to the lives of people around him. But he wasn't sure because he couldn't pin it down to anything specific. But he was sure they must have had something to do with it. Something they said maybe.

He planned to seek revenge on those teachers on a fairly regular basis, and show them just how clever he had become. How he would actually accomplish this never fully gelled in his mind. One idea he had considered was to send them something nasty in the post. But he wasn't sure how he'd get it in the envelope. Besides, it would probably seep out before it was delivered.

His revenge plots never came to fruition, as did very little else, because his concentration would waver after a few minutes, and he would become entranced by a television advert for a chat line or a refrigerator. Thirty seconds later, as with most things, the plans for revenge became a distant memory. He was a sad case.

You could describe Tucker's past as a disaster and have no fear of repercussions under the Trade Descriptions Act. But he had hopes for the future. Tucker saw himself as a comedian. He always had a filthy joke on the tip of his tongue, and had dreams of being a stand-up comic. The trouble was he had no concept of timing and zero talent. He couldn't understand why, at the few auditions he'd attended, he had never been allowed to lurch more than one minute into his routine. Some bastard always stopped him with a 'Thanks, we'll phone you.' They never did, the sods, they were bastards. Ignorant bastards.

Tucker handled these rejections with the thought that there was room for another Jack Dee in the world, there had to be. When fate whittled down the other – lesser – comedians a little, there would be space for him. Until then, he was going to show commitment to his chosen career. His plan was to keep up the practice and try to reach perfection. He believed in his talent, it just wasn't his time yet. He knew it would come one day.

In the meantime, Tucker was making do with regular employment. When he finally conned an employer that he was worth taking on, it was as a mortuary attendant. Most of the inmates didn't care and would never complain about his behaviour – after all, they could neither see nor smell him.

His tasks were menial; there was nothing in his daily routine to cause his brain to struggle too much. Just gurney pushing and large-drawer opening, and closing. Once a post-mortem was finished, he would hose down the bodies and the stainless steel tables, and wash the floors. These chores, though far from complicated, would on occasion become too much. Stress would frequently build up to such a crescendo in Tucker's life that he would have to relieve himself with a quick wank.

Wanking was the only way he could he could handle stress; the few moments of pleasure would wipe everything from his mind, rather like an electrical overload in a computer. Other people in a similarly stressful situation might go to the gym and work out for a few hours. Or take a walk in the fresh air, or maybe read a book. Not Tucker though, he would wank, preferably during his lunch break, whilst the other staff were outside in the sun enjoying a sandwich or a couple of pints in the pub.

As he stroked himself, he would be leering at one of the fresh bodies. When he reached his climax, which was usually in less than fifteen seconds, semen would fly in all directions and, because he never planned ahead more than ten seconds, a tissue was never at hand to contain the explosion. It often went down his leg. So far, he had been lucky – no one had spotted him at it. People weren't sure what the stains were. They only had their suspicions.

So it was that Tucker rather enjoyed the silent company of corpses, particularly the younger fresher ones. The sex of his companions was of no importance.

To his credit, he did have manners. He didn't stint on the pre- or post-coital conversation. He would talk to them for hours, knowing they would never answer back or turn away from him. This morning's little chat had been fairly typical.

'God, didn't I nearly break me fuckin' neck on the way in this mornin?' he had started. 'Fuckin' tripped on the fuckin' steps and woss more I'm gonna get condensation for me injuries.' He stabbed his fingers into the chest of the nearest body. 'You'll see, fuckin' government, got more money than sense anyway... Tossers.'

To his co-workers he occasionally appeared to be in a trance, as if the clientele were talking back to him. Maybe they were. Only he knew the answer to that one.

Tucker existed in a small dark basement flat in Brighton, not that the other flats in the building were dark or particularly small. Just his. It was clear that he'd never had the benefit of an interior designer looking around and giving him pointers on colour and texture.

He owned a television, a sofa, a beaten-up old chair, a few piles of rather old and by now quite sticky porn mags, and some bags of rubbish that had almost bonded with the floor.

On this particular Friday night his routine varied little. He came home, switched on the TV and was soon stuffing his face with the fish and chips that he'd brought with him from a takeaway down the road. He had a very international approach to his diet, with curry one night, Chinese the next. He didn't cook. Not even toast.

Fame was the only thing Tucker craved, apart from sex with someone who breathed – or had recently. Hence, his feeble attempts to break into the stand-up comic business. The thought that really sent shivers of excitement through him was not the telling of the jokes, or the joy of skilled delivery, timed to perfection. No, it was much more basic than that. To have several hundred people hanging on to his every word. To possess that level of control. Even thinking about it made him tremble with anticipation.

Just to have one person's attention for more than a few seconds was uncharted water for Tucker.

He had role models. He collected pictures and videos of his favourite stars, and had pasted and taped pictures all over the wall of his television room. He didn't call it a sitting room, because he wasn't sure what the difference was between a lounge and a sitting room. It was less embarrassing if he referred to it as the television room.

Loneliness and desperation usually caught up with Tucker on Friday and Saturday evenings, when he would wander the promenade and, if he was feeling bold, indulge his urge to watch couples on the beach, writhing around in the darkness.

He occasionally stood in the shadows under the crumbling West Pier. He chose this spot in preference to the Palace Pier because the seriously randy couples came here, knowing that there was less chance of being seen.

Once, a few years back, Tucker was caught dick-handed and was forced to run for his life. The bloke who'd spotted him was massive and could throw the cricket-ball sized pebbles from the beach with the force of an Olympic shot-putter. Three quite large boulders hit Tucker squarely in the back, knocking the wind out of him. He found it impossible to run fast with his trousers around his knees and a stiffy thrashing about in front. Completely ruined what little streamlining he had. Luckily for him the guy didn't give chase – he had bigger fish to fry.

This close encounter of the unwanted kind probably turned Tucker into one of the most cautious perverts in the south of England. It also kept him flat-bound for a few nights, afraid to venture out just in case the police were looking for him. Not that they would have to scour the streets for him anyway… They knew his address.

Some nights, Tucker would go to the pub and try to chat up a girl, but he never managed to get past the first all-important glance.

'One day,' Tucker screamed to the mirror in his bedroom. 'One day, they'll all wish they'd known me... Fuckin' bastards.'

When he was drunk, which was often, he would stagger around his room conversing with his reflection in the mirror. He considered the Steve Tucker in the mirror to be handsome and clever. But they never saw this one. They never came to his flat so how could they meet the handsome one? Mirror Steve was suave and sophisticated and, no matter what Tucker did or said in the real world, Mirror Steve was always smiling and approving.

Tucker's decorating skills were in evidence here too. He'd covered the edge of the mirror with snippets of wallpaper and wrapping paper to make it special. This was, after all, the door to Mirror Steve's world. It had to be special. When he was very drunk, out-of-his-skull drunk, he would creep up on the mirror and try to catch Mirror Steve unawares. Mirror Steve always caught him out though, and got there first. Tucker would tell him a joke. Which he always screwed up. But if Tucker laughed, which he always did, then Mirror Steve would laugh too. So never mind – it was the closest he would ever get to an audience.

Steve was not a well man.

Chapter 6

Tuesday, May 14, Sewel Mill, 2.30PM

Barbara Jenner parked her car in the public car park behind the main parade of shops in Sewel Mill. Babs made a beeline for the tack shop, which had been in the Tufnell family for at least three generations now. Babs was about as horsey as anyone can be without actually crossing the species barrier, so Tufnell's was her second home.

She was tall and very confident. Although not a pretty woman, she had a mature elegance and, at forty-one years of age, she still had the kind of figure that occasionally made men head-butt lampposts. Babs was far from shy about her appearance and dressed to show what she had. She was used to turning heads.

As she entered Tufnell's, her senses were immediately attacked by the glorious smell of fresh, unsoiled wax jackets. Babs wandered around for a while, content to browse. Looking to see what was new this week, if anything. Gloria, the owner, was serving another customer but it didn't look to be a lengthy transaction. When it was her turn to be served, she greeted Gloria with an air kiss past the side of her head and, after the usual pleasantries, asked if she could try on a few pairs of chaps and some jodhpurs.

'Of course you can, you just help yourself,' Gloria answered cheerfully. 'I'm sure you know where to look by now.' Gloria disappeared past a curtain at the back of the shop.

'Tea?' she called out to the sound of cups rattling.

'Oh, yes please, I'd love one, Gloria darling, but no sugar otherwise I'll never find anything in here to fit me and you'll go out of business! Couldn't have that now, could we?' Babs had a clear voice and it carried well.

Gloria came close to saying that today's modern fabrics can take unbelievable stresses and that it shouldn't be a problem.

However, she thought better of it and remained silent. In common with many people who deal with the general public for a living, Gloria had developed very good self-control over the boundary between thoughts and tongue; it was well-guarded at all times. Besides, Gloria liked Babs and she was a good customer.

Babs knew the layout of the shop well; she only ever shopped there for this kind of thing. It would have been unthinkable to go anywhere else. It must have been at least thirty years since she first set foot in the place as a youngster, when Gloria's parents were still running it. Occasionally she would buy from a farm wholesaler for feed and bits of ironmongery, but this was the shop for clothes, and she felt that people should support the local traders.

She found some chaps wide enough to fit around her generous thighs and two pairs of jodhpurs, paid for them, finished her tea, said her goodbyes and left the shop. Next stop, the butcher. As she walked down the High Street, she didn't notice the man watching her. Nobody else noticed him either. He took care that they shouldn't. He was too well-practised and too normal-looking. He was just an ordinary man in the High Street, going about his business. He attracted no attention.

Babs made her purchase at the butcher's shop – two large pork chops and some mince – and then casually wandered up one side of the street and then down the other. Still she was being watched. The man shifted his shopping bag from one hand to the other as he crossed the road. He did so in order to by-pass the extremely small branch of a building society. There was a CCTV camera pointing out at the street and the watcher was aware of this. No point in slipping up over something so trivial.

Babs had finished everything on her mental list and headed back to the car park. She'd paid and displayed for two hours and there was still over thirty minutes left. She gave her ticket to the person waiting to pull into her space. The car loaded up with the morning's shopping, Babs started the engine and pulled out of her space. At that moment, another car quite close by followed suit.

Like synchronised driving, the two cars travelled at a sensible speed out of the village, with an even more sensible gap between them.

Babs didn't even notice the other car. It wasn't a car to attract attention. The drive was not long, only about a mile, but Hazel Lane was narrow and it often took longer than you would expect. If you met another car coming in the opposite direction, one of you had to back up to a farm gate or a driveway to let the other person pass.

Babs was ruthless when it came to giving way in the lane. She had developed a very effective technique for use on those occasions when she met someone coming from the opposite direction. She would slow down and make a half-hearted attempt to pull over to one side, as if to let the other person attempt to pass. But she would in fact be stopped in the middle of the road, making it impossible for the other driver, who would then almost certainly give way and reverse back to the nearest passing place. Babs would smile in a helpless girlie way and drive on, feeling the slight thrill of triumph.

Even the vicar was subject to the same technique. Babs did attend the village church but only for hat comparisons and a bit of general socialising. Today there was no confrontation, clerical or otherwise.

Babs indicated that she was turning right about one hundred yards before her drive. The car behind her didn't need to slow down or even glance at the house. All that was needed in the way of information on the house and surrounding area had been acquired weeks ago, when no one was home.

Tuesday, May 14, 29 St Nicholas Lane, Sewel Mill, 3.30PM

Clive Marks went straight round to the back of the house. Edie was out anyway, so he didn't expect to run into her. No, it was Cecil Hayward he was looking for and Cecil was in his shed, as usual.

The envelope was ready for him, as usual, and Cecil smiled cheerfully as Marks handed over a small package in exchange. Marks nodded in return.

Few words were spoken but the two men had a regular meeting like this most weeks. The pleasantries had all been used up years ago. Now it was purely business. The arrangement worked beautifully.

Tuesday, May 14, Anvil Wood House, 3.45PM

Babs unloaded the car and walked to her front door. Anvil Wood House was a large rambling Victorian red brick building with hanging tiles from the first floor up, and moss-covered Kent peg tiles on the roof.

At the back of the property, there was a substantial yard with stabling for twenty horses and a ménage. She had inherited it from her mother, on her death almost twenty years ago. Two of the horses belonged to Babs and the others were paying guests, mostly owned by the daughters of local well-to-do folk.

She walked through the hallway then down a small flight of steps to the kitchen, put the meat in the fridge and then went out to the stables to check the horses. The groom and the two local girls who helped muck out and generally run the stables had gone for the day. Everything was neat and tidy and life was good.

Tuesday, May 14, Sewel Mill Station, 5.30PM

Poppy had left work early that afternoon and the train pulled in to Sewel Mill station on time. In her line of work, she wasn't tied to a desk from nine till five, and today wasn't a press day, so there had been no reason to hang around.

Poppy was an equestrian journalist with a mainstream horse magazine. While she enjoyed her work and the contact it gave her with horses and horsey people, what she had really wanted to be was an investigative journalist. The problem was, she never seemed to be in the right place at the right time, and no one ever tipped her off about anything. She was addicted to crime programmes and investigative documentaries on the television. She saw herself as the trusted reporter who works hand in hand with the police to bring criminals to justice, or as the cunning investigator who brings the breaking news to CNN.

Babs and Poppy had been together for twelve years, and the official story for the village was that they were cousins who were widowed young, cohabiting for company and to share expenses. Truth was they were lovers. They met one night in a gay pub in Brighton. Babs was on the prowl and Poppy was waiting for true love to come and tap her on the shoulder. Their ships came in at the same time, to the same mooring. The fact that they both had an interest in horses came as an added bonus.

Poppy kept the relationship secret from her colleagues, as she would find it too embarrassing if they found out. When the subject of men would raise its throbbing head, as it frequently did in an office full of women and a few gay men, Poppy found it hard-going. It was painful and distasteful to even think of men. She loathed them, not because of some distant trauma from her childhood or bad treatment from a relationship. She quite simply hated men and had long since given up trying to work out how or why she felt that way. She just did.

Now she was headed home. She knew Babs was taking care of dinner, as she usually did during the week.

Tuesday, May 14, Anvil Wood House, 5.50PM

In the kitchen of Anvil Wood House, Babs was preparing the pork chops. She put a small knob of butter on each one, followed by a little sage. She would add a few onion rings later. The potatoes were nearly done and the French beans lay in wait for a swift steaming. The ladies ate well.

The kitchen was big and airy with all of the original Victorian features. They both loved it. Over one corner hung a cast-iron and wood-slat clothes dryer, raised and lowered by a rope. Underneath this was a shallow butler's sink with a wooden plate rack next to it. The floor was small black and white tile, chess-board style, and in the middle was the main work surface, ten feet long by four feet wide. Halfway along one wall was the cooking range and the opposite facing wall supplied the meagre light with many quite small stone-edged gothic-style windows.

As the chops sizzled under the grill, Babs heard a sound outside the back door. It sounded like a dog, not that they owned one, but sometimes the local farm dogs went walkabout and came sniffing around, knocking the lids off the dustbins. She left her cooking to lean out of the top section of the stable-type back door so she could shoo them away. There were no dogs, it was Poppy, and she had a few harnesses and blanket samples from work to test out and write an appraisal for, and had gone straight to the stables to drop them off, rather than come in the front door.

She and Babs kissed on the lips, exchanged daily news while the food cooked and when it was time to eat, sat down to enjoy their meal. This was the best moment in their day, relaxing together and exchanging news and views. After dinner, they adjourned to the sitting room for some television and complained about the standard of the programmes. They shared a passion for Felicity Kendal and a disdain for blonde bimbo presenters, particularly the ones who made a media career out of stealing other people's husbands.

They talked horses for a while and then retired to bed at about midnight.

Wednesday, May 15, Brentwood Mansions, 12.30AM

Kate leaned against the wall as Emma fumbled with the key. Emma had taken over the task of opening the front door once Kate had demonstrated beyond most reasonable doubt that her own efforts to make it somehow fit into the lock were not likely to be successful.

Fortunately, Emma had more luck and the two of them staggered into the flat, saved from the effort and expense of going down to Claridge's for the night in the hope that the morning would see them able to operate the damn lock.

'You weren't serious about going to Claridge's, were you?' asked Emma. 'You can't have been.'

'Of course I was. You wanted to spend the night on the stairs?' answered Kate. 'I've done it before, but only once, I have to admit.'

'What, slept on the stairs?'

'No, you idiot. Mislaid my keys and gone down to stay at Claridge's. It was bloody expensive, I can tell you.' She smiled at Emma, who put her arms around Kate, as much to stop her falling over as to show affection.

'Thank goodness I was here tonight to save you from such a dreadful fate.'

'Indeed. Don't know what I'll do without you when you go back home. Speaking of which, God, it's so good to be home,' Kate breathed. 'My shoes really do need to come off right now this minute.'

'You need at least a pint of water to help dilute all that wonderful wine.' Emma headed off towards the kitchen.

'I think I could probably give up caffeine for Chateau d'Yquem,' Kate announced. She plonked herself down on her bed, kicking off her shoes.

They had been to a new restaurant that evening, one that Kate had been involved in through a lengthy renovation process. Sadly, the food hadn't been quite as good as the décor, which had been brilliant, as the two of them had frequently remarked during the course of the evening.

Yes, it was a triumph for the interior design business but not so for the catering. However, that could improve, they allowed, trying to be generous.

'So, will you call him?' Kate asked. They had discussed Paul Saxon at length while getting ready to go out earlier in the evening. They had considered the possibility of calling him after dinner – or rather of Emma calling him, while Kate disappeared discreetly to her bedroom.

Emma was happy to be with Kate but she hadn't altogether given up on her marriage. Hence, the discussions about 'will I or won't I phone him?' The marriage was certainly under a lot of strain and she knew that drastic action was required if she and Paul were to continue their lives together.

Paul was an intelligent man and she still loved him. At least she thought she did. But he didn't seem to grasp how much at risk they were. He seemed to just accept the difficulties they were facing as being normal, given his line of work. He wasn't aware that not all marriages were like theirs.

Emma shook her head. 'Too tired,' she yawned.

Both were asleep as their heads hit their respective pillows. There would be no pacing around the flat tonight.

Wednesday, May 15, Anvil Wood House, 2.00AM

The bedroom that Poppy shared with Babs was on the second floor; it was one of many. Victorians did like big families and this house was a true reflection of the architectural splendour of that era. There were eight bedrooms in total and various day rooms along with a toilet on each of the three floors. Babs and Poppy had not altered the house, preferring to leave it in its original state. Some of the rooms were empty because they didn't have enough furniture to fill them.

Heating was not a problem; they had not bothered to install

central heating. Neither of them particularly felt the cold and, if the weather took a drastic turn for the worse, they would decamp to the kitchen and huddle near the cooking range.

Even if they had been awake in their king-size bed, they wouldn't have heard the sound of feet running along the middle of the lane, fifty yards from the house. The man stayed on the hard surface, through the front gate and following the path around the side of the house to the back. He paused for breath, not from exhaustion, but from anticipation. The night was inky black, with no moon, and no streetlights. It was still warm and humid.

The horses became restless; they sensed something moving behind the house. After five minutes of total silence, all had become calm again in the stable.

The window in the kitchen opened with little effort. The sound of something landing on the tiled floor was lost in the sheer size of the house.

But Babs woke anyway; she was thirsty. And as she put on her dressing gown in their bedroom, two floors below in the kitchen, a hand was reaching for the largest of their collection of carving knives. *Take nothing with you and you'll leave nothing behind.* Poppy half woke up, disturbed by the sounds Babs was making. Babs told her to go back to sleep, and made her way downstairs, towards the kitchen. Years of living in the same house meant she had no use for a light. At the foot of the stairs, she stopped dead.

The noise she heard wasn't the usual sort of sound she would expect to hear in a house in the dead of night. It was a sort of squeaking sound, rather like new rubber-soled shoes on a polished floor. Babs started to move, slowly looking around with squinting eyes. She could see nothing and was feeling around the corner for the light switch when a hand grabbed her wrist. Babs took a deep breath intending to scream but never got there.

The knife entered her neck an inch below her vocal cords and ripped violently to her left, severing her carotid artery. She had no time to scream; even if she had the time it would have been pointless, the air escaped from her lungs before getting to her vocal cords. The hissing gurgling sound that came out of the fast-expiring Babs would not have woken a mouse.

She fell backwards onto the hall floor with a dull wet thud, blood shooting up into the air above her head and down onto her face as she hit the floor. Babs thrashed about for a few seconds, staring at her killer. Her mind was screaming "Why?" But no words came from her lips. She was dead before the killer rained another six stabs into her chest.

He climbed the stairs, slowly and silently; the visit to the house some weeks ago proved invaluable. He had an excellent memory and could have made the journey through the house blindfolded.

Quietly, he turned the doorknob to the bedroom and slid in, opening the door only just wide enough, standing in the bedroom for a few minutes, savouring the thrill of what was to happen. The voice in his head that had urged him on this far fell silent as he slowly moved towards the sleeping Poppy. He climbed onto the bed. Slowly and carefully he straddled her. He remained still, knowing that Poppy would wake up eventually.

Poppy did wake and in a sleepy but affectionate voice said, 'You know I've got an early start tomorrow.' She put up her hands to feel Babs' ample breasts, and was instantly and completely awake in blind terror. She had no idea she was feeling the smooth texture of latex rubber. All that registered with her was that there were no breasts. She screamed and struggled, but lacked the bodyweight to make any impression, the weight of the killer was simply too much for her. The nauseating smell of latex hit her nose as a large hand covered her mouth, and she started to gag.

She was still screaming as the knife blade was slipped slowly through her liver and past her spine into the mattress – then all she could do was gasp. Thirty seconds later she was dead. He was slow to climb off the still, but warm, body of Poppy. He had started to enjoy this one. Already he could hear the voice in his head. He heard the pleasure in the voice.

The killer dragged the body of Poppy down the stairs and set about carefully dismembering the victims – taking his time, he started spreading the body parts around the house.

Chapter 7

Wednesday, May 15, Saxon's Apartment, 7.35AM

Saxon was used to phone calls at this time. His days tended to start early and finish late, sometimes blending into one big day. But even on the phone, Saxon could sense the tremor in Parker's voice and he realised instantly that what he was about to hear was serious shit. Parker spelled it out in graphic detail, the horror of his words being reinforced by the shock in his voice.

While he listened to Parker's description of the scene inside Anvil Wood House, Saxon was shocked too. Not just because it was gruesome but also because it was not what he'd anticipated. Could it be connected to his serial killer? They rarely changed their MO. On the contrary, they thrived on routine and ritual. This made no sense. It couldn't be connected – or could it?

Saxon prepared himself mentally for what he would see back in Sewel Mill this time. He told Parker to keep everyone out of the house, even the forensics guys, until he had viewed the situation.

Wednesday, 15 May, Anvil Wood House, 8.15AM

When Saxon arrived at the house, it was crawling with forensics people. Superintendent Mitchell had made an early appearance, although he was in no condition to talk to anyone now, given that Saxon could see he was busy throwing up in a hedge.

Parker appeared next to Saxon as if from nowhere, visibly shaken. 'Sorry, sir, I was out-ranked; the superintendent just barged straight in there. He ordered the forensics people in, telling them they didn't have to wait for you.'

Parker gestured at the house. 'Then he skidded on a few bits and pieces lying around in the hallway…' Parker's voice faded slightly.

'Over his vomit-tolerance level, was it?' Saxon asked, not

unsympathetically. They'd all been there at some time or other. It went with the territory.

Parker nodded grimly. 'Yeah, I reckon it was.' He smiled for the first time that morning. 'He had to dash outside before he ruined parts of the crime scene with his breakfast.'

The two of them looked towards the house. 'Both of them downstairs?' Saxon queried.

'Ground and first floor,' answered Parker. 'All over the place.' He leaned forward, his hands on his knees. Saxon moved back slightly…just in case he too was about to throw up. Then he pulled himself up slowly to his full height again.

'Before you go in, sir, you've got to know. It's like nothing you've seen before.' He shook his head. 'It's like a fucking horror film in there.' His voice wavered again.

'Okay, thanks for the warning, Parker,' replied Saxon. 'So, tell me, who found the bodies?'

'The groom, sir, poor sod.' Parker had regained his composure. 'Thank Christ it wasn't one of the schoolchildren, the ones who help out here. The groom's a youngish lad, name of Peter. He's pretty shaken up. He's sitting in the stable talking to one of the local bobbies.'

'Has Dr Clarke been inside yet?'

'Yes, sir, he left quite quickly too – he just walked in spent about five minutes poking around, came out, said they're dead, and left. I guess it's quite easy to pronounce someone dead in these circumstances.'

As Parker finished speaking, Mitchell had recovered enough to walk again, and he approached the two of them, slightly subdued by the events of the past few minutes. The remains of half-digested corn flakes clung to his chin; the odd bit dropped off as he spoke. Saxon was embarrassed for him and offered him a handkerchief, which he took with a trembling hand.

'Commander,' he said, mustering as much authority as he could, given that his knees were still shaking, 'before you say anything, I must emphasise that I don't think this is connected to the other killings, completely different MO.' He paused to collect his thoughts further and to steady himself. 'We can see that clearly the other killings are almost, dare I say, gentle, when you compare them to this carnage.'

Saxon cringed inside. *Prat,* he thought. Knowing Mitchell as he did, it was obvious to Saxon that Mitchell's main concern was whether he had a serial killer on his territory. He didn't want one, not if it could be avoided. Saxon knew Mitchell would be well aware that, chances were, a serial killer was hard to trap. The crimes might not be solved and that was not going to be good for the statistics. His monthly crime figures would suffer.

Saxon wondered if it was worth pointing out that there was another way of looking at it. If Mitchell was party to solving the crimes, to catching a serial killer, then the possible rewards could be both significant and long-lasting.

However, Saxon abandoned that train of thought as a waste of time and effort. Instead, it occurred to him, not for the first time, that it must be awful to be such an arsehole; a narrow-minded one at that.

'Alex, under normal circumstances I would agree with you completely, but until I have all the facts I'll reserve judgement,' he answered quietly. 'However, I don't think we should dismiss the possibility that maybe our killer is losing control.' He gave Mitchell time to digest this possibility.

Suddenly he realised what it was that was niggling away at his subconscious. It was the smell of cooking that he was aware of, even outside the house. He called to Parker. 'They must have left the oven on. Better switch it off, before the whole place goes up in smoke.'

Then he turned back to Mitchell, who was still defending his view that the killings at Anvil Wood House were unconnected to the other three murders.

'Well, I'll be surprised if you find a connection,' he went on.

When Saxon didn't answer, he continued. 'They're not the same age group, they didn't live alone.' Mitchell was sounding more like his old self. 'Quite honestly, I can see nothing to link them to the other deaths, and the MO just underlines the fact that it must be a different killer. I have to admit I wasn't in there long enough to take a thorough look around but...'

'Nevertheless, we have to...' Saxon began.

'Yes, of course,' Mitchell interrupted impatiently. 'Nevertheless, we shall look for a connection and, if there is one, I will have to agree with you,' he said, making it obvious that he expected no such thing to happen. 'Let's hope we find it soon. I don't like this kind of spotlight on us.'

Saxon could see that there was no point at all in pursuing this line of thought with Mitchell. It was getting them nowhere. He was anxious to have a look himself and form his own opinions, so he started to step around Mitchell to head for the house. 'Shall we?' he suggested.

Saxon hadn't planned it that way, but it was this move on his part that suddenly reminded Mitchell of urgent business back in Brighton. Going into the house and looking into the crime at hand could safely be left to his staff and to the commander, who after all professed an expertise in these matters. What was needed back at HQ was a clear head to co-ordinate and manage the situation, to provide focus. Had he articulated these thoughts aloud, he would have had complete agreement from Saxon.

Mitchell got one of the patrol cars to take him back to Brighton. His uniform was in such a state that he didn't want to use his own car. One of the PCs would take his car back later.

Nobody was sorry to see him go. Interestingly, nobody was particularly snide about Mitchell's emptying his breakfast all over the hedge. Everyone there could remember their first murder scene and, although the topic hadn't been discussed between them yet, it would subsequently be agreed that they had never, any of them, seen anything quite like this before. It was the stuff nightmares were made of. Mitchell's route to the lofty heights of superintendent hadn't included much in the way of vicious killings that could have prepared him for this.

Wednesday, May 15, Newhaven, 9.00AM

Alan Turner normally sailed out of Newhaven Harbour with up to ten fishermen, or aspiring fishermen, and a cold box full of beer. He would take them to one of the many submerged wrecks to fish for conger eels or, if they weren't biting, to look for a shoal of mackerel. It was a nice little business and he enjoyed it.

Today was different and he was alone. He did this maybe twice a month and made as much money out of it as all his little chartered fishing trips put together.

He was after bigger fish today. Somewhere between eight and ten miles out, he would meet up with another small boat. Turner wasn't sure if he would recognise the captain or not. No one was expected to exchange names, so it didn't matter really. It was probably best not to know.

He didn't hang about out there. He'd be back in Newhaven by early afternoon. Better to do it in broad daylight. Less suspicious.

He didn't keep the stuff either. It was passed on the same day. What happened to it after that was none of his business. He couldn't have cared less, so long as he was paid on time.

Wednesday, May 15, Anvil Wood House, 9.15AM

Saxon and Parker kitted themselves out with gloves and shoe covers, then decided to take the advice of the forensics boys and go for the overalls as well. They were glad for the tip. As they shone their torches around, Saxon realised that the scene that faced them was surreal, no other word for it. The killer had closed all of the curtains on the ground floor, and then removed all of the fuses. He had smeared blood over the walls with a large house-painting brush and left a bath running on the first floor. The fire brigade had attended to push holes into the ceiling plaster to allow the water to drain through, before the sheer weight pulled the whole lot down.

Saxon looked around with dismay, and said gloomily, 'If there was any forensic evidence around the place, there sure as hell isn't much now – fucking place is almost washed clean.'

'Sir, do you suppose the sick bastard set out to create this kind of atmosphere to indulge some fantasy or other?' Parker asked.

'Well, either that, or he's deliberately setting out to shock us, or to try to set us off on the wrong track.' Saxon was running several different possibilities through his head. 'If this is the same killer that did Janson and the others, then the change in MO is so drastic that it really does look like the work of someone new. Don't ask me how, but I know it's the same fucker – he's out to try and fool us.'

'Maybe a robbery gone wrong? Kids who came in to nick the TV and the video, but who panicked and then got carried away when one of the women came downstairs and surprised them?' offered Parker.

'Don't think so, very unlikely,' mused Saxon. 'But why wouldn't there be the normal signs of a burglary? Let's face it, kids don't usually go round doing this sort of thing.'

'Yeah, and nothing much seems to be missing,' added Parker, as they left the sitting room. 'All the normal stuff seems to be still here, as far as I can see.' He paused. 'Oh, my God,' he said, gesturing as the shaft of light from his lamp cut through darkness and the raining drops of water.

Bits of Babs and Poppy were arranged up the stairs. Fingers were delicately planted in a large ceramic pot containing a huge rubber plant, by the front door.

They followed their noses – the slightly sickly smell of cooking was coming from the kitchen. When it dawned on everyone exactly what it was that had been cooking, several more people had to leave the building, clutching their hands over their mouths.

'What in God's name makes someone do this?' said Parker quietly, almost to himself.

Saxon stood nearby and pondered for a while. Then, thumb on one temple and fingers on the other, he said, 'It could be any one of a number of reasons, Parker,' he began. 'Abuse in childhood is supposed to be the main culprit. But people forget that some bastards are just born evil. Then it might be a desire to be noticed. Who knows?'

He looked at Parker, who hadn't necessarily anticipated a response to what was clearly something of a rhetorical question, and smiled grimly. 'You and I both know that, in more cases than not, the people who do this stuff are ordinary everyday people. Nothing particularly special about them. People that you wouldn't look at twice if you passed them on the street.' Parker nodded. 'Also, don't forget, Parker, our killer, in his own mind, might well think he's doing nothing wrong.'

'What, like he's on a mission?' Parker asked.

'Hmm. Suppose there's a link between these people that we don't know about. A connection that doesn't necessarily make sense to us, but makes sense to the killer.'

'I still think it's got to be a head case,' said Parker.

'Well, it's a safe bet that whoever is doing this isn't thinking about it the same way we would, that's for sure,' Saxon answered.

They carried on their inspection, careful not to move anything or brush up against the various body parts scattered around the house. It made for a grim progress.

They wandered from room to room, looking for clues but realising quickly that there were none to be found. The only things that told them anything were the footprints in the blood on the dry areas of the floor. They looked like stumps. Big round stumps. Vaguely foot-shaped, but more round than long. The stumps were everywhere – even places the killer needn't have gone. It seemed to Saxon that Mr Stumpy from Stumpy land had paid a visit to show off his new stumps. *We are being taunted.* The last stumpy print was on a plate, on top of the cooking range.

Wednesday, May 15, Thicket Road, Upper Norwood, 3.00PM

Keith Jenner took his car keys from the Versace dish on the hall table and flicked the remote control for the Bose sound system. Leaving the house, he used another remote for the car. His wife also had a BMW, although hers was only a 3-series.

Michelle was relaxing at the back of the house, on one of their three patio areas. Her sister was round. Again. It was beyond Jenner's understanding as to why whenever they had anything new, Michelle had to invite Carly round to see it. This time it was the new garden furniture, recently imported from Thailand via some store in Sloane Square. He personally couldn't see the difference between the old stuff and this new furniture, apart from the price tag, of course. Still, it made Michelle happy, and if Michelle was happy, she was off his back. He couldn't ask for more than that.

He looked at his Rolex – a real one, not a fake, mind. Telscombe Cliffs was about an hour and a half away. He had plenty of time before he had to meet his sister.

Wednesday, May 15, Brighton Mortuary, 4.00PM

Saxon and Parker attended the post mortems of Barbara Jenner and Penelope Field. It wasn't exactly something they looked forward to, but a post mortem could provide vital information and Saxon was desperate for something to that might kick-start the investigation again. There was no way he would have missed this particular one. He also knew the pathologist and valued his input.

The pathologist was Dr Richard Clarke. He was a powerful man with a powerful personality that often left people in his wake reeling, wondering what had hit them. Some found his presence disturbing and intimidating. Others found him charismatic and empowering.

Saxon was somewhere in the middle. He was not at all intimidated by Richard's somewhat larger than life personality, although he could easily see how it could irritate or upset some people. Saxon viewed Clarke as an equal, both from a professional and a social point of view. He also quite liked him; he seemed to be such a thoughtful sort of person. Occasionally they played squash and had a drink together when their paths crossed at the gym. Clarke kept himself very fit and Saxon rarely managed to get the better of him on the squash court.

Parker's reaction to the pathologist, on the other hand, was less favourable. He found Clarke to be loud and overbearing. Unusually for him, Parker tended to become tongue-tied in his presence and, when he could manage to utter a few syllables, they often came out in the wrong order. Nevertheless, he put his personal feelings about Clarke on one side, as always, because they were irrelevant.

They dressed for the occasion as required. Parker used to think that they looked like choirboys, but he no longer noticed. Fully togged up in protective clothing, they went to join Clarke and his team, and what was left of Babs and Poppy.

Apart from his day-to-day work as the area pathologist, Clarke was also the police doctor. It increased his workload dramatically – his excuse for taking on the extra work was that he always wanted to play Sherlock Holmes. Saxon couldn't imagine how he managed to stay so fit; Clarke absolutely radiated energy and health, no matter how many times in the week he worked twenty hours a day. He envied the pathologist.

I'll bet he does a marathon in less than three hours too. Devoting more time to getting fit went on Saxon's To-Do list every January 1st. And stayed there.

'Good afternoon, gentlemen.' Clarke looked up as they entered the mortuary. 'Welcome. Do come in.'

The early afternoon had been devoted entirely to an extensive examination of the victims as they had been found. It had taken the SOCOs quite a while in the morning to locate all the fingers in order to allow the fingernail scrapings to be done. While Jake Dalton was finishing that gruesome task, Melanie Jones had combed all the body hair of the two women, to see if anything fell out.

All orifices were checked for hidden objects. Buttons were matched and counted. Underwear was searched for any pubic hairs, which didn't match those of the victims. Stab wounds were aligned with holes in dressing gowns and pyjamas.

The surgical examination was beginning as Saxon and Parker arrived. First, the visual inspection.

Clarke spoke into a microphone that was pinned to the collar of his green overalls. 'Well, what have we here?' he went on. 'A bit of digging and poking by the look of things.' Clarke had a somewhat theatrical manner on occasions and this demonstrated itself in a tendency to perform to the audience in his theatre. It could have been irritating. But Clarke was without doubt a consummate professional and Saxon forgave him his slight lapses into actor style. He and Parker stood in silence as Clarke went about the grizzly business of examining the body parts of the two women laid out before them.

This first visual inspection took at least half an hour, as Jake stepped in periodically to take photographs, measure the width and depth of each stab wound, and remove samples for analysis. The two men worked together smoothly, with little need for instruction or questions.

Once this first part of the examination was completed, Clarke made an incision across the back of Babs' head and pulled the entire scalp over her face. This was done so that the pathologist could saw around the skull and remove the brain without messing up the face. It could all be put back so that the stitching was at the back of the head and not show if the deceased was to be viewed in their coffin. The major organs were removed after a great deal of sawing and snapping of cartilage and slicing of muscle. Bits weighed, some liquidised, and some put in chemicals. Dr Clarke worked quickly and methodically through his routine, continuing his non-stop monologue into his microphone.

Both Saxon and Parker had taken the precaution of eating well – but not too much – beforehand, but Saxon, needing an escape from the reality of the process happening before him, looked at the opposite wall and wondered if Clarke actually felt queasy when he dissected someone's remains, or whether the feeling wore off after several procedures.

On the other hand, maybe he had counselling to blank the feelings. Maybe it didn't bother him; maybe he didn't care. Far from feeling uncomfortable or even neutral about what he was doing, Clarke seemed actually to be enjoying himself.

It struck Saxon that the look on Clarke's face was similar to that of a pianist in deep concentration as he entertained a hall full of people at a concert. It was consistent with his view that Clarke had possibly missed his vocation, hence the feeling that many people expressed, both admirers and critics, that Clarke was playing to the audience.

Eventually Clarke finished both the autopsies, leaving Jake to stitch up and tidy what little remained of the bodies. Switching off his microphone, he took off his apron and threw it with his surgical gloves in the bin. He devoted some considerable time to washing his hands and spoke to Saxon over his shoulder as he did so.

'Paul, I can't tell you much I'm afraid,' he began. 'All I can tell you is that they were stabbed by a right-handed man, probably the same height as me, and that's undoubtedly what they died from. Stab wounds, a bit obvious really, don't you think?'

'Funny you should say that, Richard,' Saxon responded quickly. 'I did notice that there was rather lot of blood around the place, and it's true that both the victims seemed to have one or two holes in their bodies.'

He smiled and lowered his voice. 'They teach us to notice things like that, usually just after we join the force,' Saxon said dryly.

Clarke looked at him with eyebrows raised. 'Sorry, Paul, that's all I can say. I can only tell you how they died.'

'You're sure that there was nothing under their fingernails?' Saxon tried not to sound desperate.

Clarke just gave him a look over his glasses.

Saxon continued. 'Sorry, forget it, Richard, I'm just clutching at anything – you would have told me if you'd found anything.' He shrugged. 'It's just that we are going nowhere fast with these other cases, and I can't even tell if this bastard is the same killer.'

Clarke held up one hand, now a very clean hand. 'There is one thing that may be of use to you.' He directed them back to the body parts of Barbara Jenner and they gathered obediently around the table. 'If you look at the way her hand and fingers were severed,' he went on, 'you'll see that he cut carefully between the joints. He didn't touch the bone once.'

He looked up at Saxon. 'It's typical of all the amputations. This man knew exactly what he was doing. Maybe he's a butcher or a slaughterhouse worker.'

'Or a doctor,' said Parker hesitantly.

Clarke stiffened and looked briefly at Parker. He smiled at him and then turned back to Saxon. 'That's for you two to discover.' He stopped smiling and shook his head. 'Sometimes I think that my job is far simpler than yours.'

Wednesday, May 15, Telscombe Cliffs 6.00PM

To say that Keith Jenner was pissed off was something of an understatement. He looked once again at his watch. But no matter how expensive it was, it couldn't deliver his sister at the time she had said she would be there.

She had never missed an appointment. He would have a thing

or two to say to her when she eventually turned up.

But that wasn't his biggest worry. No, his main concern was that his reasons for failing to deliver the stuff on time would surely fall, not on deaf ears, but on the kind of ears that are just not interested in excuses, no matter how good.

He climbed out of his van, lit a cigarette and sat on the grass verge. Trying to stay calm, he looked up and down the lane and then at his watch again. He had always thought that this was a stupid place to do the handover, but he had faith in Babs and, as usual, he'd given in to her better judgement. She was always the clever one – besides he'd always held the belief that women were far more cunning than men.

She'd told him that the spot was perfect because Telscombe Cliffs was one of the few villages that could be accessed by only one road. She'd explained that this kept the flow of traffic down to the minimum. In addition, the road was cut into the side of the Downs and there were few trees in the area, so he could see well in advance if a car was approaching from either direction. His instructions from Babs were that if he saw a police car coming his way, then he was to puncture a tyre and that would be his excuse for being there.

He tried her mobile for the fifth time. Little did he know that it was trying to ring but the battery was just too wet as it swam around inside a plastic evidence bag in the storeroom at Brighton Police Station.

An hour crawled by and Jenner kicked his van a few times.

'Fuckin' bitch...where the fuck are you? Can't rely on anyone,' he shouted at the sky. He climbed back into his van and drove erratically back to London – barely able to suppress his rage and his fear.

Wednesday, May 15, Brighton Mortuary, 6.30PM

Their business at the mortuary was finished, thankfully. Parker had already disrobed and was on his way to the door, desperate for a cigarette.

Steve Tucker waited in the background for Jake to finish stitching, so that he could play with his hose.

Melanie Jones was avoiding any kind of contact, eye, verbal, or physical, with Tucker. She kept one eye on Jake, to ensure that she left with him, if not before. There was no way she was going to be alone with Tucker, not even in the interests of positive reinforcement, not even to please Jake. Being alone with Tucker and a dead body didn't count.

Saxon and Clarke shook hands, agreeing to meet up for a game of squash later in the week, other priorities permitting.

At that late stage in the afternoon, both Saxon and Parker were more than relieved to get into some fresh air. They were aware of the late-afternoon traffic: mothers collecting their kids from after-school activities; sales reps on their way home; trucks and vans heading back to base. Saxon and Parker's day was far from over. Parker lit a cigarette as they both sat on a low wall outside the mortuary.

'Christ, that man gives me the creeps,' Parker shuddered. 'It beats me how anyone can spend their working day chopping people up like that. He's got to be a bit weird.' He paused, suddenly realising that Saxon and Clarke socialised occasionally. Saxon said nothing.

Parker changed the subject abruptly. 'Don't know where we're going with this one, boss, I really don't.' As he spoke, he let the smoke out through both nostrils and his mouth at the same time, as if fumigating himself from the trials of the day, and the smell of death in the mortuary.

Saxon said nothing for some minutes, just sitting still and gently biting his lip. Without warning, he jumped to his feet and half ran to his car. 'Come on, Parker, let's get a bite to eat and then have another look at the house. Sounds daft, I know, but it's calling me, I just know it has something to tell me.'

Wednesday, May 15, 29 St Nicholas Lane, Sewel Mill, 6.45PM

Cecil Hayward looked back towards the kitchen window. He could see Edie pottering around in the kitchen, preparing dinner. They tended to eat their main meal in the evening, although his doctor had suggested that it would be better for both of them to eat more heartily at lunchtime, and then have a light supper.

'Yes, indeed,' Cecil had said. 'I remember my father used to say "Breakfast like a king, lunch like a lord, and dine like a pauper," although he never did.'

'Well it was good advice,' Dr Marks had replied. 'Very sound, and it would be a good idea if you could both apply it.'

Cecil agreed and it should have been easy, now that they were both retired. Although retired or not, Edie was still a busy woman, always running around from one thing to another. So it just wasn't practical to have their main meal at lunchtime, and they continued to have dinner at around 7PM every evening. Including this evening. Wednesdays were usually something with mince.

To tell the truth, it didn't really bother Cecil that his wife was quite occupied. Bit of a relief really. He and Edie hardly saw each other during the day, which suited him just fine. He had his regular activities. There was the garden to look after and his shed to take care of.

He finished putting his plants to bed and locked the door of the shed carefully. He fitted a heavy padlock too. All done.

He smiled as he walked into the kitchen and the smell of shepherd's pie hit his nostrils. It was one of his favourites.

Wednesday, May 15, Hazel Lane, Sewel Mill, 8.00PM

Parker was enjoying the ride as they drove towards Anvil Wood House. He had no problem being chauffeured, particularly by someone of such senior rank. The car wasn't too shabby either. They had a good view of the surrounding countryside, although it was getting quite dark now, because you're up quite high in a Land Rover Discovery. Then he noticed they were slowing down.

Saxon was usually a nervous passenger and preferred to drive himself rather than be driven. And he loved his Discovery with a passion. He was aware of Parker's quizzical look as the car slowed and they pulled off Hazel Lane onto the narrow grass verge, but he said nothing. Parker went back to his surveillance of the moonlit scenery.

As they sat there in silence, looking across towards the scene of the murders at Anvil Wood House, the fat yellow moon shone an eerie glow gently onto the roof of the house. It picked out highlights on the pine trees, trees that must have been planted close to the house over a century ago.

The dry, almost painful, bark of a fox echoed around the lanes, temporarily adding a more sinister tone to the situation. The house was impressive, even at night, a solid family house. A thought struck Parker. It was a house for an English family of Waltons. Not too many houses like that in his neighbourhood, that was for sure.

'I'll bet that place has seen a few things over the years, boss,' he said, almost enviously.

'Yeah, but nothing to match the last couple of days,' Saxon said slowly, as he put the car into drive and drove back onto the road in the direction of the house. It looked – to his tired eyes – somewhat forlorn and dejected, wounded almost. Acknowledging to himself that he needed some sleep, and soon, Saxon parked the Discovery in front of the house.

Police crime scene tape was wrapped almost completely around it. Almost as if a giant sticking plaster had been applied to the house in an effort to help it heal, it occurred to Saxon.

God, I am in a bad way. Hallucinating! Who needs drugs anyway, you can get the same effect from exhaustion.

Apart from the sound of the police radio, it was quiet, in so far as the countryside is ever really quiet. The horses had been moved to other stables already, which was not surprising in the circumstances. He could understand why nobody would want to go there so soon after such a horrific event.

Word travels fast in the country, far more so than in a town, in Saxon's experience. He knew it was possible in towns and cities for next-door neighbours never to see each other for months on end, never to meet even. His own place was a prime example. Apart from Fran, who lived in the flat below, he and Emma knew no one else in their block, for example. He shut the car door, but didn't bother to lock it.

Since it was an active crime scene, two police constables had been assigned the unenviable task of guarding the house overnight. They were sitting in their car, with the windows open. There was a smell of cigarettes and stale fast food.

More at home in the familiar streets of Brighton, the two PCs were possibly quite relieved to see the two senior officers. They both went to get out of the car but Saxon put his hand on the driver's door.

'Don't get up, lads, but smoke if you want, by all means,' Saxon said. 'Don't mind us. We're just here to take another look round.'

He looked from one to the other. 'All quiet, is it?'

'Yes, sir, no problems,' answered PC Barry Ryan, the driver, for both of them. He looked to be the older of the two, and was probably therefore the more senior. 'But I reckon if it wasn't so spooky, it would be quite boring,' he added, with a touch of bravado.

His partner, PC Michael Lucas, sat motionless on the passenger side as this exchange took place. He looked young, by anyone's standards. In an age where everyone thought that policemen were getting younger and younger, even the young constables thought Lucas looked too young to be a cop. He was very aware of Saxon's rank and to have a commander joking with you was something Lucas just didn't know how to handle. Best to sit quiet and speak when spoken to, he decided.

'I don't know. You bloody townies are all the same,' joked Parker. 'Take away the street lights and you're all pissing yourselves.' He was enjoying sounding tough and experienced to the two young constables. Saxon rarely saw this side of Parker's character and it amused him.

Parker went on. 'But watch out for Mr Stumpy, he might come back.' He didn't actually believe there was much chance of that, but he certainly wanted the two constables alert to the possibility.

They ducked under the crime tape and unlocked the front door. Saxon entered first and switched the lights on, relieved to see that the house had dried sufficiently for the power to be reconnected. The occasional drop of water fell on their heads as they made their way along the hall, making them flinch.

'So, where do we start, sir?' Parker said, trying to stifle a yawn. His approach was matter-of-fact and Saxon could see his DS had recovered his composure after the initial shock of the horror scene in the morning. The job never gave Parker sleepless nights.

He may not have been the slightest bit nervous, but Parker was at a total loss to understand why they were back at the house at this time of night, without any particular agenda. However, he knew Saxon sufficiently well to trust his judgement implicitly. Parker knew that he was not only the kind of cop who was smart and observant, he was also one who had good instincts. Parker admired that.

'I don't really know, Parker. I don't have anything specific in mind.' Saxon was already looking around the entrance hall. 'Let's just wander around for a while. Look for things that are obvious, things that tell a story about our two victims. Anything at all that the SOCO guys may have overlooked.' He shrugged. 'They don't always get it right, you know.'

Parker nodded but said nothing, wondering where to start. He'd already given the place a thorough going-over and wasn't convinced that they would find anything useful tonight.

'But don't look too hard, maybe it won't be anything very obvious,' Saxon continued, as he walked through the hall, heading towards the rooms at the end. He was definitely looking for something, but he didn't know what. It was just an instinct on Saxon's part.

The ground floor was by far the hardest part; it was vast and seemed to have no end. Babs had an office on the right as you entered the front door and Poppy had one opposite. The fact that both of them led busy lives, sometimes independently and sometimes intertwined, inevitably meant lots of paperwork.

They came back to the front door where Parker started on Poppy's room and Saxon searched Babs' office. In the latter, he found mountains of soggy receipts, twenty years of paperwork, shelves lined with files. It seemed this woman never threw anything away, he thought to himself.

An hour later, despondency was taking a firm grip of his mind, beginning to override the gut feeling he'd been so sure of earlier. Then he noticed a half-crushed box of cigarettes on the desk. The SOCO guys wouldn't have left it there, they were far too professional to be that careless. So it must've belonged to Babs. They must have been there during the morning, and he must have seen them before, but they hadn't registered as anything out of the ordinary.

But now what struck him was the absence of ashtrays. Why were there no ashtrays? *People who smoke have ashtrays, lots of them.* And there were no matches either. 'Lighter,' he said aloud, 'she would have had a lighter.' He made a mental note to get the contents of her handbag, already inventoried no doubt, down to the last safety pin and loose coin, and check to see if there was a cigarette lighter on the list.

Stuffed inside the cigarette box he was surprised to find a prescription, a very fresh prescription. Looking at the date, Saxon could see that it was only dated the day of the murders, the very morning of the last day of Babs' life.

What made it even more interesting was the signature, not that it was particularly legible, but Saxon was familiar with the name. Even if he hadn't been, the health centre stamp said it all. Dr Marks was probably one of the last people to see Babs alive, apart from the butcher, who'd been interviewed yesterday and by Gloria, who had also told of Babs' visit to the tack shop.

Saxon could see that the drug prescribed was an antibiotic of some kind but, of course, there was no diagnosis on the prescription. Deciding that enough was enough, Saxon called across to Parker who had found nothing worth mentioning, and the two of them left the house by the back door. They walked round to the front. As they passed the patrol car, Parker banged his hand hard on the roof causing the two PCs to miss several heartbeats. 'No more snogging tonight, lads, and stay awake.' They muttered something back but Parker neither heard nor cared.

Chapter 8

Thursday, May 16, Sewel Mill, 8.45AM

The next morning, Saxon and Parker drove straight to the health centre in Sewel Mill. There were several cars parked there already, the majority belonging to the doctors and staff, Saxon assumed.

It was quite a modern building and the interior was furnished in soft, warm colours. Saxon smiled to himself. *Emma would be proud of me. I must've been paying some attention some of the time when they were all nattering on about colours and moods and all the rest.*

His mood was suddenly sombre as he thought of his wife, miles away up in London with Kate, in such a very different world. A world she had deliberately chosen over the world he and she had previously inhabited comfortably together, or so he had thought at the time.

The health centre receptionist was a smartly dressed woman of around thirty-five. She had obviously graduated with honours from a comprehensive course in "How to Deal with Visitors" at the Big Dragon School of Training and Development in Interpersonal Skills.

Saxon approached the desk and she told him, without hesitation, that there was no chance of their seeing a doctor, any doctor, without an appointment, and particularly not Dr Marks, who was exceptionally busy and who therefore never under any circumstances, saw patients if they had no appointment. All the more so today, because he was running behind schedule as a result of the events of yesterday. She was sure the gentlemen would understand. She nodded at Saxon dismissively.

As this encounter was taking place at the reception desk between Saxon and the Dragon, Parker was looking over at an area quite clearly designed with children in mind. It was a much nicer health centre than the one that he and Lynne – well, mostly Lynne – took their kids to from time to time in South London. One young mother was there already, with a toddler who was engrossed in Lego.

Back at the reception desk, another woman, older but presumably more junior than the Dragon, looked up from where she was sitting behind the counter. 'We're all at sixes and seven...' she started to say, but was silenced by a glare from the Dragon, who looked back at Saxon and then down at her PC screen.

But he tuned in to the conversation between his boss and the dragon lady. He'd been in this kind of situation with receptionists and secretaries before.

Without a word spoken, Saxon and Parker both held out their warrant cards towards the Dragon, instinctively holding them not too close, in case they were damaged by her hot fiery breath.

'Oh,' she stuttered. 'I see.' She had momentarily lost her composure. 'Which doctor was it you needed to see, gentlemen?' she said, suddenly tamed. Her name badge explained that she was Mrs M. Grace. Rarely had name and manner had so little to do with each other.

'Marks,' they said together, sounding like a double act.

She phoned Marks and whispered something discreetly into the phone, told them to take a seat and wait for a moment because Dr Marks would be with them directly; and went about her work as if they were not there.

They sat in the reception area and, after a couple of minutes, started to browse through the magazines. Parker, who was flicking through the property pages of *Country Life*, looked up. 'You always find this one in doctors' waiting rooms,' he said. 'Maybe it proves that you have to be a bit sick to read it!' He laughed at his own joke.

'Just look at the state of some of these houses,' he went on. 'You'd have to be a crook to be able to afford something like that.

Oh, my God, I don't believe it, it's in Essex as well.' He laughed again.

Saxon smiled, not really paying attention to much of what Parker had said. His mind was on the interview ahead. He was puzzled as to why Clive Marks hadn't mentioned Ms Jenner's visit to the surgery on the morning of her death.

Thursday, May 16, Pike's Smallholding, Hazel Lane, 8.58AM

Andy Pike lived alone. It was his choice, completely his choice.

He'd convinced himself of this when it became obvious to him that finding a woman who was willing to put up with his strange way of living, was going to be all but impossible. He didn't like people much anyway, male or female. They were expensive and he was mean. He begrudged any unnecessary expenditure.

He was enjoying a cup of coffee. One day was pretty much like another for him. Every three or four days he shaved, if he felt like it. He didn't often feel like it. His hair was long, with a few grey streaks, and he kept it in a ponytail. Not just because it was cheaper that way, but also because he thought it made him look younger. Not to mention slightly artistic and a kind of mature countrified version of a new man, and thus attractive to women. Like the surface of his bath, his hair had not seen water for many months.

He was partial to an occasional drink, however, and didn't regard beer money as extravagant spending. He would even buy a drink in a pub from time to time, rather than at the Tesco superstore. Once, when he popped into the Red Cock Inn for a pint, someone in the crowded bar shouted within earshot, 'What is it you always find under a ponytail?' The pub went quiet and someone else shouted in reply, 'An arsehole,' to much general hooting and laughter. Pike had laughed too, along with everyone else, not realising at the time that he might have been the subject of the humorous exchange.

In fact, he didn't understand the irony until later when he got home. When it finally sank in, he was annoyed and kicked out at the first available victim. It happened to be one of his dogs, Lurch, a lurcher that was afraid of most things, even moths. The other dog, a Jack Russell called Russ, saw it coming and made a dash for the kitchen. Russ looked upon Lurch as being rather stupid and slow, with some justification.

Pike was a countryman and was only truly contented when he was out of view of so-called civilisation, ideally with something lined up in the sights of his rifle, or else maybe with a nice big trout thrashing about on the end of his fly-line. He truly believed that when the end of ordered society came, and it surely would, he and his ilk would survive, seeing as how he was a natural hunter and being in possession of the secrets of the ancient ones, including what you can eat and what's best avoided.

Around his neck, he wore a Native American charm. It was a small bag made of some natural-looking material, inside which were pieces of bone, some hair, and a few seeds. Its stated purpose, to protect the wearer from the evil spirits of the forests, seemed a reasonable one. In Pike's view, it had been money well spent during a rare outing to Brighton: not one evil spirit of the thicket at the bottom of his field had attacked him since he bought it. Now that was a bargain.

The charm was further evidence of his affinity with the new-man phenomenon. He fancied himself as a man of mystery, a bit of a Shaman. In one of his many books on the native tribes of America, he had read about the Shaman and how they travelled in the spirit world by changing their form into whatever animal they chose. For instance, one would adopt the guise of a bird to cover ground quickly. While Pike didn't fully grasp the concept of Shamanism, this aspect in particular appealed to him, because there were places on his freehold that were so overgrown with thorn trees that he couldn't get to them – even in his beaten-up old Land Rover.

The Jenner woman and that Poppy cow were his closest neighbours and they had barely spoken in twenty years. One of their rare recent encounters had been less than friendly. The Jenner woman had shouted at him, calling him a filthy, stupid bastard. She was surprisingly foul-mouthed.

Just because one of his dogs had attacked a horse she was riding. It went for the horse's legs and she nearly ended her days draped on a barbed-wire fence with her head in a ditch. Pike was pushed into a bramble bush by the horse; it was a good two weeks before he managed to remove all of the thorns, especially the ones up his nose.

That was it as far as Pike was concerned, she was a daft bitch and he would have nothing to do with her. How someone supposedly from the country couldn't understand that it was a dog's natural instinct to hunt and attack, particularly when frightened by something as big and noisy as a horse. Well, it was beyond his understanding. He dismissed Poppy as a poncey cow… Well, anyone who worked in London was a ponce in his reckoning, got to be a bit soft in the head to go to that place – full of bloody foreigners as well.

He left the cottage to drive into Sewel Mill and collect the paper and some groceries. He would call in at the butcher too. They conducted business from time to time.

Thursday, May 16, Sewel Mill Health Centre, 9.00AM

'Dr Marks will see you now, gentlemen,' called Mrs Grace, as if she had received a secret signal from somewhere. 'Surgery Two.' She gestured towards the room in question.

Saxon knocked on the door and they walked in. Marks was sitting behind his desk, slightly hunched over as he wrote, with what looked like a patient file open in front of him. He ignored them both and continued writing, presumably the notes on his most recent patient. After their dealings with the graceless Mrs Grace, Saxon was less in the mood for waiting than usual. He pulled a chair back and slumped down noisily in front of him.

Marks paused for a second then continued to write.

'Good morning, Dr Marks,' he said, more stiffly than he'd intended. 'Let's get a move on, if you please. I'm in a bit of a hurry. We've got a few murders to solve and we'd like to make a bit of progress today, if possible.'

Marks was barely ruffled, in spite of Saxon's tone. 'Yes,' he answered, barely looking up from his notes, 'of course, Commander. I'll be with you in a second.' He paused. 'We have to be careful writing these notes, don't want to go prescribing the wrong drugs to someone, do we?' He just didn't seem to be able to avoid a condescending manner, assuming he'd wanted to. He was irritating from the moment he opened his mouth.

Trying not to be impatient, but struggling, Saxon nodded almost imperceptibly. 'We need your help, Dr Marks,' he began. 'When we were looking at Anvil House yesterday, we came across a prescription. It appears to have been issued by you for Ms Jenner – on the morning of the day on which she was murdered, in fact. Would that be right?'

Marks sat back in his chair. Saxon's irritation level increased proportionately. He knew the doctor was going to be difficult.

'Well, I hardly think...'

Before Marks could say anything more, Saxon continued. 'We'd like you to confirm that she did in fact see you that morning and we'd appreciate it if you could tell us about your conversation with her. Anything at all. Whether or not you think it might be helpful.' Marks took a deep breath. Then he started on patient confidentiality, moved on to medical ethics and ended with the fear of litigation.

Saxon was about to cut him short when Parker interrupted. 'No problem, Dr Marks, we understand entirely,' he said, with a smile as sincere as he could manage, given the circumstances. 'It won't take us long to get a warrant, given the seriousness of the case. That way, you'll be properly protected from any possible criticism and we'll get the information that we need.' It was done smoothly and politely. It left Marks under no illusion. He wouldn't be able to avoid the discussion altogether, only to put it off temporarily.

Saxon was impressed by Parker's timing and style but he decided against showing it. He was abrupt. It was as if he hadn't heard Parker's assurances. 'Dr Marks, can we please cut through all this bullshit and move on? Or maybe you don't care if someone is out there killing people. Perhaps you just view it as extra work.'

Marks was clearly quite shocked by Saxon's manner. Not too many people addressed him with such evident lack of respect. Like many bullies who are used to getting their own way, he gave in, albeit reluctantly, at the first sign of any serious opposition. His tone continued to be patronising. 'Barbara Jenner was a lesbian,' he said, as if confiding a rather exciting secret. 'Or rather, perhaps I should say that she was living in a lesbian relationship.' He paused for effect.

'Ah, really, you don't say.' Saxon and Parker had been confided in to that effect several times during the previous day's discussions with neighbours and acquaintances in Sewel Mill. Saxon's feigned surprise was far from convincing, even to someone as self-absorbed as Marks.

'Commander, do you want my help or not?' he said, petulantly.

'Yes, we do. Of course we do, Dr Marks,' Saxon replied in exasperation. 'But can it be today? I told you I'm in a bit of a hurry and I wouldn't mind catching this bastard before I retire.'

Marks stood up and walked to the window. He looked out. At what, it was hard to say. He stood with his hands clasped behind his back and he rocked slightly on the balls of his feet. Saxon thought immediately of Richard Clarke.

Here's another one who lives to perform, another one who enjoys attention. What is it about the medical profession, I wonder?

At last Marks spoke, coming back to his desk and sitting

down again, as he began.

'Commander, I'm going to confide in you,' he said slowly. 'I don't know if this will help you in your investigations, but it may certainly help you understand Ms Jenner.' He smiled companionably. When he didn't resume speaking, Saxon realised that he was waiting for encouragement or appreciation, one of the two. Saxon decided to give something.

'You're so right, Dr Marks,' he said, smiling back, 'understanding the victim is usually crucial if we are to understand the perpetrator.'

Marks seemed more than satisfied. 'Indeed, Commander.' He sat in his chair again, pressed his fingertips together. He nodded gently at both men. 'Well, Barbara Jenner was an old friend of mine. We must go back more years than I care to remember; we met at the village drama society. And she, Barbara that is, confided in me from time to time.' Saxon let him get to the point, even if it seemed to be taking forever. He sensed that here was someone who knew Babs Jenner quite well. The conversation could turn out to be more useful than either he or Parker had anticipated.

'Barbara told me about all the "happenings" in her life,' Marks went on. 'When I say "happenings", you have to understand that this was a term she used to describe her sexual encounters. I'm not sure why. They weren't only with women, you know, she was bisexual.' Marks paused again for effect, clearly anticipating a response of some kind. But Saxon and Parker were skilled in maintaining deadpan expressions, even when something as unexpected as this came to light. There had been no sign at the house of any interest in men.

Slightly disappointed, Marks continued. 'The prescription was for a sexually transmitted disease. She was very sexually active and picked up infections quite frequently,' he said, very matter-of-fact about the conversation now, and speaking at normal speed, much to Saxon's relief. 'Let me put it this way,

Commander, some people join murder mystery weekends for their entertainment, others stay at home and watch television, I suppose. But Barbara Jenner didn't. It seemed to me that she travelled around with the sole purpose of picking up women. Or men,' he mused, 'depending on how she felt at the time, I suppose. More women than men, as far as I can remember'.

He looked at the two policemen, but neither spoke. Saxon raised his eyebrows, inviting further comment. Marks was more than happy to oblige. 'Another point worth mentioning,' he continued, 'Poppy had no idea about what was going on. Babs wanted it that way. Like most of us, I imagine, she always wanted someone to go home to. It certainly seemed to me that one of her priorities was not to hurt Poppy in any way whatsoever. It didn't stop her running around, of course, but she went to some lengths to cover her tracks. I think she loved Poppy, you know, really loved her. But she couldn't resist the excitement of new conquests. As I have already said, male or female, it didn't really matter to her.'

Saxon sat in silence for a few moments while Parker made notes. Then he said, 'Dr Marks, can you give me the names of any of the people Barbara Jenner had "happenings" with?'

'No, I most certainly cannot.' His manner was suddenly querulous and he very upright in his chair. 'I never met any of them, so I can't tell you any more about it than that. Even if Barbara had actually mentioned a name, I would be very reluctant to disclose it. She may not have been telling me the truth. People don't always, you know, even to their Doctors, he said, as if this were almost beyond belief, perhaps even bordering on a sin. 'Maybe there's an address book somewhere. You'll have to look. I'm afraid I really can't help you with that one. We didn't know each other quite that well, you understand.' He stood up, agitated. 'Not apart from the amateur dramatics, that is. My wife and I didn't socialise with them, of course. No.'

Marks was anxiously looking at his watch as he spoke, and

suggested that they might like to come back later when he had more time.

Saxon rose to his feet and walked to the door, turned and said, 'No, Dr Marks, next time you come to my office and talk to me. We'll need a formal statement. I appreciate the information you've given us. We will talk again. I'm sure you'll no doubt remember more as you give the subject further thought.'

Outside his surgery, an elderly man was waiting to see the doctor. He looked startled as he saw the two policemen.

As Saxon and Parker left the health centre, the graceless dragon accompanied them to the door, anxious no doubt to show that her earlier demeanour was reserved merely for common sick people. She held it open for them politely enough, but they felt her hot breath licking the back of their necks as they walked back towards the Discovery. They shuddered in unison but with a shared moment of amusement rather than any real discomfort. Parker was thinking he would tell his wife about Mrs Grace. Saxon was thinking he would tell no one, but that it was exactly the kind of story that once upon a time would have amused Emma.

'What do you think, sir?' Parker interrupted Saxon's brief moment of nostalgia.

'I think, Parker, that Dr bloody Marks is obnoxious and pompous, and I can't stand pompous bastards. But on the other hand, he's given us some useful stuff today. But I'm sure he's holding something back. First, he tells us that he's known Barbara Jenner for years, describing her as an old friend. Then later when we probed a bit, he started to disown her – saying that he didn't really know her that well. Now, call me suspicious, but he knows more than he's letting on. I want Surveillance and Technical Intelligence to watch him for a few days. We've got to find out more about Ms Jenner's secret life. It's a new direction for us to pursue I suppose.'

'However much she kept things secret from her partner,'

agreed Parker, 'she must have something somewhere that'll give us a link to these people she meets for "happenings" or whatever.'

'Sounds a bit 60s or 70s, doesn't it', laughed Saxon. 'She wasn't that old, was she. Maybe she was a bit nostalgic for the good old days of music, love and flowers, and the decades before the world discovered that there was after all a price to pay for free love.'

'My mum said the same thing, boss. Said that the whole AIDS thing was retribution for all that sleeping around that people did when she was young.'

'So she didn't buy the view that we got it from monkeys in Africa and that it worked its way into the human population and then spread around the world?' Saxon asked with a smile.

'Nah,' Parker answered without hesitation. 'My mum doesn't hold with monkeys having anything much to do with human beings, and certainly not having sex with them.'

They got back into the car.

Thursday, May 16, Hazel Lane, Sewel Mill, 10.15AM

In the light of what Doctor Marks had just given them, Saxon decided to search Anvil Wood House one more time. Maybe the voices of the recently dead could give him a few pointers in the right direction. He was sure that if Babs had secret sexual "happenings" with multiple partners, then there was a good chance that she would not have kept their details such as phone numbers in her head.

There had to be an address book. *Please let there be a book.* He was driving slowly down Hazel Lane towards the house when he became aware of another car behind them, revving loudly and using his horn... The driver beeped loudly again. Parker turned round in his seat to look.

'Not sure what he thinks he's going to achieve by that,' he observed.

'Perhaps you should ask him, Parker.' Saxon stopped the Discovery, provoking a prolonged blast on the horn of the Land Rover behind.

Parker was back in less than five minutes, smiling broadly.

'Name of Pike, boss. Andy Pike. He's their neighbour, lives up the road in the next house. I told him we'd be along to see him later.'

Saxon started the engine.

'Apparently he was in something of a rush to get back home, some kind of agricultural emergency,' Parker went on. 'But he reluctantly apologised for his behaviour when I flashed my warrant card. Hoped we'd understand, what with all the stress of the last twenty-four hours or so.'

As they pulled away, Saxon looked in his rear-view mirror but he couldn't make out the driver at all. The old Land Rover was making no attempt yet to move. 'I can hardly wait to meet the gentleman in more congenial circumstances,' he said.

They turned into Anvil Wood House, hoping to uncover something, anything, that would tell them whether or not there was a link between the first three killings and those of Babs Jenner and Poppy Field.

Thursday, May 16, The Speckled Cat, Brighton, 10.55AM

Bill Singleton was opening up for the day. The pub did great business at lunchtimes with the office workers and shoppers. In the evenings, it was one of the favourite haunts of the gay population, who referred to it affectionately as the Spotted Pussy.

Thursdays were always good. It was as if people were getting wired for the weekend. He liked the fact that although it was predominantly gay, the Speckled Cat still attracted a fair number of straight clients. Bill had his theories about this.

Well, we all like a little walk on the wild side from time to time. It takes all sorts and I wouldn't have it any other way.

His only priority was to keep it clean. He saw that as vital for the continuing success of his operation. By that, he meant no drugs and no prostitution, or at least not overtly. Not easy to achieve, but so far there hadn't been any major problems.

Thursday, May 16, Anvil Wood House, 11.00AM

The forensics team had finished their scraping and vacuuming and were in the process of shifting equipment from the house to a small fleet of white vans.

Saxon waited in his Land Rover until they were finished. He listened to the police radio, impassively taking in all the minor, although probably to the people involved, major, incidents happening in their lives.

The last member of the forensics team walked over to Saxon and handed him the keys to the house and told him the cleaners would be along in an hour or so.

Of course, less upsetting for any next of kin if the bloodstains were removed.

Once inside the house he headed straight for Babs' office, *the room of a thousand secrets*, he thought to himself. Or rather, hoped. He was working on the idea that if there were an address book, then it wouldn't be hidden in the desk, that's the first place someone would look. No, Poppy could have gone in to tidy up and accidentally found it, the way people accidentally find things when they are really looking – being nosy. It had to be somewhere else. But where would she have put it?

The office was large and filled with clutter. The certificates and photographs that lined the walls showed Babs to be a keen show jumper in her earlier years. Saxon knew that SOCO would have checked behind each one for a wall safe. But he took a look anyway. Nothing.

In the corner of the room there stood a small sofa. He sat on it to lower the level of the springs inside and then plunged his hand down around the back and sides. Apart for some small change, a hairgrip, and a tube of lipstick, there was nothing of a crime-solving nature. Frustration finally won the day and Saxon resorted to his questions and answers technique, where he would ask himself questions out loud, and come up with an answer as fast as he could. Sometimes this produced positive results, and sometimes it was just plain embarrassing.

'Right, Paul, you're in a room. It's your room, your office, but your other half is going to be in and out of it from time to time. Now, you've got secrets, serious secrets, which are earth-shattering. Or they would be, if your partner were to find out about them.' He was sweeping the room with his eyes as he berated himself. 'Having your partner find those secrets will change your life and turn it into hell. So where the fuck are you going to hide these hideous bloody secrets?'

Immediately he replied to himself, loudly. 'Under the fucking floor, where else, you idiot?'

'But where under the floor, there's a bloody great carpet covering it?'

'In the corner, you plonker, so it's easy to access.'

Feeling suddenly energised by this exchange with himself and the ideas it had generated, he examined each corner of the carpet. In a few seconds, he found the spot under the front window. When he lifted that corner of the carpet, it was instantly obvious that the spikes on the gripper strip had been flattened with a hammer to make it easy to lift. The floorboard was cut to make a small square trapdoor. And there it was in all its glory, the book of secrets, waiting to be liberated. Now they could come out to play.

Elated by his discovery, but just a bit pissed off that the SOCO guys hadn't found it earlier, Saxon placed the book in a plastic bag and was about to leave when a thought struck him. The telephone, had anyone checked the telephone?

He picked it up and dialled 1471. According to the logged time, there had been a call at 11PM last night, the night following the murders. Saxon figured the two officers guarding the house would not have heard the phone from their car with the police radio crackling away. There had been a caller, but they had withheld their number.

Two pieces of good luck in a row would've been too much to hope for.

Thursday, May 16, Pike's Smallholding, Hazel Lane, 2.00PM

Pike was sweating again and his hands trembled as he made another cup of coffee. He was trying to reduce the stress in his life, not increase it. Stress was bad for his karma. He could've kicked himself for that little encounter with the police this morning. But he kicked Lurch again instead and took satisfaction in the fact that the dog yelped and ran to hide.

He sat down, nursing the mug of coffee and rocked gently in his chair. He wondered, not for the first time, if he was going slowly mad. What with the six-foot rabbit, last night. And then he thought of the sheep. His stomach churned uncomfortably at the memory and his grip on the coffee mug tightened.

Once or twice a month, Pike would go lamping on the farm that backed up to his land. This involved driving around the fields in his old Land Rover, vintage 1963, with a powerful lamp fixed to the roof above the driver. The lamp would be swept around the edge of the field and, if there were a rabbit, its eyes would show up like cats' eyes on a road. The silencer attached to his .22 rifle ensured the rabbits wouldn't run off if he missed, as the noise it made was just a dull click. He usually managed up to half a dozen rabbits per lamping expedition, a couple to keep and one or two to pass on for a bit of loose change.

But lamping, or even the thought of lamping, brought him out in a cold sweat. One night, a few years ago, Pike had made a mistake. And it had been a huge and embarrassing mistake. He had accidentally assassinated a sheep. It was a good shot, at least 250 yards, straight between the eyes, nothing wrong with his aim, but it was very definitely the wrong target.

Pike thought of burying the evidence and saying nothing. After all, nobody had seen him. But since the farmer whose land he was clearing of rabbits had proudly told him about "the best seventy-five Kent ewes" he had ever owned, Pike decided to come clean and reluctantly told the farmer. It was probably the hardest thing he had ever had to endure in his fifty years. The shame was almost unbearable. Surprisingly though, the farmer didn't really mind; the price of sheep had dropped to an all-time low, and anyway Pike kept the rabbit population down to an acceptable level on the farm. One assassinated sheep in thirty years was excusable. And the sheep didn't suffer. However, if there were a scale of lamper's mistakes, this would have been a good fifteen out of ten.

But while the farmer wasn't too bothered about retribution, he didn't exactly hold back that evening in the pub. It was too good a story. Word soon spread like wildfire of "Lee Harvey-Oswald-Pike", the sheep assassin, and occasionally someone would "bleat" when he entered the pub.

Pike never fully realised how people saw him, with his uneasy mixture of ancient Barbour and New-Age philosophies, along with the unhappy combination of body odour and furtiveness. Over the years he had become someone who was generally to be avoided and, if that was not entirely possible, to be poked fun at. Pike was generally unaware of the effect he had on people.

His cottage was small but not unattractive, it just was in need of a lot of care and renovation, and fumigating. A great deal of the local vermin hid in the house, probably thinking that it was the last place he would look for them. The land that came with the house was approximately twenty-five acres; some of it a permanent home to wrecked cars that had been there for so long that Pike no longer noticed them anymore. Several fields were dedicated to vegetables and fruit crops, both of which he sold at the gate, and he had also invested in a large plastic growing tent where he raised flowers.

He was an accomplished horticulturist, sufficiently successful that, when combined with a freezer full of rabbits, his green fingers provided him with a steady income and self-sufficiency.

He heard a car arriving outside and his stomach somersaulted again. He was not enjoying today.

Thursday, May 16, Hazel Lane, 2.15PM

Saxon drove slowly into Pike's car parking area. He and Parker had been going over what was known about Pike and planning out their approach and their line of questioning.

'Right, Parker, Mr Pike is the nearest neighbour that Ms Jenner and Ms Field had. That's pretty much our only interest in him.' He paused. 'We know he's a pretty aggressive driver.' They both laughed briefly. 'What have we got on him?'

Parker obliged. 'Not much, boss. He was cautioned a few years ago for discharging his shotgun too close to the road, and that's all. He lives alone, never been married, keeps himself to himself. He is the owner of a firearms and shotgun certificate. He has a .22 Anschutz rifle and a 12-bore double-barrelled shotgun, both of which he uses for vermin control.'

Parker looked up from the thin file and across at Saxon. 'We may be less than welcome here, boss. It says on this report of his last weapon security check that he is unhelpful, rude and does not like the police. Surprise, surprise.'

Saxon nodded. 'Let's see if we can gently coax anything useful out of him. Chances are that he may have seen something without realising it. These rural types certainly make life interesting, don't they.' Parker got out of the car first, putting the file into a briefcase and leaving it behind the seat.

They approached Pike's cottage, only to be stopped in their tracks as Pike emerged suddenly from the somewhat weather-beaten front door.

Pike didn't waste any time. He was expecting some kind of

retribution after yesterday's little encounter down the lane and, judging by his stance, he'd decided that attack was the best form of defence. They had no opportunity to introduce themselves formally. Pike recognised Parker instantly. 'You're that fuckin' policeman, aren't you? Not that I'd need to recognise you, I can smell police from fuckin' miles away – what you bleedin' want anyway? Me guns are all locked up safe, so you can bugger off and stop harassin' me.'

They barely had time to take in the bizarre appearance before the smell of unwashed body hit them. Saxon read his body language and it told him a lot. Pike was clearly in a very aggressive mood, but he continually turned to face the other way, moving his weight from one foot to the other. In Saxon's experience, as well as in the textbooks, such behaviour is usually a sign that the person is afraid or holding something back.

Saxon opened his mouth to speak. Pike had paused for a second but then went on immediately. 'You people are always coming out here an' tryin' to catch me out so you can take me guns away, but I'm too bloody smart for you, I keeps them safe don't you worry. They's always locked up properly when I'm not using 'em.' He paused for breath and turned his attention to the "For Sale" display, aggressively tidying up his potatoes and carrots.

Having read the file, Saxon guessed that the best way of establishing control over the interview was a return bout of aggression. He visibly lost patience. 'Mr Pike, listen for just a minute, will you. We are not here about your guns. We couldn't give a toss about your sodding guns. And what's the matter with you people out here, are the farmers spraying something on the crops to make you all bloody-minded?' It worked. Pike stood momentarily silenced and open-mouthed.

'I'm Commander Saxon and this is Detective Sergeant Parker, we would like to talk to you about the murders at Anvil Wood House.'

Pike tried desperately to regain some appearance of composure. He realised his original approach had been uncalled for. Backtracking quickly, his aggression was now challenged into what passed for wit in the Pike household. 'Oh, well I never, a commander no less. And what's a bigwig like you doing out 'ere then, talking to the likes of us peasants then?' Pike was visibly relaxing as it dawned on him that he was in no immediate danger of being arrested, or losing his guns.

He motioned them to follow him into the cottage. 'Don't want to be seen standing out here talkin' to the likes of you,' he muttered, as they followed him in. Saxon was still exercising extreme self-control, as he often had to in his job. Parker on the other hand seemed to be finding the whole thing amusing. He was, in fact, toying with the idea of doing an impromptu gun inspection, just for the hell of it. But he stopped seeing the funny side when Saxon caught his eye, and he returned to being a policeman on a murder investigation again. Winding up the Andy Pikes of the world was not on the agenda for today, tempting though the idea was.

Pike's muttering had turned to his views on his recently deceased neighbours. As they entered the cottage, he was making it clear that he had little liking for either of the ladies and no sympathy for their passing. Nor did he have any time for their unnatural lifestyle. Shouldn't be allowed, as far as Pike was concerned. Saxon let him talk. Neither he nor Parker would have dreamt of interrupting Pike at this stage.

They took in their surroundings. The fact that Pike didn't offer them anything like a cup of tea wasn't a problem. It was a relief. Pike's exterior appearance would have told them that the cottage wasn't likely to be any cleaner or more wholesome. And indeed, it wasn't. If anything, it was worse than they could have anticipated. The place was just disgusting and the smell of dog piss nearly made them keel over. Even the surface of the sink had stalagmites.

Pike sat down and made himself comfortable. He didn't offer them a seat, for which again they were both grateful. All the more so when they noticed the two dogs hadn't stopped scratching for one second since they arrived, and the chairs were likely to be the hive of whatever it was that was biting today.

Saxon thought he'd detected a slight smile on Pike's weathered features when the murders were mentioned. It was hard to put an age on Pike, just by looking. Their records showed that he was just past 50 but he looked quite a bit older.

Pike became more talkative the less the two policemen said. This was a ploy Saxon used when suspects with room-temperature IQs weren't forthcoming with information. Just as nature abhors a vacuum, so the vast majority of people dislike silences during a conversation.

While Saxon stood as far from Pike as was practical within the small confines of his front room, apparently giving him his undivided attention, Parker wandered around, generally eyeballing the place. He had two reasons. The first was to look for anything incriminating and the second was the hope that maybe, if he kept moving, the Jack Russell would stop trying to shag his leg.

Pike seemed unable to concentrate on both of the men at the same time and this was clearly worrying him. Several times during his monologue, he glanced behind to check that Parker was not too far away.

'Mr Pike,' interrupted Parker, 'are you a birdwatcher by any chance?' Parker looked down at the ever-persistent Russ, as he tried to shake him off his left foot, wishing at the same time that he had some anti-riot CS gas spray.

Suddenly, Pike lurched forward, delivering Russ a firm swipe across his hindquarters. 'Will you leave that man's fuckin' leg alone you daft little bugger – you don't know what you'll catch.' Russ yelped and ran out through the front door. Pike continued, 'What do you mean – birdwatcher?' he said incredulously. 'I ain't got no time for that sort of rubbish. I watch 'em for a second or two just before I blows their 'eds off, if that's what you mean.' Pike grinned at his little joke.

Parker tried to laugh, in the interests of furthering the information flow, but found he couldn't. 'Well, Mr Pike, it's these binoculars here,' he said, indicating an expensive-looking pair on the windowsill. 'Big, aren't they?' He picked them up and came to stand beside Saxon so that the two of them were facing the sitting Pike. He leaned forward. 'I'll bet you can see right into your neighbours' sitting room with these,' he said, in a low and conspiratorial voice.

Pike was taken aback, both at the sudden friendliness and the implied suggestion that, unusually for him, he picked up on immediately. 'I don't know about that,' he said quickly. 'Never looked, did I. Mind my own, don't I.' Pike began to squirm. And it wasn't just from the broad spectrum of animal life inhabiting his chair and quite possibly his underwear too.

Parker persisted. 'Come on, Mr Pike, they were sitting here, right by the window, and I'm sure that if I look through them I'll be able to see Barbara Jenner's house quite clearly.' He took a couple of steps back to the window. Pike half stood out of his chair. Parker noticed but continued to put the binoculars up to his eyes. 'Oh my, there it is,' he said, trying to sound as sarcastic as possible. Parker had a perfect view of Anvil Wood House. From Pike's front-room window, the drive and the front door were both in plain view.

Saxon pressed Pike on this point saying. 'Surely, Mr Pike, there must be nights when there's not much on the telly.' Pike didn't answer. Saxon turned to Parker. 'Wouldn't you say, Parker?'

Parker turned back from the window. 'I'd say that happens more often than not these days, what with the soaps and the cookery shows and the garden makeovers.' He laughed, almost sincerely.

'Makes you wonder why you pay for a licence, doesn't it, Mr Pike?'

Pike started at the mention of the word licence, just as Parker had intended he should. It was irresistible. Pike held his breath.

Saxon was aware of the diversion and a part of him shared Parker's amusement, but he wanted to pursue the binoculars theme because, with no evidence that could help them pinpoint the killer, anything at all that Pike might have seen could be useful and could even change the course of the investigation.

'So, you're bored with the telly,' Saxon went on, 'and you happen to see the binoculars there, by the window. Why wouldn't you look through them, just to see what's going on out there. After all, if you don't like quiz shows and you're not into ideal homes, there's nothing much on the box that's worth watching, is there?'

Pike breathed again. They weren't going to pursue the licence question, thank heavens.

'Well, no, s'pose not, but…' he started, with relief.

'…Nobody's going to arrest you for looking, are they', continued Parker. 'After all, it's your window, it's your view,' he said.

'Well, all right, I might've took the odd peek, now and then,' Pike admitted. 'And I 'ave seen things, you know, comings an' goings from time to time.' He warmed quickly to this new subject. 'Mostly I was keepin' a lookout for crooks and the like. Someone might come and nick me plants or me chickens or something.' He was almost indignant. 'We gotta look after ourselves out 'ere, you know. By the time you lot turn up, we could all be murdered an' dead.'

Saxon smiled to himself. *He's on a roll now; there'll be no stopping him with a bit of luck.* He remained silent, as Pike continued to reinvent himself as the guardian of the neighbourhood watch.

'And did you see any comings and goings last night?' Saxon

asked him.

'No, I didn't, I wasn't 'ere.'

'Where precisely were you, Mr Pike?' asked Parker.

'Out.'

'Fine, that's a great help. Where out?' Parker pressed him.

'I was rabbitin' with a lamp.'

'Come on, Mr Pike, you can tell us more than that – we need to know exactly where you were rabbiting, or maybe it wasn't rabbits you were after.' Saxon paused for a second. 'Maybe you were out killing a couple of dykes, Mr Pike. You didn't like Barbara Jenner, did you, Mr Pike? You didn't care for Ms Field either. I don't think you're telling us everything.' Saxon fixed Pike with a stare that made him think, for some reason, of the rabbits that were caught suddenly in the light beam when he went lamping.

'Bleedin' 'ell,' Pike shouted. 'What you accusin' me of? I ain't done nothin'. I wasn't even 'ere. I told you.' Pike was in a panic all over again. He suddenly realised he'd been having a long conversation with the enemy. Not like him at all. And look where it had got him. With a policeman at close quarters either side of him, Pike was feeling somewhat overwhelmed. The questions seemed relentless, and so fast.

These bastards 'ave 'ad talkin'-fast training, an' I'm getting into trouble 'ere. Another wave of fresh sweat was added to the several already coating his body.

'We're not accusing you of anything, Mr Pike,' said Parker quickly but not too reassuringly. 'It's just that we want to be very clear that you understand how important it is that you tell us the truth here.'

'We need to be able to cross-check your information with that we receive from other witnesses,' said Saxon, planting the thought in Pike's mind that there was little point in lying since they were already in possession of a great many facts. By suggesting to Pike that his information would only be used to corroborate something they had already heard from somebody else, Saxon hoped to prise more out of Pike than the latter would normally have felt comfortable disclosing.

'You can see how it would look to a suspicious policeman's mind. If you can't explain where you were last night, and what with people knowing that you didn't exactly get on with the two ladies, well, people might put two and two together…' Saxon paused for his words to take effect.

Pike looked up. 'Give me a minute to get me 'ed together, you's confusing me somethin' rotten.' He paused to gather his thoughts. 'I might have seen something last night, I was out, but I wasn't snooping. I never done nothin' like that. I ain't never bin no fuckin' pervert. I wasn't watchin' the poof women, and they was poofs you know; I don't 'old with that, you know.'

He nodded across at Saxon, as if any right-thinking man would be agreeing with him. 'I was in the field behind their 'ouse, down the far end. I done a sweep with me lamp and I seen some eyes. But there was something different about them they was in the wrong place – too high they was.' He shuddered. 'Not many six-foot rabbits round 'ere I can tell you. Fair gave me the shits.' He shook his head, as if the memory was still too real. 'At first I thought it was an owl flyin' in my direction like, but it never moved, just fuckin' hovered there, like it was lookin' at me – nearly crapped me self, I did. Then suddenly they was gone.' He stopped and Saxon waited to see if anything else was forthcoming.

Pike obliged. 'I come 'ome fuckin' fast, I can tell you, like shit off an 'ot shovel.'

Saxon felt encouraged by this information. 'Tell me, Mr Pike, if you thought you saw someone lurking around your field at that time of night, why didn't you ring the police? You could have saved the lives of those two women.'

Pike shrugged with a look of total disbelief. Saxon went on, 'How do you know it wasn't an owl sitting in a bush, Mr Pike?

Looking in your direction? Maybe it went to sleep, that would account for the eyes suddenly vanishing.'

Pike was quick to respond. 'Shows what you fuckin' townie people know, don't it?' said Pike, triumphantly. 'Owls don't nod off to sleep at night, they fuckin' 'unt, don't they? Starve to death otherwise, wouldn't they? Don't you know nothing about the countryside?' It was so clearly a rhetorical question that neither Saxon nor Parker felt called upon to answer.

Pike hadn't finished. 'And there ain't no trees in that spot for one to perch on anyway. No, that weren't no owl, that was someone standin' there watchin' me. I know the countryside, an' I know country people, they don't go an' stand about at night unless they're poachers, and there aren't none of them round here, or they've lost their bleedin' nuts. An' if I 'ad called you lot, 'ow long would it've taken you to fuckin' get here? Answer me that.'

'Mr Pike, do you think that if it was someone watching you that they would have recognised you, bearing in mind that the light would have blinded them temporarily?'

Pike looked slyly at Saxon. 'Don't be daft, if it was a local person they would know I goes lampin,' but if it was a stranger all they'd 'ave to do is follow me tyre tracks across the fields to 'ere. But don't you go worryin' 'bout me, I've got me dogs and if it comes to it I've got me guns too.'

'But of course, Mr Pike, we can't condone the use of guns in that sort of situation. If you have any worries then you must call us,' said Saxon, handing Pike his card.

'What's the good of that, you lot only hurry to help rich people in big 'ouses.' He was belligerent again, sensing that the interview was coming to an end and that somehow, against the odds, he had survived much better than he'd expected to. 'I can look after meself. You keep yer card and give it to someone who needs it.'

Saxon took the card back but placed it next to the phone,

which was by the front door, underneath what looked like a dead chicken.

'Well, I'll just leave it here. Let's just say you can use it if you think of anything that may be of interest.'

Saxon could tell that for all his bravado, Pike was a frightened man.

Lurch was staring up at his master, they clearly had an unspoken bond. The poor dog was picking up on the fear that Pike was exuding and it too had a frozen expression of blind terror etched on its face. Lurch farted nervously and audibly, and the smell, combined with the odour of dog piss permeating the cottage, was too much for the policemen. Russ, who had crept back into the cottage and was dozing on the remains of a rug, was oblivious, whimpering gently from time to time in his sleep as he no doubt fantasised about policemen's legs.

They thanked Pike for his help, told him that he would have to make a statement and were quickly out the door to the safety of the car. Saxon spoke first. 'Christ, Parker, what does that dog eat to make that kind of smell?' They both breathed deeply, grateful for some relatively fresh air.

'Right,' Saxon went on. 'I want SOCO to take a look around that field – get the charming Mr Pike to take them to the exact spot where he saw the phantom eyes. There may be some interesting footprints, but then again, it is a bit dry maybe for footprints.'

'Yes,' Parker answered. 'We've ruled out sleepy owls and we never did believe in six-foot rabbits,' he laughed. 'So there's got to be some other explanation.'

'But even if there's the remotest possibility it's our killer,' Saxon said, 'why on earth would he go into the field in the first place?'

'God knows, sir. Maybe he heard Pike's Land Rover cruising around the field and just wanted to check in case he'd been seen.'

Saxon paused for a moment, then said with a wry smile,

'Shame Pike didn't get a twitchy trigger finger and accidentally blow his brains out.'

'Come now, sir, that would never do would it?' Parker paused for a few seconds. 'Not a bad idea now you mention it.'

Friday, May 17, Thicket Lane, Upper Norwood, 11.00AM

Keith Jenner was speechless. This was not his normal condition. He put the phone down on the policeman and slumped into a chair. He had made no response to the condolences offered, but the police were used to dealing with people in shock and didn't take it personally. Not that Jenner would've cared about offending a policeman.

His mind was working overtime. Vaguely aware of the news reports the day before about murders in Sussex, he had never imagined that it could have involved Babs. His sister was dead.

His stomach shrivelled at the thought of any incriminating evidence the police might find at her place. *Please, God, let her have been careful.* She would've been. She was clever. She was the bright one. Their mother had seen to that by getting her into a decent school.

When Mr and Mrs Jenner had parted company, Keith had had no hesitation about going with his father. He knew which side his bread was buttered on. Dad was much more fun and life would be better with him. He occasionally wondered how his life would've turned out if he'd stayed with Babs and his mum. Well, at least he was alive, even if he was apprehensive about what the next few days had to bring.

He wondered about her will.

Friday, May 17, Cookbridge, Sussex, 4.30PM

Gertraud Bishop held a tissue to her mouth, struggling to understand what had been said. She'd been dreading a phone call like this, ever since she'd seen the news report. How could it have happened? How did they know? What would Angus say if this was all resurrected? How was she going to keep it quiet from him? Why had she ever got involved?

She needed a Prozac.

Saturday, May 18, Dingmer Gliding Club, 4.30PM

Jake Dalton made a tight turn, and he looked to his right as the wing of his glider bowed and strained under the G-force. Jake was a more than competent pilot, and from his early childhood had dreamt of being a fighter pilot. However, the opposition from his parents was overwhelming, causing him during his teens to run away several times, weather permitting of course.

Mr and Mrs Dalton senior were both doctors, his mother was a consultant orthopaedic surgeon and his father a plastic surgeon. Money was not a problem. It was made clear to Jake that they would be so proud if he followed the family tradition and embarked on a career in medicine.

He caved in, reluctantly at first, but after a few months at St Thomas's he realised that medicine could be a lucrative career and maybe it was quite interesting too.

Jake was six feet tall and handsome. Friends used to joke that he resembled an Action Man toy, sporting a similar haircut, and always wearing combats. He was fit and strong, a keep-fit fanatic who regularly worked out and attended martial arts classes.

This time of the year the weather was perfect for gliding, plenty of thermals meant it was possible to keep your glider in the air almost indefinitely, or until nature called suggesting you sat somewhere else. Jake decided to glide until the light started to fade, running through a routine of rolls and loops and a spot of hill soaring.

He worked well with Dr Clarke and found him intellectually stimulating, he knew so much, with his years of experience. While Jake was struggling to find the solution to a problem, Clarke would sometimes pre-empt him by not only knowing the answer but also the question before it was even asked. He had a knack for knowing, and a definite talent for anticipation.

For three years, Jake had been Clarke's assistant, finding the job both interesting and challenging, but also enjoying the fact that certain stresses of operating as a normal doctor were removed. He didn't actually have to keep any of his patients alive. It was a bit late for that. And the job gave him loads of time to fly.

The view from the glider was breathtaking. From his 3,000ft perch, he could clearly see from Ditchling Beacon to Eastbourne, and he thought that if he climbed another 2,000ft or so, he would easily be able to see France quite clearly. The wind speed was more than enough for him to angle the glider in such a way that it stopped moving forward. It was a strange sensation, a bit like flying on a kite by a non-existent wire. You couldn't really describe it to someone, you had to show them.

Jake held the aircraft there for a few seconds until it stalled, the nose dropped and it started to lose height. Then he went looking for thermals. These are found over freshly ploughed areas or cornfields on a sunny day as they reflect the heat of the sun. Once he located his thermal, he turned to the right and dug the wing that was being buffeted by the rising hot air into the thermal, and pulled back on the stick gently as the warm air lifted the glider.

Soon he was at 6,000ft, the only sound coming from the wind as it skimmed over the glider. Total silence only came if the angle of the aircraft was acute enough to slow it down to stall speed. The nose would then drop and the glider would gain speed and back came the noise.

When the time to land arrived he lost the first 5,000ft with what could only be described as a power dive. He bottomed out at 1,000ft and at 600ft he started to operate the air brakes, strips of wood or glass fibre, which at the pull of a lever protrude up out of the wing and disrupt the flow of air, causing the glider to slow down and lose altitude.

The glider stops and drops in a series of steps, until you have it correctly positioned for landing. You didn't get a second chance, so it had to be good. It was. He made his turn and the glider's speed was perfect; he was lined up well with the grass runway and it was a textbook touchdown. All his landings went well, and he was a natural pilot, if such a thing existed. The glider bumped along on its single front wheel for a while and had completely come to a stop before it gently tipped to the left and settled on its wing. Perfect.

The weather was fine with hardly any wind. Jake and a fellow pilot dragged the glider to its parking space, threw over a tarpaulin, and pegged it down. Often at the end of a long flight he would go to the clubhouse, and socialise with the other pilots and rather like fishermen exchange stories of the biggest thermals or the strongest crosswinds and how they fought them. But tonight, Jake was tired and decided to go home and slob out. Saturdays were a big night in Brighton but he wasn't in the mood right now.

The track from the gliding club to the main road was long and extremely rural. His car was not really suited to it, and he was forced to drive from side to side and avoid the potholes. Either side of the track the terrain was typical Sussex, one side the flatness of the Weald, and the other, sheep-cropped Downs dotted with dark green gorse bushes and the odd chalk pit. Once Jake hit the main road, he smoothly joined the flow of traffic and sped off in the direction of Brighton and home.

Saturday, May 18, Pavilion Square, Brighton, 8.19PM

Saxon punched in the four-digit code to unlock the main outer door of the house. He checked his mailbox without enthusiasm – bills as usual – and entered the large circular hall. In the middle was a small two-person lift with a concertina slide door surrounded by a cage. Around the lift was the main staircase, the original one having been ripped out long ago. The house was an unusual mixture of Regency style with a touch of 1920s Art Deco. He rather liked it. Every window seemed to contain a stained-glass peacock or a sleek woman holding a fan.

His flat was on the top floor and often he ran up the four flights of stairs; it was part of his somewhat limited keep-fit regime. But not tonight. He was on automatic as he took the lift. As he approached the third floor, a voice startled him.

'Good evening, caged cop. And how are we today?' It was Francesca, his neighbour on the floor below. She was taking rubbish to the chute and she waved at him as he headed skywards. She smiled up at him as he opened the door of the lift at the top.

'Fine, Fran, I'm fine.' Then he smiled back, realising that it was a while since anyone had actually cared how he was. He could hear voices coming from her flat. 'Well, actually I'm frustrated and exhausted, but bearing up. And how are you?' He put his key in the lock.

'I'm all the better knowing there's a big strong policeman in the place. I count on you to protect us all from the bad guys.' She laughed.

He laughed too. 'Not so much emphasis on the big, if you don't mind,' he answered, patting his stomach.

Francesca took in the small paper carrier bag he was holding in his other hand.

'Is that your dinner?' she asked with raised eyebrows. 'You're very welcome to join us, you know. Neil and Gary are here. You met them before when I had a little party to introduce you both to all the other inhabitants when you moved in.' She paused. 'Some company might help.'

She was still smiling. He'd always had the impression that Fran was one of life's happy people. He thought, not for the first time, how attractive she was. He wondered how she knew that Emma was still away. The thought of Fran keeping an eye out to see who was in residence and who wasn't momentarily irritated him. Then he mentally slapped his own wrist. Bringing a takeaway home for dinner on a Saturday night didn't exactly look like normal married life, did it? And it was nice of her to notice and to care, wasn't it.

'But, it's okay,' she was saying. 'I would understand if that was a problem right now.'

'Thanks, Fran,' he said, turning the key in the lock and pushing the door open, 'I appreciate the invitation. Maybe another time.'

'Of course, it was just a thought.' She seemed very relaxed. It helped.

'My regards to the lads. They're okay?' he asked.

She nodded. 'Mmm. We're planning a brochure for the next exhibition, so we're going through a creative phase tonight.' Voices were raised slightly inside Fran's apartment. 'I'd better get back in there before it gets too heated,' she laughed.

'Enjoy your evening,' he said, suddenly hungry for a social life that had once been quite busy but seemed to be non-existent these days.

'Yes, you too,' she answered, walking back towards her own door from the chute. 'But come down and join us later if you want a coffee or a nightcap.' She looked down at her wrist, but there was no watch there. 'I was going to say, it's only early, but that would have to be a guess on my part, since I don't for the life of me know where my watch is!' She laughed again.

He raised his hand in farewell. 'Well, okay, I might just do that. Thanks. Not sure that I'll be able to add much to the creative process, though.'

She lifted her own hand in response. 'No creativity required, we're overflowing with it,' she laughed. 'Did you know,' she asked, in a deep and serious voice, 'that there is a direct correlation between a good Chianti and the creative process?'

They both laughed and he was still smiling as he closed his door. Saxon stood in his hallway and his smile faded. The mess was clearly out of control, growing a bit more with each passing day. He was beginning to think that if he didn't clean up soon, a new life-form would evolve from the mess and jump on him one night as he slept, rip him to pieces and add him to the mess. He hoped that there might be a message on the answerphone from Emma but there was nothing.

He looked at the takeaway but couldn't summon up any appetite for it. When he found his kettle, he made some tea and switched the TV on in time for the local news. The main story of the day was the murders at Anvil Wood House. No doubt, it was headlining on the national news too. The report played heavily on the gruesome nature of the killings, although the police withheld any reference to the fact that the victims had been dismembered, or that body parts had been spread around the house, including in the oven.

The phone number of the police incident room was flashed up on the screen, and that was it.

A couple of other items of local news and then it was the weather forecast. At least the prospects were not so gloomy on that front. A heat wave was on the way.

He flicked off the TV and, with his mug, climbed the stairs to the roof. Saxon was fortunate that his flat was at the top of the building. He and Emma had built a staircase up to a skylight and converted it into a door to the flat roof, where they could sit and look at the stars and think. Saxon leant on the stone balustrade, and looked out over Brighton to the Palace Pier.

Saturday night in Brighton was a busy time for policemen. The London crowd still descended on the town in droves at weekends. Inevitably, a few of them drank too much and needed to be mopped up and rescued, although only a small few were grateful for that kind of help. Some weren't and managed to get into fights. Saxon was glad at times like that he was no longer a beat cop.

The phone ringing in the apartment below broke his rooftop

meditation, and he dashed down the stairs. He grabbed it as the answerphone kicked in.

'Paul, it's me.' Her voice was soft. He was filled with a mixture of relief that she'd phoned and dread at what she was about to say.

'Hi, Emma, how's things?' he said, with slight hesitation.

'Fine,' she answered. 'Well, you know.'

Saxon sensed immediately that the news was not going to be good by the tone in her voice. Emma would not have made a good negotiator; her voice gave too much away.

She went on. 'I saw the news report about the murders. You're handling that one?'

'Yes, that's me. It's all mine,' he answered.

'It sounds really bad, even by your standards,' she said, sympathetically.

He was puzzled by the turn the conversation was taking. 'Well, without revealing any state secrets, I'm not making much progress at the moment,' he said. 'We've got sod all to go on. He's a cunning bastard, as well as an evil one.' His voice trailed off. He wasn't going to discuss the case with her and they hadn't spoken in a week, so there were other important things to think about.

Emma wasn't as anxious as he was to move on to other things.

'Or her,' she offered.

Saxon's response was emphatic. 'No, I don't think it's a woman. Unlikely anyway, it's usually a man. I don't get any female vibes from this one. Plus, the amount of physical strength used makes me think it's got to be a man.' He realised that he was going into lecture mode and Emma hated that so he changed the subject abruptly.

'When are you coming home, Emma?'

She made no response for a few seconds, taken aback by the sudden change of subject.

'I'm not...not yet anyway,' she said slowly. When he didn't answer, she went on. 'Paul, I need time to think things over.' Still he said nothing. 'And it'll do you good, give you time to reassess.'

Saxon stopped holding his breath.

'What on earth do you mean, it'll do me good?!' he shouted. 'It's pissing me off, that's what it's doing. It's telling me you don't want to be here.' He instantly regretted losing his temper and apologised. This was followed by a long silence as if neither of them was prepared to be the first to speak.

Emma gave up first. 'I have to go; I'll call again in a few days,' she said. 'Look after yourself.' The phone clicked, and she was gone.

The apartment was deadly quiet. He went back up to the top of the stairs to the roof and locked the door. Saxon was depressed by Emma's apparent lack of compassion. He couldn't tell for sure but he sensed that she didn't really care too much how he felt. Although she hadn't said that it was all over, he wondered if she might've done, if the murders at Anvil Wood House hadn't persuaded her that now was maybe not a good time to hit him with more bad news. Maybe she was being considerate. He pushed the thought to the back of his mind and went into the kitchen, where he dumped the takeaway, still in its carrier, into the bin.

He spent the next two hours on the floor below, drinking better coffee and helping Fran, Neil and Gary with their creativity by giving them constructive feedback about their efforts so far. He didn't think about Emma once.

Chapter 9

Monday, May 20, Brighton Police Station, 9.00AM

Parker arrived with his usual Monday-morning eagerness. Usually Saxon liked that little quirk about his DS, but this particular morning it was a bit irritating. The weekend had made its mark and the conversation with Emma was still echoing around inside his head. Not to mention the conversations with Fran.

'Morning, boss,' said Parker, his tone cheerful and his tie bright. 'Summer's here at last.'

Parker was happy. They'd made some progress on the case at the end of last week and he'd had a great weekend with Lynne and the kids. Today was going to be useful, he just knew it. Life, in fact, was pretty good.

He sensed that Saxon wasn't in quite such a positive mood and retreated discreetly, returning in ten minutes with two steaming skimmed-milk lattes.

Back to business. 'Boss, you know that the address book you found under Barbara Jenner's floor contains a few business contacts and an awful lot of names and phone numbers of what could be friends,' he started.

Saxon nodded. 'Have you had any success working out the stars? Are there any other codes?'

Parker shook his head. 'No, we've tried various ways of looking at them, but I think we're going to have to assume that the stars are just a personal rating that Babs used.' He couldn't help smirking slightly. 'Since we know from Dr Marks that she was pretty highly sexed, I suppose it's safe to assume that she was giving them marks out of ten.'

Saxon didn't laugh. 'One, it's never safe to assume, Parker, you know that. And two, just because you got laid at the weekend, doesn't mean everyone else is only interested in sex.'

'Yes, sir.' The smirk had disappeared from Parker's face. 'Er, we know that most of the names are female; about sixty percent, I would say.' He put the photocopied sheets onto Saxon's desk and pointed at two separate entries.

'Two of those female names have been crossed out, both with "BITCH" written across them. We've been trying to get through to that one in Camberley since Friday, but up to now, no reply. Could be on holiday, I suppose.'

'Or away for the weekend,' Saxon offered.

'A WPC is checking the address this morning. Physically going round there to have a look. We should hear later today.'

'Did you have any luck with the other one?' Saxon looked at the entry. 'The one that's in Cookbridge?'

'Yes, boss. She's a married woman, a Mrs Gertraud Bishop. She's a German lady, apparently, married to a Mr Angus Bishop. They're long-term residents of Cookbridge. She was very upset when we spoke to her, very cagey and didn't want to talk on the phone. Apparently, her husband wouldn't understand. And I can't say I'm surprised.' Parker smirked again, but wiped the smile off his face as Saxon looked up at him, eyebrows raised. 'She's coming here to talk to us this afternoon at about four. She was anxious to come to us rather than have us go to their place.' Parker was still amused, however hard he tried to hide it.

'And what about the other names?' asked Saxon.

'The Yard team are working their way through the other names, all the data is in the computer and we'll see what it spits out later.'

'Oh, we've found the brother,' Parker continued, looking even more pleased with himself. 'One Keith Jenner. He doesn't sound the most pleasant of people. When I phoned him on Friday afternoon, he didn't seem too bothered that his sister had been murdered.' Parker shook his head in disgust. 'More interested in coming to view the property, which I suppose, he will inherit. He'll be dropping in here tomorrow. Lives and works as a scrap dealer in South London. He does very nicely, thank you. Big house at the nice end of Upper Norwood and, as a special bonus he's got a bit of form. Small-time gangster, by the look of things – likes to rough people up a bit sometimes.

'He's done time for GBH – got three years for beating up some poor bastard who owed him money. The original charge was attempted murder due to the extent of the injuries, but the victim changed his testimony during the trial and said that he attacked Jenner first. Prosecution thinks the family of the victim were threatened to keep him from testifying; CPS decided it was unsafe, so the attempted murder charge was dropped. Two years ago he was arrested for insurance fraud but the charge was dropped, not enough evidence.'

'Well, at least we have someone who is not totally straight to talk to,' Saxon said, showing his pleasure at the progress the team was making. 'Not likely to have much of a motive for killing her though. It sounds as if he's worth more than she is.'

'Yes, boss, but I'm not making any assumptions about that,' he said, keeping a straight face. Parker collected the papers and put them back on his desk. He was good at records, kept things in order. He never lost a piece of paper. It was one of his strengths. 'As I said, Mr Jenner will be here for a chat tomorrow afternoon at 2PM.'

'Great stuff, Parker, keep digging up as much as you can on him between now and tomorrow, I want to see what you have a good couple of hours before we talk to him, okay?'

Parker took the lid of his coffee and inhaled the smell.

Saxon was thinking aloud. 'You never know, it could be a hit for gain, and maybe I've got it all wrong. It's possible that we have two killers. One weirdo who's bumping off the gays – and the Anvil Wood House killer, who's just killing for profit. It would be neat and tidy if it was Jenner.'

'Yes, boss.' Parker switched on his PC and binned his empty cup. His boys had been on at him to stop using the paper cups and take a reusable cup in each time instead. Knowing he was addicted to Starbucks, they'd even bought him one for his last birthday, one with a lid, specially marketed by the coffee company for exactly that purpose and to placate the green lobby at the same time. But the reusable cup was somewhere at the Yard, waiting for a good wash.

Parker played devil's advocate. 'But would he kill Barbara Jenner's friend as well, just to inherit a house?' Parker leant back in his chair and gazed at the ceiling for a moment. 'A bit savage, even if you leave out all the chopping up of limbs and planting of fingers in potted plants. And dare I mention the cooking bit?' He looked across to where Saxon was sitting. 'He'd have to have a reason for doing that, it can't just be to get the house.' He paused. 'No, boss, my money's not on Jenner as the killer.'

Saxon stood up and turned round. He walked across to the window and opened it. The temperature was rising fast. The weather forecast was spot on. He held on to the sides of the open window with his hands above his head and cooled himself in the draught, thinking to himself for a few seconds.

'I don't know, Parker. People will do unbelievable things to each other for money, usually to their own family. Maybe our second killer, if indeed there is a second killer, is devious enough to try to blame the Anvil Wood House murders on the current weirdo doing the rounds.'

Parker nodded. 'Could've been a spontaneous thing, taking advantage of the timing of the other murders,' he agreed.

'If only we had at least one clue about the killer.' Saxon sounded exasperated. 'But there is absolutely sod all.' He rubbed his face with both hands in frustration and slowly wandered back to his chair. He sat down and leaned forward on his elbows.

'We know a bit about the victims, mostly about Babs though. Strange isn't it, Parker, how some people lead interesting, and fascinating lives. They get up to all kinds of escapades, some good and some not so good. The more the person interacts with other people, the more you'll learn about that individual. Then you come across Miss Penelope Field, and there's bugger all to say about her – not even a speeding ticket. If it weren't for a few photographs in an album, you'd never have known she'd even been on the planet. We don't even have a clue who she was involved with before she met Babs. But I suppose if we look on the bright side, we'll know even more about Babs Jenner after these next two interviews. But I doubt it will tell us anything about the killer,' he said despondently. 'Come on, Parker,' he went on. 'Suggestions, please. Why is it that we have no forensic evidence? Does our killer not have fingerprints? Or come to that, does he have any hair? Is he bald all over? As for the footprints, I just don't know what's going on there. When he does have them they are non-human and what does he do for the rest of the time…hover?'

Parker shrugged and suggested another drink and left the office, he returned a few minutes later with two cups of water. And, after placing one on each desk, he took off his jacket, complaining mildly about the heat. Saxon interrupted his meteorological comments.

'You know, Parker, the more I think about it the more I'm convinced that this guy, whoever he is, is definitely a serial killer. I'm sure we are after one killer, not two. He is very clever, and he's deliberately not keeping to the rules. You know as well as I do that with serial killers, they tend to follow the same routine when they kill. Almost like a ritual.

'They always take trophies, such as clothing or other personal items. Some of them even try to interact with the police. They can't help it, the compulsion overwhelms them.'

Parker was knowledgeable about the field too. 'The Rillington Place bloke, Christie, kept pubic hair, teeth and sometimes underwear from his victims,' he said. 'You don't get much more personal than that.'

Saxon nodded. 'The psych guys will tell you that the reason

they do this is so that they can relive the experience at a later date. Either they toss themselves off or they just enjoy remembering the power they possessed over their victims before they killed them.'

In their database, the Unit had extensive records of every serial killer ever traced as well as information on the as-yet-unsolved crimes.

Saxon continued his musing. 'There is also plenty of evidence to show that some serial killers like to revisit the crime scene,' he said.

'Yes, boss,' Parker agreed. 'They could do a walk past as we arrive and we'd never know.'

'The more I think about this case, the more I'm sure that what we have is a very bright and unusual serial killer who can change his tactics and twist the so-called rules,' affirmed Saxon.

'But does that mean he's doing this for fun?' asked Parker. 'How else does he overcome the irresistible urge to follow a pattern, like the usual serial killer?'

Saxon was confident. 'I reckon it's because our guy knows that if he does that, then we'll get him. It means that not only is he clever but he's also educated and, specifically, he knows about serial killers. He's probably studied them.'

Parker saw it too. 'So you're saying that he knows what to do so that he doesn't get predictable?'

'Afraid so... I think we should get Professor Roger Ercott to do a profile based on what we know so far. He's done well in the past.' Saxon looked through his address book for Ercott's number. After a minute of searching, he threw the book on his desk. 'I can't find it – see if you've got it somewhere. He's getting on a bit though, and he doesn't take on all work that comes his way. Good enough to pick and choose I guess.'

Parker was rummaging through his notes desperately trying to find Ercott's address. 'Ah, found it. That's handy,' he said. 'He lives in Worthing, boss."

'Right. Call him and arrange a meeting as soon as possible, I don't want to waste time on this. Ask him if we can talk with him this afternoon, and after that we'll be back here to talk to Mrs Bishop at about four o'clock.' Saxon switched on the fan on his desk and then opened his office door to let the air flow through.

'What's next? How about our friend Dr Marks, anything on him?' Saxon so wanted there to be something juicy on Marks.

'He's being checked out as we speak and breathe, sir. We've had Surveillance and Technical Intelligence put a minor tail on him over the weekend but as he's not a major suspect, we haven't been searching his rubbish bins yet. But he does frequent some interesting pubs. Let's say the kind of places where you and I would stand with our backs to the wall while we drank our beer.'

'And what pubs would these be, Parker?' Saxon paused for a second. 'Is he married by any chance?' he continued.

'Oh yes, sir, he's married all right but, I suppose he's a train that uses both tunnels if you'll pardon the expression. His main drinking, and apparently poking, hole is the Speckled Cat, over in Kemp Town. It's outside his catchment area for patients so he's unlikely to be thrust up against anyone he knows. By the way, sir, his name appears in Barbara Jenner's book with the number seven next to it – whatever that means.'

'Okay, Parker, ensure STI stays on him wherever he goes for the next week, and I want hour-by-hour updates. If he goes back to the pub, they are to follow him home afterwards. If he picks anyone up, I want his name and address as well. We need to be sure that he's tucked up in bed every night.'

Monday, May 20, Victoria Tube Station, 11.00AM

The London Underground is a good place to be lost. That is, of course, if you want to be lost. The man knows that he can blend into the sea of humanity that surges through the turnstiles every day, and never be noticed. His goal is to be seen only when he wants to be seen. He is confident that he can achieve this at will.

He is jostled slightly in the crowd and resists the temptation to push back at the tourist who pushed his way through the crowd, with no care for who he knocked aside on the way. The man follows the backpacker briefly along the platform of the Circle Line, but turns aside when he sees him join a group of three other similarly clad and equally well-laden young people.

There are as usual so many people that if he looks everyone in the face as they pass by, even just for a moment, then he will get dizzy. Endless faces, moving across his line of vision. After a few seconds, his perception shifts. They are no longer individual people, but just souls that are clean or dirty.

He feels faint. He mustn't pass out. Because to do that will draw attention to himself. He can't afford that. The cameras are everywhere. Being spotted by the Transport Police – because he is acting suspiciously – would be a disaster.

His weakness is not a sign of poor health. Far from it. The master ensures that he is fit, that his body is in perfect condition. Every day, the man is awakened by the master's voice urging him to exercise, to do push-ups and sit-ups, to use the equipment at home for an hour every morning. He must maintain himself in peak condition.

He pauses for a moment by a vending machine, studying the contents. He breathes slowly. The mission is too important for him to fail. It's all down to him and he knows it. Right now he has to look and act like every other normal person.

Standing there, nobody notices him. He is almost invisible. He knows the true secrets of camouflage and it comes from within the body as well as on the exterior. His clothes are not his own. They would never be found in his home simply because he stores them underground somewhere in a wood in Sussex, sealed in a waterproof container. Each time he decides on the persona he will adopt, he can dress accordingly.

Even if someone should happen on his hidden wardrobe, the clothes are not traceable. The labels have all been removed and a receipt or two, picked up in the street, has been placed in one or more of the pockets, to throw any meddling police who become involved off the scent. *The emperor's new clothes make the emperor invisible*, he thinks to himself triumphantly.

Of course, the British Transport Police are just doing their job, much as he is doing his. On the other hand, it could be said that they were not doing their job. He knows that they see what he sees and still they take no action. But he also knows that they would stop him if they could, if they knew what he was doing.

The man shakes his head. It is so wrong. Because if he were to be stopped, then who is going to save them all from what is obviously already happening to the world? Perhaps it isn't their fault. How can they be expected to understand? Nobody else does either.

It worries him sometimes though. Is he really the only person called upon to deal with this?

He moves on from the vending machine, having purchased a carton of juice and sits to drink it. The trilby hat he's wearing doesn't look out of place. It hides his hair and much of his forehead. His glasses are twenty years out of date and tinted to hide the true colour of his eyes. Subtle use of makeup has changed his facial structure and his moustache is of a suitable standard for close-up filming. Yes, he has control of how he is seen by others. He is grey and rather dull. Why would anyone look twice at him? He is boring and slightly hunched. Satisfied that nobody has noticed his moment of hesitation, he looks around.

The people to be cleansed are here, just as they are everywhere. No need to look too hard for them. And he knows better than anyone that the population need to be dealt with.

The master is surely using others too. But why then is it only his achievements that are announced in the press and on TV? Are the others working in secret? No, it seems he is alone. It is up to him to prevent the impending disaster with his own contribution.

Is it enough though? Will it ever be enough? Sometimes he wonders how many innocent lives he has already saved.

He functions with no remorse for his actions, no pity for his victims or their loved ones. They are bringing it on themselves with their selfish lust for pleasure. Pleasure at any cost to themselves, even at the cost of bringing a curse to humanity. To Her.

Then he sees the girl. She is sitting at the side of the platform; her dog slumped forlornly against her side. They both looked pathetic. Several people appeared to have made a donation but the girl was unresponsive, her expression glassy, her pupils dilated. Her soul was dirty and the master would be pleased.

Monday, May 20, Brighton Police Station Canteen, 12.30PM

PC Michael Lucas always wanted to be in plain clothes. He decided that one way to make his mark and be noticed would be to catch a killer single-handed. He figured that if the killer was targeting gays, and he went to the Speckled Cat, maybe the killer would try to pick him up and he, PC Lucas would catch him all by himself and be a hero.

He ran the idea by PC Barry Ryan as they tucked into pasta and chips.

'You can't be serious, Mike,' Ryan said, incredulously. 'We would be in big trouble if we were found out,' he argued.

'I am very serious. Couldn't be more serious, Baz,' Lucas answered with a smile. 'And we definitely wouldn't be in trouble if we were instrumental in catching a killer that everyone is struggling to get anywhere near.'

'But we'd stick out like sore thumbs in a gay pub, wouldn't we?' Ryan didn't like the idea at all. 'We're not gay and they'll notice.'

'But the killer might not be gay, so how's he going to know?' replied Ryan. 'No, I think it's a great idea. Someone's probably already planning something like this, it's just that we'd be ahead of them if we do it sooner rather than later.'

Their conversation was interrupted when they were joined by a couple of other PCs. The conversation turned to the weekend's football.

Barry suggested a beer after work in the nearest sports bar and they agreed to meet up there. 'See you there, Mike,' he said pointedly to Lucas.

Lucas smiled. 'Yeah, okay, see you there.'

Monday, May 20, Worthing, 3.00PM

'Ah, gentlemen of the constabulary, you are very punctual, welcome. Please come in, and make yourselves at home. Tea? We have tea. Or coffee, if you would rather? Let me see. Or could I offer you a cold drink.' Ercott radiated boundless energy as well as, at this precise moment in time, genuine hospitality.

He was a thin and gangly six-foot-two of dignified hyperactivity. His hair was still thick but it was completely white. It had been cut but not recently. It had been combed but quite possibly not today. And, although nearly seventy-three, his appearance somehow managed to give him the air of a schoolboy on occasions.

Ercott had gone into psychology in the days when people raised their eyebrows whenever a shrink was mentioned. He had long since forgotten how many times he had heard – and ignored – someone say, "Anyone who sees a psychiatrist needs their heads tested." He had moved over to criminology simply because, as an overgrown child, he saw it as jolly good fun. A bit of a wheeze.

Offender profiling was now his main passion, and he once amused his grandchildren by boasting that he could tell which milkman was doing which shift, by the position the bottles were placed on his doorstep. And he was right. His grandchildren thought he was way cool.

Ercott led Saxon and Parker down the hallway to his study, which apparently was not confined to one room but spread over the entire ground floor of the house. The main walls had been knocked out so that a large gentle arch divided each room. At the back of the house were large French windows leading out to a patio and a long garden with a well-trimmed lawn.

'Please come into my study, gentlemen. And have you decided, tea, coffee or lemonade?'

They settled on coffee and Ercott passed on the order to a small round woman wearing an apron. She had appeared as if by magic, just as he turned to look for her. Saxon guessed she must be roughly the same age as Ercott. She nodded at both of them.

He smiled at them, inclining his head towards her. 'Oh, I'm sorry. Forgive me. I didn't introduce you to my housekeeper, Hettie. She has been with me for a long time, and you know I really can't remember exactly how long. Sign of my age I suppose. Hettie, my dear, these gentlemen are from the police.'

Hettie nodded again and disappeared in the direction of the kitchen. Social graces were not her forte.

Ercott's old world ways and courteous manners struck Saxon immediately. Ercott wore an off-white colonial-style suit, with cuffs that had definitely seen better days; he resembled Saxon's idea of a British embassy official in the 1920s, somewhere tropical. As he spoke to Saxon, he repeatedly removed his steel-rimmed glasses and held them up to the light as if he couldn't believe there was nothing on the lens restricting his vision. Periodically he wiped them and put them back on only to remove them a few minutes later for another polish.

Every inch of wall space was covered with bookshelves starting at floor level, and the top books touched the ceiling in places. Saxon was able to see at a glance that they were mostly books on psychology, criminology, and true-life crime – particularly murder.

While Ercott dithered around trying to find somewhere sensible to put the papers and books that had covered the sofa, Saxon and Parker stood in the centre of the room like two boys in the headmaster's study, waiting for a good talking-to about something found stuck under a desk.

Eventually Ercott lost patience with himself and swept pretty much everything from the sofa to the floor. He apologised for the apparent chaos, but explained that he knew where everything was and could generally lay his hands on what he needed. So the filing system – or lack of it – suited him very well. He gestured for them to sit down in the newly available space.

'Now, officers, what is it that I can assist you with?' Ercott seemed exhausted as he slumped in his desk chair.

Saxon slowly expounded the entire story so far, as Ercott made careful notes, stopping Saxon every now and then so that he could catch up and occasionally clean his glasses. The only real pause was when Hettie reappeared with tea instead of coffee. Nobody said a word, other than to thank her. They didn't want to cause any embarrassment to the old woman.

'I'm sorry, gentlemen, but she never quite gets it right,' Ercott apologised. 'Can you suffer with your tea instead of coffee?'

'No problem, I'm sure it will be fine, Professor.' Saxon felt sorry for the old dear.

'Do call me Roger. After all, that's what I was christened, not Professor,' Ercott said, beaming at them.

Saxon could tell even from that first short meeting that he and Ercott were going to have no communication problems at all. He liked Ercott; indeed, it was difficult not to like him.

'Right then, Commander. Or can I call you Comm for short?'

'You can call me Paul, I wasn't christened Commander either.'

Ercott took his glasses off again, and polished them. He squinted at Saxon. 'Right, Paul, what I need from you at this stage are the names of everyone you have come into contact with regarding this case.' He looked through the bottom of the glasses and then put them back on. 'And details, as many details as possible about those people. For instance, have any of them changed their names either through marriage or by deed poll? I need to know where they live and where they lived for the last five years at least. Is there the slightest chance that their paths have crossed before? Is this quite clear, Paul? It's very important that you follow my instructions to the letter otherwise we will all be wasting our time.' He pressed his fingers together, almost as if he were praying.

'I will need to see photos of the crime scene… And, by the way, how were the locations left after the murders?'

'Extremely tidy, except for the last one, I found that very strange,' Saxon said with Parker nodding in agreement.

'Yes, but what did the "tidy" tell you, Paul? Did it say clinically tidy or just average tidy?' Ercott sat leaning on his knuckles looking intense.

Saxon paused. 'I would say clinically clean and tidy.' He looked across at his colleague. 'Would you agree with that, Parker?'

'Yes, sir, I'd say it was spooky how clean and tidy. Too bloody tidy. Up to the last murders at Anvil Wood House, that is.' Parker was relieved to be included in the conversation at last.

Ercott stood up and wandered around the room with his head back so that he could focus through the bottom of his glasses. He scanned the shelves of books as he went.

'Oh I can't find the damn thing, I'm sure Hettie comes in here and moves things about when I'm not here,' he mumbled in an irritated tone. 'Ah, wait, got it.' With a swipe, he grabbed a heavily read book and flicked through the pages.

'If it is the same person committing these crimes then his MO is obviously changing, which is unusual to say the least. Most serial killers have a set pattern that they stick to religiously and if one of these killers becomes active, you realise this phenomenon is quite rare don't you, gentlemen? Of course you do, silly me, you are policemen after all. Maybe in this country, we will only come across two or three serials every couple of years. But due to the predictability of their actions and your detection talents, they can usually be caught.'

He held up the book with his thumb marking the spot with the elusive information.

'A colleague, or rather should I say, ex-colleague, he's dead now, wrote this book in the fifties. Very ahead of his time, had some radical ideas and wasn't afraid to speak up. In those days, very brave, very brave indeed. Anyway, as I was saying, he worked with the police on several occasions. Some of the more forward-thinking high-ranking officers realised that if, as they called them then, "a homicidal maniac", was on the loose, then maybe someone who understood the workings of their minds may be able to help catch them. The author's name was Alan Gittings. Poor chap had ginger hair, and we called him Ginger Git. Never mind though, he's probably forgiven us by now.'

Saxon was hoping that Ercott would hurry up a bit and come to a conclusion, but Parker was completely entranced like a small boy in awe of a favourite teacher. Ercott was striding around the room in full lecture mode, although totally unaware of it.

'The point I'm making, gentlemen, is that Gittings came across one particular killer during his long and varied career. It was, I think in 1958; yes it was indeed '58.'

He spoke slowly as he checked it out.

'This murderer, a charming fellow by all accounts, by the name of Clive Williams, a bit grand, thought highly of himself, a journalist apparently. After first killing three ladies of the night, by strangulation, Williams changed his MO and suddenly started to stab his victims. For a serial killer this does not come easy. They have set routines where they feel safe because in their minds they have practised over and over the events that will happen during their attack. They meticulously plan for all eventualities, including, for example, their escape route. Back to Williams, after two knife killings he decided to try smashing the skulls of his victims with a hammer. Only one – thank goodness. He was caught because he dropped his hammer after running away from his last attempted murder.

'His prints were all over it and he was apprehended about a week later. At his trial, Gittings referred to him as a man who changed his personality as he changed his choice of weapon. As his personality changed so did his physical appearance, by that I don't mean he turned into a werewolf or anything like that. It was his bearing that changed. One personality, the hammer man, was hunched over and almost goblin-like, while the strangler was tall and quite aristocratic.'

Ercott sat down and looked Saxon in the face.

'Gittings gave him a very trendy cognomen, a "shape shifter". Have you come across that term?'

'Not sure I have. It sounds like something out of science fiction. So, you're telling me that you think our killer could be one of these shape shifters?' Saxon stood up, walked across the room and gazed out at the garden. 'What you're saying, if I've got this right, is that the killer is going to change tactics so much and so well that unless he screws up, then we haven't got a chance of catching him?'

'I'm afraid so, Paul.' Ercott began counting off points on the fingers of his left hand. 'He is more than likely very smart and very controlled. He also seems to have a good knowledge of forensics by the sound of things. Believing that what he is doing is right and everyone else is wrong, he is probably convinced that the rest of the world is evil. This is a way, or should I say a mechanism, to justify his actions.' Ercott shook his head. 'I have to say, this man is an awfully disturbed individual,' he said.

'Well, we'd have to agree with you there, sir,' said Parker. 'Going by what we've seen, he's probably the most disturbed criminal I've ever come across.'

Ercott smiled grimly at him. 'Yes, my lad, but what is even more disturbing is that when you finally catch up with him you will be surprised at his normality.' He looked back at Saxon. 'Paul, he could be your young colleague over there. He could be that normal.' Parker was pleased that he was deemed "normal" enough, by someone who clearly knew was he was talking about, for him to be considered as an example of normality. The urge to preen himself slightly was irresistible, and he smoothed back his hair.

'If you could hear the way he talks to his computer you wouldn't say that,' laughed Saxon.

'Oh, very funny.' Ercott laughed heartily and the sudden effort brought on a choking fit. After the spasmodic coughing, that only men of a certain age are capable of, had finished, he continued. 'This man would under normal circumstances be a loner, most serial killers are. However, if he is a true shape shifter he may not be the typical run of the mill "catch-me-if-you-can-I'm-a-loner-type-of-serial-killer-come-and-get-me". I could go on but someone may have to hyphenate this if I'm ever quoted one day,' he chuckled. 'One thing I should say to you about this person is that whoever he is there will be certain characteristics that he won't be able to hide.

'He is almost certainly going to be suffering from paranoia, of which there are several symptoms, like for instance: a tendency to bear grudges persistently, that is – he will never forgive someone if they dare to cross him. An excessive sensitiveness to setbacks and rebuffs. A tendency to experience excessive self-importance, meaning in laymen's terms that he considers himself to be right in everything, and I mean just that – everything he does in his eyes is perfect. There are about seven recognised symptoms. If he suffers from only three of them, then he is paranoid. The paranoia will make him obsessive about everything he does. It will make him careful.'

Saxon had expected light to be shed by Ercott. He had hoped for something to help them focus their search. Instead, much as they were receiving an extraordinary amount of relevant and interesting information, the waters were muddying rather than clearing. He couldn't help but feel slightly despondent and it showed.

'This doesn't make me feel very optimistic, Roger. Until he leaves some forensic evidence, I'm screwed. He leaves nothing, no prints, no hair, and not much hope. All I can do is wait for him to make a cock-up. Try telling that to the family of his next victim.' He hung his head.

Ercott sympathised. 'Sorry, Paul, I do understand. Not much else I can say at this point. When I've studied the photos and read the pathology reports, I may be able to tell you more. What I can tell you, however, is that he will make a mistake – they always do, and when he does, we will be there.'

Saxon arranged a time to have the photos of the crime scenes along with all the other information he had requested sent to Ercott, and they agreed to meet up a couple of days later when the profile was completed. As they made their way down the hall, Hettie appeared and asked them if they would like another cup of coffee before they left. They thanked her but declined the offer.

Monday, May 20, Brighton Police Station, 3.57PM

She walked nervously up and down the road outside the police station. Being early was not a situation Gertraud Bishop was particularly familiar with. In fact, she was a notoriously tardy woman under normal circumstances, much to the extreme annoyance of her husband. Today was different. Being late would mean prolonging the agony, so it had been out of the question.

Mrs Bishop did not like police stations; she found the very idea of them intimidating in the extreme. Four o'clock had approached painfully slowly all day. All weekend, in fact. She had watched the hands of the clock circling inevitably towards her appointment with the police, and it had been one of the longest weekends of her life.

She would have been willing to see them on Friday afternoon

and get it over and done with, but as luck would have it, Angus was not working and had played golf, so he planned to be home relatively early. He had left again on Sunday for a long trip, so she had to reluctantly wait until today.

One minute to four and Mrs Bishop entered the outer door and had to pause as the duty officer took a brief look at her to see if she was the sort of person he should admit. A second later and she was in, and the constable at the desk informed her that Commander Saxon was not back yet, but expected soon. She was shown to a seat and offered a cup of something from a machine. It was called tea but tasted like nothing she had ever come across before.

The waiting prolonged her torment further. She endured it with a superficial calmness. The whole situation she found herself in was to her, an intensely private and shy person, pure purgatory. Suddenly without warning, the door flew open and in strode Saxon followed by Parker. The PC caught his eye as he passed and nodded towards Mrs Bishop, who by now was in such a state of anxiety that she was trembling and had given up on the tea-like substance.

Saxon walked over to her and gently shook her hand.

'Mrs Bishop? I'm Commander Paul Saxon.' She rose to her feet as he approached.

'I'm sorry to have kept you waiting like this,' he went on. 'I do appreciate how very difficult this must be for you.'

She was almost the same height as him. She was elegant and stylish. He was struck by her stunning blue eyes and expensively cut hair. She was beautifully dressed too. She was chic, he thought. Not a word that seemed to be used much these days, but that's exactly the effect she had on him. Even if she was at a disadvantage right now because of the circumstances, she still exuded it.

'Would you please follow me? We can talk in my office. Much nicer than the interview rooms believe me.' Mrs Bishop said nothing but followed Saxon. She sat down obediently in front of his desk. Parker sat behind her by the door, and Saxon stood by his chair. A WPC stood by the door.

'Thanks for coming, Mrs Bishop. I will try not to keep you here for too long. I do understand that this is not easy for you, but I do have to ask you some questions regarding your relationship with Barbara Jenner.'

Mrs Bishop sat bolt upright with her head slightly inclined, unable to make eye contact.

'Thank you, Commander, you are right – I'm not enjoying this at all.' Her English accent was almost perfect.

Saxon turned to gaze out of the window, thinking that it might make the situation less stressful for her. 'First, I would like to get straight to the point, Mrs Bishop, and there is no reason at all for you to feel embarrassed. Were you at one time having a sexual relationship with Barbara Jenner?'

'Yes, Commander, I was. But it was over a year ago, it is all finished now.' Her breathing became faster and she started to shudder. Saxon saw the signs that the floodgates were about to open and handed her some tissues.

'When you are ready, Mrs Bishop, take your time; I know this is difficult for you. You can leave out the "Commander" bit, it is quite a mouthful'. She calmed down after a minute or so.

'Thank you, you are very understanding, unlike my husband. He was not at all understanding. But I think that not many times it happens that a wife tells her husband that she is leaving him for a woman, is it?' She looked at him with appealing eyes.

Saxon remained silent, and she filled the waiting vacuum.

'I met Babs two years ago. I had decided to take up riding. You see, my husband is spending a lot of time away and I was bored and needed something to fill up my time. One day I was driving down Hazel Lane and noticed that Anvil Wood Stables was a place where you could have lessons in riding. I stopped and went in and the moment I met Babs I knew she was gay, it was quite obvious really. As for me, I always had a feeling that I had made the wrong choice in life. I should never have got married in the first place.' She paused for a few seconds and Saxon handed her a few more tissues.

'How long had the relationship progressed before your husband found out – or did you tell him?' Saxon said with genuine concern. He felt that she was being totally honest and deserved to be treated with respect.

'Three months, I think it was, yes three months. You see, Babs led me on, making me think that she would end her relationship with that Poppy woman. I thought she wanted me to move in with her and that's when I told him, and of course, he went crazy, smashing up the house and throwing things around and at me. Then when he calmed down he said that he would kill Babs and he called her an "effing bitch", and that he would sort her out, you understand?'

'Yes, Mrs Bishop, I think we understand what that means,' said Saxon, slightly bemused at her coyness. 'And do you think he is capable of carrying out a threat like that?' Saxon scented a possible suspect.

'Yes, I think he could. He can be very aggressive and quite boorish sometimes. Angus has a violent temper, with a lot of shouting and breaking up of the furniture, although he has never harmed me in any way whatsoever. It took him many months to really start talking with me again.'

Saxon was pleased that his gentle approach was producing results. He continued. 'Why would Barbara Jenner have written the word "BITCH" across your name in her address book?'

Mrs Bishop looked shocked, and paused for a moment. 'I was upset when it happened. When we separated, I mean. It was so hard to accept, when I had taken such a risk for her. And I'm ashamed to say that I kept on phoning her and I wrote some unpleasant letters – which I now regret. She threatened to call the police if I didn't stop. So I stopped.'

'What did you write in these letters?'

'Just that I might tell her friend, Poppy, what had been going on between us, that's all.'

'And did you?' Saxon asked.

'What, tell her friend?' Mrs Bishop seemed surprised. 'No, of course not. I wouldn't have dreamt of telling her.'

'Mrs Bishop, what does your husband do, what is his job?'

'He is an airline pilot, a captain. He is based at Gatwick and sometimes he's away for long times. All over the world he is flying.'

Her accent was holding out but the order in which the words came out seemed to be controlled by her stress levels. Saxon asked her to excuse him for a moment while he briefly stepped out of the office. Next door was the operations room and Saxon stuck his head around the door and told one of the PCs to check out Angus Bishop now, and phone him immediately with the details.

He was hardly back at his desk before the phone rang. Bishop was clean apart from a few old speeding offences and a drunk and disorderly fifteen years ago. It had taken five policemen to get him into the van at the time, and even more to get him from the van to the cells. Saxon put down the phone and turned to Mrs Bishop.

'Where is your husband at this moment, Mrs Bishop?' Saxon asked her, conversationally.

She looked at her watch and calculated mentally, the way people do when they are used to operating in different time zones. 'He's in New York, but he won't be back for two weeks; in fact he's back on the second of June. He's on a training course.'

'Do you think he is capable of murder, Mrs Bishop?'

'Who knows what people will do when they are upset. I don't feel that I really know what he could do, I just don't know.' She started to lose her self-control again. More tissues. The WPC raised her eyebrows questioningly at Parker. They would be through an entire box of tissues in a minute and she could imagine Mrs Bishop's solicitor complaining of unreasonable pressure on his client.

Saxon must have been thinking along the same lines. He decided to end the interview; at least the wavering finger of suspicion had someone to point at.

'Okay, Mrs Bishop. I will be talking to him about this matter when he returns from the States. If he is at all difficult later please ring me.' He handed her a card with his work and mobile phone numbers. She looked him in the eyes and thanked him. It was a look that lingered. She held his eyes without expression. Then she gave a hint of a smile before she turned and left. The WPC went with her.

After they left the office, Saxon said to Parker. 'Okay, Parker, get in touch with his employer, whichever airline it is, and check that he has turned up where he's supposed to be in New York. If not, get on to the FBI and maybe they could be kind enough to shoot him for us.' He was cheerful that they had something substantial to get their teeth into.

He was aware of a pregnant pause in the room.

'What's on your mind, Parker?' he asked. 'You've been shifting from one buttock to the other, what's bugging you?'

'The truth?' Parker said tentatively.

'The truth will do, spit it out.'

'I think she could be setting us up to think that maybe her husband is the killer. Could be a handy way of getting rid of him. Apart from his money, it doesn't sound as though she has much use for him. And there was something else, sir.' Parker paused wondering whether or not to go on.

'Well get on with it, Parker, we haven't got all day.'

'I did have the feeling that she was flirting with you just a bit, sir.'

'Don't be ridiculous, Parker.' He thought about it for a second. 'Your imagination's working overtime.'

Saxon felt himself blush as he looked away and walked over to the window to open it.

Monday, May 20, The Speckled Cat Pub, 8.20PM

Lucas had adapted his plan, reluctantly at first, to exclude Baz Ryan. He was disappointed in some ways, but then on the other hand he was also quite looking forward to getting all the glory, rather than having to share it. His intention was to wait in the hope that maybe people would eventually talk to him. He didn't have to wait. Quickly, he'd found himself in the position of fighting off advances from several of the regulars, and learnt the true meaning of cruising, as he was asked if that was what he was doing at least a dozen times.

He wondered if that was how it felt to be a girl. He was confident in his sexuality and confident in his appearance. He knew that he was attractive and he quite enjoyed the idea that the part he was playing was one that required no effort. He just had to look good. Nevertheless, he couldn't help but be a bit nervous.

Lucas walked up to the bar and sat casually on a barstool. The music from the jukebox was a steady drumming drone as if the band that produced it had recently bought an electronic drum synthesiser - and just left it on for too long. He didn't care for that kind of music. Lucas looked around.

It was early evening so the pub was quite empty. The after-work crowd had mostly gone home. There were a few really keen, but sad-looking individuals, either on first dates or just out to be the early birds after their worms. Lucas ordered his drink from what he thought was a rather attractive barmaid, and indeed, he had decided to flirt a bit. This plan was thwarted when a man approached the bar and asked "Eric" if he could have a large gin and tonic.

Lucas moved away from the bar and sat in a corner with a good view of the door. Fifteen minutes dragged by and a few more people came in, but nobody who seemed worthy of any particular attention. Lucas was considering calling it a night, when a man came in who caught his eye immediately. He was tall and rather thin but he had his head down and was looking unsure of himself. He ordered a drink and sat down at the next table to Lucas.

For twenty minutes, they sat sipping but not speaking. Nobody else of any interest came in. The man glanced in Lucas' direction often, but seemed too shy to instigate any form of conversation. Lucas was convinced he had a possible suspect in his sights. He was acting suspiciously, his manner was furtive. Lucas was wondering how to engage him in conversation when suddenly the man rose to his feet, and Lucas realised he was possibly going to leave.

Lucas had to act quickly. 'Can I buy you a drink?' he asked. The man stopped and smiled hesitantly at Lucas. 'Yes, all right, thank you.'

Lucas sensed his relief and flushed with embarrassment himself. Deep down, he knew that what he was doing was totally against his nature and probably illegal to boot. He should be out having a good time with his girlfriend or over at the Fox with Baz and the others. Alas no, here he was trying to pick up a man, who could be a serial killer, in a gay pub. But the thought of him, a lowly PC, catching a serial killer gave him the will to persevere.

The man wanted a pint of bitter. Lucas was surprised and relieved. He'd been expecting the man to ask for a pink gin or some cocktail or other with a daft name, like a "long slow screw up against a wall". His girlfriend and her mates used to go for drinks like that just to see him and his mates squirm with embarrassment when they had to ask for them at a bar. He smiled at the thought of his girlfriend. She rarely asked him about his work and he didn't mind that at all, but he knew she would not believe what he was doing tonight. He rather thought she would be impressed though, if it all went according to plan.

The man joined him at his table and the chat was stilted and matter-of-fact for about ten minutes, but gradually the subject turned to sex. Lucas had given it some thought over the weekend while he'd been planning the exercise. He'd decided to play the part of a man who was new to the gay scene, just coming out of the closet, as it were, and didn't really know what he wanted. The man seemed to accept the situation but didn't look too happy. It occurred to Lucas that his "date" was trawling for sex and was therefore almost certainly hoping for someone experienced rather than someone he might have to coax along. Lucas was going to play the situation as an innocent.

'So, what do you do for a living?' he asked.

'I'm a medical journalist,' the man answered easily. 'I work freelance. It gives me a lot of freedom of choice about my hours of work. I really like that.' The story was either true or very well-rehearsed, since it sounded very plausible. 'How about you? What do you do?' he asked.

'Me,' answered Lucas, with a smile. 'I don't work. Don't need to. My father made a lot of money and I have a trust fund. It gives me enough to pay for clothes and the car and for going out.' He laughed. This was his and Bazzer's favourite fantasy. So, in a way, his story too was well-rehearsed.

By 9.30PM the pub was filling up with people of every sexual orientation Lucas could think of, and a few that he was unsure of. As the numbers swelled, so did the thumping music. The more chattering voices, the louder the music became.

But Lucas was frustrated. It was hard to coax anything of interest out of the man. He seemed to withdraw whenever Lucas asked anything personal. Lucas could foresee a situation in which they simply said goodnight at the end of the evening. He was determined not to let that happen. They took to discussing the other people in the pub. Since they were both conventionally dressed, albeit a generation apart, they could observe together. Body piercing was popular and every possible permutation of rings and studs and body parts seemed to have decamped into the pub during the last hour. There was enough leather upholstery in there to furnish a sofa warehouse. They soon ran out of conversation.

Lucas found this situation was totally alien to him and he needed time out. He told the man that he had to take a piss. The toilet was a long way away now that the pub was full, and the surge of people was overwhelming. People he didn't really want to be in close proximity to. The journey was, however, uneventful, apart from a few men who tried unsuccessfully to lure him with their eyes. Once inside the toilet, a large man almost walked into him and seemed to blot everything from his view. He had time to utter two words, 'Sorry, mate.'

The attack was so fast, and so violent, he could do nothing. The man was strong enough that Lucas was lifted clean off his feet and pushed against the wall. The last thing he heard was a soft voice say, 'Die, carrier.'

Then he was dead. The knife had ruptured his aorta and the dramatic drop in blood pressure was so swift that he didn't have time to blink.

The killer dragged Lucas' body into a cubicle, carefully arranging it with trousers around ankles, and Lucas' head down the toilet bowl, hands tied behind the down pipe.

After he had cleaned the area around the body, he left via the fire escape, which was inside the toilet. He was happy with his handiwork. If anyone had seen him enter through the pub, when he was not worth remembering, they certainly didn't see him leave, when he was well worth recollecting.

The even sadder thing was, if a cubicle was closed in this pub, the inhabitants were never disturbed. Lucas' body was not discovered until well after closing time.

Chapter 10

Tuesday, May 21, Pavilion Square, Saxon's Apartment 1.05AM

'The phone...oh shit, damn the fucking phone,' muttered Saxon, as he dragged himself from what had promised to be the best night's sleep he had experienced in a long time.

'Sir?' Parker's tone was solemn.

'Yes, Parker, what is it?'

'Bad news, sir, very bad, there's no easy way to say it.'

'For Christ's sake, Parker, don't dither; I hate it. Spit it out.' Saxon was wide-awake.

'It's Constable Michael Lucas boss. He's been topped. Some bastard's killed the poor sod. I can't understand it, boss.'

'Slow down, Parker.' Saxon was shocked. 'Tell me what you know. How did it happen? Where was he?'

'Don't know too much yet, boss,' Parker said. 'He was killed in a pub called the Speckled Cat. Apparently, it's a gay pub. What the hell was he doing in a place like that for fuck's sake?'

Saxon was firm. 'I know the pub, Parker.' He was already out of bed and on his feet. 'Your guess is as good as mine as to what he was doing there. Perhaps it was his local. Fill me in on anything else.'

Saxon broke several traffic laws on the route to the Speckled Cat, noticing on arrival that Superintendent Mitchell was already there, talking to a man Saxon didn't recognise. As he approached them, Mitchell ushered the man away.

No chance of an introduction here, thought Saxon, suspiciously.

Mitchell beckoned to Saxon and Parker to join him. He was agitated and his voice was low but insistent. 'Right mess this is, I don't need to tell you. But we can survive this; we can limit the damage.' He looked around. 'What the bloody hell was Constable Lucas doing in this place? That's what I want to know.'

He looked accusingly at Saxon.

'Did you have anything to do with this, Commander? Was he working with you? Because if that's the case, I didn't authorise the use of one of my men.' Mitchell spat the words out.

Saxon and Parker stood silent. Mitchell was sweating heavily. The night was warm and humid. Saxon could feel his own anger and frustration building up inside. Parker sensed an explosion coming. 'He wasn't on our team, sir,' he started to say, but he didn't get to complete the sentence.

Mitchell continued as if he hadn't heard. 'You had better leave this to me. With respect, Commander, you be the policeman, I'll be the politician. I have a feeling I am the better diplomat, and believe you me, I know what everyone thinks of my policing skills. I'll talk to the press; no one else is to breathe a word about this. Understand – not a bloody word.' His breathing was fast and loud.

Saxon had had enough. 'Okay, Alex. That will do,' he said, concerned to end the tirade and get on with something more constructive. 'I have no idea what Lucas was doing here – he certainly wasn't working for me. For all we know he may just have gay friends, which we all know is not illegal. Let's base things on that assumption at the moment but keep open-minded to other possibilities at the same time.'

Saxon gestured with his head for Parker to leave them and then put his hand gently on Mitchell's arm. 'Alex, perhaps you had better go and tell his next of kin, in your diplomatic way. We'll examine the crime scene and see if we can catch the bastard who did it.'

Mitchell looked at Saxon, still hostile. But he seemed to have used up his supply of vitriol and he strode off, without saying anything further, towards the un-introduced stranger, who had been waiting patiently in the back seat of a patrol car.

Parker, who had waited at a discreet distance during the final exchange, approached Saxon to lead him to the back of the

Speckled Cat.

'Who's the suit Superintendent Mitchell was lurking with, boss?' he asked, looking over his shoulder at the patrol car, as Mitchell conferred with the stranger, who was blowing smoke rings into the night air. The smell of cigars carried easily. 'I didn't recognise him. Do you know him?'

'Beats me, Parker,' he answered. He had a feeling it might be significant, but right now it wasn't the priority. 'Let's get on.'

They made their way through the dark pub, across the now-deserted dance floor. The only people around were three PCs and some SOCO guys, waiting for the order to start their examination.

One of the constables approached Parker nervously. 'Sarge, I don't understand, that's Mike Lucas in there. We had no idea he was gay. He never...' He didn't get any further.

Saxon had walked on and didn't see Parker firmly push the PC to the wall and say with reserved calm, 'We don't know if he was, son. Gay, I mean. We don't care. Just because he was here doesn't mean he was gay. The point is, he's dead. Murdered. He's one of ours and we are going to get the bastard that did it.'

Parker poked the constable in the shoulder. 'Tell me you understand, Constable.' The shocked PC nodded and was released.

Parker caught up with Saxon as he entered the toilet area. They both slowed down at the same time.

'Where is Dr Clarke?' Saxon demanded, of nobody in particular. 'Has anyone even bothered to call Clarke?'

'I've called Jake Dalton,' Parker answered immediately. 'As soon as I heard about it, I tried to contact Dr Clarke, but there was no answer on the contact number we have for him at home. Dalton's getting hold of him.'

Saxon was anxious to get on, to focus on the details and get some evidence. It was too much of a coincidence, this one. It had to be connected to the other killings. A gay pub, maybe a gay policeman. In spite of the shock, he couldn't help feeling a surge of anticipation that maybe, just maybe, there would be a clue here. Something they could go on.

'Until he's pronounced dead we can't progress.' He looked at Parker impatiently. 'Can someone please find Clarke. Call Dalton again.'

Memories of his father's death and the helplessness of the situation momentarily flooded his thoughts. As usual, these images were pushed to the back of his consciousness.

'Fuck this, it's obvious he's dead,' he said. 'Come on, Parker. We're going to look around, just don't touch anything'.

They put bags on their feet and slipped on a pair of latex gloves but, in the confined space of the toilet cubicle, it was immediately apparent that there was little they could do or see until Lucas' body was moved.

For a start, it was hard to tell how he'd been murdered. There was nothing round his neck, and no visible signs of any wounds or bruising on the body.

Parker straightened up and looked at Saxon. 'Do you suppose,' he began hesitantly. 'Do you think he was raped, boss?' he said quietly.

Saxon shook his head. 'I don't know. Not our department. We need someone who knows what they're doing to tell us that. God, I hope not,' he answered.

'Poor bastard,' Parker murmured.

'Yes, poor bastard.' In spite of his sympathy for Lucas, Saxon was anxious to get the investigation focused. 'Let's leave that one for the pathologist. We'll know soon enough.'

He stood still and stopped looking around. 'What can you see?' he asked Parker.

'Well, there's not much blood in here, for a start, is there,' he answered. 'And that smell is disgusting,' he added.

'It's bleach,' Saxon said. 'Think we'll find it's bleach.' He looked back outside the toilet. 'Must be gallons of the stuff around in public toilets.'

'So the killer set out to clean up and he tipped bleach everywhere?'

Saxon nodded. 'It would clean up the blood superficially, but forensics will be able to detect if there was any here, and it would probably take away any traces of the killer's presence.'

'Assuming there were any to begin with, boss,' said Parker, shaking his head. 'If it's our man, then he probably didn't leave anything at all.'

'Well they all slip up at some time or other,' Saxon answered grimly. 'The professor said it, so it must be true!' They both knew it was a wish rather than a statement.

They stepped backwards out of the toilet cubicle and had a look around the area.

'There's the locker where they keep the bog rolls and the cleaning stuff,' said Parker. It had been broken open. Not a difficult task.

Fifteen minutes later Jake Dalton arrived to a very impatient reception. He was clearly flustered by the fact that the pathologist hadn't yet arrived.

'Jake, at last. Thank goodness.' Saxon made no attempt to hide his irritation. 'What the fuck is going on?' He looked over Jake's shoulder and then back at Jake. 'Where's Dr Clarke?' he demanded accusingly. 'We don't have all night to fart about here. Tell me something I want to hear, please'.

'Sorry, Commander, I rang him a minute ago, when the PC at the door told me he wasn't here yet. But I just got his voicemail again.' He shrugged his shoulders slightly, while already looking around at the crime scene. He looked back at Saxon and Parker. 'This is not like him at all, you know. Normally he's frighteningly prompt.'

Jake craned his neck slightly to see inside the cubicle. He could make out the kneeling form of the victim. 'I can make a start if you like,' he offered. He didn't wait for an answer, stepping around Parker and crouching down to start his initial examination, before the photographer moved in.

'Yes, sir,' Parker added. 'Same thing happened when I tried to call him.'

Saxon thought for a moment. 'Well maybe Dr Clarke has a life outside work and fitness after all. Who knows – anyway, keep trying his number.'

They left Jake alone to get on with his work and walked back into the main part of the pub, exchanging the smell of bleach for stale booze and cigarettes. Parker lit a cigarette himself and stood in silence, surveying the scene. Saxon inhaled deeply and toyed with the idea of joining him. He had quit smoking some time ago, mostly because Emma didn't like the smell or the taste. He enjoyed the habit and right now, it seemed like more than a good idea. Parker seemed to read his mind and offered the pack without speaking. Smokers like to share their habit.

Saxon caved in without hesitation. He felt the rush of nicotine and that taste that you never forget. *Why don't they all taste like this?*

As they stood in the dim lighting, Parker filled in Saxon with all the details of the evening.

'We've got three witnesses as of now,' he said. 'Although we'll get plenty more tomorrow, I know.'

Saxon was surprised. 'What happened to everyone else?' he asked. 'This place must've been packed last night.'

Parker laughed quietly. 'Well, boss, it seems that everyone disappeared as soon as they heard that there was the wrong kind of stiffy in the bogs,' he said.

Saxon frowned. 'Yes, I can imagine that one went through here like wildfire,' he agreed. 'So where are they, our three witnesses?'

'Upstairs, boss. In the landlord's flat, drinking coffee,' Parker answered. 'He lives on the premises and he suggested that we use his place.'

'We'll need a word with him too,' Saxon said.

'Name of Billy Singleton, boss,' Parker answered. 'He seems okay. Very concerned, of course. Anxious to help, he says. At least he's sober, as far as I can see.'

'Okay, let's make a start,' Saxon started, but stopped as Parker interrupted him suddenly.

'Boss, I forgot to tell you. The STI guys are outside. You won't believe this, but Dr Marks was in here.'

'You what?' Saxon was astounded. 'Any more vital news that you've omitted to tell me?'

'I'm sorry, boss, I forgot for a minute in all the excitement.'

'Well, Dr Marks,' Saxon said through gritted teeth. 'Looks like you did have more to tell me, after all.' He smiled at Parker.

'There's a turn up for the books.'

'Sorry, sir,' Parker went on. 'We don't have anything very useful yet. All we know from the STI guys is that he was in the pub. The landlord says that Lucas went past the bar on his way to the bog and never returned. He's not sure of what time, but he's trying to fix that in his mind. We'll have to talk to him.

'One of the witnesses says he was at the next table to Lucas, and he noticed him particularly because both Lucas and whoever he was sitting with looked to be having a difficult time. You know, not much rapport or whatever.' Parker paused for a moment. 'Our witness fancies himself as a bit of an amateur psychologist, I think.

'Anyway, whoever Lucas was talking to – and we don't know yet if it was Marks – stayed for a while then, when Lucas didn't come back, this man scarpered, according to this chap.'

'Maybe he thought his date had had a better offer,' Saxon mused. 'Or maybe he followed him out to the toilets?'

'According to the witness, boss, it was some time after Lucas went off that this man suddenly jumped to his feet and left in a bit of a huff.'

'So we need him to have a look at a photo of Marks to see if he's the man Lucas was talking to.'

'Yes, boss. I'm on it. Not sure how worthwhile it'll be though, because our witness had sunk a fair few vodkas during the evening, by the look of him.' Parker shook his head again, his despondency showing.

Saxon was sympathetic but they had no time for sentiment right now. This was the biggest breakthrough – potentially – that they'd had on the case. He'd had a feeling that Marks was being evasive when they spoke to him at the health centre. His helpfulness could well have been intended to throw them off the scent entirely. Now here he was at a murder scene.

'They found Lucas at chucking-out time, right? And when did Marks leave?' asked Saxon.

'Marks had left slightly before then and the STI guys followed him the moment he left the pub.' Parker looked across at Saxon, his eyebrows raised. 'He went straight home to his wife, sir. Poor cow.'

'Christ, Parker,' Saxon muttered, stubbing out his cigarette in an overflowing ashtray. 'A cop is murdered in pub and STI are sitting in a car outside all the time, probably unaware that Lucas was even in here. And why, for Christ's sake didn't they go inside and watch Marks? Doesn't make us look too clever does it?' Saxon paused despairingly.

He continued slowly. 'So if he's not our man, maybe he has no idea that there has even been a murder committed.'

'Right, boss,' agreed Parker. 'He certainly left before it was public knowledge.'

Saxon recognised an opportunity when he saw one. 'Then we want to see Dr Marks first thing in the morning, don't we, Parker.'

'We'll go round to the health centre when it opens then?' Parker asked.

'No, I think we'll call in at the house before he even leaves for work,' said Saxon.

'See him in front of his wife, you mean, boss? Up the ante a bit?' Parker saw the way Saxon's mind was working.

'Exactly.'

'Maybe his missus deserves to know where she stands, boss,' Parker agreed. 'She might catch something she doesn't want...' he finished, the thought just having occurred to him. 'What a bastard! How about we go and have a word with him now?'

Saxon declined. 'No, Parker, tempting though it is. Mrs Marks certainly doesn't deserve to hear this sort of thing from a couple of cops in the middle of the night – bad enough in the daytime.'

He thought about it a moment, anticipating the interview to come with some pleasure. 'Parker, believe me, Marks will be begging us to hear any information we want. The bastard knows a lot more than he would have us believe. We'll have a word with him just after he's heard about it in the press or on the morning news.'

They didn't have an opportunity to continue their rehearsal of the interview with Marks because Dr Clarke arrived. They heard him before they saw him.

'Sorry, everyone, I know you've been waiting for me. Many apologies – I'm deeply embarrassed, if that helps. I've been unwell,' he announced.

Saxon and Parker walked towards him. Clarke lowered his voice slightly, but not much, at their approach. 'I heard my phone ringing,' he went on. 'I was throwing up and couldn't answer – must have been the mussels, nothing worse than a bad mussel. Okay now though. Right, where's the body? I trust nobody has touched anything,' he said as if they didn't know any better.

Jake backed out of the cubicle to allow Clarke to have access. Saxon and Parker climbed the stairs behind the bar. The smell of stale cigarette smoke and beer followed them as they went to interview the witnesses. It turned out that the only person sober enough to be interviewed was the landlord.

Parker escorted the three others back downstairs so that they could be taken to their various homes. He emphasised that they would be expected to make statements in the morning. At least the coffee had sobered them up enough for him to be reasonably confident that they would remember.

As he came back into the bar, Dr Clarke finished his examination. He disappeared quickly, saying that he still felt a bit under the weather, but as usual he would only speculate on the cause of death until the post mortem.

SOCO stayed at the crime scene to finish their examination and Parker went back upstairs.

Tuesday, May 21, Billy Singleton's Flat, 1.45AM

They knew the landlord was forty-five, but he didn't look it. He had an average build, but was well-toned. He wore his hair in a small plaited ponytail, but that was it as far as body adornment went. As far as Saxon could see, Mr Singleton didn't go in for body piercing. Or at least, not anywhere that showed.

Saxon introduced himself and Parker.

Saxon winced slightly at the strength of the handshake and withdrew his hand as quickly as possible. They both sat down on the leather sofa, at their host's invitation.

'Thanks for helping out with the witnesses earlier,' he started.

'So, for the record, your full name is?' Parker took out his notebook.

'Bill Singleton, but everyone calls me Billy. You can call me Billy.' He walked over to the sideboard and picked up a bottle of Scotch and some glasses. He offered Saxon and Parker a drink. They declined for the usual reasons.

'Yes, I understand,' he said. 'I never drink on duty either.' He was sympathetic. 'But I hope you don't mind if I do now,' he said, as he took a mouthful. 'It's the first one of the day.' He put his head on one side. 'Er, yesterday, I mean.'

Billy sat himself down in a comfortable armchair facing them. He looked from one to the other. 'I'm glad this sort of thing doesn't happen every day,' he sighed. He looked at his watch and then took another sip of his drink.

'Okay, Billy,' Saxon said. 'Tell me what you saw. Take your time.'

'Well, it was busy,' he said. 'Thursdays always are. I come down again at around six o'clock and I'm here till closing time. It was quiet to start with tonight, I mean last night,' he corrected himself. 'There were a few office groups, a couple of people left over from lunchtime too. But it always perks up later. To tell the truth, it just seemed like another normal night.'

'Yes, go on.' Saxon really just wanted to listen.

'Anyway, I saw the young man come in – Lucas, right?' he queried. 'Poor bloke. So sad.'

He paused for a minute but nobody spoke. Billy went on. 'It must've been sometime around eight o'clock or maybe a bit later. I noticed him because there weren't too many other people around them and also – I hope this doesn't sound ridiculous – I noticed him because I thought he looked a bit lost.'

He leant forward slightly. 'You have to understand, Commander, that a lot of the people who come in here are a bit full of themselves. You know, they swagger a bit. So that's what made him stand out a bit.'

Saxon just nodded.

'Well, he sat down all alone with his drink. Looked a bit nervy to me, took no notice of anyone else. Not what people usually do here. I wish more people came to drink instead of just looking.'

Parker interrupted. 'Did you notice anyone talking to him for any length of time?'

Billy thought for a second. 'Well, it got quite busy around nine o'clock so I didn't pay any particular attention. For a while he was chatting to someone else though. Older man, quite conservative-looking. Dark hair, if I remember rightly. But I couldn't be sure; it's a big pub and with people milling about all the time, coming and going, he may have just been sitting at the same table. Are you sure I can't tempt you to a drink?'

Saxon smiled. 'No thanks, Billy. Personally I'd love one but, knowing my luck at the moment, I'd probably get stopped and breathalysed on the way home.'

Billy laughed good-humouredly. He continued at some length about the regular clientele, their drinking habits, and their social groups. Most of his information was of no interest to Saxon, until Billy mentioned the man who seemed out of place.

Saxon felt the hairs on the back of his neck start to move.

'Man, what man?' he queried. 'And why did he look out of place?

'It was just a glimpse; I didn't really get a good look at him. I have got a very busy pub to run you know. Everybody wants to be served at the same time. But there was just something about this man. You see, I'm used to some of the people who come in here being a bit, well, furtive. Especially if they're here for the first time. It can be a bit intimidating, you know. You want something, so you want to be here, and yet you don't really know what to expect when you come here for the first time, maybe.'

'Right,' agreed Saxon. He thought he understood. 'So this man you're talking about was furtive?' he asked. 'Why did that seem out of place then?'

'Well, that's just it,' answered Billy without hesitation. 'He wasn't furtive, not really. He was more, well, secretive, if you see what I mean. It's hard to say, hard to describe exactly.'

'No, go on,' said Saxon encouragingly. 'You're doing a great job. I just want to be sure we really understand what you're getting at.'

'Maybe I wouldn't have noticed him normally, but I looked across at the door just as he came in. He didn't hesitate. He didn't look around to see who was here. Well, that's odd for a start. Everybody does that. Either so that they can go straight up to someone they know and say hi, or so that they can avoid someone they don't want to see. Anyway, this man just came in and went straight through to the toilets. But he looked straight ahead and didn't meet anyone's eye as he went.' He paused. 'I can tell you, that's not normal in here. Maybe if that poor boy hadn't been murdered, and in our toilets, I wouldn't have given Mr Mystery Toilet Man a second thought, but as it was, I thought I'd better mention him. I don't suppose it's any help at all, is it?' he added apologetically.

'Billy, you never know,' answered Saxon. 'It could be just the break we're looking for. We can check it out with the other people we interview. Maybe something will come of it.' Saxon was telling the truth. 'Anything else you can tell us about him?'

Billy didn't hesitate this time. 'The only thing I can say for sure was that he wore a hat and glasses. I think the glasses were tinted, but I couldn't be sure.'

'Hat colour and type?' asked Parker.

'God knows, grey I think. It looked like a trilby,' said Billy. 'The kind of thing my father used to wear.'

'How tall was he?' Parker asked.

'Not small, definitely not small. Quite big, I think, and strong-looking. I didn't have much time to study him because, as I said, he was in through the door and then into the toilets. Besides, he was the other side of the dance floor and there was a lot of writhing bodies between him and me, not to mention the smoke.'

'And it definitely wasn't the same chap that young Lucas was talking to?'

'No, definitely not.' Billy was firm.

'Billy, did this man enter the toilets before or after the young man who died?' Saxon was almost holding his breath.

Again, Billy didn't hesitate. 'Oh, definitely before – I think, but I couldn't say exactly how long, maybe ten to fifteen minutes.' He shook his head and shrugged slightly. 'Christ knows.'

'Okay, Billy, did you see the man come out again?'

'No. No, I didn't. Unless I missed him, of course. But if he was avoiding anyone seeing him, he would probably have used the fire escape. You can get to it from the toilets, you know. They're one-way doors, so you can only exit through them.'

Parker confirmed that. 'The SOCO boys checked the fire escape while they were waiting for Dr Clarke to arrive, boss. They didn't find anything out there.'

Saxon leant forward. 'Billy, this is so important, I can't begin to explain how important. If I tell you that this might be a very significant lead, maybe the first lead we've had on this weirdo...' He looked at Billy intently. '... What you've told us is very helpful. Very helpful indeed. But anything else you can remember – even if you think it means nothing or sounds stupid, I want to hear it.'

'Well, I'm sorry; if I could tell you any more, don't you think I would?' Billy was defensive. 'I really don't like the idea of some crank killing off my customers. Bad for business, you know. The only other thing I think – but I'm not sure, he was so far away – is that he had a crew cut or was bald. He was moving quite fast.'

Saxon's full attention was fixed on Singleton. This was the best bit of evidence so far in a list of almost nothing. Saxon and Parker exchanged quick glances. Too soon to celebrate, but they both had a strong gut feeling that they might have something to go on.

Parker was puzzled though. 'If he was wearing a hat, how do you know he was bald or had a crew cut?' he asked. 'Was his hat tipped right forward?'

'No,' said Billy. 'It's just that from where I was standing at the bar, I could see right into the toilets. Just as he went through the door, he took his hat off and just for a split second I saw that he was either bald or cropped.'

'If you saw him again, would you know him?' Saxon said, already knowing the reply.

'Sorry, gents, I have to say no.' Billy was apologetic. 'To be honest, he looked like a bit of everyone who doesn't come into pubs like mine. He was too ordinary and boring.'

Parker resorted to an alternative approach. 'Did he look like anyone you might've seen on television or in a film, maybe. In a magazine? Did he remind you of anyone famous?'

Billy looked at Parker and inclined his head. 'Hmmm, good question.' He thought for a moment, picking up a packet of cigarettes from the low table in front of him. He offered them round and lit one up for himself. 'No, not really, I couldn't say he did. He didn't make that much of an impression on me for the way he looked. It was more the way he was behaving. But I'll tell you what...' he began, standing up and walking over to the window. He opened it and they were aware that it was raining softly. '... This is going to sound funny. His clothes were too old for his body – I notice things like that you know. One other thing did strike me though, I did think it strange that he should be wearing such heavy, tweedy sort of clothes – especially in these temperatures and in a place like this.'

Saxon and Parker took this in.

'How about CCTV? Do you have security cameras in the bar?' Saxon knew that he was clutching at straws, but decided to give it a shot.

'Good heavens, no.' Billy was amused and affronted at the same time. 'Do you think I'm made of money? But I have been meaning to talk to the bank about a loan for some refurbishments. I suppose that might be one thing we should consider. But then you never expect something like this to happen, do you. Sorry, that isn't much help to you is it?'

Saxon stood up. 'To be honest, Mr Singleton, Billy, you've been very helpful. We'll leave you to it now. We very much appreciate your help.' Saxon handed him his card. 'We'll need a formal statement, of course, as soon as possible. If you think of anything else that struck you, either about that man, or anything at all, please don't hesitate to call me.'

Billy placed the card on the mantelpiece and turned to Saxon and Parker, as they were about to leave. 'I understand the young man was a colleague of yours, Commander.'

'Yes, he was – why do you ask?'

'Oh, no real reason. But we do get quite a few policemen and ladies in here from time to time. Refreshing really, isn't it? Now that it's not a crime anymore.'

Saxon smiled and shook hands with Billy as they left.

Saxon and Parker headed back to their cars, cutting quickly through the small groups of onlookers. There were still a few stragglers out on the street, even at that time, and some had stopped to study the commotion, only to be moved on by the uniforms.

They reached Parker's car first and paused. Parker turned to Saxon. 'Not a bad bloke, is he, boss,' he said.

Saxon couldn't help but agree. 'The description of the man Singleton reckons he saw talking to Lucas certainly sounds like Marks,' he said. 'We'll have a picture later and we can show him that to confirm it, one way or the other, hopefully.'

'But even if it turns out to be Marks, he might not know anything at all – it could all be circumstantial,' Parker said.

'You could well be right, Parker, but you have to admit it's a very strange coincidence, if that's all it was. And I'm still going to squeeze him as hard as I can. If he knows anything, he'll be begging to talk by the time I've finished with him.'

They said goodnight and Saxon continued on to his car. He needed sleep. He could only recall one other night as sleepless and depressing that compared to this one. That night was back in his childhood. And that's precisely where he would leave it.

Saxon drove home slowly, the long way, cruising the streets. He was hoping against hope that he would see the killer roaming the back streets with a dripping knife. How neat and tidy that would be. And how bloody unlikely!

He shook himself mentally and physically and pointed the car homewards. He needed some sleep. Otherwise, he wouldn't be entertaining these thoughts in the first place. He got home without further diversion, realising that there wasn't much of the night left. He was asleep before his head hit the pillow.

Tuesday, May 21, Saxon's Apartment 7.00AM

It felt as if it were only minutes later when the alarm clock was screaming at him to get up. He knocked back two cups of strong coffee as he towelled himself dry from the shower and gulped down toast with marmalade – no plate, as he couldn't find a clean one. *Must wash up tonight, and that's a promise.*

When he left his apartment, precisely fifteen minutes after he'd got out of bed, he didn't notice the card that had been pushed under his door. As he ran down the stairs, two steps at a time, he did notice Francesca, who was on her way up. But as she spoke, he cut her off before she'd managed more than 'Hi,' calling back up to her, 'Morning, Fran.' He waved. 'Got to rush.'

Francesca stood motionless and watched him disappear down the stairs. She heard the front door slam seconds later. She got to her door and checked to see if he'd pushed a note under it earlier. No, there was nothing there. *So how am I supposed to know if you're going to make it tonight or not?*

Men were very difficult sometimes.

Parker sat in his corner of their temporary office, his eyes glued to the computer screen, barely responding when Saxon strode in.

'Morning, sir,' he mumbled, not looking up from the mesmerising information in front of him.

Saxon was feeling quite good, in spite of less-than-adequate sleep. 'We have Mr Jenner later today, don't we?' he asked.

'Yes, boss. Keith Jenner's in for questions this afternoon at two o'clock.'

'Ah, yes, should be interesting. Can't wait.' Saxon was aware of something he'd missed back at home. Fran's face and the expression on it. He had seen it for a second or two but it had registered. Now it occurred to him that she had been about to speak to him, and she'd looked surprised when he rushed past her. Maybe she'd wanted to say more than just 'Good morning.'

A criticism that Emma had made, to the effect that he often ignored her – too often, as it turned out – resurfaced from wherever he had temporarily filed it in his brain.

He found Fran's business card in his index and dialled her number. She barely had time to say her name before he interrupted her.

'Fran, hello, it's Paul. Sorry I was in a screaming rush this morning.'

She started to speak but he barely paused for breath. 'Didn't have time to stop. Have I missed something important?'

'The card, did you see the card on your doormat?' she said, with the usual laugh in her voice.

'Uhm, no...sorry, you'd better tell me what it's about.'

'Well, maybe if you're so busy, you probably haven't the time to have dinner with me tonight,' she teased.

It was so unexpected that Saxon was at a loss for words. 'Well, yes, that would be great, Fran,' he stammered. 'But don't expect too much of my tantalising personality, I haven't had a lot of sleep lately.' He paused. 'One of our lads was murdered last night, so it's frantic here.'

'Oh, I'm sorry, Paul, it must be awful. Maybe you'd rather put it off for a while.' Her voice was sincere and concerned. He couldn't believe his luck. She was asking him out. Before he'd even had time to wonder if it was the right thing to do for him to ask her out. Problem solved before it happened.

'No, don't worry. It's fine,' he said quickly. 'Even policemen need some time to relax. Could be my last chance for a while. I really enjoyed the other evening.'

'Great. I'm glad you did. I had a great time too.' She hesitated. 'I can ask Gary and Neil to join us if you want a repeat,' she offered, laughing.

'No, no,' he said quickly, hoping she wasn't serious. 'I just meant it was more fun than I've had in ages. I would love us to have dinner. Even without them.'

'Okay, I know. I was kidding.'

'Well, it'll be hard, being deprived of their company,' he retaliated. He loved the fact that she had a sense of humour. Emma didn't, not really, when he thought about it, which he wasn't about to right now.

'You'll give me a ring when you're through tonight then?' Francesca asked.

'Of course. I look forward to it,' he answered.

'Unless something comes up at the last minute. I know the case comes first. Specially, when it's one of your own.' She was very serious again. 'I'll understand,' she said.

'I'll see you later. I'm looking forward to it,' he said. 'And, Fran, thanks for asking me.'

The phone call ended and Saxon nursed the handset for a few seconds before replacing it. He sat down at his desk and glanced across the room. Parker was smiling to himself. Smirking, even.

'That's enough of that, Parker,' Saxon muttered. 'Get on with whatever it is that you're supposed to be doing. You don't get paid to laugh.' In spite of the sharp words, Saxon was smiling.

Parker's own smile turned into a grin as he rose to his feet and suggested coffee. 'No muffin for you today, boss. I suppose you'll be eating later.' He retreated hastily before anything could be thrown in his direction.

When he came back with two coffees, both with extra shots of caffeine, he had an update on station news.

'You know, boss, apparently the superintendent is in pretty bad shape this morning. Didn't get much sleep at all, by all accounts. They're saying he spent most of the night with Mr and Mrs Lucas,' he reported.

Saxon raised both eyebrows as he gratefully took charge of a steaming coffee. 'So, he didn't delegate it? Maybe not such a total wanker after all then, Parker,' he said.

'Maybe only ninety-percent wanker, boss,' Parker ventured.

'Whatever,' replied Saxon. 'He must possess some higher-life-form genes, even if he doesn't get to demonstrate it too often.'

Tuesday, May 21, Anvil Wood House, Sewel Mill, 12.40PM

Keith Jenner used his BMW for the trip to Sewel Mill and Brighton. He'd spent the late morning looking over the Anvil Wood House property and he wasn't too unhappy with what he'd seen. In a rising property market, he knew he was safe in assuming it should fetch a bob or two. Of course, not everyone would be interested in a house with such a history but he didn't exactly need to advertise that aspect, and all he needed to do was close the deal before the buyers heard about the murders. His mind was racing ahead already.

It had been such a relief to find out there was no will. Since he was her only relative, it made the whole question of her estate very straightforward. He'd been worried that she might have left all her worldly possessions to some daft horse-rescue charity or, even worse, to that Poppy cow. Thank God she didn't get round to it. There were no complications.

He told the agent he'd be in touch as soon as the arrangements had been finalised, and got back into his car for the short drive to Brighton.

Tuesday, May 21, Brighton police Station, 1.05PM

Saxon called a progress meeting, but it was like no progress meeting that any of the officers had ever attended. When there is no evidence, what do you discuss? Several officers had been doing the rounds of gay pubs, asking if any strangers to the area had been spotted. No one had much to offer. A few of the people questioned said they were getting frightened at the prospect of a killer stalking gays in and around Brighton. A minute's silence was held for Lucas, and then it was back to the daily grind.

Tuesday, May 21, Brighton police Station, 1.30PM

'Mr Keith Jenner is in reception, boss.' Parker passed on the news to Saxon, after a call from the front desk.

Saxon looked up. 'Good,' he answered, glancing at the wall clock. 'He's early.' And he looked back at the papers on his desk.

Parker hesitated. 'You want me to get him now, boss?' he queried.

Saxon shook his head briefly, and didn't take his eyes off what he was looking at. 'No, I don't think so. He can sit there and sweat for half an hour.' Saxon wasn't feeling merciful, and besides, it could only help the interview. From what he knew of Jenner in advance, it was not likely to be a particularly pleasant experience.

By the time Jenner was taken to the interview room, he was purple with rage. Saxon paused the moment he set eyes on Jenner. This man was a bottom feeder and a mouth breather, who possessed none of his late sister's finer points. In fact, he was the epitome of what a South London scrap dealer would look like in the hands of a particularly savage caricaturist.

Overweight, over six feet tall, fifty-three, with greying hair and nicotine-stained fingers, Jenner wore shorts that fit snugly under his belly. His yellowing string vest could do nothing to restrain his girth. His trainers had never been subjected to the trauma of a good run, but they did show clear signs of having had both food and beer spilt on them in many a pub. He sported an identity bracelet and matching medallion, with too many rings on his fingers. This combination of attire, with not a splash – but a tidal wave of cheap aftershave, was painful to the eyes and noses of Saxon and Parker.

Before Saxon introduced himself, Jenner started to shout and prod his finger aggressively towards Saxon's chest. 'I've come here of my own free will and, I might add, in my work time, to talk to you bastards and you keep me bleedin' waiting half a fuckin' hour. I have got better fuckin' things to do than sit on my bleedin' arse in a piggery half the fuckin' day. I'm losing income by being here. What about compensation then?' Eyes bulging and red-faced, he stopped when he realised that he wasn't getting the required attention.

'I'm Commander Saxon, this is Detective Sergeant Parker.'

Jenner cut in. 'I don't care who the fuck you are, I'm not putting up with this sort of treatment, fuckin' liberty-taking shitbags.'

Saxon stopped him with almost a whisper. 'Jenner, I'm so sorry you have been so terribly inconvenienced and made to sit on your fat arse for a full half hour. You did arrive early didn't you? But people are being murdered, your sister for instance – remember her? One of our lads was killed last night too, so if you really think that I am even mildly concerned about you, Jenner, you are very wrong, so shut the fuck up and follow me."

Jenner's mouth had stopped mid-sentence and hung open. It took the wind out of his sails completely. Saxon led the subdued Jenner to an interview room. He lumbered along behind them and Parker mumbled something about knuckles dragging on the ground. Saxon pretended not to hear, but couldn't help a little chuckle to himself. He and Parker sat facing him in one of the interview rooms.

'No need for a tape of this little chat, Mr Jenner, as you have not been charged with anything – yet. I am right, am I not, that you would like us to catch whoever killed your sister. Or maybe there is something that you would like to tell us?' Saxon looked down at some papers on the table in front of him and appeared to ignore Jenner. Eventually what he had said sunk into Jenner's consciousness.

'What do you mean – are you accusing me of bumping off my own sister?' Jenner looked genuinely astounded.

'People do some very bad things, we see it all here, nothing surprises us. You'll feel much better if you get it off your chest.'

'You can fuck off, the pair of you… I've never done anyone in and you know it.' Jenner started to get up, but sat down after Saxon gave him a look that left him in no doubt that he would be stopped and kept there for far longer than necessary.

'Okay, Mr Jenner, tell me about your relationship with your sister.'

'Never had much to do with her, and if you must know, we didn't get on – stuck up bloody cow, she was.'

'Why not?' said Parker, studiously making copious notes.

'Give me a break will you. She's, I mean was, a fuckin' dyke, and I don't want to mix with dykes and poofs do I?'

Saxon sat calmly with his hands clasped on the desk. 'Did you kill your sister?'

Jenner sprang to his feet shouting. 'No I fuckin' didn't…and if you think I did then you're fuckin' wrong and you must be fuckin' barmy. I can account for my movements anytime you like, you just have to ask my old woman.'

Saxon, without looking up from the piece of paper he was studying, said, 'Yes or no will suffice, and please will you sit down, you are making my sergeant very nervous. Believe me, Jenner, we don't want to make him nervous…he's not a nice man when riled – are you Detective Sergeant Hard Bastard Parker?'

'No, sir, I get nasty, stitch people up, and hurt them badly.'

Saxon cut him short. 'That's enough, Parker, just because we have more power than the normal police and the Inland Revenue and Customs and Excise put together, combined with the ruthlessness of the triads, we don't want to be forced to abuse that power do we?'

'Not really, sir, not if we can help it, it upsets our weekends – gives us extra work. Lots of explaining to do.'

Jenner returned to his seat again and began to sweat heavily. 'All right, you bastards, I can account for my movements. I was out with the wife. We had a drink and a curry.'

'And your wife's name is…?' Saxon paused. '… Please fill in the gap, Jenner, your wife, her name is?'

'Okay not my wife…a friend.' He looked down at the floor; his voice carried the tone of a man crushed.

'A friend is it? What is the name of your friend, bearing in mind that we will be checking out this friend very thoroughly?'

Saxon didn't want Jenner to have an alibi. Of all people, this fat loud-mouthed bastard would do nicely.

'Lizzie, her name's Lizzie, she's an old friend of mine, bit of a slag but…'

'I understand, Jenner, spare me the sordid details, you don't need to explain.' Saxon's hopes flew out of the window. *Shit, he has an alibi. Shit. He wouldn't have admitted to having a meal with his slag if it wasn't true.*

Parker looked coldly at Jenner and asked, 'What is the full name and address of your slag?' And then threw in, 'Are you the sole beneficiary in the event of your sister's death?'

'I don't know do I…well I suppose so…haven't really thought about it.'

Saxon stopped taking notes and looked up.

'Come off it, Jenner, we may look a bit simple but we're not daft. Your sister dies suddenly – and shame on me for thinking this, but she owned a very big house in the country, with stables and a fair bit of land. In fact, not a bad little earner. Dare I say this could make you a very wealthy man? You can't blame us for thinking such things? You've already admitted that you couldn't stand her. I repeat, Jenner, we are not daft, and you, I know, are a cunning bastard. For all we know you may have decided to have her topped. We know everything about you and your business and the sort of people you mix with and your entire past all the way back to ten minutes before conception. Tell me, Jenner, what's the going rate for a hit man down the Old Kent Road these days – a hundred quid, five hundred?'

Jenner lit a cigarette, blew the smoke towards his interrogators and folded his arms, fag in mouth.

'You two are going to look like a couple of right fuckin'

wankers – I didn't kill my sister, but I'll tell you what – I'm glad the bent bitch is dead. She was a cow, and if it keeps you arseholes busy for a while, all the bleedin' better. If you want to talk to me again I want my solicitor with me.'

Saxon paused and made notes long enough to make his victim twitchy. As Jenner was about to speak, Saxon interrupted him. 'Well, thanks for your time, you have been entertaining to say the least, and don't worry about your solicitor, next time we will come to your home...maybe your wife could help us with a few details regarding your whereabouts on certain days and nights. Perhaps we could get your wife and your slag together to discuss some of the finer details of your business activities. Help us fill in the gaps if you know what I mean. Oh, and please correct me if I'm wrong, but of course, I know I'm not, I do believe you have been questioned in the past regarding fraud. Maybe we can take another look at that case while we are at it. Spent some time banged up for violence too: attempted murder, reduced charge not enough evidence – yeah right. We'll be in touch – can't wait to meet the wife. You can go now, Mr Jenner, thank you for cooperating with you friendly neighbourhood police service.'

Jenner banged his cigarette on the table near the ashtray and moved towards the door. Parker called him back.

'Not so fast, Mr Jenner – I want the address and phone number of your slag, if you don't mind.' Jenner scribbled it down on a piece of paper and pushed it across the table. He then left quickly and without a word. But they both heard the outer door slam. The interview room was supposed to be soundproof.

Saxon slouched back in his chair and lit one of Parker's cigarettes. He wondered idly if Francesca smoked. He hoped so.

'Delightful chap, Mr Jenner,' he said to Parker. 'But it's obvious he didn't do it. For starters, he's not clever enough – the man's a Neanderthal. He certainly doesn't fit Ercott's profile.' He tossed a copy across to Parker.

Saxon blew smoke contentedly into the air above his head. He leant back and watched it disappear.

Parker looked up from the report. 'So, we should be looking for a professional man between the ages of thirty-three and forty-five, boss,' he quoted.

Saxon nodded. 'How the hell he came up with those numbers I'll never know, but I guess he knows what he's talking about.'

Parker ran through the points Ercott had suggested. 'Right, apart from the age group, he'll likely be an educated, even cultured type, exceptionally cunning.'

'How do we spot cunning, I wonder, Parker?' Saxon mused.

'Says here that's he's possibly very right wing,' Parker added.

'And he would seem to be someone who has his life in good order,' Saxon interrupted. 'In good order, that is, apart from this little quirk which prompts him to murder people from time to time.'

'What did it say about medical knowledge? I know there was something,' he asked.

Parker found the place. 'Yes, the professor says he will almost certainly have medical knowledge of some kind. Also that he's physically very strong. And obviously, he has a big grudge regarding gays.' He read on in silence.

'I was interested by what Ercott said about the killer's attitude to his victims,' said Saxon. 'The method he uses to kill them indicates that he likes to attack them from the front, and that's a dead giveaway, apparently.' He stubbed out his cigarette and kept crushing it even though it was never going to smoulder again.

'So,' he went on, 'what are our possibilities? Could it be that our killer is gay but not out of the closet yet? Or maybe gay, but brutalised by his parents as a result. Or maybe a close relative of his has either contracted AIDS and is sick or has already died from it.'

Parker had a suggestion. 'Maybe we could contact all of the

hospitals in the area and start looking for men who have lost either a wife to the disease or even a child?'

Saxon nodded. 'Go on.'

'But to start with, we're only interested in men who fall in the age group that Professor Ercott has suggested.' Parker was thinking as he went along. 'It could be that the killer himself has the disease from a blood transfusion, or possibly, he is a doctor or male nurse and has been accidentally pricked with an HIV-contaminated needle.'

Parker stubbed out his cigarette and stood leaning against the wall. 'It won't be easy though, the hospitals and hospices don't like to give out that sort of info.' He lit another cigarette after Saxon declined one. Parker inhaled deeply. 'If the killer is big and strong, that excludes that tosser Marks then, doesn't it, boss,' he said.

'What makes you say that?'

'He may be tall, but he's built like a right nancy,' said Parker, in a tone that expected no disagreement. None was forthcoming.

'Which reminds me, sir, isn't it time we went and had a few words with him? He probably can't believe his luck – he must have seen the news by now surely. There's got to be some major movements going on in his bowels at the moment.'

Saxon laughed aloud. 'You're right, Parker, although it hardly seems worth it – we know he didn't do it. The only good thing that could come out of talking to him is that he may have seen the man with the hat and glasses just before he did his Jack the Ripper routine on Lucas. We'll go and talk to him this evening at seven. I think it's only fair that Mrs Marks knows what her husband gets up to in the evenings.'

They left the police station and wandered down to the promenade looking for a suitable fish and chip shop for a real policeman's lunch. It was the high season for tourists and the queue at the fish and chip shop was heaving, so they found a pub and settled for a sandwich and a couple of pints instead. Saxon bought the first two and carried them out to Parker who was sitting under a parasol, but still baking.

'Any bright ideas on what to do next?' said Saxon, as he sat down heavily, exhausted by the heat. He put away most of his pint in one swig.

Parker looked lost. 'I'm sorry to say I haven't the foggiest idea what we can do. It's really frustrating; we've absolutely nothing to go on. It's as I feared, we have wait for him to kill again, and hope for him to make a cock-up. Not the most proactive way to go about things though, is it, sir?'

Saxon sat sipping his beer and looking out towards the Palace Pier. 'And if he stops killing, we will never know who he was. And that would never do, would it, Parker?'

Tuesday, May 21, Wychwood Cottage, Sewel Mill, 6.55PM

Saxon's Land Rover crunched over the gravel drive to Dr Marks' cottage, slowly coming to a halt in front of the garage. The surroundings were idyllic, Sussex Weald with the South Downs as a backdrop. The cottage – built during the reign of Henry VIII, had stood the test of time well. The only sign of any interference by modern man showing on the roof – the thatch was just a little bit too new.

They walked across the drive to the front door and Saxon tried the doorbell, but got no response. Several loud law-enforcement-style knocks on the door proved fruitless too, so they followed the path around to the back of the property. The garden was extensive and well-maintained, covering roughly four acres of well-tended lawns and flowerbeds.

They found Marks and his wife lounging on sun beds, on a large patio, next to an impressive swimming pool.

Mrs Marks was a slim attractive woman with jet-black hair; she was forty but looked a young thirty. Saxon noticed at once that she appeared shaky and withdrawn. Her hand, holding a very large gin and tonic shook as she put the glass to her lips.

Marks saw them before his wife, and sprang to his feet with a look of dread on his face. Saxon didn't waste any time, and before Marks could introduce his wife, Saxon launched his attack.

'Dr Marks, where were you last night? Think carefully before you answer.'

Marks stood his ground and decided that attack may be his best form of defence. He shouted at Saxon.

'How dare you come here and talk to me in that manner. I will not tolerate this sort of treatment. I am not a criminal and I refuse to be treated as one. Now, please leave.'

Saxon remained calm. 'I repeat, where were you Dr Marks? If of course you refuse to answer my questions, we can discuss this matter at Brighton Police Station.'

Marks remained silent as if he couldn't bring himself to speak in front of his wife.

Saxon turned to Mrs Marks, who appeared to be in a semi-drunken state, with the intention of introducing himself. She got there first.

'Clive, who are these people, and what do they want?'

Marks looked down at his wife. 'Nothing for you to worry about, darling. You sit there and relax. I'll go inside and talk to these gentlemen – I won't be long, I'll bring you a cold drink.'

'Clive, you haven't been naughty again, have you?'

This comment from Mrs Marks stopped everyone in their tracks. She looked up at Saxon and Parker, with a slightly confused expression on her face.

'Police, you're policemen aren't you?'

'I am Commander Saxon, and this is Detective Sergeant Parker, we are investigating several murders, the one that we wish to talk to your husband about happened in a gay pub in Brighton – we know that he was in the pub in question, at the time of the murder. The victim was a police officer and your husband may have been the last person to speak to him. We are here to talk to him, not to arrest him.'

Mrs Marks' face took on a stunned disbelieving look with considerable anger beginning to boil up.

Saxon turned to Marks, whose face was growing redder by the second. He continued. 'Dr Marks, I don't really care what you get up to in your private life, I just want to catch whoever it is going around chopping people up. You can answer my questions here or we can go to Brighton. Here is much more pleasant, believe me. You decide.'

Mrs Marks hurriedly put down her drink, stood up, stripped off her gown and dived into the pool.

Marks sat down and motioned the two policemen to sit.

'Okay, what do you want to know, Commander?' Please excuse my wife, she's been rather unwell. She seems to live on booze and tablets at the moment. She had a nervous breakdown a few months ago, never really recovered. She has boyfriends, you see. The latest one turned out to be a bit of a pain. When she tired of him, he wouldn't take no for an answer and he started to stalk her. It all got a bit nasty, and she couldn't cope with it. And before you ask me why she has boyfriends, I suppose I'd better tell you. You'll find out anyway I suppose.' Marks paused and looked down and said nothing for too long.

'Yes, Dr Marks, we're still here waiting for you to tell us something earth-shattering. But I think you are about to tell us that you are gay…is that right?'

'No, Commander, bisexual would be a better description.'

'Amounts to the same thing if you ask me,' interrupted Parker.

'Well, we are not asking you, are we, Sergeant?' Marks spat.

Parker backed off, but was unable to hide the slight smirk on his face. Saxon shot him a glance, which clearly told him to shut up.

'This is all very interesting, but I need some answers regarding the night of the murder. First, I think we have established why you were in the Speckled Cat pub – what I want to know is if you spoke to him, what did Constable Michael Lucas say to you during the evening, and did you see anyone who looked out of place?'

Saxon took out a picture of Lucas and pushed it under Marks' nose.

'Did you speak to this man?'

Marks studied the picture, but showed no reaction at all.

'Yes, Commander, I did. He didn't say much at all really, just that he was wealthy and didn't need to work, and he said he was unsure of his sexuality – huh, times I've heard that one. I had no idea that he was a police officer, Commander, none at all. Anyway, we sat talking for a while and he said that he wanted to go to the toilet. That was the last I saw of him. He didn't come back and I got tired of waiting, so I left. And no, I didn't see anyone with a badge that said "murderer, pay attention", written all over it.'

Saxon rolled up his shirtsleeves another couple of inches, wondering if Marks would offer a cold drink – he didn't.

'Dr Marks, why didn't you come forward and talk to us sooner?'

'Oh, for Christ's sake, grow up, Commander, what would you have done in my shoes? I'm a GP in an English village. There are Victorians alive and well still living in Sewel Mill you know. If word spread that I'm bisexual, where do you think all of my patients would go? They would go to the first doctor they could find who was straight and who wouldn't infect them with gay diseases with just one touch of his hands – Christ, people are so stupid, and I would be out of a job.'

Saxon admitted to himself that Marks was right.

'Why does your wife tolerate your lifestyle?'

'Are you going to charge me with anything, Commander Saxon, because if not then I would like you to go now.'

Marks suddenly changed from being cooperative, to sullen-faced and withdrawn.

'You have to understand a few things about police work, Dr Marks – we collect facts and information, then we put it all together and see what it all adds up to. So, as I said earlier, we can talk here in these pleasant surroundings, or I can charge you with leaving the scene of a crime. Perhaps I could try to get you on wasting police time, or maybe withholding evidence. The list could get longer during the drive to that rather unpleasant smelly interview room at Brighton Police Station. You do get my drift, don't you Dr Marks? Talk to me now and the village may never even know about you private life. Give me all the information you can and I may forget about you being in the pub in the first place – you have to admit that's a good deal. But don't lie to me, I'll know if you do.'

Mrs Marks finished her swim and climbed out of the pool, picked up her drink, smiled at the three of them and said that she thought she may have caught a little bit too much sun and was going to go inside and lie down. Saxon and Parker tried not to stare too much at her not-too-shabby figure as she tottered by and disappeared through the French windows.

'Up to you, Doctor, what do you want to do?' Saxon was becoming more impatient and finding it harder not to show it.

'You don't really give me much option, I'll have to take you up on it, Commander,' Marks said admitting to himself that it was a good deal. 'My wife, Anne, likes the lifestyle – the house is paid for. I inherited some money and bought it outright, so no mortgage worries. A GP's salary isn't too bad, plus I do some consultancy work, four days a month, which almost doubles my money. Anne knows that if she left me she would get nothing, one of the advantages of a good solid pre-nuptial agreement, I suppose.'

At last, Marks asked Saxon and Parker if they would like a drink, and went into the cottage to fetch some iced water. From the garden, they could hear a heated exchange of words flying out of the sitting room. After a couple of minutes, Marks returned with a large glass jug tinkling with ice cubes. He looked angry.

Saxon downed his first glass in one gulp and as Marks filled it up Saxon started to work on him again.

'Did you murder Christopher Janson?'

'Don't be ridiculous, I'm not a killer, I'm a doctor!' shouted Marks.

'So were Crippen, Mengele and Shipman,' Saxon shot back.

Marks scowled like a spoilt child and took a sip from his drink.

'Dr Marks, did Janson know that you are bisexual, and was he perhaps blackmailing you? You have to admit that if that were the case then you would have a pretty good motive.'

'No, Commander, I haven't killed anybody, next question,'

'In Barbara Jenner's house I found a book of names and phone numbers. Your name is in the book with the number seven next to it. Can you perhaps tell me why that seven is there?'

Marks stiffened and tried to look deeply uninterested. 'I have absolutely no idea, Commander, perhaps you can tell me.'

'I hope I will one day.' Saxon and Parker stood up, finished their drinks, and turned to walk away. Saxon turned as he spoke. 'That will do for now, but I want a piece of paper delivered to my office tomorrow morning with all of your alibi's very carefully listed. Don't get it wrong, Dr Marks, we will be checking it thoroughly.'

As they climbed into Saxon's Land Rover trying not to burn themselves on the hot interior, Parker turned to Saxon. 'He didn't do it – the only thing he's guilty of is being an idiot. If he intended to bump someone off he'd use poison, the man is too much of a wimp to use the kind of physical strength our killer has used.'

'Agreed, but I thought he may be able to give us more useful information than he did. Maybe I'm clutching at straws, Parker, I think I'm losing my touch. We are getting fucking nowhere. I'll tell you what's bugging me right now though – the number seven next to his name in the book. What the hell could that mean?'

Parker's mobile rang with a sound similar to a very loud frog croaking, and he answered it as quickly as possible when he saw the look of disbelief on Saxon's face. 'Sorry, sir, kids have been playing with it – DS Parker, yes, Jim.

'Shit, how many?'

Parker listened for almost a minute, 'Thanks, Jim, I'll pass on the good news, bye.' He flicked the phone off and sighed.

Saxon gunned the engine and they started to move off slowly down the driveway. 'Break it to me gently, Parker.'

'Sergeant Groves has been in touch with all of the hospitals in the South East of the country. They gave him a few statistics – do you have any idea how many people became infected with HIV in this country, during the last year alone?'

Saxon looked left and right, and pulled out into the lane. 'Enlighten me.'

'Nearly three and a half thousand, that's how bloody many – so if we go back say four years, well we don't need a calculator to work that little lot out. Then I suppose there are private clinics, and if we want to make it even more depressing, maybe we should look into all the AIDS-related suicides. Sorry to sound so defeatist, sir, but it would be a never-ending task.'

'I know, Parker, I know,' was all Saxon could say as he pulled into a lay-by and dialled Francesca's number.

'Am I too late for that dinner you promised?' He paused. 'Sounds good to me...see you in about forty minutes. Bye.'

Parker looked out of the side window and smiled.

Chapter 11

Saturday, May 25, 11.15PM

Andy Pike drove slowly across the furthest of his fields from the house. It made him feel like a real landowner when he patrolled his small estate. His old Land Rover had admittedly seen much better days, but he was confident it still exuded effortlessly an image of ancient, solid, county aristocracy.

Pike, although happily fostering for as long as he could remember a deep hatred of rich people and everything associated with them, did on occasions allow himself the self-indulgence of feeling, and he took for granted, looking, quietly regal – but only when he thought nobody was watching.

He had been feeling uncomfortable at the thought of lamping. The night of the murders, with the strange eyes staring at him, had given him a few sleepless nights. But the local butcher had asked him for a couple of dozen rabbits and he'd used the magic word. 'We're talking "cash" rather than "please".' That was all it took for him to overcome his fear. Besides, he had his gun and his dogs, and surely, no harm could come to an armed man in the British countryside. Particularly one who was on his own turf.

Slowly, he pulled over in the bottom corner of his largest field. His fields were small by modern-day standards. His land had never been flattened into vast corn-growing plains, as had a great deal of farms in the south of England. Pike's smallholding hadn't changed since medieval times, and he was proud of that fact.

The other side of the hedge from where he parked, there was a small stream, the noise of which would help to drown out any sound that he may accidentally make, which might in turn scare the rabbits away. Not that he would be likely to make such amateur mistakes, of course – Pike was an old hand at lamping, and was capable of moving through crisp dry undergrowth without any sound.

With his rifle loaded and resting across his lap, he made a sweep of the field with the roof-mounted lamp; Russ and Lurch both jumped up, keenly looking out of the side window following the beam of light.

'Shit,' Pike muttered to himself. 'Nothin' there, where's them fuckin' rabbits then?' The dogs heard and maybe they noticed his irritation. Russ ignored him as usual, but Lurch detected the change in the tone of his voice and looked back and forth from master's face to beam of light, as if to say "Don't blame me, you can't get me for this one."

Pike was puzzled, the weather was perfect, and there should have been plenty of rabbits out nibbling away for most of the night. Usually this field was home to at least fifty or so. He told the dogs to be quiet and to keep still. He grabbed a large torch and his gun and left his Land Rover to walk along the hedge for a few hundred yards.

He thought that possibly the sound of the engine had startled the rabbits and they had bolted underground. His plan was to use stealth and creep up on them. Although underfoot was dry and firm, Pike always wore rubber Wellingtons – he was, through past experience, well aware that if there was anything undesirable to step in, then he would be the one to find it. The boots made walking tiresome, but at least his feet were always dry and clean.

After three hundred yards of shining his torch up and down the field and still nothing to be seen, he stopped to roll a cigarette. Had there been any rabbits this would be okay, as he was downwind from where they should have been. Temporarily blinded by the glare from his lighter he felt slightly disorientated as he screwed up his eyes waiting for his optical nerve to kick back into gear.

As he let the smoke slowly escape through his mouth and down his nostrils, he tried just one more sweep of the torch before giving up for the night. He regretted this decision almost immediately. Across the other side of the field he saw a pair of eyes reflecting the light back, but they, like the eyes on the night of the murders, were in the wrong sodding place and were too high off the ground and moving as if the head of the person was slowly rotating. Pike panicked, his heart thumping heavily against his ribcage. At first, he was paralysed, not being too sure which way to run. Then, suddenly, the desire to run became overwhelming, but he had lost his bearings, and he ran into the hedge.

The barbed wire didn't stop him – he fell over it headfirst and crawled where the rabbits couldn't go. It was the brambles and blackthorn that not only stopped him from reaching the next field, but also prevented him from going anywhere. He tried to reason with himself, but it didn't work, so he settled for panic again. He had lost the torch along with his rifle and, unfortunately, it must have either broken or switched itself off as it hit the ground.

The night seemed to close in on him as he thrashed around collecting thorns in most parts of his body. Instinctively, he closed his eyes to protect them from ending up like olives on cocktail sticks. His fear and will to survive, closed down the pain receptors in his brain. His heart beating wildly, he was in a near state of collapse brought about by rapid breathing.

Hyperventilating momentarily caused him to stop and assess the situation. He knew he had to regain his bearings and his control; gradually he talked himself into being calm. Convincing his body to stop producing so much adrenalin he started to feel pain; thorns were everywhere, even in his groin.

Stuck in a half-crouching position, seemingly surrounded by an impenetrable wall of thorns and in total darkness, he reached into his trousers pocket, took out his lighter and flicked it on. The light it provided was just enough to allow him to see in his immediate area of about two feet in any direction.

This made Pike feel even more isolated and more vulnerable – it, whatever it was out there, could now see him, but he couldn't see it. His father, told him stories of when he was a soldier during WWII, of how he was taught that if you use a torch at night, then you are not the only one who can see. They, meaning the enemy, could see you. Better to bump into the odd tree than get killed. Was someone trying to kill him – closing in on him? More waves of panic started to overwhelm him again as he started the tedious task of trying to free himself from the hedge.

Several minutes passed before Pike managed to back his way to the fence and freedom. Once he was safely out of the undergrowth and back in the field, he started to crawl around looking for his torch, which to his immense relief he soon found. It was with his rifle but was not broken; the thing had indeed switched off when he dropped it.

Fully armed and dangerously angry, Pike quickly flicked off the safety catch and plucked up the courage from somewhere to shine the torch in the direction of the eyes. At first, it seemed that they had disappeared, then as before, they slowly appeared as if the person was looking in the other direction and turning to look towards him.

Pike raised his gun towards the eyes and lined up his sights.

'Right, you fucker, I've 'ad enough of you, you've 'ad it now, you bastard.'

The silenced gun barely made any sound at all, and Pike immediately ran across the field to inspect whom, or whatever he had killed. He wasn't a clever man, but as he ran, he started to imagine what he would have to say to the police if he had killed someone. Shining his torch carefully on the position of the shot, he slowed down cautiously as he approached the spot where he expected to see a body. But all he found was a length of string hanging from a tree and a large turnip lying on the ground with a neat hole between a couple of cats eyes that must have been gouged from a stud in the lane.

Pike would have laughed if he had not been in considerable pain and bleeding from so many different places. Puzzled, he turned to head back to his car. In the distance he could hear Russ and Lurch barking and noticed the interior light was on. *Enough is enough,* he thought to himself. *What a fuckin' awful night.* He sighed, and started to jog across the centre of the field.

The dogs had stopped barking, but he could see Lurch's tail in the air as if he had his head down and was eating something on the back seat. Pike shone the light in the side window and could see that the dogs were eating a dead rabbit that had been hacked to pieces.

He opened the door slowly and stared speechless – then he heard a slight noise behind him causing him to turn suddenly. Frozen with fear at what he saw standing six feet away, urine crept down the inside of his pants. A large human form, it appeared to have rough skin covered in bumps and grooves with a small hole for a mouth and a couple of hard eyes that didn't seem to blink.

Pike wanted to raise his gun and shoot it, but was unable to move other than shake. He stood frozen as the humanoid shape moved closer; holding a rabbit snare with both hands and quickly slipping it over his head. Pike's eyes bulged, staring with disbelief as the wire suddenly tightened around his neck. Still paralysed, his Wellingtons filled up with urine as his eyes rolled up and his lips turned blue.

He was found two days later with the snare still around his neck and his head shoved down a rabbit hole. Something had eaten most of his face. Russ and Lurch had finished the rabbit, and were ready for more.

Monday, May 27, 8.00AM

Saxon trudged across the field with DS Parker; jackets left in his car, both were wearing one-piece paper overalls with bags over their shoes and rubber gloves. And they were hot; the heat wave had arrived with flying colours. There was even talk in the village that there would soon be a water shortage. Ten years ago, during another equally hot spell, the local pub had run out of lager, nearly causing a riot. Right now, what the two policemen wanted more than a hot stinking walk across a field to poke around a hot stinking corpse with the probability of not finding any clues, was at least a couple of pints of cold lager.

Pike's Land Rover had been fenced off with crime scene tape – the dogs had been rescued just in time, if one of the windows had not been left slightly open they would have surely cooked in those temperatures.

'Who found the body, Parker?' Saxon asked automatically.

'Dog walker, nothing sinister as usual – an old chap who comes out here once a week or so. Thank God for dog walkers – where would we be without them?'

'Very true, where indeed.'

They walked beyond Pike's car, through a gap in the hedge, along a short path that followed the stream and over a small makeshift bridge. They continued on guided by the sound of the SOCO people, fighting off mosquitoes the size of small mice. As they cleared the trees and looked to the other side of the valley, thirty yards up the path was Pike's body, spread-eagled, face down with his head in a rabbit hole. Dr Clarke and Jake were just finishing their initial examination after SOCO had examined Pike's clothing, hair and nails. Parker was the first to speak.

'Sir, why the hell does our killer have to be so theatrical – I mean, why doesn't he just do the normal thing and just leave his bodies lying around, or stuffed in car boots or even just buried?

'There's the man who can probably answer your question better than I, Parker,' said Saxon, pointing towards Professor Ercott who was wandering around the fenced-off body of Andy Pike, making notes and sketches, and occasionally talking into a small tape recorder. Parker wandered over and repeated his question to Ercott.

'I'm glad you asked me that very interesting question, young man; it's a fascinating one too. Firstly, the killer always has time to arrange his victims, because he plans absolutely everything down to the finest details. I dare say, that you will have noticed that all of our victim's heads have been hidden or covered in some way. Well, the reason is usually very simple. The face covered is normally a sign that the killer knew the deceased and can't bear the thought of being looked at by his or her victim. However, I don't think that is the case with our man – I am convinced now that it is a man, a very strong man: I think Pike was killed by his car and then carried here by the killer – no, our man has none of these feelings of guilt; just hate, and he wants to confuse us as much as possible. As I think we shall see, he will continue to change his MO with each murder.'

Saxon cut in, taking a cigarette from Parker's hand as he was about to put it in his mouth.

'What about forensics – anything at all?' He didn't expect a thing.

Ercott's eyes lit up.

'There is one thing, Commander, but you won't like what I'm going to ask you to do.' Ercott looked over his glasses at Saxon and motioned him to follow. He lifted the tape to allow the two policemen to approach the body.

'Now, Commander, and you, young man, come on; he won't hurt you, he's dead. Kneel down next to the unfortunate Mr Pike and smell him – I know he's a bit smelly but there is another pong apart from the usual decaying flesh.'

Saxon and Parker looked at Ercott with a lot of disbelief, and then at each other with even more.

'You have to be bloody joking.' Parker would have none of it and suggested that it would be better if he and his commanding officer just took Ercott's word for it.

Saxon wasn't too impressed with the idea either, but he trusted Ercott's judgement, and knelt down and took a cautious sniff. At first, he almost gagged but held on.

'Rubber, I can smell rubber. Go on, Parker, smell it, you may have to back me up in court one day.'

'Oh, sir, for Christ's sake, must I?'

'Get it over with, Parker, don't be such a wimp.'

Parker reluctantly gave in and took his sniff, then dashed off to the bushes to throw up. He returned several minutes later with a cigarette in his mouth.

'Sorry, sir, can't abide the smell of rotting bodies, but the rubber smell is there, I agree – quite strong too.'

'Well done, Parker.' Saxon put his hand on Parker's shoulder and walked around the body to speak with Ercott.

'Ok, Roger, so what are we looking for, a man wearing a scuba-diving suit or some kind of fetishist who covers his body in condoms? He should be easy to spot whichever one he is.'

'Your guess is as good as mine, Paul. Maybe he used a rubber tarpaulin to cover the body while he carried it. Don't really know.'

'What makes you think Pike was killed over by his car?'

'I didn't spot it myself; sorry to say, it was one of the SOCO girls, nice young thing too. Anyway, she noticed that dent in the back of his head. You will find that the corner of Pike's Land Rover with a bit of his scalp hanging on it, is a perfect match for that dent. Dr Clarke agreed with me when I spoke to him earlier, that combined with the wire around his neck, that blow would most probably have killed him. There are also a few traces of him being dragged a short distance before being hoisted up onto the killer's shoulders.'

'And footprints, or are we looking for flipper marks?' enquired Saxon.

Ercott smiled but otherwise ignored the joke. 'Sorry, Paul, no footprints, ground's too dry, and if there were any over there by the stream, he must have gone back and cleaned up afterwards. He's thorough – I'll say that for him.' Ercott wandered off cleaning his glasses.

Sergeant Green, a short fat policewoman, one of the SOCO team, approached with a dog handler.

'Commander Saxon, could you come and take a look at something we've found at the top of the field?' She led him back across the stream, past the Land Rover. By the time they reached the area where all the interest was emanating from, they were sweating and exhausted. The dog handler showed Saxon the remains of the turnip with the cat's eyes, telling him that the dog had picked up a scent that started at Pike's vehicle and it seemed strange that there should be a direct line of scent between the Land Rover and the turnip with eyes. Saxon could only agree and suggested that the hole through the middle of it could be from a bullet. It didn't take them long to find a hole in the trunk of the tree that lined up perfectly where a bullet would have travelled from the Land Rover.

Saxon pondered. 'So these cat's eyes could have convinced Pike that someone was watching him from up here; the hovering eyes. He must have been seriously spooked to take a pot shot at them, and while he was doing that, the killer jumped on him and snared him, banged his head on the car to finish him off.' Reasonably satisfied that they had interpreted the evidence correctly, they stripped off their overalls and walked slowly back to Saxon's Discovery.

'Next time we have a situation like this, Parker, please remind me that I have a four-wheel-drive sodding car and that we can drive to the crime scene.'

Parker was too hot and still feeling too sick to laugh or answer.

Thursday, May 30, 9.20PM

Jake Dalton parked his car, grabbed his takeaway curry from the passenger seat and made his way across the private car park to his apartment. He'd lived in Brighton Marina for three years; he liked it and to his delight found it to have a friendly village atmosphere. The correct balance of white-haired weekend sailors, London yuppie executives, and local Brighton residents had been reached successfully. It was surrounded on three sides by the English Channel, which occasionally tried to crash over the fortress-like walls, and reclaim the land. And with a garage, some fishing tackle shops, fast food and supermarkets, and easy access to the pleasures of Brighton, he was content.

The light was starting to fade; gone 9PM but still oppressively hot. Even the seagulls were taking it easy, just the odd shriek in contrast to the screaming aerial display that usually greeted him. Jake punched in his security code and entered the communal hallway. Finding it unusual that the light didn't work, he fumbled at his front door juggling curry, briefcase and keys. As he touched the lock with his key, the door moved slowly open.

Putting everything on the floor, he cautiously pushed the door inwards and reached inside for the light switch. His mind racing and his body ready to fight he burst into his apartment. 'Shit, bloody little bastards!' he shouted, not caring who heard. His next-door neighbour James did hear and appeared at Jake's door.

'You all right, Jake? What's happened?'

'Sodding kids that's what. Look at the graffiti, got to be kids with all that shit on the walls.' He reached in his pocket and took out his mobile and started to call the police.

'Well, I'm amazed, sorry, mate, I've been working all day just the other side of that wall and I haven't heard a sound. The state this place is in you'd think that there would have to have been some noise,' James said almost apologetically, scratching his head.

Half an hour later a couple of local PCs arrived and told Jake that someone would call in the morning to take his fingerprints for elimination purposes, and then see if the "little bastards" had left any of their own behind. Meanwhile, they asked him to make a list of anything obvious that was missing. Jake decided that the mess was so overpowering that he would make the list after the fingerprint person had finished. He spent the night on James' sofa.

Jake awoke early next morning with a jolt, the realisation of the previous night's dilemma hitting him squarely between the eyes. He dragged himself off the sofa, splashed water on his face and went to his apartment to survey the damage in the cold light of day.

Sergeant Tony Palmer, the SOCO man, arrived an hour later and started to lift prints from under the toilet seat. Jake had met him several times, as their paths had crossed frequently during the last few weeks.

'It's the place they tend to forget to wipe clean, if our burglar is a pro of course – kids just piss on the floor usually, but it looks like kids' stuff to me.' Palmer had a bored drone in his voice as if he'd said it all a thousand times.

Jake handed Palmer his list of missing items. 'Strange, I don't understand this at all.' Jake stood hand on chin looking at the list.

'From what I can make out, the only things missing are some shoes, a sweater and a hairbrush. Nearly everything else is just trashed – they didn't even take the stereo or TV.' Palmer eyed the list suspiciously. 'Why would anyone want personal items like this then – say, Jake, you haven't got a stalker have you? Someone who wants something personal of yours to snuggle up to maybe?'

'Very amusing, but not that I know of, I've not noticed anyone following me if that's what you mean?'

Palmer wandered off with his fingerprint brush dabbing here and there. 'Well, could just be the beginning,' he droned with a touch of "you mark my words, and watch your back". 'At least it can't be one of your patients, they're all bloody dead.' Palmer laughed from the bedroom. Jake muttered something under his breath about it not being particularly funny and set about tidying up. Once this task was completed, Jake and Palmer sat down to drink a cup of coffee and to take Jake's fingerprints for elimination.

'You do realise, don't you, that chances are that we won't find any prints other than yours?' said Palmer. Adding, 'It's not like on the telly you know, never as clean cut – we have to find the prints first and then they have to be clear enough to identify. It used to be that we had to find at least twelve points of reference on the print before it was even admissible as evidence. Nowadays, it just takes the testimony of an expert to say that in his opinion, the prints match.'

Palmer explained that he had found a few good "dabs" as he called them, but they were more than likely Jake's. He would wait until he got back to the forensic lab and call Jake later with the news either way.

Chapter 12

Wednesday, June 5, Bottle Walk, Hampstead, North London

Fabio Gerard was the sort of person who stood out in a crowd. Not because of his physical size or his good looks, both of which were impressive. But he had presence and charisma oozing from every pore. A Parisian – staying in London for a week with his friend Kris with a "K", it was Chris with a "C" really but in the hairdressing business, Kris seemed to be more memorable to the clientele – Fabio was loud, camp and proud of it. But unfortunate on this day, that he was so noticeable.

His first couple of days had been idly spent lounging around in bed, occasionally getting up to eat; watching television and playing at "French Chef", for Kris when he came home after a hard day in the salon.

Kris was no ordinary run-of-the mill hairdresser, owning a chain of salons around London with branches in Monaco, where he had an apartment, Milan and New York, all highly successful. His home was in Hampstead, North London and he drove a yellow Ferrari as a symbol of his business prowess. Fabio ran the Paris salons of which there were three. They met twenty years ago when they were both young apprentice hairdressers and had been together ever since. Fabio lived in Paris for most of his time but they both regularly travelled to the different establishments to check that standards were being adhered to, and to soak up as much of the glory of being the owners of their joint, highly successful venture as possible.

Fabio was recovering from a vicious bout of flu and pacing himself carefully. No way could he have ever have been accused of overexerting himself – the slightest illness, even a cold, was capable of almost confining him to a wheelchair. Years of pampering and self-indulgence had seen to that. He had decided that what he really needed more than anything was time off. He had worked hard all his life, and he felt that he deserved it. He intended to spend the next few days sightseeing around London.

Kris's house was not big, although if he had so desired, he could have purchased a small mansion – even at London prices. No, his house was modest and in a sought-after area of Hampstead down a small almost unnoticeable lane just a few yards down the hill from Hampstead Underground station. The row of semi-detached houses were set back from the road and raised up, so that anyone walking past would be unable to see in the ground-floor windows, and with about forty feet of garden in which to grow suitable cover, the houses seemed to disappear in the summer when the foliage was dense.

Fabio liked Hampstead. Back in the late 70s he'd lived in Highgate and frequently spent nights in the many gay pubs and bars that were there; illegal, but there just the same. Often, afternoons were idly spent trawling Hampstead Heath for the odd sexual encounter, undertaken with great care as "queer bashing" was occasionally practised by a few stragglers from the Stone Age. It had never happened to Fabio, so he only had his friends' stories to go by, and he secretly thought that maybe they were exaggerating anyway. He was quite blasé and believed that no harm would ever come to him no matter what he got up to. Although he had been with Kris for a good few years, he still strayed, enjoying the thrill of cruising for sex with a stranger, combined with the chance of danger.

Kris knew Fabio well and although he'd have preferred the relationship to be more one to one, he too strayed from time to time. They were both of the opinion that if a relationship wasn't too broken, and it still worked, then don't try to mend it.

Fabio had started his day with a trip to the British Museum, followed by the National Gallery, mostly for Monet, but he thought a top-up of culture never hurt anyone. Soon, thoughts turned to shopping and Fabio caught the Tube to High Street Kensington, and Fabio shopped as if that was the last day of shopping before the seven headless horsemen called a halt to everything. The temperature was high, making the trying on of clothing tedious and uncomfortable, so if he liked something, a guess was enough to decide yes or no. Money was of little or no importance – if it didn't fit or look good later, then it was thrown away.

A few hours of high-octane shopping started to take its toll on Fabio's fingers so he hired a taxi to take his mountain of goods home. The housekeeper, Mrs Lyons, was there all day and Fabio gave the driver a large tip for his trouble.

Unburdened and in a summer mood, Fabio was game for adventure. The taxi left him at High Street Kensington and Fabio was hungry. Always aware of his figure, he opted for a fruit squeeze, followed by a Starbucks. These purchased, he walked along Kensington Gore towards the Royal Albert Hall, crossing the road and strolling into Hyde Park. All of the benches were taken so Fabio found a spot in the shade near some bushes and arranged himself on the grass.

Apart from the distant rumble of London and the odd shrieking child or whining toddler, all was peaceful in Fabio's world. But the heat was now becoming intense and oppressive. He carried a mid-sized shoulder bag, which made a passable pillow. A few hours' sleep wouldn't hurt. After all, he was on holiday and he hadn't been well. It would probably do him a bit of good.

The snivelling children, buzzing flies and occasional laughter faded away as Fabio drifted into sleep.

His awakening was sudden. Just a cough, but a cough engineered for the purpose of alerting someone of another's arrival. To Fabio though, it wasn't just a cough, it was a man's cough. The gender of the cough was all-important. Fabio prided himself on the fact that he could spot a gay man instantly. Not for nothing did the gay community adapt radar to gaydar. He could never understand his friends who made mistakes and hit on a straight man from time to time. But when he looked around for the source of the cough, the man lying on the grass ten feet away didn't give off the right signals.

The stranger looked up from his book and smiled pleasantly at Fabio, but not seductively. There was not the slightest element of flirtation in that smile. Just a hint of danger. The man's eyes were cold.

Oh, this one likes to be on top, Fabio thought to himself, with a shiver of anticipation. The very idea sent waves of excitement all through his body and his original impression that this man was not likely to be interested was washed away in the flood.

Fabio didn't like the idea of cheating on Kris, but he was weak. He enjoyed the thrill of conquest, or rather of being conquered. Besides, he knew that Kris had the occasional fling. If they both took sensible precautions, then surely no harm was done. He knew that if he could keep thinking along those lines then everything would be okay.

Fabio had no rigid timetable, he didn't have to be anywhere in particular, didn't have to answer to anyone. Kris had gone to the States for a few days on business, so the house would be his playground. Mrs Lyons would be going off on holiday that night, cleaning her own house until Kris returned.

He rolled onto his front, head turned away from the man, and after a few minutes of courage building, he turned suddenly to start spewing out his much-used chat-up lines – but the man was gone. Fabio sat up looking around, not a sign of him. It was as though he was never there, not even a mark on the grass, he hadn't even any litter. Feeling deflated, he picked up his bag and headed back towards Kensington High Street. The man was still there, but chose not to be seen.

Fabio took the Tube to Hampstead, he in one carriage, the man two carriages away standing by the sliding doors, checking each stop to see if Fabio was still on the train. As the doors opened at Hampstead, the man saw that Fabio had reached his destination and rushed to the lift catching the one before Fabio. He slipped on a baseball cap and dark glasses and waited on the corner opposite the station entrance knowing that Fabio would appear in a couple of minutes. He stood with his back to the street, using the reflection in a shop window to keep track of Fabio's movements.

Fabio appeared, stood for a brief moment, swept his hair back and turned left down Hampstead High Street, and turning left almost immediately, he walked down Bottle Walk. The man followed, keeping his head down, never looking up at the CCTV cameras for even an instant. The walk to Kris's house took no more than two minutes. Fabio entered as Mrs Lyons was leaving. They exchanged pleasantries on the doorstep as the man walked by making a mental note of the house number as he gently fondled a plastic bag containing a large knife, some hair, fibres and a surgical glove in his jacket pocket.

The man spent the next four hours wandering around the Hampstead area carrying what appeared to be shopping bags. These bags contained old clothes with no labels. Ordinary, plain, with no distinguishing marks. Every hour the man changed his appearance by swapping his jacket, trousers, hat and glasses in the public toilets. He even changed the way he walked. If he were caught on camera, which one of his shadows would the police pursue?

When darkness came, he walked along Bottle Walk, stopping outside the house and looking up and down the road to check if he had been seen. The place was deserted. Strange, he thought, how quiet the side streets of London could be. He walked up to the front door and listened. The television was on and he peered in through a gap in the curtains. Sitting on a sofa with his back to the window, he could see Fabio, wine glass in hand watching a film.

From where he stood, the thick bushes surrounding the front door obscured the road. 'Perfect,' he said quietly, as he took an eight-inch butchers knife from the inside pocket of his jacket. He rang the doorbell.

Fabio jumped to his feet and peered through the spy hole in the door. He thought that he recognised the distorted face, but wasn't sure until he opened the door.

'My God, you're the guy from the park, how did you know where I lived?' But as he said the words, the alarm bells in his head started to sound off. The speed that the man used as he lunged forward towards Fabio's chest was anticipated well by Fabio. He deflected the blow to his left. The killer hadn't intended to enter the house, but he was given no choice. Fabio was big and fit. He grabbed the man by the wrist and fell backwards pulling his assailant with him. As Fabio hit the floor still holding tightly to the man's wrist, he put his foot in the man's groin and launched him over his head.

The man crashed into the television, which fell in a shower of sparks against the far wall. Fabio was on him before he could recover, and punched him hard on the side of the head. Suddenly, Fabio saw the knife as the man brought it up slashing him across the chest. He felt no pain – his senses numbed by the adrenalin rush. He leant back in shock and that was all it took for the man to grab his chance. He pulled himself up onto his knees, and pushed his forearm into Fabio's throat and pinned him to the wall. The pain started to come now and Fabio gritted his teeth. The man stared into his eyes as he quickly pushed the knife into Fabio's heart. His surprised look only lasted a second before he slumped to the floor.

The killer found the bathroom, picked up a nailbrush and scrubbed Fabio's fingernails. Then he ran a comb through his victim's hair, in case any of his own had become detached from his head during the struggle. Next, he dabbed Fabio all over with strips of duct tape to remove any fibres. After removing his own clothes in the bath, he changed into one of the clean outfits from his bag, and then set about cleaning up the room. All of the surfaces he had come into contact with during the fight were cleaned thoroughly. He took out the small plastic bag from his pocket and put a few hairs in the palm of Fabio's hand, and a few fibres from his collection he put on Fabio's lips.

In a cupboard under the stairs, he found a vacuum cleaner and vacuumed the entire carpet. He removed the dust bag and carefully put it in a plastic bag, which he took with him when he left. He closed the front door behind him, pausing to post a tape cassette through the letterbox. Carefully wiped clean of any fingerprints...of course.

The killer missed the last train from Victoria Station, so he opted for a minicab. It proved to be an expensive trip, but he thought it was well worth it to remove some more scum from the world. He told the driver that he was very tired and that he would go to sleep.

This gave him good reason to keep his head down and also to avoid too much conversation. When they drew near to the place where he had left his car, he made sure that the driver saw him walking up the path to a house that was not his.

When the minicab was out of sight, he backtracked along the lane to his car. He drove to a narrow lane where the normal traffic didn't venture, particularly at that time of night. He knew the lane well, for in the woods he kept his wardrobe. A water-tight container buried just under the surface. He took with him, a trowel and some surgical spirit, and dug a hole big enough to take the blood-spattered clothes. The spirit and a match destroyed that bit of evidence. When the fire died down he changed into his everyday clothes. His other "mission clothing", as he called them were sealed in the underground container. He removed all signs that anyone had been there and walked back to his car.

The difficult part was how to explain the bruises on his face.

'But there is always makeup,' he said to himself.

Tuesday, June 11, 7.30AM

Saxon parked his car in Mitchell's space at the back of the police station. Mitchell had willingly given it up for his superior officer, probably thinking that it would go on a report at some time mentioning how considerate he could be. As he walked through the reception area, the desk sergeant, Ian Dowling, stopped him.

'Excuse me, Commander Saxon, CID have been trying to get you on your mobile – something about a possible crank call, but they said to tell you that it was very interesting. Apparently, it contains stuff that we haven't given to the press. Detective Sergeant Parker has a tape of the call in your office.'

Saxon smiled at Dowling. 'Thanks, Ian, just what I've been waiting for – anything.' He ran up two flights of stairs as fast as the temperature allowed, to find Parker intently listening to the tape. Parker stopped it when Saxon entered.

'Morning, sir, how do you want to start, with the good news, or the bad news?'

'Both will do and I don't care how they come.'

'Right, the bad news is that it's a digitised voice so no chance of a voiceprint. Whoever made this tape must have typed it first and then got his or her computer to read it back, so it's a completely mechanical voice, a bit like that Stephen Hawking chap. My guess is that either he used a laptop and took it to the phone box, and held the phone close enough to pick up the sound, or he re-recorded it to a small tape recorder and used that. Less chance of being seen I suppose.

'Now, the good news is interesting. It has to be genuine. He talks about things that we haven't released to the press; this bastard would have to have been there to know what he knows. There is more good news – he is giving us clues or maybe a puzzle to solve regarding his next murder. God knows why he would want to do that though, beats me.'

Saxon sat grinding his teeth for a moment, digesting the flood of information.

'Could be that he wants to be famous. Most serial killers want that. If he is never caught, he can never be famous. Let's hear the tape.'

Parker flicked the switch.

Dear Boss,

Don't worry, Commander Saxon, I am not another Jack, my subjects are more deserving of their punishment. Did you like the planted fingers in the dykes' house, I was wondering. Have they grown into anything yet? And did Mr Pike's dogs enjoy the rabbit I left for them? No doubt, you think that you will catch me soon, but although you are clever, you will not get me until I am ready and finished my work. For your entertainment, I am going to give you a few clues. These clues will not lead you to me, but may help you to save my next subject. For the time being, at least. If you are late solving these clues then the subject will die. If you save the subject, I will kill him later. Did I say him? Could that be the first clue? Pay attention Mr Policeman, here are the other clues.

First. Like the trunk of thirty-four and the man involved, this may not be solved. But this man will not get away.

Second. Castle of justice, motte and old...

Third. Subject wears a wig in public and in private.

Four. Subject will be in a skip to get to Heaven or more likely Hell.

Easy isn't it, Commander? Or maybe, not so easy. You will judge for yourself, no doubt. The problem for you is to solve this riddle before midnight tomorrow. Good luck.

Parker switched off the tape recorder. 'It seems too easy, sir, although there are a few bits I don't get. What's all that stuff about a trunk?'

'Don't you ever read anything, Parker? Call yourself a detective? Right, history lesson, pay attention. First of all the "Dear Boss" bit is the way Jack the Ripper addressed his letters to the police – if it was indeed he who wrote them in the first place.

'Then we have the first clue, back in 1934, a trunk containing a head and some limbs was left at Brighton Railway Station. The main suspect was a man named Mancini. He was never charged regarding that particular crime as he had a good alibi, but he did happen to have the body of his girlfriend Violet Kaye stored in a trunk in his flat. He even had the nerve to take her body with him when he moved house. He was charged with murder, but convinced the jury that she had died accidentally in a fall, and that he kept her in the trunk because he had a criminal record and didn't think that he would get a fair trial. God knows how, but he was found not guilty and discharged.'

Parker stood staring at Saxon. 'Excuse me for saying this but, does sir need to get out more? How on earth did you know all that?'

'You're excused this time, Parker. I have a comprehensive library of crime books.' He paused. 'Don't look at me like that, Parker – some people collect stamps and butterflies, I just happen to collect crime books, and maybe it's just as well because I think the "man" in the first clue probably refers to a present-day Mancini, who is more than likely the next victim.'

'How about the second clue? The only thing that springs to my mind is Bailey, as in Motte and Bailey,' Parker said sounding slightly unsure of himself. 'Castle of justice has to be the Old Bailey.'

'That's pretty obvious, Parker, and I think the third clue has to be referring to a judge, and if the judge wears a wig in private, then he's probably telling us that the judge is gay.'

'How about the skip to get to Heaven, sir?'

'That's the bit that worries me, Parker. I don't think our friend is warning us about an impending murder at all. I think he's already killed the poor sod. He's not going to risk capture, not just yet anyhow. I think the bastard has already done it. Call it instinct if you want, but I just know it. Get me a list of all High Court judges in the country and I want a search started now of all builders skip's within a half-mile radius of the Old Bailey. Any skip trucks that have picked up loads within the twelve hours are to be traced. But my feeling is that we will find a body in the closest one to the courts.'

It didn't take long to locate the list of judges, and to see that one was named Bernard Mancini. Two members of Saxon's team, Sergeant's Brian Anderson and Jim Groves raced to his home address in Chislehurst; they tried to phone him on the way but got no reply. The house was located in a quiet road near Chislehurst woods, a large mock Tudor, complete with roses round the door and brick paths.

The car skidded to a halt and Groves jumped out. He grabbed the gate and flung it open with a crash as Anderson revved up the engine. Groves hurled himself back into the car and in a cloud of flying gravel they sped up the lengthy drive to the front door.

The house was silent and dark, with no signs of life. Anderson ran around to the back door while Groves first pressed the bell button followed by several hard bangs on the door. The front door was solid, but the back door gave up the fight easily after a couple of kicks from two pairs of size tens. Mr Justice Mancini was not at home.

Meanwhile, back in London, teams of constables searched for builders skips in the area of the Old Bailey. The search only lasted twenty minutes. A skip less than thirty yards from the law courts attracted their attention quickly. On its side, large sprayed-on lettering which read, "NOT FIT TO JUDGE" in bright red.

A tent was erected over the skip. Mancini was found lying under a double mattress in his full courtroom regalia except for the wig, which was blonde with long flowing curls. Bright red lipstick was smeared around his mouth, giving the appearance of a large gaping wound, the sight of which made the SOCOs, even with their experiences of far worse horrors, draw back in shock when the mattress was removed.

Saxon and Parker arrived at midday, during the forensic search of the body, while the entire contents of the skip were removed bit by bit to another skip that was now parked within a few feet of the first one. One of Saxon's team, Dave Hope, a gangly shaven-headed detective constable, showed them a plastic bag containing a few strands of hair.

'Found them in the deceased gentleman's hand, Commander, they're short and there's only a few of them but some have part of the hair root attached so there's a chance that they may be okay for DNA testing.'

'Thank God for that, at last we have something,' said Saxon wanting to give Parker a "high five" but restraining himself in front of the crowd, which was growing by the minute.

'There's more, Commander, a few fibres caught on a fingernail – looks like wool to me.'

'I couldn't give a toss what it is, so long as we can match it to someone's clothing. It's the hair I'm interested in. However, it's one thing to have DNA, but if you don't have a suspect to match it to, you are well and truly screwed.'

Parker who had been lurking around the edge of the skip suddenly called for a long probe of some kind, having spotted something tucked down below the body and next to the edge of the skip. He was handed a wire coat hanger, which had been opened out to form a long hook.

'Christ, call this the high-tech age, I suppose it'll do though,' he muttered as he groped around trying to hook the object. After several minutes of cursing and heavy sweating, he retrieved it. And there it was dangling on the end of Parker's low-tech hook, a single surgical glove.

'Parker, you know, I think I will keep you after all. Well bloody done, that man deserves a medal. Right, I want that bagged and

I want to know whether the fingerprints inside the glove are useable, and I want to know within the hour. I also want everything there is to know about Mr Justice Mancini. What cases he has presided over for the last five years; has his life ever been threatened? That sort of thing; and I want it on my desk just after you tell me about the fingerprints. Understood? Good. See you in my office.'

Parker looked as though he had been sledgehammered, and wandered off to complete his tasks. He stopped after a few yards and turned back towards Saxon.

'I've been thinking, but it may sound daft.'

'Spit it out, Parker, I don't care how daft any ideas are at the moment.'

Parker paused as if too embarrassed to even contemplate what he was intending to say.

'Okay, but I'm clutching straws here.'

'For heaven's sake, Parker, part of good police work is being able to use one's imagination. If it sounds daft I'll tell you, and it won't go on your record.'

'Right,' began Parker nervously, 'the mystery phone call came from a phone box in the Brighton Marina, and you know who lives there, don't you?'

'Enlighten me, Parker – I don't feel like a pub quiz just now.' Parker shifted about uncomfortably.

'Jake Dalton, he lives in one of those little wanky designer flats. What's more, as we both know he has medical knowledge.'

'Well, he would wouldn't he; he's a bloody doctor. But he's also not a fool. Don't you think it would be a bit daft, to say the least, to use a phone that's close to his home to make a call to the police warning them about a murder he was intending to commit. Doesn't make sense, the guy's too bright. He'd know that we would trace the call.'

They stood in silence for a few moments, finding the heat almost unbearable. Parker broke the silence. 'By the way, sir, did you know Jake was burgled the other day?'

'No, I didn't, but what's it got to do with this?'

'Nothing much was taken, apart from some old clothing, and odd worthless stuff, strange things like a hairbrush, which you have to agree is pretty weird. But the interesting thing, sir, was that the place was wrecked and the guy next door didn't hear a thing. Now you have to admit, that's unusual; a big-time mess with broken furniture and graffiti usually means some noise, if not quite a lot.

'The local boys think it was probably kids, but what if it was meant to appear that way. Suppose it was someone looking for specific items.' Parker thought for a moment, wondering if maybe his imagination was getting the better of him. 'Forget it, sir, I'm probably fantasising.'

Saxon stood with his chin resting on the heel of his palm.

'Please tell me they took his fingerprints for elimination, and that they haven't been destroyed yet.'

'They did, and they haven't.' Parker's eyes lit up. 'Are you thinking what I'm thinking, sir? The surgical glove from the skip?' Saxon pulled out his mobile and dialled the station. He told them to hold. He looked at Parker with growing excitement in his eyes.

'Who's the fingerprint man at Brighton nick?' Saxon asked Parker.

'Palmer…just ask for Pinky Palmer, they'll know who you mean.'

Saxon was told that Palmer was off duty and was given his mobile number. Palmer didn't mind being interrupted during his afternoon's gardening, and he confirmed that he hadn't destroyed Jake Dalton's fingerprints yet.

'Bring the glove, Parker; we are going straight back to Brighton, I want Pinky Palmer to check this out while we stand over him. If the prints are Jake's then we arrest him immediately.' Saxon was starting to smile to himself as they climbed into his car.

Parker was the first to speak. 'I have to say, I find it difficult to believe Jake Dalton is our man. Jake for Christ's sake, we both know Jake, he seems so normal.'

'I know what you mean, Parker, but remember what Ercott said – he could be as normal as you, Parker. But we can't be sure it is him yet…we could be jumping the gun. We'll know within three hours.' Saxon drove through South London, weaving in and out of the back streets; until he hit the M25, then it was cruise control all the way to Brighton.

Tuesday, June 11, Brighton Police Station, 2.30PM

Pinky Palmer was waiting in Saxon's office when they arrived. He almost snatched the bag containing the rubber glove from Parker's hand, and they followed him to his office; the walls of which were decorated with posters and diagrams of fingerprints showing whorls and spirals, all with points of reference clearly marked.

Palmer talked to Saxon all the way through the process of extracting the fingerprints from the inside of the surgical glove. Although Saxon was fascinated, he just wanted the result, not the lecture.

All of the prints were good. Palmer explained that the reason why they were so good was because the glove had been removed carefully, and not in the way that they were usually pulled over the wrist. He thought that the reason for this was that the glove had been covered in a considerable amount of blood, which had now dried, and the wearer would not have wanted to splash himself.

Palmer made up two slides, one with Jake's thumbprint from his flat, and the other from the glove.

Saxon could hardly contain himself.

'Well, does it, or doesn't it match, tell me for Christ's sake.' Palmer took a deep breath, and looked sideways at Saxon, he looked disappointed.

'Perfect match, I couldn't wish for a better set of prints...and he's supposed to be on our side.'

Saxon had a look of elation, but it turned to exasperation quickly. 'I agree, I've known him for a few years – it's hard to believe it, but how else can you explain the appearance of that glove in the same skip in which we find a body in London. I'll keep an open mind on this one, and if there is an explanation I really can't wait to hear it.'

Saxon left Palmer's office and found Parker chatting to Ian Dowling, the desk sergeant. He told Dowling to send a car with two PCs and a SOCO unit to the marina and wait for him around the corner from Jake Dalton's apartment block. Under no circumstances were they to approach him or even be seen by him.

As Saxon left, he shouted back to Dowling, 'And no radios, Just mobiles...understand? The press will probably be scanning our frequency; we don't want any vultures circling.'

The traffic through Brighton had almost reached gridlock. Thousands of tourists were out on the town, but Saxon didn't want to use sirens. Didn't want anyone spooked. The heat became even more intense with the car hardly moving, combined with the fact that there was no wind. Thirty minutes later, they arrived at their destination, driving down through the concrete-lined approach road on to the reclaimed land of Brighton Marina.

The two PCs covered the fire escape while Saxon and Parker pressed the button on Jake's front door. There was a pause and then a mechanical voice said, 'Hello, who's that?'

'Jake, it's Paul Saxon, can I come in and have a chat with you?'

'Sure.' The electronic lock on the door clicked open, and Saxon and Parker climbed the stairs to Jake's apartment. He was waiting for them by his door looking slightly shocked.

'Oh, I didn't realise there was going to be two of you. This can't be about the burglary, surely a commander wouldn't concern himself with a mere burglary for heaven's sake.'

Saxon didn't hesitate. He didn't relish the task at hand, because he was having big trouble believing the facts that had been presented to him.

'Jake Dalton, I am arresting you on suspicion of the murder of Mr Justice Bernard Mancini.'

Before Jake could speak, he cautioned him and told him to hold out his right hand so that he could be handcuffed to Parker.

'This is a joke, isn't it? You have to be kidding.' Jake started to shake. 'I don't understand. Paul, what's going on? I haven't murdered anybody. For goodness sake, the handcuffs aren't necessary, I'm not going to make a dash for it am I?'

'I hope not, Jake, because you wouldn't get far, we are not alone,' said Saxon, feeling quite strong doubts about the situation, and hoping that there was a good explanation for the evidence. He had arrested many criminals during his career, and Jake was not giving of the vibes of a guilty man.

'Can I get a few things to take with me, at least a change of clothes and underwear? And wait – what about my cats. Can you get my neighbour to look after them for me?'

'No, you can't have a change of clothes, I'm afraid you have to come as you are – we will need your clothes when we get to the police station. You will be given something to wear, and you can make all the relevant phone calls when we get there. Don't worry about the cats, they'll be well looked after.'

Saxon decided to leave the cuffs on, Jake was a fit and strong man and if he decided to bolt, he could probably outrun all of them. Parker called the two PCs on his mobile and they were waiting by the front door. Parker remained chained to Jake in the rear of the squad car with Saxon following in his Land Rover.

Jake was strip-searched, given paper overalls and slip-on shoes, and went through the usual process of fingerprints and photographs. He phoned his parents followed by his solicitor, Miss Sarah Wright, who arrived promptly and demanded to see Jake the minute she arrived. The duty officer took her to see Jake in his cell before Saxon and Parker started their interview. She wanted to know when the interview was scheduled to start and was told that she would be contacted in due course. For the time being, she could speak to Jake for as long as she wanted. The police were still busy gathering evidence.

Saxon and Parker returned to Jake's apartment to assist with the search. The press had arrived, and were so keen for any information that they jostled Saxon as he made his way from his car to the apartment block. He stopped at the door and held up his hands in surrender.

'I'll make a brief statement, then I want you all to go away. I will give you all further press releases as and when I have something for you. For now all that I can say is that, we have arrested a man in connection with the recent spate of murders in and around Sewel Mill. I am not naming the individual at this time as he has not yet been charged.'

A voice from the press pack shouted Jake's name, but Saxon chose not to be drawn. He disappeared through the door and two constables barred anyone from following. Once inside the hallway, he and Parker kitted themselves out in the usual crime scene garb and began searching the place slowly and methodically.

All of Jake's clothes were individually bagged; samples of hair were taken from brushes and even the dust bag was taken from his vacuum cleaner. Telephone bills showing itemised call records were collected – in fact every scrap of paper in the apartment was put into bags for analysis; even the top blank sheet of paper from a notepad was carefully removed so that tests could be carried out on it to show what had been written on the sheet that had preceded it.

Parker called from the kitchen. 'Sir, I think you should take a look at this.'

Saxon looked up to see Parker standing in the doorway holding a plastic evidence bag containing a single surgical glove.

'Found it stuffed inside a roll of paper kitchen towel. Correct me if I'm wrong but they usually come in pairs, I believe.'

'You're right, but why hide it there – if I were him I'd have thrown it away,' said Saxon, looking surprised.

Parker thought for a moment. 'He may have overlooked it at the time, and thought we would find it in his rubbish bags and decided to dump it later, in a public trash bin somewhere.'

'Could be,' said Saxon, looking at a long and well-stocked bookcase. 'Have a look through that lot when you get through with the kitchen – see if there's any homophobic stuff – you know, right-wing Nazi crap, that sort of thing.'

'Yes, sir… I think we have a visitor,' Parker said, looking out of the window. 'Dr Clarke on the starboard bow.'

Saxon sighed. 'Shit, I don't really want to see anyone at this moment in time.' But he was left with no choice.

Clarke appeared at the door. His voice boomed. 'Paul, I won't come in, I see you're busy. What's all this I hear about you arresting my assistant? Can't be true, good solid bloke, what evidence have you got?' Clarke trampled over anyone's chances of speaking in his usual manner until he decided that he had finished.

Saxon didn't need this. 'Hold up there, Richard, I wouldn't have arrested him unless I had good reason, and believe me, I think we have him dead in the water. Good forensics and not too much circumstantial. I will need to talk to you in the next few days, Richard, I trust you aren't thinking of going off anywhere for a while.'

'Oh good heavens, am I a suspect as well, is it open season on pathologists?'

'No, of course not, don't worry, Richard. I'll just need to talk to you about Jake, that's all. His behaviour lately – anything you may have noticed. But right now I have to get on with my job here, so if you will excuse me.'

'No problem, Paul, I'm at your disposal any time you want.'

Clarke left as abruptly as he appeared, and Saxon turned to Parker. 'Please go and tell the two constables who are supposedly guarding the door, that when I say keep people out I mean it. And spit venom as you say it.'

Parker went downstairs and Saxon heard his voice clearly telling them that, 'There isn't a body so we don't need a pathologist,' followed by some remarks about demotion and traffic wardens. Parker did have a way with words when required.

Wednesday, June12, 8.30AM

Jake sat in the interview room, looking totally bewildered. A fixed expression of disbelief deeply etched on his face. His solicitor, Sarah Wright, looked cool and composed, apart from her hands clasped tightly on the desk. Saxon and Parker walked in and sat down in front of them. As he flicked the switch to start the tape recorder, his mobile phone started to ring. He stopped the tape and apologised, although Ms Wright was not pleased – showing her displeasure with an icy glare. Saxon chose to ignore her; she was young and inexperienced at glaring. He answered his phone.

He looked at Parker, who had sensed the seriousness of the call by the look on Saxon's face. He sat listening for some moments, taking notes. He thanked the caller and hung up.

"Sorry, I'm going to suspend this very short meeting for a while. Seems we have another body – in London again. I'm going to have to keep you on remand, while I take a look at the evidence... Have you been to London lately, Jake?'

Ms Wright put her hand on Jake's arm and said with a frown on her face. 'You don't have to answer any questions, bearing in mind the tape is not running and this is no longer a formal interview.'

Jake leant forward towards Saxon. 'You know I didn't do it, you know I'm not a killer, don't you?' He looked Saxon in the eye as he spoke.

'Jake, I've known you some time now, and I have to say you always struck me as being a completely sane sort of person. But a shrink told me recently that when I catch whoever it is committing these crimes he will appear completely normal. You fit that part of the profile. We have good strong evidence against you – the fact that you have no alibis for any of the killings, is in itself, very damning for you. If you are innocent, then it's downright incredible, I would say unheard of in criminal history.'

Saxon stood up and walked to the door, he turned back and looked towards Jake and his solicitor.

'I have to go and look at a body now. We'll continue this interview on Friday.'

Saxon and Parker drove to London and parked outside the house in Bottle Walk, where Mrs Lyons had discovered the body of Fabio Gerard. As usual, there were people in white overalls, taking photographs, and others lifting fingerprints and taking samples of almost everything. Saxon spoke to sergeants Brian Anderson and Jim Groves. They told him that Mrs Lyons, the cleaner, had returned after a few days off to find Monsieur Fabio Gerard lying there with an acute case of shortness of breath. A joke that Saxon didn't find at all funny at the time…later, maybe.

Saxon wandered around the room and muttered, 'Dog walkers and cleaning ladies, maybe they're the ones we should be after,' but no one heard him.

He stood in the middle of the room and addressed the team who were working the scene. 'Right, listen up, you lot. I don't want any mistakes; I know you are the best in the country. Probably in the known universe, come to think of it. But I have to tell you that we have a man in custody.'

A subdued cheer went up, mingled with a few shouts of 'Yes!'

'Okay, settle down, and remember, if we are to make the evidence stick, it has to be solid. I want no room for doubt. Understand? Good…get on with it, and find me something, if you can't find anything then for Christ's sake don't let anyone see you planting it.' There was a general grunt of approval from the team before they continued with their work.

Parker had located Mrs Lyons; she had fled next door to call the police, and drink tea to calm her nerves. Saxon found her in a state of near collapse, trembling and about to start demolishing a large glass of whisky. He stopped her – saying that he needed her to have a clear head while she answered his questions. She reluctantly agreed.

The neighbours, Mr and Mrs McCormack, a young married couple, sat in the corner on a sofa overawed by what was unfolding before them.

Saxon sat down beside Mrs Lyons and gently put his hand on hers. He spoke softly, hoping this would calm her down.

'Mrs Lyons, I know that this has been a terrible shock for you, but as usual in situations like this, questions have to be asked. Please tell me, in your own time, exactly how you left things next door. By that I mean, how was Fabio when you last saw him – did he seem edgy or different in any way?'

'I left here last Wednesday, just for a few days off. He seemed to be okay. Quite capable of looking after himself, he was. And, no, he didn't seem at all edgy; not at all, he was his normal self. He was such a lovely man, queer as hell but that didn't matter to me, I don't care what people get up to – nothing to do with me anyway.' She paused and gazed at the large whisky waiting to be of medicinal use to someone.

She added. 'Poor Chris, that's Chris with a "K", they are hairdressers you see – apparently you can do that with your name if you're a hairdresser. He's out of the country at the moment, on business in America; he's going to be so upset. Do you think I should phone him? He said I should call him if there were any problems.' She started to cry so Saxon handed her some tissues.

'Don't you worry about that, Mrs Lyons, we'll take care of it for you. Now, have you noticed anyone hanging around lately, or have you had callers saying that they are looking for someone who you have never heard of, for instance?'

She controlled her tears and offered Saxon the tissue she had used. He let her keep it.

'I wouldn't notice if there was someone watching from the street because of the bushes. You can't see through them during the summer because the leaves are too thick, and no one has called that I know of.'

'Okay, you are doing very well, Mrs Lyons. When you found Fabio, did you enter the house?'

'You must be kidding; I nearly wet myself when I saw him lying there. I opened the door and reached in to put the light on – I always do that in case there's someone behind the door. I've always done it, call me silly if you want, it's just a habit of mine.'

Saxon smiled at her. He was relieved that she hadn't entered the house. If only other people were more cautious, less chance of the crime scene being spoiled.

'I don't think you are silly, Mrs Lyons – I'm just glad that you stayed away from any evidence that may have been lying around.'

Jim Groves appeared in the doorway holding a sample bag containing a tape cassette. 'Found this wedged behind the door, Commander, it may be just a music tape but you never know.'

Mrs Lyons looked up with a puzzled frown on her face. 'I can assure you that if there isn't a label on it, then it doesn't belong to Kris. He's very methodical about things like that, and I wouldn't have left it on the floor. I'm a professional cleaner; I don't leave things lying around. I'm very particular about things like that, I'll have you know.'

Saxon stood up and walked towards Groves.

'Any prints on it?

'None, it's like new, sir.'

'Let's play it and see what delights it holds. Mr McCormack, do you have a tape machine that we can use for a moment?'

Mr McCormack took him to the hi-fi, and Saxon pushed the tape in and set it to play. Nothing happened for the first ten seconds, then the same mechanical voice as the Mancini message.

Dear Boss,
Me again. The policeman in the pub was a mistake, he should not have been there. He knew me and I had no choice but to kill him. I cannot be blamed. I am told what to do by the voice of the master. I have no control over what I am told. You can tell his family that he wasn't a fucking queer. I think he decided to go bounty hunting, and look for me on his own. A very foolish thing to do. It was not my fault. He walked in at the wrong moment. He was not meant to be next.

They stood in silence for a moment to make sure there was nothing else on the tape. Saxon rewound it and placed it back in the bag. He thanked Mrs Lyons and paid another brief visit to the crime scene, and then he and Parker drove back to Brighton with the tape.

They hardly spoke during the journey. Neither of them could remember such an eventful and stressful day.

Chapter 13

Thursday, June13, 7.20PM

Steve Tucker sauntered along the seafront with a smile on his face. He had several reasons to be happy. Jake Dalton had been arrested for murder – this made Jake a celebrity, which in turn made Tucker one too because he knew him; worked with him, no less.

Tucker was on his way to meet his friend Lee Fry, who was a small, bald and painfully thin man, unfortunately for him. Like Tucker, school had been a dreadful experience for Lee. Children being often quite cruel, the inevitable nickname was soon to rear its head, "Small Fry". As nicknames go this was not so bad, especially to the kids who were called "Shithead" or "Arse Face".

Fry didn't care about the other children; he was an only child and only really cared about number one. He still lived with his parents, who were now retired – living on a council housing estate on the north edge of Brighton. He had known Tucker for most of his life; they were in the same class at school and shared the same interests – sex, drugs and booze. Both of them were frequently hauled up in front of the headmaster, literally because they were incapable of walking – being either stoned out of their skulls or drunk.

Tucker was planning to meet Fry at a pub called the Old Ship. It was a "Goth" pub: you weren't allowed in unless you wore a combination of black or black, with the usual leather and silver rings, either through your ears, nose or nipples. The less visible piercings didn't count. The place was patronised by art and university students, and had a reputation for being a "hard" pub. But with modern youngsters, a fight usually constituted a bit of slapping and some bad language.

The hard reputation was gained during the 50s and 60s when gangs of Teddy Boys, Mods and Rockers fought their battles on the beach, briefly stopping to tank up in the pub. Then back to the beach to slash a few more of the enemy with a flick knife or flog them with a bicycle chain.

Tucker arrived to see people standing on the pavement drinking. The place was throbbing. This was heaven for Tucker – he saw it as a chance to squeeze through the mass of bodies to get to the bar. He thought to himself that an orgasm followed by a nice cool lager was what he needed after a long day "at the office" as he called it. However, this little pleasure of his was not without risk.

Tucker was well-known at this pub; the regulars didn't like the smell of him, and they, like the people he worked with, were naturally suspicious of him.

Tucker thrust his way through the mass of drinkers, attracting some shocked glances from almost every woman he came into contact with. A few of the men scowled at him as well. Possibly something to do with the way he used his groin. He was smirking by the time he got through.

He found Fry sitting in a corner on his own. Lee Fry was similar to Tucker in many ways – not physically, but they shared an almost identical IQ. Unfortunately for them, two low IQ's didn't make a genius. This was a fact that puzzled Fry from time to time.

He was born in Liverpool, but his parents moved south when he was seven years old; he was there long enough to pick up the accent. But he didn't remember much else. For years, he had listened to stories from his father about the early hard years back up north; he used it to get sympathy by stating that he never had the chances that other people had.

Apart from being stupid, his main handicap was drink. The planet earth didn't have enough of the stuff to satisfy his thirst. The one thing that slowed down his drinking was lack of coordination – due to drunkenness. His sexual preferences were similar to Tucker's, but only if money was due to change hands. He had several convictions for gross indecency. He viewed that as a rather unfortunate occupational hazard.

Tucker flopped into the seat next to Fry. They nodded to each other – not smiling, they were being cool and manly. To the disgust of the people around them, they blatantly eyed up the women nearest to their table. Until that is, the men who were with the women made it obvious that to continue would be dangerous for them, and could even have an effect on the style of wheelchair they would have to choose several weeks hence.

'Don't like this fuckin' place,' said Tucker, as he finished his pint noisily, slurping down the last dregs.

'What's wrong with it?' grunted Fry, looking at Tucker under heavy eyelids – he was at least four pints ahead of his friend.

'Fuckin' tarts aren't friendly.'

'They never are with you – wanker.'

'Why is that, Lee? I'm the same as anyone else, ain't I?' said Tucker, with genuine puzzlement in his voice.

'Yeah, mate, but you do stink a bit, don't ya?'

'I don't fuckin' stink, you drunken fucker, I 'ave a bath every now and then – even if I don't need it.'

'You stink of death, probably from where you work; but you stink of sweat all the time anyway. So the death stink adds to it, dunnit?' Fry wasn't exactly expecting an answer. And one was not forthcoming. He tried to explain further. 'I mean, no tart in her right mind is going to want some smelly git like you stinkin' of death an' sweat givin' her one an' slobberin' all over her, is she?'

'Bitches don't know what they're missing,' Tucker threw in, before forcing his way through the crowd to get another couple of pints.

They drank and smoked and openly leered until closing time and were the last to be asked to leave the pub. The landlord was firm but polite to them – after all, they, with their regular drinking, paid more than enough for his once-a-year trip to

Majorca. And though there were other regulars to the pub, these two were the fastest drinkers he had ever come across in his life.

They staggered from the pub to the beach, which was well lit. It was a full moon and, like children, they threw stones into the waves, then they threw them at each other until it hurt too much. A couple of times they misjudged the size of the waves as they broke on the beach, and their shoes filled up with water. Although the temperature of the air was high, the seawater, as usual around the coast of Britain, was not particularly warm.

When their feet became uncomfortable, they climbed up the beach to the sea wall, sat down, looked at the pier and smoked. The youth of Brighton was still out and about, couples walked on the beach holding hands and a few lay on the beach courting – a few had gone beyond that stage and were practicing egg fertilisation.

Tucker was the first to speak. 'I think I'm turnin' full-time normally sexualised – I've like started to notice strange things about meself. I don't fancy blokes any more. Know what I mean?'

'No,' said Fry looking the other way.

'What do you mean, no? You're fuckin' thick as pig shit, you are.'

Fry looked at his friend aghast. 'Me…thick, give me a fuckin' break. I remember when you bought that E tablet from the bloke in the disco… Steve, an M&M sweet turned sideways don't make it into an E tablet for Christ's sake. Twenty fuckin' quid for a sweet…no wonder he told you not to chew it – you'd have found the fuckin' peanut if you had, you bleedin' tosser. Anyway, I'm not thick, I'm dislaxtic – or somethin' like that, well, that's what they told me anyway. You've always been a bit bent you dick 'ed, you don't just get over it like that,' Fry said with a look of authority. 'It's not like guts ache yer daft git. Anyway, what's brought this on – your periods stopped or somethin'?'

'Funny man, bleedin' wanker,' said Tucker quietly, looking the other way, trying to cultivate an air of mystery by letting the smoke escape from his nostrils slowly. The effect was lost due to the fit of coughing it induced.

'There's a tart I work with, I think, no, what I mean is, she fancies me.'

'Oh yeah, and what makes you think that, you tosser?'

'Well, for starters, she don't complain about me as much as some of the others.' Tucker allowed himself a little smile at his joke.

'Melanie's 'er name, fuckin' good tits on 'er too. Someone I work with said she looked like a dead heat in a ziplin race – whatever that's supposed to mean. Are they big?'

'Are what big?' said Fry, not really interested.

'Ziplins or whatever the fuckers are called?'

'How the fuck am I supposed to know, you toss pot?' Fry said with a whine in his voice. 'Steve, she don't fancy you – why the fuck should she, you're just a stiff scrubber. That's all you do all fuckin' day, is scrub stiffs.'

Tucker started to sulk. He couldn't think of anything to say. He wanted to be cool. He wanted to crush Fry with his wit but a suitably damning reply eluded him. He gave up. Looking down at the beach, he let some drool drop from his continuously open mouth to the pebbles below.

He remained silent for some minutes – until the memory of why he was sulking faded into insignificance. It was one of his few redeeming features. He wasn't one to harbour a grudge. Then, suddenly with no warning, Tucker stood up and walked off.

Fry was startled. He wasn't used to unpredictable behaviour from Tucker. 'Where you going, Steve?' Fry called after him but Tucker didn't stop or even glance back.

Tucker crossed the road, bumping into a few people and banging his hand down hard on the roof of a passing car, causing the driver to stop and consider whether it was worth getting out and kicking him around the road for a while. But no chance –

Tucker had stalked off. By this time, Fry had decided that he didn't want to be left alone, so he ran after his friend and caught up with him after a couple of hundred yards.

'Well, tell me where you're going then?' whined Fry, having to run to keep up with him.

Tucker smirked. 'I'm going to see my Melanie…you can come as long as you keep the noise down.' Tucker's face took on a determined look and he quickened his pace.

'What are you talkin' about?' said Fry, amazed, even through the haze of alcohol. 'It's nearly one o'clock in the fuckin' mornin', she'll be in bed.' He had visions of Melanie, assuming she really existed, calling the police to complain about unwanted late-night callers.

Tucker turned to Fry, with a look of superiority on his greasy face. 'Don't you think I don't know that, you fuckwit? Of course, she'll be in bed, how else am I going to be able to see her at this time of night – fuck, I wish I was famous, then she'd want to come and see me, in the daytime as well I suppose.'

It dawned on Fry that the plan was to see the place where this Melanie lived and maybe try to look in through the window. So now, they would get done for prowling rather than causing a disturbance. A little incoherent voice in the back of his head tried to tell him this was not a good idea. But Fry wasn't really listening to his inner voices. Tucker was his friend, after all.

So Fry didn't answer, he just lit a couple of cigarettes and handed one to Tucker. They walked in companionable silence for ten minutes, ending up in School Terrace, which ran parallel to the seafront, up behind the hospital. At the end of the terrace, Tucker led Fry up a narrow passage leading to the back of the tall Victorian houses. At the end of the passage, Tucker turned to the right and gestured for Fry to be quiet. They walked for about fifty yards and Tucker pushed open a wooden door that took them into the back yard of one of the houses.

Up against the building stood a fire escape, which led up to the roof. It looked to be a bit rusty in places, but Tucker knew that basically it was secure. His confidence was growing by the minute.

Fry had to say something. He whispered, 'What are we doing here, Steve? We'll be right in the shit if we get caught.'

'Shut yer face. Melanie lives up there – an' we're going to see her – well I mean, I've seen her. I'm going to show her to you.' Tucker bent down to undo his laces.

Fry wasn't too keen on heights. 'I'm not sure I want to see her that badly. I mean, I'm sure she's really nice an' that, but let's fuck off, Steve, before we get in trouble,' he said in his most appealing tone of voice. 'If the police get me again, they're not gonna let me off with just a caution next time,' he whined.

Tucker was struggling with a knot.

Fry wasn't going to give up. 'Anyway, what do you mean "see her"? You think we're just going to climb up Mount fuckin' Everest here and knock on her window an' say, scuse me, Miss Melanie, wake up please, this little pervert what you work with wants to say hello an' show you to his friend at whatever fuckin' time it is in the fuckin' morning? Oh, and while you're standing up, please show us yer tits? Do me a fuckin' favour.'

Tucker clamped his hand over Fry's mouth. 'Shut yer fuckin' face. I've done this loads of times,' he hissed. 'She sleeps with the window open in the summer. All I do is look in through the window – she never wakes up. Now, just follow me an' don't say nothin', there's other bastards livin' here as well as her.'

Tucker took his hand away. Fry gasped in a lungful of clean air. Tucker didn't wait for a reply; he'd already taken his shoes off and put them against the wall. He started to climb the steps. He had to concentrate on keeping his mouth shut, although that was a struggle, given the extra oxygen needed for the climb.

Several of the other occupants had decided to keep their windows open due to the heat wave, so Tucker took extra care not to make a sound. Fry, being stupid and, as usual, quite incapable of making his own decisions, followed a few seconds later. Without the bright moonlight, the climb would have been tedious and a great deal more dangerous, but the light was strong enough for them to see the steps and tread more confidently.

Melanie's flat was on the top floor and, sure enough, her window was open. They crouched down either side of the window and Tucker gently lifted the blind. Melanie, however, was not in bed. She was in her sitting room quietly reading.

'She's not fuckin' there. Shit, she must be out,' cursed Tucker under his breath.

'Yeah, she's probably out with 'er real boyfriend, who's givin' 'er one up against some wall, right now.'

'Don't say that. I don't like it when people say things like that,' said Tucker, looking at Fry with real anger in his eyes.

Fry missed the message in his eyes and went on, 'Yeah I'll bet 'e's got 'er up against a wall somewhere, all groanin' and sweaty.'

Tucker could feel the anger and frustration rising fast. He pushed Fry in the face with the flat of his hand. 'Just you fuck off – she wouldn't do that, not my Melanie. Not while she's interested in me, that is.'

Fry shrugged, roughly pushing his hand away, and stood up. 'You need serious help, you do – I'm goin' 'ome, you do what ya want.'

Fry started to climb down the stairs, leaving Tucker to make decisions. Not an ideal situation. He sat down and thought for a while and slowly the idea crawled into his head that if Melanie was out, then he could creep into her bedroom and borrow some of her underwear. She would never guess that it was he who took them. As he grew more excited by the idea, the bolder he became.

The smell of her perfume wafting from the room made him tremble with anticipation, this combined with the element of danger was almost more than he could bear. The idea of her suddenly coming into the room, and seeing him there caused his already erect penis to shoot him in the groin as usual, somewhat earlier than expected. He fantasised himself throwing her on the bed, tearing her clothes off and giving her the best fuck she could have ever wished for. She would beg for more, but he would be manly and tell her to wait while he laid back and smoked. Just like in the movies.

Melanie finished her book; she was sleepy and the big decision to be made was – sofa, where she had been lying for the last three hours, or bed, which required much more effort. Bed won.

Tucker had his hands in her panty drawer as she walked in. She screamed when she saw the outline of a person against the moonlight which streamed into her bedroom. Tucker was relieved that she didn't stop to switch the light on. She ran one way and he ran the other. His flight through the window and back onto the fire escape almost ended in disaster for him. He banged violently into the railing, nearly toppling over the edge.

Melanie ran to the flat below, and hammered on the door until her neighbour woke and opened it. By the time he was on the phone to the police, Tucker was heading back to the beach where he decided to lay low until all the sirens stopped. He took out his mobile phone and called Fry.

'Lee,' Tucker panted down the phone, 'I fucked up, I need some 'elp, where are you?'

'I'm nearly at me pad – what happened, you toss pot?' Fry laughed.

'Fuckin' bitch walked in as I was standin' in 'er room, didn't she,' he gasped.

'Oh, what happened to "my Melanie" then? Now she's a fuckin' bitch,' Fry teased.

'I don't think she saw me, cos she never put the lights on – so I legged it down the fire escape and now there's pigs all over the place. I need somewhere to stay for the night so I got an alibi,' Tucker said in a grovelling tone.

'No, don't even think it, you can't come 'ere, you wanker. I'll meet you by the old West Pier. I don't want you to be seen arriving here at this time of night. I'll bring a few cans and if anyone asks, we can say we were there all night.'

Twenty minutes later Fry found Tucker huddled in the doorway of an old derelict fish and chip stall. The West Pier was crumbling into the sea and most of the surrounding amusement stalls and small souvenir shops had failed because of it. The majority of tourists to Brighton gathered around the Palace Pier, which was still a thriving enterprise. The only reason to look at the old pier was to see the starlings, as thousands flocked above it at sunset.

Fry handed Tucker a couple of six-packs, and said, 'Follow me, dick 'ed.'

Slowly, they climbed the steps from the lower part of the promenade up to the street level. After a few minutes of standing by the barred gate to the pier – trying not to look suspicious, they squeezed through a hole in the barbed wire.

Fry had been there many times. Usually to smoke a few joints, but when he was younger, to sniff glue. The journey to Fry's little den of vice was precarious – a large percent of the floor was missing, and the sky was visible in many places.

More imaginative people would have heard the echo of the past, the sounds of holidaymakers, singing to the tune of a great Wurlitzer or just tapping their feet to a brass band. The atmosphere was wasted on them. They just walked.

Tucker followed behind, carefully treading in the same places as Fry – the last thing he wanted to do was to fall through the floor. If he fell, and survived the fall, the water would finish him off. He was to swimming, what Vlad the Impaler was to political correctness. Fry took Tucker to a corner and they both sat on an old bench and started to drink.

'We ought to stay here for a while, at least until the pigs go back to the piggery,' said Fry, trying to appear worldly. 'They never come here. Fuckin' good place this, it's a bit spooky at first, but you get used to it.'

Tucker didn't respond; he just sat looking insecure. After an hour, they were both very drunk, but the adrenalin was still coursing through them. They discussed the merits of taking a stroll together along the seafront and maybe rolling some innocent bystander for a bit of cash. Serve them right for being out at that time of the night. The idea seemed good enough and they set off along the pier. The fact that he was so drunk prevented Tucker from feeling the pain he inflicted on himself as his leg suddenly disappeared into the void beneath the pier. Blood trickled down from a gash below his left knee, but he ignored it and started to laugh hysterically.

A few minutes later, they emerged, falling through the barbed wire and turning left to walk in the direction of Hove.

They didn't have to go far before they saw a potential victim. Sitting in one of the wind shelters was a man. He had his feet on the seat, with his knees drawn up in front of his face and his head resting on his hands. His black baseball cap covered his face. He seemed to be quite small, but the light was not good, and his clothing was dark – making him difficult to judge size-wise. Fry always carried a small knife, although he had never actually used it on anyone, it was more to give him a sense of security.

They decided that the best way to handle the mugging was for the pair of them to jump the guy, and hold his hat down over his eyes. They would then let him have a quick look at the knife, take his wallet and run. They split up and approached the man from both sides. Fry grabbed the back of his head and pushed his cap over his eyes, as planned. Tucker said nothing; he merely stood close to the man with the intention of keeping him on the bench.

It didn't work. The man sprang to his feet. He was much bigger than they had estimated – much bigger, and he was strong. In a flash, he grabbed them both by the back of their necks, squeezing so tightly that neither of them could utter a sound, and ran pushing them towards the railings. His strength, combined with the precision of his grip on a particular nerve, overpowered them immediately.

With the speed they were running, all it took was a gentle push to launch them over the railing headfirst to the lower pavement thirty feet below. The last sound they heard was a voice that one of them thought he recognised, a second before their skulls smashed into the concrete below. 'Leave the planet, scum.'

Friday June 14, Brighton Seafront, 5.30AM

Saxon dipped under the police tape and walked over to Parker who had been at the crime scene for thirty minutes already. They nodded to each other, then, Saxon lifted the sheet that covered, first Tucker then Fry. He grimaced at the injuries. Parker handed him one of the plastic cups of coffee he had been holding.

'One of them looks familiar, Parker. Who is he?' he said trying to stifle a yawn.

'The ugly one, is one Steven Tucker, he's an attendant at the mortuary – or was, I should say. The uglier one is Lee Fry – small-time crook, rent boy, several convictions for mugging, burglary, buggery and thuggery; he's known for carrying a knife occasionally. There is a knife over there, and I would say that by the position of it, it came from his hand when he made contact with the planet.'

Saxon sipped his coffee, 'What about Tucker, what do we know about him?'

Parker removed his jacket and draped it over the edge of a small rowing boat, which had been drawn up the beach. 'Tucker is a bit more interesting – like Fry he was bisexual, but he never charged for his services. He is well-known by the local police for basically being a pervert and a pain in the arse. Bit of a Peeping Tom – he was barred from most of the pubs in Brighton for lewd and inappropriate behaviour. Educationally sub-normal, or I suppose I should say, educationally challenged. There was something interesting in his pocket, sir.' Parker took a plastic bag from one of the SOCOs. 'One pair of ladies' pants. This is where it gets even more interesting – last night a call came in that a girl living in School Terrace reported a prowler in her flat. She was adamant that the prowler took a pair of her knickers from her bedroom, counted them I suppose.'

Saxon felt the warm glow of pride in his sergeant. He had obviously been busy since the crack of dawn. 'Okay, Parker, but what has that, got to do with this? They could be his girlfriend's pants, maybe he carries them with him for good luck – believe me, people do stranger things.'

'The fascinating bit, sir, is that, one: the girl worked with Tucker. Two: Tucker was bisexual, Fry was the same, and now they are both dead. Three: Jake works at the mortuary.'

Saxon cut in. 'It does seem to be centring on the mortuary. But I can't for the life of me, understand why.' He paused, and added, 'Jake, as we both know, is in custody and couldn't have done this. So the question has to be – were these two killed by a new fresh killer, or was it the old one, who has possibly done an excellent job of framing someone else?' He walked over to the two bodies. 'How certain are you that these two didn't have a fight up there and just topple over the edge?'

'It's the distance, sir, they are too far from the wall to have just fallen – they flew some distance as you can see, and what's more, they are too far apart. If they were fighting, they would be closer together.'

Saxon had surmised the scenario already. He wanted Parker to come up with the same theory. 'Did the girl identify Tucker as the perv who nicked her knickers?'

'No, sir, she only caught a glimpse of him, the light was off and he was out through the window as soon as she walked in on him,' said Parker, taking another sip of coffee.

Saxon looked up to the railings at the crowd of people who

had gathered. He gestured to a constable to move them on. 'What about a time of death, have we got one yet?'

'Yes, about two hours ago, although it's a bit tricky to tell in these temperatures, according to Dr Clarke, who has been and gone,' Parker said, tipping his coffee on the beach.

Saxon and Parker climbed the steps to the upper promenade.

'Parker, get some PCs and talk to the security people in all of these hotels and find out if any of them have CCTV cameras that would cover this area. Also, get on to traffic; there's a chance that one of the road cameras might have picked something up.'

Saxon strode off calling back to Parker, 'Right, Parker, I think it's time we finished our interview with Jake Dalton, let's go and wake him up.'

Friday, June 14, Brighton Police Station, 7.00AM

Jake was already awake. He had not slept well since he was arrested. To be incarcerated, knowing that you are innocent, had to rank among the top three most frustrating situations a human being may have to endure. He had his own theories of why it had happened to him of all people. Life had been too easy for him for the major part of his life.

His parents were wealthy, which in turn gave him wealth. The higher-than-average intelligence genes had been successfully handed over to him in the process of cell division. Jake was healthy, strong and handsome. The shit had to hit the fan one day. That day, as far as he was concerned, had come with a long weekend attached.

When Saxon appeared at his cell door, Jake was pleased. At least it gave him the chance to have his say, and he knew that Saxon was a reasonable man and would listen with an open mind. He also knew that if it was up to Superintendent Mitchell, the key to the cell would have been thrown away days ago – if the evidence was there, that would do for Mitchell – even if he thought it was not quite kosher.

Saxon entered the cell; he sat on the end of the bunk and proceeded to tell Jake about the events of the morning. Parker stood leaning on the doorframe with his arms folded. When Saxon finished, Jake said something, which finally made him realise that Jake was not guilty of murder.

'Paul, there are elements in this morning's murders that seem to connect a group of individuals, who just happen to work in the same place – it doesn't prove anything much. It certainly doesn't conclusively prove that I'm innocent of the other murders. Unfortunately,' he added with a half-smile.

Saxon shifted about uncomfortably. He wanted to let Jake go, knowing deep down that he was innocent. Having him there was a complete waste of time.

'Right, Jake,' Saxon said standing up, 'let's get your Ms Wright in, and have a formal interview for the record. Then I'll decide what to do.' He smiled at Jake and stopped at the cell door. Turning, he said, 'Pack your bags, Jake; I think you'll be going home later.'

Sarah Wright arrived with her usual businesslike manner, with a smattering of rudeness thrown in for good measure. Most of the officers who came in contact with her, held the opinion that she had seen too many crime thrillers on the television, and was behaving in the way that a brief was supposed to. None of them could be bothered to tell her that this was real life and all she had to do to get good service was to be polite.

Saxon was called the minute she arrived. He talked with her in the interview room while Jake was brought up from his cell. Parker sat next to him and sipped tea. Saxon outlined his thoughts to Ms Wright; she was shocked, but pleased to hear what he said.

'Commander Saxon, you surprise me…I don't understand – the evidence, according to you, is so strong. Why on earth are you letting my client go? Could it be that you are a new breed of policeman, one who is capable of thinking for himself? I'm impressed.' She smiled sweetly, adding, 'You're not a bad bloke for a copper.'

Saxon blushed, and smiled back. 'Thanks; I just know he didn't do it. I usually trust my instincts and they haven't let me down so far. I'm just going to ask him a few questions and then he's a free man.'

Jake was brought into the cell. He took his place at the table.

'Jake, good morning, I want to ask you about the burglary – it says here on the incident sheet that personal items were taken. Tell me about it in as much detail as you can remember.'

Jake took a deep breath. 'I arrived home at about twenty past nine. The first thing that struck me as strange was the fact that my front door was open, but not forced. The lock had been either picked or the burglar had a key. You don't need me to tell you, that kids would do that – they'd force it open. Then there's the state of the place. Why didn't James my next-door neighbour hear anything?

'I'll tell you why, whoever smashed up the place, did it carefully, and they didn't leave any fingerprints. Kids who do that sort of thing aren't that bright, they would have left prints all over the place. I'm sure this is a set-up, Paul. Someone's out to get me.'

Saxon leant back in his chair and blew air noisily through his mouth, then meshed his fingers behind his head. After a pause, he said, 'It struck me as strange that there was no evidence at all, not even one hair in any of the victims' hands and nothing under their fingernails. Until after you were burgled, that is – then suddenly bits and pieces of you started turning up all over the place. Okay, this is the way I see it…' He paused. 'It seems pretty obvious to me that Mr Killer broke into your apartment with the sole purpose of gathering a few items of clothing, and I see on the list, a hairbrush was taken, so that he could extract samples to plant on his victims, thus framing you. Now, the question is who would want to do this to you. Any ideas?'

'None that I can think of at this particular moment, but whoever it is knows about forensics,' said Jake, knowing he had stated something obvious.

Parker stood up and removed his jacket, and added. 'But with all the crime shows on the telly, anybody with a bit of intelligence has a rudimentary understanding of forensics. Everyone surely knows that DNA can be extracted from hair and skin, and stuff like that, and that if we find fibres at a crime scene then we can match them to wherever and whatever. Don't have to be a rocket scientist to digest that, do you?'

Saxon looked squarely at Jake. 'Tell me what you know about Steven Tucker.'

'You can't be serious – the bloke was a complete idiot. He worked in the same place as me, as an attendant and cleaner down at the mortuary. He would have been totally incapable of planning a crime that involved anything more complex than grabbing and running.'

'There was another body found near his. A young man named Lee Fry – does the name ring any bells?'

Jake shrugged. 'Never heard of him. Do you think they were bumped off by the person who's trying to set me up?'

'I can't say, because I simply don't know. They were both bisexual and that appears to be the only connection at this time. It could merely be a coincidence. Back to my original question – are you sure that there isn't someone way back in your past who's got it in for you?'

Jake sighed. 'Sorry, but there is no one that I can think of – I guess I'm just too good to be true.' He smiled, and glanced at Sarah Wright, who had sat through the entire conversation without saying a word, and she was smiling too – a lingering smile that kept his attention longer than usual.

While Jake was preparing to leave the police station, Saxon organised STI to follow him for the next week – as much for his own protection as to check on his movements. Saxon knew he wasn't a killer but it wouldn't hurt to be doubly sure.

Superintendent Mitchell was not too happy to hear of Jake's release, but being a creep, he argued for the standard amount of creeping time, and then he eventually conceded and was happy to just obey orders.

Jake had no idea that he was being watched. The STI department were so skilful at their trade, that Jake never realised that two men suddenly occupied the empty apartment opposite his, with a fancy camera and a taste for fast food. And whenever he drove anywhere, the cars following him were rotated, so that if he looked in his rear-view mirror, the same car would never appear more than once. Since the death of PC Lucas – STI were trying even harder this time.

Parker walked around the office fanning himself with a few sheets of paper, moaning about the high temperature. 'They say the weather is going to break soon, sir. A good downpour, that's what we need. It'll freshen everything up.'

Saxon was reading, he stopped and looked up at his sergeant.

'Thanks, Parker, meteorology later, crime now if you don't mind. I don't like it, Parker, we appear to be back at square one again. I feel as though we are sitting around waiting for another body to fall out of a cupboard.'

Parker's mobile rang and he listened for a minute and mumbled a thanks and hang up. 'That was Sergeant Groves. Apparently Judge Mancini, as expected, presided over hundreds of cases over the past five years – only seriously threatened once, and that person is still banged up. But wait for it. He was gay.'

Saxon frowned, 'Why aren't I surprised?'

The phone rang and Parker answered it after one ring. He turned to look at Saxon with an intense expression, becoming more serious as the seconds ticked by. 'When did this happen?' Followed by, 'Are you sure it was him – do we have a positive ID on that? Good.' Then there was a long pause, until Parker said, 'Okay, keep me updated on this – thanks.' He hung up the phone and sat down.

'Keith Jenner, Mr Charm himself, has knifed a farmer for driving his tractor too slowly along the lane outside Anvil Wood House. According to Sergeant Dowling, Jenner pulled out from the house into the lane, the driver of the tractor just managed to nip in front of him. There were two people on the tractor, anyway Jenner followed for about a mile beeping his horn and flashing his lights.

'When they came to the junction with the Cookbridge Road, Jenner jumped out of his Jaguar and started swearing at the farmer. Apparently the farmer swore back. Jenner went to the boot of his car and produced a baseball bat and a carving knife, and wait for it – a pistol. Not the subtlest of people is he? Anyway, he stabbed the driver of the tractor, after beating him about the head – then he hit the other chap several times, but didn't hang around to knife him. Nice of him.'

Saxon sat slightly stunned. 'What about the driver of the tractor – what's his condition?'

'Touch and go at the moment. Not much hope.'

Dowling knocked on the door and entered without waiting for a reply. 'They've spotted him, sir, we've got a helicopter following him, and he's heading for Newhaven.'

Saxon jumped to his feet. 'Come on, Parker, I want to be in on this one.' Parker was tall, and considered himself to be a fast runner, but he had a problem keeping up with Saxon. As they dashed through the police station, they attracted a certain amount of attention – nobody had ever seen a commander run before.

Saxon gunned the engine of his Land Rover as Parker reached out of the passenger window and attached the magnetic blue light to the roof. He then picked up the microphone and told the control room to patch the helicopter through to their car. Saxon was a fully-qualified pursuit driver and quickly pulled out from the police car park into the stream of traffic. Parker switched on the siren, causing a great swathe to open up before them.

The drive along the A259 to Newhaven was fast, Saxon pushed the Land Rover close to the limit. The V8 engine was capable of greater speeds, but unfortunately, the road planners hadn't allowed for police chases. They had built roundabouts, which Saxon considered driving over to save time, but he had an ingrained respect for the law and couldn't bring himself to do it.

The running commentary from the helicopter gave them a blow-by-blow account of what Jenner was demolishing in his bid to escape. So far, he hadn't run anyone over, but the police were aware that this could happen at any time. If the situation warranted it then the tactics they could use would be as deadly as a police marksman. They would drive him off the road and over a cliff if necessary.

As Saxon and Parker approached the town centre, they asked the helicopter pilot for a precise location of Jenner's car. He told them Jenner was heading alongside the river, opposite the ferry terminal, and that there were two patrol cars chasing him and an armed-response unit. Saxon checked his mirror – nothing behind him was moving. Most of the drivers in Newhaven realised that something big was going on and had pulled over to the side of the road. By this time almost every squad car of the East Sussex police, was heading for Newhaven town. Saxon realised that he was travelling in the wrong direction and did a spectacular handbrake turn and went the wrong way around the one-way system. 'So, let them arrest me,' he muttered under his breath.

He drove over a traffic island and sped along the riverside road. Ahead, he saw the helicopter hovering over Jenner. 'Gotcha,' said Parker, more than ready for a little action. Saxon had to slow down; the road was narrow, one mistake could send them skidding to the left, ending up in the river. To their right were small boathouses, made of concrete.

'I don't know why, sir, but he's heading for the beach. There's nowhere to go this way. Either he doesn't know Newhaven or he's panicked and gone the wrong way.' Parker had his hand ready to release his seatbelt the second they came to a halt.

Jenner cursed himself and slammed on his brakes the moment he realised that he had made a mistake. The road had literally come to an end. Some men who were standing on the edge of the harbour, fishing, turned to complain about the gravel that his car sent flying at them, but backed away when they realised that the helicopter hovering overhead was very much to do with him. He found himself in a large rough-surfaced car park with a few small untidy souvenir shops. On one side was the English Channel and the other side, chalk cliffs. Down the far end of the car park, there was a concrete pier, at least four hundred yards long, that stretched out into the Channel. There was nowhere else to go. It would delay the inevitable and give him time to think.

He slammed his Jag into gear and raced to the pier.

Once there, he jumped from his car. Leaving the door wide open, he ran as fast as his weight would allow. People who were fishing off the pier watched in stunned disbelief at the events unfolding around them. The helicopter hovered low, as the pilot spoke through a loudspeaker, telling everyone to vacate the pier immediately. Most of the fishermen complied when they noticed the pistol in his hand.

As Jenner worked his way along the pier, people waited for him to pass them, and then they made their way back to the car park. Except one, and as Saxon said later, 'There always has to be one who thinks he's Bruce Bloody Lee.'

This particular man, who had fished from the same spot for the last twenty years, fancied himself as a bit of a martial artist. Even Jenner paused in amazement as the hapless man attempted to disarm him with a flying kick. He sailed through the air past him, screaming something that sounded vaguely Chinese, a second before he landed in the sea.

Saxon stopped his car next to Jenner's. The armed-response

unit arrived seconds later – Saxon and Parker signed for a weapon each, they donned bullet-proof vests, attached earpiece radio microphones and started to slowly follow Jenner along the pier. Flanked by two marksmen as they walked, they kept a wary eye on Jenner who was backing away and stumbling occasionally. The helicopter pilot positioned his aircraft at the end of the pier – hoping to make it plain to Jenner that there was nowhere to go. The pilot repeatedly broadcast a message, warning Jenner that there were armed police approaching him, and ordered him to put down his weapon and to lie down on the ground.

Jenner chose to ignore the warning and continued to make his way further along the pier. By the time he reached the end, all of the anglers had managed to get to safety. The helicopter moved further away in case Jenner decided to empty his gun in their direction – they were unable to land on the pier because of its irregular shape.

Saxon put up his hand to stop the officers either side of him and called to Jenner.

'Keith, don't you think it's time to stop now. I'd hate to sound like one of those cops on the television – but there really isn't anywhere for you to go. Why don't we all go back to Brighton and have a talk about this?'

Jenner looked around, breathing heavily through his mouth and wiping the sweat off his forehead with his shirtsleeve. He continually pointed his gun at the four policemen before him one after the other. Parker spoke as he stared into Jenner's eyes along the barrel of his gun. 'Nobody's been seriously injured yet, Keith. I've heard that the farmer you stabbed is okay – just a flesh wound. Now is the time to call it a day – but if you continue to point that thing at us, someone is going to lose their nerve, and believe me these officers will shoot to kill.'

Jenner backed away a few more steps. Saxon lowered his gun slightly – not taking his eyes off Jenner for a second. Jenner turned to look at the helicopter, which had moved even further away to ensure that the people on the ground could hear what each other were saying. Saxon could see that Jenner was starting to breathe more slowly. As much as he disliked him, he didn't want him dead, he wanted information. There had to be a reason why Jenner became so agitated as he left Anvil Wood House.

The radio Saxon was wearing crackled into life, and he got the message that the tractor driver was dead. Saxon decided to try another tactic.

'Keith, look at me, have you got any children?'

Jenner seemed surprised at the question. The situation he found himself in had thrown him mentally and physically. He seemed to be unable to comprehend where he was and what he was doing; he even looked at the gun in his hand from time to time as if it was nothing to do with him. It took him a good twenty seconds before he managed to utter any words.

'Two, I've got two – two boys. Why, what the fuck's it got to do with you?'

'It isn't about me, Keith. What are they going to do if you are killed? We should end this now – sure, you've made some big trouble for yourself, but at least nobody's been seriously hurt up to now.' Saxon took a few steps closer, but stopped dead when Jenner suddenly put the gun into his mouth. 'Keith,' he shouted, 'get wise for once – what are your children going to think of you when they hear about this on the television. What will happen to them at school when all the other kids take the piss about their dad blowing his head off? Do you want that to happen to them? I don't think you do – you're not that sort of bloke are you, Keith?'

Jenner held the gun in his mouth for what seemed like an eternity, and then slowly he removed it and gazed at it with a look of disbelief as he pointed it at the ground.

Parker walked forward, still pointing his gun at Jenner's chest. Gently, but with a firm tone he told Jenner to put the gun on the ground and then to take three steps back. Jenner complied. The two armed-response officers quickly moved forward, pulled Jenner to his knees and then flat on his face, and handcuffed him.

Saxon stood in front of him as he was helped to his feet. 'Keith Jenner, I am arresting you for murder. You do not have to say anything. But it may harm your defence if you do not mention, when questioned, something which you later rely on in court. Anything you do say may be given in evidence. Do you understand?'

Jenner's jaw dropped. 'But you said he was okay – you fuckin' lied you bastard.'

'Sure did,' said Saxon. 'But I can live with that – not really as serious as murder though, is it?'

The solicitor representing Jenner was late. Saxon was irritated by the time he turned up. He didn't seem to fit the usual mould that solicitors seemed to pop out of. To Saxon, Mr Christian Haines was more barrister material. He seemed to be a bit grand – even stately. As usual, he spent some time with Jenner before the interview was started.

An hour after Jenner was brought into the police station and processed in the usual way of photographs and dabs, he was taken to the interview room. Saxon left him sitting there long enough with his solicitor to become even more apprehensive than normal.

Eventually, after Saxon decided that Jenner had simmered enough, he strode in with Parker following behind. He sat and faced Jenner but did not look directly at him – he sat in silence reading from a file on the table in front of them.

Haines became agitated and started to drum his fingers on the table. 'Oh really, Commander Saxon, can we make some progress here. I don't think these delaying tactics are really necessary.'

Saxon ignored him for another minute, and then he suddenly looked up. 'Okay, Jenner, for your information the man you murdered this morning was married, with three grown-up children, and two grandchildren,' Saxon said, withholding his emotions as much as he was able.

'That was a mistake – an accident, I didn't mean to do it.' Jenner was looking down at the table in front of him, sounding like a spoilt child.

Saxon slid out a sheet of paper that had been hidden inside a folder on the table. 'Says here that Mr Philip Barnard – that's the name of the gentleman you murdered this morning, in case you didn't know that – had been hit several times about the head, with a baseball bat, and then stabbed with a large carving knife. I see here,' he paused while he read the sheet again, 'that you stabbed him twice in the chest. Now, correct me if I'm wrong, but that doesn't sound much like an accident to me.' Saxon raised his voice, 'Once, maybe we would have just slapped your wrist and sent you home – but no, that wasn't enough for you was it? You just had to make sure the poor sod was dead didn't you?'

Haines put up his hand and glared at Saxon. 'I don't think we need to shout, do we, Commander?'

Saxon didn't take his eyes off Jenner. 'Answer the question please.'

'He got in the way,' mumbled Jenner, sullenly.

'He got in the way – I see, and did the other gentleman, Mr Varnham, also get in the way?'

'I lost my temper. I do that sometimes – I just can't control myself when I blow.'

Saxon managed to calm himself. 'Why were you in such a hurry when you left the house? You know the lane is narrow and has a lot of dangerous corners. Why the big rush?'

Haines moved closer to Jenner and whispered in his ear. 'You don't have to say a word, Mr Jenner.'

Saxon threw in a passing comment. 'Oh, by the way, we know that you were looking for something – but we found it days ago.'

'You found the book?' replied Jenner quickly.

Saxon's trick had paid off. 'So, that's what this is all about, the book. Oh yes, and we are steadily but surely going through all of the names, one by one.'

Jenner looked across at Saxon with a knowing look. 'If you've got the book, you won't need me to tell you any more, will you?'

Saxon, still trying not to give away the fact that he didn't know fully what the names in the book represented, added, 'It will help your defence if you cooperate more.'

Jenner sat back and folded his arms. 'You've got no fuckin' idea what the book is all about – you think it's just a load of names, don't you?'

Saxon didn't respond.

'You and your sister were in it together, weren't you?' added Parker, with even more bluff.

Saxon continued to use the same tactics. 'We know that you and Barbara were not as estranged as you would want us to think. We found plenty of evidence in the house – and then there's the fact that you have been watched for the last six months, and I suppose I should add... Well, no maybe I will keep that bit of information to myself, because if you refuse to help us, I can bring it up in court and the jury will not be at all lenient. You'll go down for a very long time – and Liz, your slag, as you so politely call her, will probably go off with some other thug.'

Haines, who was making notes, paused and threw his pen down.

'I really must protest, I don't think that sort of attitude is called for, do you, Commander?' Saxon didn't answer.

Jenner turned to his solicitor, and they conducted a whispering session for about a minute. Parker leant over towards the tape recorder. 'For the record, Mr Jenner is whispering to Mr Haines.' Then he looked at them both as if to infer that it was not permitted.

Saxon started to drum his fingers on the table. 'Please can we get a move on? If you wish to confer with your client, Mr Haines, then we can stop the interview for half an hour and resume when you have got yourself up to speed.' He knew that would hurt.

Haines showed no emotion. 'Commander, I will take you up on the offer – half an hour it is then.'

Saxon walked out of the room, leaving Parker to make the relevant comments to the tape recorder. He then followed Saxon and found him waiting along the corridor.

They walked out onto the fire escape and found a shady spot. Saxon smiled and gently punched Parker on the shoulder. 'Good move, Parker; I think you have the makings of a fine detective.' Parker, not quite realising what the compliment was for, took out his cigarettes and offered one to Saxon – who took it eagerly. There was a moment of silence as they topped up their nicotine levels. Then Parker had to speak.

'Which bit, precisely was the good move, sir?' he said hesitantly.

'Don't be a twit – the bit about him and his sister, being in it together. I must admit, that angle hadn't occurred to me…' he paused, '…yet, at least. Anyway, he now thinks we know a lot more than we do. In fact, let's face it, Parker, we know sod all. Let's keep bluffing – he may end up telling us everything, whatever everything is.'

'What do you suppose they're planning in there, sir, maybe a plea?'

'If they are, then they won't get far. That bastard in there murdered a man because he was driving his tractor too slowly down a country lane. He's going down for murder. We can pretend to go along with the idea of him taking a lesser charge, but however we do it, Shithead is going to be off the streets for a long time.'

They returned to the interview room. Jenner and Haines were shouting at each other. Saxon's appearance was enough to make them stop. Parker moved to start the tape. Haines asked him to wait a second or two, and then looked over the top of his glasses.

'Commander Saxon, before we make this interview formal,

my client is willing to give you as much information as he is able. He also regrets greatly the events of earlier today and feels that he is in need of psychiatric treatment to help him curb these uncontrollable outbursts of temper. Mr Jenner has remarked to me that his memory of what happened this morning is already becoming a bit of a blur. Therefore, if a plea of second-degree murder, on the grounds of diminished responsibility were to be accepted, then he would benefit more from the justice system if he was committed to a secure hospital where he could receive treatment.'

Jenner looked up at Saxon with pleading eyes. Saxon half smiled as if he was sympathetic to him. But shook his head slowly, giving the impression that with a little more persuasion he may be tempted to change his mind.

'Mr Haines, you of all people should know I can't go around making that kind of promise. Besides, your client may just tell us everything we already know. He probably can't help us very much at all. Now, I think we should stop all this time wasting and get on with the interview before everything becomes a total blur, don't you?'

Jenner had started to shift around in his seat as he saw his chance of avoiding prison floating out through the window.

'Wait,' said Jenner quietly, 'I'll tell you everything.'

Saxon leant forward and cupped his hand as if he were slightly deaf. 'I'm sorry, I didn't quite hear you.'

Jenner increased the volume. 'I said, I'll tell you everything you want to know, but I need guarantees.'

'You are in no position to ask for anything, Jenner, or have the events of this morning blurred into total insignificance? If you help us, we can make recommendations, but that's all. We'll see what we can do if you help us sufficiently – do you understand? We can only do so much, but you'll be in a better position if you cooperate fully. Now let's get moving,' he said sternly.

Parker flicked the switch, and he and Saxon sat back to listen.

They waited for Jenner to compose himself. 'Well, first of all Barbara and I met up once every two months for the handover of the stuff.'

Saxon looked up. 'Stuff, what stuff. Please be specific for the tape please?' he said, gesturing towards the recorder.

'The drugs – coke mostly, some grass but some shit as well, lots of E, in fact, fuckin' shedloads of the stuff. A friend of hers gets it from another friend. He's got a small fishin' boat. It gets passed from boat to boat out in the Channel, so if one of them was checked by Customs and Excise, chances was that by that time, the stuff – the drugs, would have been passed to another boat. It was wrapped in heat-sealed plastic bags, which were wrapped in even more bags, lots of them anyway, and they was washed each time, it's done like that so the sniffer dogs can't even tell if the stuff 's been on the boat in the fuckin' first place.'

Saxon couldn't help smiling. In one day, he had caught a murderer and stopped a fairly substantial drug route into the country. 'Of course, you can supply me with names, Mr Jenner?'

'Only one – the bloke who owns the boat, Alan Turner, I never heard any other ones.'

Saxon scribbled the question: "Find out if the drug squad knows anything about this", on a piece of paper and slid it to Parker. He nodded to acknowledge it, got up and left the room.

Saxon continued, 'I thought you hated your sister.'

'I had to make you lot think I had nothin' to do with 'er, didn't I? For all I knew, you might 'ave been on my arse.' Jenner was sweating heavily, sending splashes across the table every time he shook his head. Saxon slid his seat backwards – out of range.

'What quantities of drugs are we talking about?'

'As much as you can get in a horse box – one of them double ones. You know the ones what takes two horses.'

'So then, what happened after your sister picked up the drugs from her fisherman friend? Did she distribute any of the stuff, or was that one of your little hobbies?' Saxon tried in vain to hold back the sarcasm.

'She supplied some to 'er friends. You wouldn't believe how many so-called respectable people are users, believe me. I picked up most of it and took it up to London. Don't ask me for any names – if I tell you, I'm as good as dead.'

Saxon decided to leave that little task to the drug squad. 'So tell me, why the rush this morning, why were you in such a hurry to leave Anvil Wood House?'

'Barbara had a pile of money for me that I was supposed to pay the dealer in London with. It has to be in the house somewhere, but I looked everywhere and I couldn't fuckin' find it. I was frightened when I left the house and I was seriously thinkin' about doing a runner. If you owe these people money and you don't come up with the dosh, they kill you. Simple as that.'

Parker entered the room and asked Saxon to follow him out into the corridor. Saxon suspended the interview, telling Haines that he would be back in a few minutes. Parker was looking pleased as he gave Saxon his news. 'Drug squad have no information regarding this at all. They had absolutely no idea what I was talking about, and they were, understandably a bit cagey at first, wanting to know everything now. But I told them it was early days yet and when we have more information, we'll get back to them.'

'Good, they can't have him until I've finished with the bastard. Then they can do whatever they want with him.'

They returned to the interview room. Saxon started the questions. 'Does the name Jake Dalton mean anything to you?'

'No, never 'eard of him. Should I 'ave?'

'How about Clive Marks, he's a doctor?'

'Now you mention it, yeah, 'is name rings bells. Babs was always sayin' that she mustn't forget to get his stuff to 'im on time, otherwise he got really pissed off.'

Saxon struggled to hide his glee. 'Did Barbara ever say why

Dr Marks needed drugs?'

'Yeah…now you mention it – somethin' about some of his patients needed shit…you know, cannabis for muscle problems. I think it was Muscular Sclur… Sclera… fuck it, I don't know how you say the bleedin' word.'

Saxon said nothing. *I don't think I'll be pursuing that one then.*

'What about Gertraud Bishop – ever heard of her?'

'Nah.'

'Christopher Janson?'

'Yeah, I heard 'er talk about 'im.'

'In what context?'

'What? I don't understand.'

'In what way did she talk about Christopher Janson?'

'Why didn't you say that in the first place? She just said that he told 'er that he was hoardin' the drugs she sold him so that if he got cancer or somethin' like that, he was going to top 'imself with it.'

'Did your sister's friend Poppy have any idea what was going on?'

'Not a fuckin' clue – shit for brains that one, I can tell you. You see, most of the drugs never got to Babs' house – we transferred it all to one of my vans in a lane somewhere in Sussex. Daft bitch didn't know what planet she was on half the time. Couldn't stand the cow.'

Saxon stopped him. 'I'm not interested in your personal opinion of her. Is there anything you would like to say before we end this interview?'

'No, except my fuckin' 'ead 'urts somethin' rotten – I must 'ave a mental disease and I feel a bit dizzy,' said Jenner slyly, thinking that he really had convinced them that he was suffering from some kind of mental disorder.

Parker ended the recording. He and Saxon sat while Jenner was taken back to his cell. Haines packed up his papers and left without a word.

Parker slumped down next to Saxon and offered him a cigarette.

'Thanks, I must buy some, I seem to always be smoking yours,' said Saxon as he drew in the smoke.

Sergeant Dowling entered the room looking pleased. 'Good news, sir, Mr Varnham is going to be okay – hospital just called. They're going to keep him in overnight and tomorrow morning and probably take him home during the afternoon.'

'Thanks, Sergeant, so we have a confession and a witness. Things are improving. All we need now is a something to go on regarding our shape-shifting friend. The rate he's been bumping off his victims, we should hear something very soon.'

Chapter 14

Sunday, June 16, 8.00PM

Saxon sat alone in his apartment. Again. He hadn't heard from Emma for some time and, although this upset him, he didn't feel the pain of the separation in the same way anymore. In the beginning, particularly during the first month after she left, he would pace around, listening to sad music, almost swamped by his misery, occasionally drinking too much wine, and certainly regretting it the following morning.

Sometimes the despair he felt would be so all-encompassing that he almost cried with pain. However, as usual with him, the safety switch in his head would kick in and push the pain away.

The weather was still freaky. There were reports in the news of water shortages, and of the ground drying up so much that the foundations of some rural buildings were becoming unstable. It made him think of his childhood – were the summers really hotter? Or was it the fact that children overheat faster than adults, and that memory, more often than not, plays tricks?

He didn't have the answers. Just memories. Some of which he preferred to store in one of the deeper recesses of his mind. But like a nagging pain; they would always surface just when you don't want them. One of these unwelcome memories was of his father – the father he had hardly known – the father he had been deprived of. Saxon was so young at the time of his death that the majority of his memories comprised of Saxon senior telling him a few stories of the war, combined with glimpses of days in the country, growing up in idyllic surroundings and living in a Tudor cottage in Sussex.

Richard Saxon was an enigma. He was a quiet man with great inner strength and had led an eventful life. During WWII, he was a squadron leader, flying Spitfires, Hurricanes and occasionally Lancasters, on bombing raids deep into Germany. Once, he was shot down near Berlin but, remaining calm, he managed to walk out of Germany, into France and eventually, after meeting up with the French Resistance, was smuggled back into England. Only to be given another aircraft – a brand new Spitfire – in which he was shot out of the skies by an anti-aircraft battery on the south coast of England. Apparently, one of the ladies who were plane-spotting on that day thought his aircraft sounded like a Fokker. Not exactly the word he used, but close enough.

Saxon loved to hear his father describing his fighting escapades. He thought that it was really what every little boy wants – the memories of his father from a child's point of reference, without seeing the imperfections that all children start to see as they get older and realise that their poor father was not Superman after all.

The slightly inebriated reminiscing was abruptly halted by a knock on his door. He didn't bother to look through the spy hole; after all, he was a big tough policeman, so why bother.

Francesca stood looking nervously at him. She handed him a bottle of red wine. 'You seemed to like this wine the last time we had it, I thought maybe you'd like to try it again.' This comment was followed by one of her warm smiles, which Saxon had to concede, was extremely endearing.

He had trouble hiding his joy at seeing her and invited her in. She walked through the hallway into the sitting room while Saxon wandered around trying to remember exactly where he had left the corkscrew. *I hope it's not in the sink.*

He found it, at last, and he opened the bottle of wine, relieved that the cork came out smoothly. They climbed the stairs to sit on the roof. They sat together in companionable silence, looking out towards the sea.

Saxon was rehearsing a number of things to say, but not finding the right one, when Francesca turned to him. 'Well,' she said, 'this is very pleasant, isn't it, sitting here like an old married couple.' She smiled at him and they both laughed. He opened his mouth to reply but she turned back to look at the sea and went on speaking. 'Paul, I hope you don't mind me saying this, but here goes – why don't you go and see Emma and just ask her what she's playing at. Surely, she must know that going off like she has and not contacting you for weeks on end is hardly fair to you.'

She paused and turned back to face him. 'There, I've said it. Now I suppose you're pissed off with me?' Saxon remained silent. She closed her eyes and let her head fall backwards. 'It's none of my business, is it?' she said.

Francesca waited for the ticking bomb to explode. Saxon waited for the light to stop reflecting off her hair as it fell back with the movement of her head.

There was no explosion. Saxon looked at her and smiled, but it was a sad smile.

When he spoke, it was slowly. 'Fran, you have every right to ask. To tell you the truth, I've all but given up on her. I came to the conclusion that no matter how much I felt sorry for myself, and moped around being depressed…' He shrugged. 'Well, what good was it doing me?'

She was looking at him now. 'The answer is none,' he said. 'It wasn't doing anyone any good, but particularly not me.' He shook his head.

Francesca reached her hand across the six inches that separated them and touched his fingers briefly. He looked up and nodded in acknowledgement of her touch. She took her hand back and sipped the wine.

'You know something, Fran?' It was clearly a rhetorical question. He was smiling now. 'I was happy before I knew her, so I can be happy now that she's gone.' He sighed with evident exaggeration.

Francesca laughed. 'Good for you,' she enthused. 'Let's go out and have dinner somewhere – on me,' she added, smiling broadly.

'Wouldn't dream of it, why on earth should you pay?'

'Oh, I suppose because I'm a woman, you think you have to pay for everything.' She emptied her glass. 'Well I've got news for you, Mr Tough Big Macho Cop.' She stood up, straightening her skirt slightly as she did so. 'I'm not a dependant little woman. I've got money, and I'm going to buy you dinner – so just this once you just stop being a commander and do as you're told and follow me.' She walked towards the stairs. Then she glanced back over her shoulder. 'I mean it,' she said, with a mock severity. She climbed carefully down the spiral staircase, taking the glasses and bottle with her. He followed, feeling quite pleased with himself and life and the universe in general.

As they left his apartment, Francesca suggested they use the lift rather than the stairs. The lift was small, with barely enough room for two people. They neither of them commented on the fact, although they were both intensely aware of it. His hand brushed hers as he followed her into the lift and turned at her side to face the door.

The journey down took less than thirty seconds but they were a long, slow thirty seconds. He was aware of the faint perfume she'd put behind her ears. It was subtle, but already responding to the warmth of her skin. He inhaled it but not too obviously. It was lovely. It wasn't one he knew, but it smelt vaguely old-fashioned to him. Emma had once observed to him that the new perfumes tended to be too brash for her taste, too in your face, literally in your nostrils. He shared her preference for the softer, gentler fragrances.

Now here he was, reflecting on Fran's choice of perfume. And it didn't seem at all odd. But his heart was thudding against his chest. How strange to be in such a state of anticipation over a simple dinner. He held back to let her leave in front of him, and then closed the lift door.

Francesca smiled and waited for him. Something in the way she was standing, with her hand at her side, just made it very easy for him to link his fingers with hers. She leaned into him slightly and squeezed his hand very gently. Then she started walking towards the door. He hoped desperately that his hand wasn't clammy. His heart rate had increased.

'So,' she said, 'what are you in the mood for?' She had one of those wonderful voices that sounded like laughter, even when the speaker is only smiling. He loved her voice.

'In the mood for?' he answered. The question was unexpected. Never normally at a loss for words, he was suddenly off-balance.

'Food-wise. What are you in the mood for food-wise?' She raised her eyebrows. 'What do you fancy, Italian, Indian? We're going out to dinner, aren't we? That implies an element of choice. We have to decide what we want to eat. Just because I'm treating you doesn't mean that you've surrendered all control. I wouldn't want you to think that.' She held his gaze momentarily; her head tilted very slightly on one side, and then she set off down through the square to the sea front.

He pulled gently on her hand to slow her down so that they were walking side by side. 'I surrender all control,' he laughed. 'Until further notice, that is.'

Rottingdean, Sunday, June 16, 11.00PM

He sat in the middle of the room. The lights were off – he had no need for light. Everything he needed to see happened behind his eyelids – if he opened his mind sufficiently to allow the images to be projected in the right place. Controlling his breathing, slowing it down to six breaths per minute, it would take five minutes before the voice would come – would decide to come, if he was considered worthy of a visit.

Sometimes the voice refused to be heard. Sometimes, when it had not been forthcoming, he fell to his knees, pleading to know – to be told, that he was completing his tasks satisfactorily. If approval was withheld, then so was sleep as questions spread wildly through his mind. Had he done something wrong? Maybe the wrong person had been cleansed. Should he have searched harder and longer for more of them to send to the master? Would the master become tired of him if he made mistakes? If so, then what would he do?

But now, his mind was open, searching, probing for the right frequency. When the voice came, ecstasy flooded his body causing him to convulse. And now, he became tense as the first wave hit him in the chest and surged up through his shoulders. Then, as it shot up through his neck, he felt it explode to every part of his being.

He found himself looking around a laboratory, brilliant white, so bright he could barely stand the pain. Such was the pain to his eyes; he was unable to focus fully. Around him he could just make out desks – he was aware that there were people sitting at the desks, but everything was so out of focus they appeared to have no features. He wanted to blink. But there could be no escape from the pain to his eyes as they were already closed. If the master had chosen this to be the image he had to see, then who was he to object.

The voice came at last, so soft and reassuring, with the words he had wanted so much to hear. He was doing well, it told him. He was doing far better than the others. They didn't have the same background as him, so how could they be expected to perform with the same degree of expertise. The master knew he had chosen well.

However, more work was demanded. More filthy souls were to be sent to the master. His hunger was great. He was told that the meddlers who tried to stop him, were as bad as the rest of them. They must be persuaded, using all methods at his disposal, from their incessant meddling.

The voice faded away, but he was still in the white laboratory. The light faded sufficiently for him to pull his eyes into focus. Gradually everything sharpened up, and he realised that people in white coats occupied all of the desks, but their heads were skulls. Traces of skin and hair hung off all of them, at least the ones he could see. The room had grown to massive proportions, disappearing into the distance in all directions. Each desk was covered with test tubes and various-shaped glass containers. All were overflowing with blood.

He stood transfixed as the skulls first turned to gaze at him. Then, as though all were commanded, they turned to look in the direction of a lone figure in the distance, which appeared to be walking in his direction. Unsure at first, because of the distorted perspective – but eventually, at a distance that he couldn't begin to guess, he realised that it was a woman, a small woman.

His eyes stung and watered. He wanted to rub them hard, but the voice gently told him to wait. Suddenly his vision seemed to telescope to the face of the approaching woman.

He tried to run forwards as her emaciated face filled out to regain the beautiful features he had known when she was his wife. His legs refused to respond. He called out her name and she smiled, lifting her arm in the air over her head. She began to wave to him, but the flesh on her arm started to decay and drop onto her face. She looked up, surprised and frightened. Her face contorted, as in the split second that precedes a scream.

The scream came as she put her hands to her face. It was a scream that no one could ever forget. As she removed her hands, her face came with them. Her skull looked down at the dripping mass of rotten flesh.

He turned to run away but his legs were not his to use. Turning back to his wife, he almost gagged as the remainder of her flesh slipped to the floor. The cadavers at the desks turned to face him as the blood in their test tubes overflowed onto the floor. Like a vast red carpet, it travelled from the furthest reaches of his vision to the grotesque skeletal figure that was once his wife. As the first drops touched her feet, she slowly regenerated, causing him to experience an overwhelming feeling of elation.

He attempted to move toward her again, but she raised her hands to stop him. Her mouth made the movements of speech, but the voice that he heard was that of the master. 'This is why I must have the blood and the souls.'

Suddenly, there was nothing. He found himself on the floor beside his chair. He shook violently. Feeling the nausea welling up inside him, he staggered to his bathroom, falling over a coffee table on the way, and emptied the contents of his stomach down the toilet.

His understanding of why he was chosen for the quest now made more sense than ever before. The master had never shown him anything like that before. Surely his reward would be the return of his wife. Apart from removing the disease from the world, the energy from the souls along with their blood would save the innocent ones who had contracted the filthy disease through no fault of their own.

He knew there would never be a cure for AIDS – all that was required was a cull. He reasoned that diseases like that don't just happen. They are sent. *If something or someone sends these things to decimate humankind, then there must be a power that can destroy them.*

That power was surely working through him.

Rottingdean, Monday, June 17, 12.30AM

He had no time for sleep. A list had to be drawn up of the meddlers. But no, a list could be found – how would he explain that. Best to keep it in his head. These people would need to be removed, because they were unwittingly assisting the spread of the disease by attempting to stop him. A moment of panic overtook him. The thought of not being able to complete his work frightened him. Fear was an emotion he hadn't experienced since his childhood – sweat trickled down from the back of his head and his hands grew moist.

It didn't help that the weather had changed. The heat wave was losing its lust for life, making the air heavy and humid. For the last couple of nights there had been faint, distant rumbles of thunder out over the Channel. But so far, there had been nothing with enough power to clear the air.

He wandered around his house. Twenty rooms in total – not large rooms, but still twenty of them just the same. At one time, when his wife was alive, the house appeared to be so much smaller. There were always friends dropping in for a chat, dinner parties that went on into the night. Sometimes the guests would stay overnight if the alcohol intake careered out of control. With twenty rooms, it was not a problem.

Even when he and his wife were alone in the house, working on the décor and in some parts, rebuilding it together, such was the size of her personality that the house, regardless of its size, seemed to shrink. Her musical laugh would echo from room to room. He and his wife were keen members of the village amateur dramatics society, both accomplished actors, both highly intelligent.

But now he was alone. If silence had a sound, it echoed around the house. The friends no longer came, and he couldn't blame them – maybe they were more her friends than his, or possibly they were too embarrassed to come. Some people couldn't deal with death. Or the change that he had gone through made others uncomfortable. He was different now, only smiling when it was expected and only with his mouth, never his eyes. He covered his true feelings with his brash personality, but he thought that maybe he was losing his touch; maybe he was no longer as convincing as he used to be. Whatever was going on behind his eyes was gradually becoming more evident in his expression.

His mental list was complete. But when and where, that was the problem that occupied his mind now. He just had to wait until the voice answered those questions.

Chapter 15

Wednesday, June 19, 8.50PM

The phone on Saxon's desk rang. Parker slowly leaned over from his computer and grabbed it, 'Commander Saxon's phone, can I help you?'

Silence.

Irritated, he slammed down the receiver and moved back to his console. It rang again almost immediately. 'Commander Saxon's phone – who is it?'

More silence. 'Whoever you are, this is a police line and the call is being traced; now talk to me or piss off, I'm a very busy man.' Then, a second before he was about to slam it down again, he heard the mechanical voice. Instantly he hit the record button. The message was short. The second the caller hung up, he dialled Saxon's mobile. *Shit, no signal.*

He quickly rummaged through his address book, and found Saxon's home number and tried that one. Just an answerphone – but it would have to do. The phone beeped. 'Sir, Parker here, call me urgently, we've had another message from the killer. It involves you. He has made threats against you. I'm sending some lads to your apartment to check it out. I will keep trying your mobile.'

He hung up the phone, and for a second he paused. *What if the killer is pulling the same stunt as he did on Mancini? What if he's already got to Saxon?* As this thought struck him, he heard a long distant rumble of thunder.

It took several attempts but Parker eventually managed to get a signal on Saxon's mobile. Relieved, he left pretty much the same message on his voicemail. The decision to be made was whether to stay in the office or to go to Saxon's apartment. He opted for the apartment. On his way past Sergeant Dowling, he told him to patch any calls through to his mobile, and if Saxon was to call in on the off chance, then tell him to watch his back as Mr Weirdo was out to get him.

As Parker drove into the square where Saxon lived, he immediately recognised the unmarked police car that seemed to be lurking in the shadows. Much to his annoyance, he had to park his car two hundred yards away as there were no free spaces. PCs Ryan and Ellis stood waiting for Parker to arrive and put out their cigarettes as soon as they saw him approaching.

'Seen anything?' asked Parker, gazing up at the elegant Regency building.

'Not a thing, Sarge. Now, I hate to sound defeatist but how are we going to get in…have you seen the size of that door, and it's rock solid,' said Ryan, with more than a touch of despair in his voice.

'That's why I'm in plain clothes, Constable – why didn't you ring one of the other door bells for Christ's sake?' Parker couldn't believe how stupid some of the beat cops could be sometimes. He ran up to the door and pressed the button for the ground floor. After a few moments, the light came on in the hallway and a tired-looking late middle-aged woman half opened the door. She blinked a few times as Parker thrust his warrant card through the gap. She grabbed it and then closed the door. After what seemed like an eternity, she opened the door and was nearly knocked off her feet as the three officers pushed past her.

'Sorry, love,' Ryan called back to the grumbling woman who was fast disappearing back into her apartment. 'Which floor, Sarge?' shouted Ellis, as he started to run up the stairs.

'Top,' answered Parker, deciding to take the lift and at least be left with a little bit of strength by the time he got to the top. They all arrived at Saxon's door at the same time – Ryan and Ellis gasping for breath. The first thing that sent waves of concern to the pit of their stomachs was the red cross that had been painted on the door, in what looked like blood. It was still wet.

Parker tried the handle, but it was locked. He hammered on

the door as loudly as he could. 'Sir, Commander Saxon, are you in there?' Silence.

'Right, lads, let's not fuck about, get this door open and fast.'

Parker moved out of the way. He was the taller, but the pair of uniforms were built like rugby fullbacks. It took three well-aimed kicks under the door handle before they heard the cracking of timber as the doorframe and hinges gave way. The door fell flat on the carpet of Saxon's hall.

Cautiously, Parker felt inside for the light switch and flicked it on. No one there. Quickly, they went into every room, looked in wardrobes and checked the roof – the place was empty. Ryan and Ellis walked back to the hallway and stared at the demolished door.

'The commander's not going to be too pleased about that,' said Ryan, picking up splinters of wood that had travelled to the sitting room.

'I think the sodding door is the least of our problems at this point in time,' said Parker sarcastically. 'Right now I'd like to know where Commander Saxon is.'

'Why would you like to know that, Parker?' called a voice from what was left of the door. All three of them turned sharply to see Saxon standing in the doorway with Francesca. 'And what the hell have you done to my door?' he continued, kicking bits of wood out of his way.

Parker was almost speechless with relief. 'Sir, thank Christ you're okay...we were about to call out the helicopters and the dogs and start scouring the countryside for your body. Where have you been? I tried to get you on your mobile, but it was switched off. Didn't you get my message when you turned it back on?'

Saxon walked through the hallway with Francesca following behind. 'Flat battery, I'm afraid. But I'm here now so tell me what's going on.'

Francesca started to walk to the kitchen. 'Tea all round,' she said as she disappeared through the door.

Parker filled Saxon in on the phone call from the killer. 'Basically, sir, he said that the time had come to stop the meddlers from trying to stop his mission and that number one on his agenda was you. He also said that it would be fruitless to try and stop him because higher powers were at work – usual loony stuff. I couldn't contact you so that's why we came here. Then there's the symbol painted on your door.

Ryan and Ellis lifted the door up and leant it against the wall so that Saxon could see for himself. 'Ok, your motives were good – I won't sue you for damages this time,' joked Saxon. Francesca appeared with tea for everyone. The two constables, who obviously had asbestos throats, finished theirs first and stood up.

Ryan's radio crackled into life and he moved out into the hall to answer the call. He came back quickly. 'Got an incident – sorry, sir, we have to go.' They didn't wait for permission.

Parker drained his cup and hauled himself up. 'Right, sir, I'll organise someone to keep an eye on your flat. I can get a uniform to sit out in the corridor all night if you want.'

Saxon interrupted him. 'Absolutely not, Parker, the killer knows where I live, which is interesting in itself. How does he know my address?' He pondered, 'Does he know me, I wonder? What does worry me, is that if he's been watching me, then he more than likely knows about Francesca.'

Parker looked at her sitting on the sofa next to Saxon – perhaps too close to be just friends he thought to himself. 'Oh, sir, I er, see,' he said, instantly regretting having said anything at all.

Saxon put him out of his misery. 'Yes, Parker, we've been out to dinner and I suppose you could say it was a date – so end of subject okay?'

Francesca beamed a smile at Parker who was now blushing heavily, but managed to return it, albeit sheepishly.

Saxon continued. 'As I was going to say, Francesca, before the interruption from Miss Marple here, I think that you should stay in one of our secure houses for a while. It's nothing special – just a house where you'll live with a couple of WPCs until we can be sure that it's safe to come back here. As soon as the door is fixed, I will be back in here waiting for the bastard to pay me a visit. What I don't want is lots of obvious police all over the place frightening him away.'

Francesca turned to look at him and he could tell immediately that she was not going to cooperate. 'But, Paul, what about my work? I'm a photographer. When I'm not out taking pictures, I live on my phone looking for work, and besides, all my equipment is downstairs. How am I going to earn my daily crust? It's out of the question – I won't be driven out of my home by some stupid nutter.' Saxon knew he'd met his match when he first laid eyes on her.

Too damn cute, this one – she'll always get her way.

He couldn't order her to move out. He had started to feel very protective towards her and thought maybe gentle persuasion would convince her. Parker, who was dog-tired, and really wanted no more than to get to his bed, decided it was time to make his contribution to the minor domestic argument that was unfolding before him.

'Miss,' he began…but she stopped him.

'That's okay, you can call me Francesca. You don't have to be so formal.'

'Thank you, Francesca; by the way, my name's Guy. I'm sure that we can transport your equipment to the secure house, and any phone calls you make can be paid for by you, as the bills are all itemised as a matter of course. We would all be much happier if we knew that you were safe.'

Francesca thought about the situation for a moment. 'Guy, you have a way with words. Let me just go downstairs and check my phone messages. I'm expecting a big job any day – my agent may have left the details for me. I'll only be a minute.' She stood up and walked across the room. Parker found it impossible not to notice her trim figure. Whatever she had, she oozed it.

Saxon smiled at Parker. 'Calm down, Parker. Don't forget you're a married man.' Parker in turn was about to state the obvious, but thought better of it and merely nodded and grinned.

Two minutes later, Francesca suddenly ran back into the room, her face as white as chalk. She was trembling as she spoke. 'Yes, okay, this secure house you were talking about sounds like a nice place – shall we go there now please?'

Saxon stood and put his arm around her shoulders. 'Fran, what's happened? Don't worry, we are here, nothing can happen to you.'

Parker had immediately dashed downstairs to her flat and reappeared a couple of minutes later. 'Sir, you have to come and look for yourself.' They all walked down together – understandably, Francesca didn't want to be left on her own. When they entered her apartment, Parker closed the front door. Written on the back of the door, again in what looked like blood, were the words "AND HIS FRIEND". Underneath it was the same red cross as on Saxon's door.

Saxon turned to Francesca. 'Okay, well I think that just about settles it. If you don't voluntarily accept police protection then I will arrest you for knowingly putting your life at risk. Can we do that, Parker?'

'Oh yes sir, we can,' said Parker slowly.

Francesca looked at them both and held out her wrists. 'Cuff me.'

They hung around for a while as Francesca packed a few things into a suitcase, and left after a couple of PCs arrived to guard the building. The thunderstorm crashed and flashed as weeks of pent-up energy was released. Thunder spots splashed down on their heads as they ran to Saxon's Land Rover. They drove down the road and stopped next to Parker's car. He jumped out and met up with them at the secure house later.

They stayed until Francesca was safely settled in with her two WPCs. One of them was a dog handler – she felt safe as Ralph, the dog, took an instant liking to her and after a licking frenzy decided that he wanted to sleep at the end of her bed. Then they returned to Saxon's apartment. Parker told the PC who had been on guard duty to make himself scarce, and after he and Saxon had propped the door up to look as normal as possible, tried to sleep on the sofa.

The thunderstorm continued for most of the night, causing both of them to wake periodically. But eventually the sound of the heavy rain on the skylight lulled them into a deep, well-earned sleep.

Thursday, June 20, 8.15AM

Saxon walked into the canteen at Brighton Police Station. Several officers stood when they saw him, but he gestured for them to sit. One of the perks of rank, he mused. Parker was already there, tucking into the full cardiac arrest fried breakfast. Saxon was one of those people who didn't need to eat sensibly. Anything was fair game to his stomach. Emma used to say that she could have fed him wire wool and it would have no effect on him. He pushed any thoughts of Emma to the back of his mind. She was making no effort to contact him, so why bother with her.

He loaded up his plate and sat next to Parker. 'Heart attack by lunchtime then, Parker?'

Parker smiled, 'Yes, sir, but bloody worth it…do you suppose we could charge the cook with murder if one of the people in here dropped dead from eating too much cholesterol?'

'We'd never make it stick, Parker, unlike that blob of yolk you've got stuck on the front of your jacket.'

'Shit, it was on clean this morning,' cursed Parker as he tried to scrape it off with his knife, but managing only to spread it out a bit.

'Right, let's get down to business. I have some questions that urgently need answers. One: how did the killer know my address? Two: how the hell did he know about Francesca? Three: how did he get into the building? And four – and this one really disturbs me – is how the fuck he got into her apartment? Any ideas will be listened to.'

Parker finished a large mouthful of his breakfast. 'The only answer for your first question, has to be that he knows you. Simple as that.' He took another mouthful.

'Not that simple… I know lots of people – call me foolish, but I don't think any of them are killers. But then again, would I really know? Remember what Prof Ercott said, and I quote, "You will be surprised at his normality". Tell me, Parker, what do you get up to in your spare time?'

Parker wasn't sure whether to laugh or not, so he smiled nervously. 'Sir, he must have been watching you to know about Francesca. I work with you, and I had no idea you had…er, started a relationship with anyone. I did notice that you seemed less grumpy lately though.' Parker's mind flashed, *Oh shit, why do I say these things?*

'Me, grumpy? I'm never grumpy,' snapped Saxon.

'Sorry, sir, anyway, as to gaining entry to the building – all he had to do was to either follow one of the other residents through the front door, or ring a bell and say the magic words "Gas Board, checking for leaks" and he could gain access to Hades if he wanted to. If brainless thick criminals can do it, then our killer who seems to have an IQ of about five hundred would find it a piece of cake.'

Saxon looked up from his plate. 'Carry on, Parker, you talk – I'll eat, if I have anything interesting to add to the conversation I'll tell you.'

Parker continued after taking another mouthful of bacon and egg. 'One thing has been bugging me ever since we heard the first voice message from our shape shifter. I have been looking into the type of computer that can simulate the voice he's using. I've been doing a bit of research and the nearest match I've come up with is an artificial voice called "Bruce"; it's a free bit of software that comes with an Apple Macintosh computer. So he either owns an Apple Mac or he has access to one.' Parker dived in to his breakfast again before he was asked to talk any more.

'Impressive...does Jake Dalton have one of these Apple computers?' said Saxon, as he chased the last bits of his breakfast around the plate.

'No, sir, I've already checked,' he said, pleased that he had pre-empted one of Saxon's questions. 'Anyway, sir, STI said that he couldn't have popped over to paint things on your door yesterday because they had him in their sights all day. He got up, drove to work and stayed there. Then he drove home, and there was no evidence to suggest that he had a pot of blood and a paint brush on or about his person.'

'Does he have access to one where he works?'

'Now that, I don't know – but I suppose there would be blood in a mortuary. But I thought we'd decided someone was setting him up?' said Parker.

'Actually, Parker, I meant does he have access to an Apple computer, not pots of blood. But that's an interesting point...I suppose there would be plenty of blood in a mortuary. Maybe, someone he works with is jealous of his position.' Saxon sounded unconvincing.

'I hardly think that's the answer, sir, have you seen the state of them down at the mortuary? Besides, Jake is a very popular bloke. They all seem to like him a lot. It's geek and nerd city rolled into one – a physical impossibility, there's not one of them that could lift any one of our victims single-handed.' Parker added, 'I was wondering, sir, what are you intending to do about your personal protection while this threat is hanging over you?'

Saxon pulled open the front of his jacket to show the handle of a standard police-issue handgun tucked under his left arm. 'Just this, plus I'm thinking that maybe I will leave my apartment door open tonight in the hope that I may get a visit from the friendly neighbourhood murderer.'

Parker finished eating and pushed his plate away. 'I think, sir, that I should stay with you – just in case.' He knew what the answer would be…and he was right.

'I appreciate your concern, but if he's watching me – and I have no doubt he is, then we don't want to frighten him off. If he saw you anywhere near my apartment, there's no way he'd show up. I'll be okay, Parker, because you, my friend will be sitting in a car watching my front door from the seafront with a nice big pair of night-vision binoculars.'

Parker was about to say what he thought of the idea. He didn't relish the thought of spending the night cooped up in his car on the promenade. Apart from the obvious attention it would draw to him, as he sat there looking inland instead of out to sea. If he were needed in Saxon's apartment quickly, how long would it take him to drive up the square – would it be quicker to run? He didn't like the sound of it at all. 'But, sir I don't think—' was all he had time to utter as his mobile started to play a tune by Mozart. He answered it as several officers on adjacent tables chuckled at his choice of ring tone.

'Sorry, sir,' he muttered. 'Parker,' he said abruptly into the phone. 'Shit, okay when? – we're on our way.' He stuffed the phone back in his pocket. 'Quick, sir, we've got to get to the so-called safe house. Someone's pinned a wreath and a note to the front door.'

The colour drained from Saxon's face as he raced across the canteen and out to the car park at the rear of the station. As soon as they were on their way through the traffic, Parker called for a SOCO to meet them there. Saxon then handed him his own phone. 'Call Francesca, the number's programmed in – find out where she is and tell her to go to the nearest police station and wait for us to pick her up, and tell her to trust no one. It doesn't matter how familiar or friendly someone may seem to her, she's to wait for us – understand?' he shouted over the sound of the siren.

Parker was holding on to the handle over the door with one hand and operating the phone with the other, and trying not to look too stressed. At least breakfast appeared to be staying put. Saxon drove skilfully but faster than Parker was used to. 'God, I hate mobile phones,' yelled Parker, unable to get a signal. He picked up the police radio, gave control Francesca's phone number and told them to try a landline. After a few minutes, they were successful and patched the call through. Parker relayed the message and fortunately, Francesca had been out on a photographic assignment with one of her WPC minders. They were driving back to the secure house. Parker told them not to go back to the house – they were to go to Brighton Police Station and wait there. He and Saxon would be along later to explain.

Once they were out of the centre of Brighton, Saxon turned the siren off and slowed down. Soon they pulled into the quiet leafy suburban road where the secure house stood, looking just like all of the other rather plain-looking medium-sized houses. The only thing about it that would give anyone cause to take a second look was the wreath hanging on the front door. Saxon parked the car and with Parker behind, walked up the path to the door. Winnie Short, one of the WPCs who lived in the house, opened the door when they were halfway along the path.

'Hello, Commander, Sergeant.' She looked grim. 'Well, I guess we aren't as secure as we thought we were.' She shrugged.

'No, I suppose you could be right there, Winnie,' replied Parker, lighting a cigarette and looking up and down the road. 'I guess you didn't hear or see anything.'

'Sorry, Sarge, not a thing – I was in the kitchen and the washing machine was going. The old lady next door popped round to offer her condolences, then I noticed it...not that you could miss it. Shame the dog wasn't here, he'd have kicked up a hell of a stink even if someone opened the gate.'

'Not your fault, Winnie,' said Saxon as he examined the envelope attached to the centre of the wreath. The bastard must have followed us here the other night. 'How do you feel about staying here now that this has happened?' said Saxon sympathetically.

'I didn't join the police to go hiding away if things got a bit sticky, Commander. I'm quite capable of taking care of myself. But, I am trained to carry a gun, if that's all right with you, sir.'

'You'll have one within the hour – how about your colleague?' said Saxon as he looked up and down the road wondering where the SOCO had got to.

'Jenny – she went for dogs, and I went for guns,' she said with a smile.

Saxon took a pair of rubber gloves from his pocket and slipped them on. He carefully lifted the edge of the envelope and looked at the other side. 'Shit!' he exclaimed. 'He didn't seal the damn thing, so no saliva to check for DNA; and I'll bet there's not a single print on it either. Bastard, why can't you make one tiny mistake – not much to ask for is it,' he mumbled.

They didn't notice Pinky Palmer park his white van three houses up the road and they certainly didn't hear him walking up the garden path. 'Oh, what have we got here then?' he said loudly, causing Saxon's hand to move towards his gun for a brief moment. Parker's reaction was more verbal. 'Fucking hell, Pinky, you know better than to creep up on armed police officers, and where've you been; we've been waiting for you?'

'Sorry, Sarge, got stuck in traffic.'

'Just get on with it, Pinky, and for Christ's sake find something, anything will do; especially a large thumbprint.' Parker had started to see the funny side of what had just happened.

Pinky put his briefcase on the ground and opened it; he took out some tweezers and pulled at the envelope, which was attached to the wreath with a strip of sticky tape. 'Well, there are no prints on the tape – not even marks from a rubber glove. He must have pulled a long strip from his roll of tape and stuck it to the envelope, then cut off the excess with a sharp knife or a scalpel.'

'Why do you say that?' said Saxon, moving forward to take a closer look.

'It's simple – if you stretch a piece of tape and then cut it with a pair of scissors, the cut will be straight. If you do the same thing, but use a blade – like a scalpel for instance, the cut will have a slight wiggle in it. Believe me, I run tests like that in my spare time...and before you say anything, Sarge, yes I know I need to get out more.'

Parker didn't react. 'What about the lettering on the envelope?'

'It looks like the sort of typeface you'd get built into a computer; it's called a System Font. It's called Courier. It could have come from any computer, but the good news is that it can only have come from one particular printer. If you can find the printer, there's a chance I may be able to match each individual letter – could be his first mistake.'

Saxon was hearing the sort of news he had been waiting for and was impatient to read the note inside the envelope. 'Sorry, Commander, I don't think I should open it here; there's too much chance that the evidence could become contaminated. I should bag the whole thing up and take it back to the lab.' Reluctantly they could only agree and they helped him to bag it.

Saxon took Parker to one side. 'Get some uniforms out here and have them do a house to house. I want to know if any of the local curtain twitchers saw our friend delivering the wreath.'

Back at the police station, the first thing on Saxon's mind was to check on Francesca. He found her sitting in the canteen with WPC Jenny Hedges and Ralph, one of the largest German shepherd dogs he'd ever clapped eyes on. Saxon asked her to finish her lunch and then he would be back to figure out a better protection plan for her. Francesca smiled as he put his hand on hers. She looked up at him and said, 'And I feel safer now I know you are here.'

Saxon blushed and smiled back. As he left the canteen, he thought he heard Jenny laugh, followed by, 'I can't believe you said that.' But he wasn't sure.

He went back to the lab where Pinky had already unwrapped the wreath and laid it out on a large sheet of white paper. He gave it a gentle shake to see if anything fell out. There was nothing to fall out. As Saxon and Parker looked on, he opened the envelope using two pairs of tweezers. Inside was a sheet of A4 paper. On it, a few lines of writing. But no ordinary hand had written it. It was in reverse.

Pinky checked it for prints, but it was possibly the cleanest piece of paper in the country. 'The problem with this writing is that it isn't written with ink – not this copy anyway,' Pinky said leaning over a light box and gazing through a small magnifying lens.

'Run that by us again, but in English this time,' said Saxon, feeling that it was time to make progress a little faster.

'It's a photocopy of some writing, so we can't check each stroke of the pen. With handwriting analysis, it's important to see the ink build-up on each side of a stroke of the pen as well as the overall character of the writing. By making a copy of the text, he has wiped out any subtleties. All we have are solid black lines.'

'And the fact that it's written in reverse – what does that tell us?'

'Commander, I think you'll need to get a shrink to answer that one. But at least we can read it.' Pinky flipped the paper over on the light box and, as if holding it up to a mirror, the words became legible.

Commander Saxon,
By now you have surely realised that when I decide to act, then nothing will stop me. You are meddling in my affairs. Obviously, you can have no concept of the importance of my mission, but listen well, Commander, no matter where you put your new friend I will find her. I could have killed her today, but I am willing to give you one more chance. It is within my power to grant you that. It would be hard for me to kill you or your friend, as neither of you is a carrier – it causes me physical pain, to cleanse a non-carrier. But if you force me to do it, the responsibility will be yours. Believe me, I have suffered immensely to attain the level that I have reached. Any more meddling and I will systematically wipe out you, your new friend, and the rest of them.

'Wow, sicko bastard or what,' exclaimed Parker.

Saxon poked the wreath with a pencil. 'Looks as though it's seen better days.' He moved his face closer. 'Looks like mud and a few blades of grass here.' He teased the grass out of the wreath and it fell onto the paper. 'The clever bastard must have picked this up in the cemetery, so there's no way we can trace it to him. God, this shithead is pissing me off – why can't he just slip up once?' Saxon turned to Parker. 'Get on the phone to Prof Ercott, tell him what we've got here and fax a copy of the note to him, he may be able to see things that we can't.'

Pinky photocopied the note onto a sheet of clear film, and then from that, back onto a piece of paper to reverse it. Fifteen minutes later Ercott was on the phone to Saxon.

'Hello, Paul, well, one thing I can tell you is that he is showing all the signs of paranoia. The main one being, excessive self-importance – he isn't interested in the truth. Do you see how he's shifting the responsibility onto you? He's without a doubt…completely barking.'

'What about the fact that it was written in mirror writing?' added Saxon.

'Now, that is interesting, your sergeant didn't mention that – but, you've told me now so don't reprimand him too much. This phenomenon is very rare indeed, very rare. I've only come across it once or twice and that was years ago. Children can quite often do it, some of them don't realise that they are doing it. Sometimes the ability carries over into adulthood and when it does, the person is usually ambidextrous, and has a high IQ. But we already knew that he was clever anyway.'

'What about the writing itself, I suppose I'll need to find a handwriting specialist for that? I don't suppose you can recommend one?'

'Sure can – me. I spend a good chunk of my time nowadays, working for multi-national companies, checking job applications from people who have applied for top executive positions – sort of, spot the crook before he's in control of your finances stuff. Before I can do anything more I'll need to see the actual document though; the fax you kindly sent me isn't good enough to do a proper analysis on. Be with you in about half an hour.' Click, and he hung up.

'Oh okay, Prof, see you soon,' Saxon said to the dead phone in his hand.

Saxon made his way back to the canteen. Francesca was still in the same spot, sipping a cup of what they called tea. Ralph sat at her feet with one paw on her lap and his chin resting on her knee.

'Lucky dog,' muttered Saxon as he sat next to her. She giggled quietly.

'For God's sake, don't let anyone see you laugh – if they start to think I have a sense of humour, they'll never take me seriously again,' he said in a mock serious voice…but not too loudly.

Then he became genuinely serious. 'Right, Francesca, I understand WPC Hedges has made it clear to you why you couldn't go back to the safe house.' She nodded.

Saxon continued. 'The problem, as I'm sure you know, is that we're dealing with an immensely dangerous man – he's not just one step ahead of us, he's about ten at the moment. Now, the reason the bastard's after you, is to get at me. He thinks that if he threatens you, I will stop going after him. He doesn't seem to realise that if it weren't me, it would be someone else. My problem is that I've always had more faith in myself than in other people, so I thought that if the nutter is going follow you then maybe, if we stick together, I would be there to protect you. Along with Parker, who would play a minor role in the background of course. How does that sound to you?'

'You mean I'm bait?'

'Sort of. But I have got this.' He opened his jacket enough for her to see the gun.

'Now you're talking, Commander. I've always thought it was a daft idea to give policemen sticks to defend themselves with.' She hesitated for a moment. 'Uhm, I was wondering, is Guy Parker's gun bigger than yours?'

'I'll talk to you later,' he said as he left the canteen – trying as hard as possible not to laugh.

The phone on Saxon's desk rang just as he was about to start wading through a well-earned cup of tea. 'Professor Ercott in reception, sir,' announced Sergeant Ian Dowling.

'Good, show him the way to Pinky Palmer's office please. And tell him I'll be down in a couple of minutes.'

Professor Ercott was leaning on the desk with his arms folded, peering through the bottom of his bifocals and nodding his head gently. He stood up when Saxon walked in. The two men shook hands. Ercott's manner was friendly but businesslike and he greeted him with a friendly respect. Rather as if, it occurred to Saxon, they were wearing the same old school tie.

'Good to see you again,' started Ercott, before Saxon had a chance to say a word. He held the photocopy of the killer's message out in front of him. 'I've had a quick peek at the note you gave me.' He looked up and nodded at Saxon. 'And it tells me all kinds of very interesting things.'

Saxon was relieved but still anxious that the information should turn out to be useful, and even more; he needed it to stand up in court. 'Glad to hear it, Roger,' he said. 'I've been looking forward to getting some feedback from you. What can you tell us about our man?'

'Well, for one thing, even though it's written in reverse, you'll see that it's amazingly tidy. Most people don't have particularly clear handwriting, do they, even when they're just writing normally.' He raised his eyebrows, and Saxon nodded to show he followed.

'But what...?' Saxon started to ask.

Ercott interrupted him. 'Legibility is a good thing, of course, but sometimes it can mean that the person who wrote it is trying to be a bit of a goody-two-shoes. In other words, the person can be a bit of a wolf in sheep's clothing.'

'So our man isn't necessarily walking around with "KILLER" printed on a tee shirt, but we didn't think he would be. This guy's no idiot, is he.' Saxon was disappointed, he'd been hoping for some new light.

Ercott went on, hardly noticing Saxon's reaction. 'There are certain traits that are quite evident in the writing. For instance, the way that it seems to jump about rather than follow a definite base line indicates what we call a hysterical personality – by that I don't mean the person is funny. Quite the reverse in fact; it usually means the person is out of control and is on the edge of some kind of manic breakdown. One other thing, which is quite obvious to me, is the backward slant of the letters. This tends to show that the writer literally spends most of his time living in the past. An event in his past has had such a profound effect on his personality, that he can't forget it.

'Now, I could rant on for hours about this writing. But that would of course be a waste of time, wouldn't it. What I can't do is give you his name and address, based on the note you have here.' He chuckled. 'But,' he went on, all humour disappearing from his manner, 'if you find the man and give me a sample of his handwriting, then I'll be able to match it to this. I don't think the writer realised that mirror writing doesn't disguise the writing; it merely reverses it. Could be his one fatal error.' He stood up. 'Let's hope so. Anyway, I'm off, got to buy some food from the supermarket. Hettie, my housekeeper, normally does it for me, but lately she's been coming back with all kinds of foreign stuff that even I can't recognise.' The two men shook hands again.

'Thanks very much for that, Roger,' said Saxon. 'It was helpful. And we'll bear in mind what you said about comparing the handwriting if we get a serious suspect.'

Ercott started to move toward the door, and then stopped. 'By the way, Paul, I understand you know Dr Richard Clarke quite well.'

'Yes, I've known him for a few years, why do you ask?'

'Oh, just wondered, no particular reason. Other than, I used to know him years ago. Nice chap, really good actor, he used to belong to his local theatre group, as did I at one time. I was wondering how he's doing. He wasn't very talkative when I bumped into him the other day while we were examining the unfortunate Mr Pike's body.' Ercott paused. 'You know, he used to do some wonderful things with makeup; he had this latex stuff, which he plastered on his face. He would completely change his features, and some of the other players let him do their makeup as well. Yes, he was quite a leading light in our little acting world.' He shook his head. 'I thought we might lose him, you know. I was glad to hear he was working and doing well for himself.'

Saxon was puzzled but not particularly interested. He held the door open for Ercott, his mind already racing ahead to what he would be doing in ten minutes.

Ercott put his hand on Saxon's arm. 'Tragedy sometimes does it for people, and other times they survive. You can never tell how it will work out. But Richard and Helen were so close, an ideal couple, it was hard to imagine how he would pull back after she died. It was so tragic.'

'Really? I'd no idea. What happened?' asked Saxon.

'Well, he withdrew for ages, you know. We hardly saw the man, he stopped coming to rehearsals altogether. Incidentally, he is a member of the same club as that poor Judge Mancini and me. Although I haven't seen him there for a long time.'

Saxon froze. Ercott didn't realise it but he had Saxon's complete attention. 'His wife died?' asked Saxon.

'Yes, very tragic it was. Such a shame.'

'And what did his wife die of?' asked Saxon, almost in a whisper.

'It really was very sad. She was a lovely girl; like a breath of fresh air, it was as if she was always pleased to see you. It seemed as if she was well one day and then suddenly she was gone. We hardly had time to realise she was ill before we heard she had died.'

'Yes,' said Saxon. 'I can see how that would have been very sad. But do you know what she died of, Roger?'

'Actually, I'm not sure of all the details, Paul. And poor Richard was in such a terrible state that nobody liked to press him too much at the time. From what I remember, she had a problem with her stomach – I don't know all of the details, but the long and the short of it was that she needed a blood transfusion, and that's when it all went wrong.'

'It was infected blood?' asked Saxon. 'She was given HIV-positive blood?' His flesh was crawling.

'Well, screening then wasn't what it is today. Yes, that's exactly right, the blood was indeed infected with HIV. She didn't last long after that.' Ercott sighed.

'AIDS,' breathed Saxon. 'Good God, AIDS.'

'Yes, exactly.' Ercott patted his arm and turned back towards the door. 'Such a tragedy. Such a waste.'

Saxon was almost speechless and his heart was thudding in his chest. Suddenly, out of nowhere, had come the biggest lead in the case. 'Roger, I can't thank you enough,' he said. 'You've been a great help.'

'Don't mention it, my boy.' Ercott raised a hand in farewell. 'Glad to have been of help.' They shook hands again. 'And do give my regards to Richard when you see him. I really am glad he's all right now.'

The door shut behind Ercott and the two policemen looked at each other. Pinky stood transfixed. 'It all adds up, doesn't it, Commander?' he said slowly. 'It has to be him, it feels right – you can't beat that old gut-feeling.' He patted his stomach.

'I know exactly what you mean, Pinky – I have the same feeling.' There was nothing slow about Saxon's response. 'Find Parker for me. Meeting in my office. Now.'

Thursday, June 20, 9.00AM

'Could just be circumstantial,' exclaimed Parker. 'It all sounds too good to be true, and what do we do now? We have no evidence, and as for the motive, we might as well put him in the list of thousands of other people who have lost family or friends to AIDS as well. Anyway, he seems so normal…'

'Quite,' interrupted Saxon, 'he does, doesn't he? I want to know where he was at the times of all the murders, but I don't want him to think we're on to him – he mustn't get a sniff that anything is going on, and that is going to be bloody difficult.'

'Where does he live, sir?'

'He's got a huge detached pile over in Rottingdean. I've never been there, but he mentioned it to me once. I think, Parker, that it is time Richard Clarke and I had another game of squash,' said Saxon as he picked up the phone and dialled the number of the mortuary. He got through to Clarke's secretary who told him that Dr Clarke was on holiday.

'Oh, of course,' said Saxon as if it had slipped his mind, 'and just remind me would you, he did say he was going abroad – is that correct?' he added.

The secretary told Saxon that Dr Clarke definitely wouldn't have been leaving the country, because whenever he did that, he left it up to her to organise his itinerary for him. She was sure that he said he would just be travelling around Britain, staying in guesthouses and doing a bit of sightseeing. Saxon thanked her and asked to speak to Dr Jake Dalton.

'Jake, how're things?'

'Fine, you're not going to arrest me again, are you?'

'No, don't worry. But I do need you to come to the station for a chat – how about this evening at six?'

'Sounds intriguing, I'll be there.'

Saxon hung up the phone and looked at Parker. 'Hopefully, he may be able to give us a few pointers into Clarke's movements over the last few weeks.'

'Sir,' said Parker like a small boy who was contemplating something naughty. 'If Dr Clarke is away supposedly travelling at the moment, and someone thought they saw a shifty-looking devil climbing in through one of his windows, then that someone should be a good citizen and call the police to check it out. Now, if you and I were the only two officers available – then I guess we would just have to drop everything and get out to Rottingdean as fast as possible.'

'Shame on you, Parker, but that's not a bad idea. Now go outside to a phone box and call me…just so the record shows that such a call came into the station – on your way, don't dawdle.'

Ten minutes later, they were driving along the coast road to Rottingdean. There was no need to hurry; the fictitious "shifty devil" was probably long gone.

The house was set back from the road. The wrought-iron gates were unlocked; the key was probably mislaid decades ago. They drove slowly along the drive, which was "S" shaped, ending at a quite large roundabout at the front entrance to the house.

Saxon stopped the Land Rover under a large fir tree that looked as though it had been providing shade for carriages for at least a couple of centuries. The house was partially castellated and it was evident that the owner had restored it sensibly; nothing seemed to be out of place.

Parker stood transfixed, such was the contrast between his own modest two up, two down and the mansion he stood before now.

'Sir, I'm thinking of making a career change. If this is what you get for poking around dead bodies, then I'm game for it.'

Saxon just nodded in agreement, and walked up to the front door. 'I guess we'd better try the bell just in case he has a housekeeper.

There wasn't one. They checked the garage for Clarke's car – it was open and empty. 'Okay, Parker, I think we need to find the window that the alleged burglar might have used.' Saxon looked left and then right. 'You go that way, I'll go this way and I'll meet you around the back. If you find a window that looks as though it could be the one, call me.'

A second or two after Saxon disappeared around the corner, Parker heard the sound of breaking glass and he ran to see if Saxon was okay. He found him carefully brushing tiny fragments of glass from his elbow. Saxon had broken one of the small diamond-shaped panes of glass and reached in with his hand to release the catch. 'I think this is the one, Parker – in you go and I'll meet you at the front door,' he said in a matter-of-fact sort of way.

'I just hope he's not at home, sir, we'd have a lot of explaining to do if he is.'

'So would he, Parker…so would he – now get a move on.'

Saxon returned to the front door as Parker unlocked it. The interior had not been maintained to the same standard as the exterior. It had been a long time since the place had been dusted; cobwebs hung down from the corners of the ceiling in long strands. There were potted plants in abundance, some small and some several feet high; when they were alive at least. They walked from the hall to what appeared to be the main drawing room; the floor was uncarpeted and looked as though it was original. Underneath the thin veneer of dust, it was evident that at one time someone had lavished a lot of care and attention to it.

In the corner stood a grand piano with the lid closed. It was covered with various sizes of silver frames, but that was the only difference between each picture – they all contained the same image, a photograph of an attractive, smiling woman.

In among the pictures, stood a tall, fluted silver vase, which held a single red rose. They walked over to the piano. 'Sir, it looks as though this rose is fresh, so he's only just left here recently.'

Saxon lifted it out of the vase. 'It's made of silk, so it tells us nothing except that this is his altar – this is where he comes to brood over the death of his wife. What we need to find is where he keeps his trophies...they always keep trophies.' He thought for a moment. 'Here's what we do, Parker, search but don't disturb anything – put your rubber gloves on. When we find something, anything incriminating, we get out of here and I'll get a search warrant, understand? Now there's got to be a cellar, these old places always seem to have one, let's try there first.'

There was a cellar, Parker found it when he opened what resembled a cupboard in the kitchen. He switched on the light and they cautiously made their way down the steps. The ceiling was vaulted with brick, and every ten feet or so, stood a pillar. In between the first and last of the four pillars were racks of dusty wine bottles. The floor was also brick, laid out in a herringbone design.

Around the edges of the cellar were odd items of old

furniture, some of which looked as though it may have been built at the same time as the house. As Saxon and Parker stood at the bottom of the stairs, they noticed a large white plastic bucket with a snug-fitting snap-on lid. Next to it on the floor were several empty boxes. Saxon picked one up and read the front. 'This is very interesting,' he said as he held it towards Parker. 'What we have here is rubber skin – makeup artists use it to build up people's faces and to make masks.'

'I don't understand, sir.' He paused and sniffed the box. 'But I remember the smell – Andy Pike's body, it's the same smell; but why would his body smell of this stuff?'

Saxon pulled the lid off the bucket. 'Watch and learn, Sergeant.' He dipped his finger into the off-white solution, and quickly replaced the lid. His finger was covered with a layer of latex, which was drying rapidly. Within a couple of minutes, it had hardened so much that he had to pull at it quite hard to remove it.

'Imagine, Parker, if you covered your entire body with this stuff, except for your eyes of course, and a breathing hole for your mouth. You could even build it up around your feet and make any foot shape you wanted – even take an impression of someone's shoe. But you know the main reason for this stuff, don't you? It's so bloody obvious now. If you went into a person's house to kill them with this plastered all over you, including your hair, then nothing would be left behind. How could it – everything would be glued down. And that's why we've not found any DNA. What's more, Clarke is always the next person to get close to a victim after it's been discovered, so he can check again to see if he's missed anything first time round.'

'It explains why we couldn't get him on the phone after PC Lucas copped it,' said Parker. 'He would have probably still been off somewhere to peel off his kinky rubber suit. If only we could find out what he does with the stuff after he's finished with it…'

'I wouldn't worry about that, Parker,' Saxon interrupted.

'Unless he tells us, we haven't a chance of finding it. He's no fool, he will have disposed of it, or should I say them, after each murder.'

The light in the cellar was not good and it took their eyes a while to become accustomed to it. Looking into the dim light, they noticed a door to their left. Parker tried to open it but it was jammed – there was no lock, it was swollen damp wood that prevented it from opening.

'Shit, why is nothing easy,' he said despairingly, and gave it a hefty kick. It crashed open.

'Well done, Parker – good job there aren't any neighbours...in you go.' Then Saxon pulled Parker out of the way. 'Only joking, I wouldn't send the troops anywhere I wouldn't go myself,' he said as he pushed past him. The unpleasant smell that assaulted his nose was faint, just a hint of what was to come. There wasn't a light in the room, so he took his torch from his pocket. The space was about two thirds of the size of the main cellar, it was void of anything except for a pickaxe and a spade. Saxon noticed that the smell was getting stronger as he walked to the centre of the room.

Parker followed, and shone his torch on the floor. 'Sir, the bricks look as though they've been disturbed here.' He knelt down and directed the beam further across the floor. 'Look, sir, there's several places like this.' He moved a few of the bricks out of place, it was then the smell suddenly hit them both as if it was waiting just under the floor to be released.

Parker fell backwards. 'God, that's disgusting,' he said, almost unable to catch his breath.

Saxon helped him to his feet. Parker was coughing and trying not to throw up. 'Right, Parker, I think we both know what that smell is – question is, who is it?'

Parker was the first up the stairs and out into the open air. Saxon got on the radio and was about to call in when a thought struck him. Did he really want the place to be crawling with police just yet? Wouldn't it be better to leave it as they found it? He ran back into the house and tidied up the broken glass where Parker had climbed in through the window. He moved a dead potted plant to hide the fact that a piece of the window was missing. Then he returned to the cellar to replace the few floor bricks they had moved out of place.

Parker watched as he leant on the Land Rover, smoking a cigarette; he was trying to replace the smell of decay that was lingering in his nose with an alternative odour. Saxon walked across to him. 'Here's what we are going to do...precisely nothing.'

Parker looked up, surprised. 'What about the bodies under the floor? We need to get some SOCOs up here and start a thorough search of the house. We can't just leave it...can we?'

'We can, Parker. Let's get out of here, and bring your cigarette butt with you. I don't want there to be any signs that we've been here – let's play him at his own game. Just because Clarke told his secretary that he'd be travelling around the country, doesn't convince me that he will actually do that. He's no more on holiday than we are. If he is stalking Francesca, and me, then I don't think he will be admiring the views in the Lake District, will he?'

Parker looked uneasy. 'What are you proposing, sir, that we lie in the bushes and wait for him to come home?'

Saxon started the engine and as they pulled away, he smiled at Parker, who was looking even more puzzled. 'No, nothing so crude, I have a plan, Parker...a very good plan.'

When they were back on the road to Brighton, Parker threw his cigarette butt out of the window and turned to Saxon. 'What I'd like to know is why after all the trouble he's taken not to leave any evidence, does he then decide to bury a few bodies in his cellar. It doesn't make much sense to me at all – in fact, it seems bloody stupid.'

'We'll find out soon I think, Parker. Meanwhile, use your

mobile, not the radio. I don't want anyone overhearing you. Call the station and tell STI that I want to talk to them when we get back. I've got a little job for them.'

As Saxon and Parker hurried through the reception area of Brighton Police Station, Superintendent Mitchell was on his way out looking flustered. Saxon could tell by the expression on his face and the half-open briefcase full of files, that he was well into bureaucrat mode. 'Ah, Commander Saxon, could I possibly have a word if you're not too busy?'

Saxon didn't stop. 'I'm too busy – talk to you later.' He didn't need to talk to anyone, particularly a paper-pusher like Alex Mitchell, so he kept going. Mitchell followed Saxon along the corridor to the incident room, but Saxon was speaking to Parker in hushed tones. 'Find out what make of car Clarke owns, and tell traffic to get off their arses and find the bloody thing. Then check on Francesca to see if she's okay, as quickly as possible.'

Mitchell interrupted. 'I'm sorry, but I have to insist, Commander. The chief constable has asked me how you are progressing…I need to tell him something, he can be quite difficult you know.'

'Alex, if you have to tell him anything at all, you can tell him that I'm not close to making an arrest, no more than that. I don't want any press releases flying about all over the place. If the media gets wind of what's going on, then so will my prime suspect and I don't want him to know that I'm on his tail. If the CC gets awkward then you can tell him that I will talk to the commissioner and he'll talk to the Home Secretary, okay? That should keep him off your back.'

Saxon turned and walked away and left Mitchell standing with sheets of paper fluttering to the floor from his briefcase.

Inspector Mike Honeysett, who was in command of the Surveillance and Technical Intelligence squad, was waiting in his office. Saxon knocked and entered the room. Honeysett was a fastidious man – in his line of business, he had to be. His entire working day revolved around not being seen. Often fellow officers would pretend to bump into him and say things like, 'Sorry, guv – didn't see you there,' or they would stand in front of him and ask if anyone had any idea where Inspector Honeysett was. He stopped finding it funny years ago but still they did it. Nowadays, he hardly reacted. Just a slight roll of the eyes and a cold stare, it usually stopped them for a while at least.

Honeysett jumped almost to attention as Saxon entered the office. 'Commander, good to see you again – I hear through the grapevine that you have a job for me.'

'I do. I have a house in a rural setting. The person who lives there, is away at the moment – however, he may come back at any time. I want to know when he returns. But I don't want your people crawling around in the shrubbery. The target is extremely dangerous. His favoured weapon is a knife, but he has killed several people with his hands. If he even gets a sniff that we're on to him, he may vanish. He is too clever and too dangerous to be allowed to escape. That's it…what can you do for me?'

Honeysett barely moved his lips. 'Remote camera…in a tree, pointing at the front of the house. Simple, I'll rig it up myself. Are you sure the target isn't in the house?'

Saxon was amazed at Honeysett's calm approach, it was as though the man had no emotions. 'As sure as I can be, Mike – all I know is that he's on annual leave, and that he's supposedly gone away for a few days. But that, we know is bullshit. He's in the area and could be back in the house at any time.'

'No problem, I'll do it tonight after dark. The camera will have a night-vision lens, which automatically switches over from the normal one when the light drops below a certain level. Where is the target house?'

Saxon filled him in on the exact position of the house using an Ordnance Survey map.

Honeysett added, 'If you want, you can come along with me – you could be my van driver, we usually do this sort of thing in pairs so that someone can keep an eye on things while I'm in the grounds setting up the camera.'

Parker knocked on the door and entered the room. 'Sir, Clarke owns a – and you're not going to believe this – a Morris 1100, early 70s model in the exciting colour of dark grey…hardly surprising nobody ever noticed it. Oh,' he continued, 'Francesca and WPC Hedges have left the building.'

'What do you mean, left the building?!' he shouted. 'I told them both to stay here. Get WPC Hedges on the radio now. She's to bring Francesca back here immediately – what the fuck was she thinking? Do it now, Parker, don't just stand there…get moving.' Parker was long gone before he heard the tail end of Saxon's wrath.

'It's not her fault,' said Francesca looking at the floor, 'I needed a few things from home and besides; we had Ralph with us all the time. He'd have bitten the nuts off anyone who came too close.' She looked up with appealing eyes, and continued, 'I gave her no choice in the matter – I told her that as I'm not under arrest I can come and go as I please.'

Saxon didn't only find it hard to be angry with Francesca…he found it impossible. Besides, he was so pleased to have her safely back in the station, he had trouble hiding his pleasure. He tapped his pencil on the edge of the desk and did his best to look annoyed.

'Well, please don't go off like that again… I worry about you,' he said shyly. 'So if you do need to go anywhere, tell me, and I will go with you.'

'I'm flattered – it's been a long time since anyone worried about me. It's rather a nice feeling.' She gave Saxon a lingering smile.

Ian Dowling, knocking on the door, broke the spell. 'Yes, Sergeant, what can I do for you?' Saxon said trying not to gaze at Francesca in such a goofy manner.

'Sorry, Commander, Jake Dalton in interview room one, for his six o'clock appointment.'

Saxon slumped down opposite Dalton and lit a cigarette. 'I know I should quit, but I've got a lot on my plate... It helps.' Saxon squared up some notes that he had on the table. He paused tentatively; then he stubbed out his cigarette after a couple of drags.

'The reason I've asked you here is going to come as a shock to you.'

'You have my attention, Paul – fire away.'

'How do you get on with Dr Clarke?'

'Okay, but why do you ask?' He thought for a second. 'Now, wait a minute – you can't be suggesting that he's now your next suspect.'

'When you hear what Sergeant Parker and I saw this afternoon I think you'll agree that he's our man.' Saxon had a way of communicating matters of a serious nature without trying too hard.

'You're not bullshitting me are you. I can tell – you're deadly serious aren't you?'

'I haven't got time for bullshitting anyone, Jake. Parker and I went to Clarke's house and took a peek inside. Tell me, have you ever been to his house?'

'No, he's never invited me. In fact, he doesn't socialise with any of the staff. And tell me what was it you found in his house that makes you think it might be him?' Jake said with a hint of sarcasm in his tone.

'Oh that, yes it was the bodies in the cellar that did it for me, and I think Parker would agree with that.'

'Bodies...right.'

'Well, we didn't actually see any bodies, but it's evident that the floor in the cellar has been recently disturbed – and there's the smell. The smell, which you and I have sampled too many times in our careers – you know the one, the dead body smell. Now to move on a bit, did Clarke tell you where he would be going for his holiday?'

'Not a word, he never tells anyone where he goes – and he never sends postcards to the office.'

'If I give you a list of dates, could you tell me whether he was in the mortuary or not?'

'Sure can, but I'll need my diary to check it properly... I'm having trouble believing this. I've worked with the man for some years now and he always seemed so...'

'Normal,' added Saxon. 'That's the trouble, Jake, they always do. How about gays, has he ever mentioned gay people in conversation?'

Jake thought for a few seconds. 'Once, he talked about Steve Tucker and said that he shouldn't be working in the mortuary, because he was too bloody thick and he was a disgusting little shirt lifter. I was quite surprised when he said it because it was such a sudden outburst. Not his way to go about things normally. He's usually very calm about most things – loud occasionally, but that's only when he was feeling a bit theatrical.'

'Do you know if he has girlfriends?

'No, I don't think he has any – I don't think he ever got over the death of his wife.'

Saxon stood to stretch his legs and leaned against the wall. 'Yes we know all about his wife. But I only just found out about that today. I wish I'd known sooner. I'm sure that's what started him off on his killing spree.'

Jake helped himself to a drink from a water dispenser. 'I don't know if there's any more I can say that will be of use to you. If you think of anything I can do to help, you will let me know?'

'Of course... There are two things you could do which would be useful... I need a sample of his handwriting, because by the time I get pathology reports they are typed, and by the way, is he left- or right-handed?'

'He's both, I've seen him change hands often during a post

mortem.'

"Good, the other thing you will probably know is; does he have a laptop computer, and if so, what make is it and, where is it?'

'I'm pretty sure it's in the office and it's an Apple Macintosh Power Book.'

Saxon was starting to feel as though he'd chosen the right career again. 'Thanks, Jake. Parker will meet you at your office later – say about 9.30 when it's dark – and pick up the computer and a sample of handwriting. Obviously, if Clarke phones in to the office or tries to contact you in any way, try not to show that you know anything. We have evidence that he's still in the immediate area and is stalking someone he considers to be a hindrance to his "mission", as he calls it. But as far as I know, he doesn't realise we're on to him. I want it to stay that way. I don't want you to put yourself at risk – if you think he's on to you, don't hesitate – call me.'

'I think I can manage that, Paul. Strange to think it was him who burgled my apartment so that he could frame me,' said Jake as he made his way to the door. Saxon shook hands with him and suggested he leave by the back entrance.

Thursday, June 20, 9.30PM

Jake Dalton was apprehensive as he pulled into the mortuary car park. He noticed for the first time how dark the shadows were in the more badly lit areas. The small alleyway, where the rubbish bins were stored next to the side entrance, which the staff used, seemed to grow darker as he stood fumbling for the right key. Once through the door, he had to walk several paces to the light switch. Why didn't they put a switch by the sodding door? Then as the lab lights flickered on, he wondered if he was being watched again. He felt like a goldfish in a lit-up bowl. Quickly, he found the computer and a handwritten note that Clarke had made for his secretary to type for a pathology report.

As he looked around for a large envelope, he thought he heard a noise from the corridor. Or was it from the cupboard next to the door to the corridor? The hairs on the back of his neck started to prickle. He was fit but had never actually been involved in any kind of combat situation. *Will I be able to defend myself?* He quickly looked around for something that would make a suitable weapon. If he had been in the surgical theatre there would have been an ample choice of hardware such as knives, hammers and saws.

But where he stood there were only chairs. That would have to do. Lifting a chair over his head, he positioned himself next to the door. The noise from the corridor turned into footsteps getting louder – but he was ready…tense, but ready. Parker started to talk before he appeared in the doorway…lucky for him.

'You there, Jake… Oh, are you rearranging the furniture…and was that meant for me?'

'Sorry – just a tad jittery,' he said as he lowered the chair. Jake handed over the laptop and an envelope containing the note.

'Whatever you do, don't erase anything from it. There's months of information on that thing,' said Jake nervously.

'Don't worry,' replied Parker. 'The stuff I'm looking for will more than likely have been trashed. I've got some software that can retrieve information that's been deleted – providing nothing has been written over it, that is. We'll need to hang onto it for a few days at the most.'

Jake switched the lights out and they left together. Parker let Jake drive away first, neither of them noticed the man standing in the darkness of the alleyway.

Chapter 16

Thursday, June 20, 11.00PM

Saxon sat in the back of a transit van, parked in a muddy farm gateway two hundred yards along the lane from Clarke's house. The exterior of the van displayed an interesting series of mid-sixties floral designs. Honeysett had told him, before he left to go and rig up the camera, that he was thinking of getting it resprayed, because he was sick of the traffic cops stopping it for spot drug searches.

The interior had no affinity with the flower-power era whatsoever. High-tech listening and looking devices from floor to ceiling hummed quietly in the background, as he sat looking at a small monitor, which at that time showed nothing but static. When Honeysett positioned the camera, and switched it on, Saxon should see the front of Clarke's house, and with Saxon's guidance, would fine-tune the exact angle so that they would have a view of the garage and front door.

Honeysett didn't believe in using front gates – especially when there was a perfectly good tree to climb, which happened to be just the right height for the wall he intended to scale. He dropped almost silently behind some rhododendrons and waited for a minute without moving. Not that he thought he might have been heard, but he'd found through experience that if the lights didn't come on during the first minute, then it was okay to assume that there was nobody home, or that they were asleep.

He unclipped the night-vision goggles from his belt and slipped them on. There was no moon that night and certainly no street lamps close enough to be of any help – not that they would have helped. The whole point of that kind of operation; is not to be seen. He was never happier than when a certain amount of crawling around in the undergrowth was called for. It brought back memories of his army days.

The extensive lawn in front of the house hadn't been trimmed for some time, so it was important to keep to the edges. From the house, which was raised up slightly, anyone who looked out across the lawn would have seen his footprints the following morning, where he'd trampled on the grass. He made his way to the biggest fir tree and threw a rope up ten feet to the lowest branch, carefully, and without a sound, he hauled himself up and sat astride the branch. He opened his small rucksack and took out the camera, which was slightly larger than a cigarette box. Using thin plastic ties, he fixed it to the tree, called Saxon on his mobile for the final adjustments and shimmied down the rope.

Four minutes later, he was back in the van looking at the monitor, which displayed a grey picture with some detail picked out with a sort of greenish glow. Saxon studied the image. 'Is that as good as we get, Mike?'

'Afraid so, but it will be just like a normal picture when the lens switches over from night-vision during daylight. You get used to it after a while, and we don't need to worry about the batteries because it's solar powered.'

'How about the range, can we monitor it from Brighton nick?' said Saxon, hopefully.

'Not really, Commander, the signal won't reach that far. I'll drive along the road and find a quiet spot and keep my eye on things until daylight, then I'll get someone to relieve me.'

Saxon decided to walk down the lane to the town. He asked Honeysett to call Parker and tell him to pick him up by the yacht club. As Saxon opened the door to leave, Honeysett called him back. 'Have a word with traffic for me – tell them to keep away and not to turn up in the wee small hours banging on the side of my van…it frightens the shit out of me.'

Parker was waiting for Saxon by the time he found his way down the lane. He told Saxon about the computer and how he'd managed to run the software and retrieve everything that had been trashed from the hard disc.

'I've found the notes he keyed in regarding Mancini, and the one where he threatened you and Francesca.' Parker could hardly contain his elation.

'Parker, you are a fucking marvel – we've got the bastard, that's all the evidence we need; all we have to do now is find him... Francesca okay?' he added, trying not to sound too concerned.

'Don't worry, sir, she's safely tucked up in a cell for the night, and she can't go wandering off again, because I told the custody sergeant to lock her in,' he said, laughing to himself.

Saxon smiled at the thought of the one person he truly cared about, being securely locked up with good, honest decent criminals.

Back at the police station, Saxon sat in front of the laptop and read the two documents that Clarke had written. He yawned. It had been a long day and he still couldn't see an end in sight. He sipped black coffee as Parker copied the text from each document into Simple Text format, and moved the cursor up to the top of the screen. Under the menu, "Sound", he selected "Speak all", and there it was – the mechanical voice, the same as the three phone calls.

'What's more, sir, is that each of these documents has a date attached to them. The computer records when they were made. All we have to do now is contact the phone company, to find out when the first call was made from the marina to here. Then it's just a case of proving Clarke was out of his office at that time. He has to have been recorded on CCTV at some time.'

Saxon stood up and put his hand on Parker's shoulder. 'You've done some good work today – now go home and get some rest before anything else happens.'

Parker gladly agreed and started to head for the door, but stopped and turned. 'What are going to do, sir?'

'I'm just going to go to my apartment and get a change of clothes and a shower – check my messages and possibly get a bit of sleep.' He knew what Parker was going to say about that.

'I have to say, sir, with respect, that unless you have some kind of back-up, then that is about the most stupid thing I've heard, since I really don't know when.'

'I thought you might say that, but I can't see how we can draw him out into the open. You have to realise, he's got to believe that he can get to me without getting caught in the process. By all means, be in the area, but I know, Parker, that if he sees you, or anyone near me, then he won't make a move.'

'I don't like this one bit, sir. If you get attacked in your apartment, it would take me several minutes to get to you.'

'Give me a break, Parker, I'm not without a few physical attributes – I can defend myself you know…it's one of the many skills they teach us in the modern police service, you know.' He reached under his jacket and pulled out his gun. 'And I still have Big Bertha here, so don't worry – maybe he'll try to get lucky…and make my day.'

Parker was hesitant about leaving. But he knew how Saxon worked, and he was also well aware of how stubborn he could be if he thought he was being pushed around. He decided that an argument wouldn't solve the problem. And he thought maybe a night spent in the car munching on fast food and cigarettes, wasn't such a bad thing. Reluctantly he agreed.

'I'll be just around the corner, sir, if you need help press speed dial on your phone and I'll be there as fast as I can – just watch your back. That's all I can say. But I still don't fucking like it one bit.'

'Thanks, Parker, I'm a big boy now, so just go and don't worry.' Saxon gathered some papers from his desk and shoved them into his briefcase; he slipped his mobile phone into his trouser pocket. As he walked past the duty officer, he stopped for a second.

'Sergeant Dowling, please tell Miss Francesca Lewis that I will be back at about 7.30AM, and if she's been good she may get parole.'

Dowling laughed and said goodnight. Saxon walked slowly to his car, hoping more than anything that he was being watched. Such was his desire to catch Clarke, that he had lost almost all regard for his own safety. He pulled out of the station car park and took the coast road, along the promenade for about a mile, turned left, into the square and pulled up almost directly outside his building.

He gathered his things together, but didn't notice that his mobile phone had slipped out of his pocket and was nestled between his seat and the central console.

He walked to the door. His natural survival instincts, which were something that worked with his subconscious, didn't warn him of any immediate danger, but were working just the same, ticking over in the background of his mind. He punched in his entry code and the automatic lights came to life. He took the lift. Much too tired for the stairs. Slowly, it carried him to the top; he opened the metal concertina door and walked across the landing to his apartment. He was apprehensive…not everyone had a serial killer stalking them. He felt his fear – it was tangible. It was like a fog that seemed to surround him. He took comfort in the fact that he knew Francesca was safely locked up in a police cell. Quite frankly, he wouldn't have minded being in the same situation right now, particularly if he was in the same cell.

His keys seemed to have a mind of their own as he pulled them out of his pocket and dropped them on the floor. *Idiot*, as he bent down to pick them up. So far, so good, he'd made it to his front door and the killer hadn't appeared out of nowhere brandishing a knife.

'It's not going to be like it is in the movies,' he said out loud, as he entered his apartment.

Parker was sitting in his car eating a Big Mac, when his mobile rang.

'Yeff,' he said, struggling with a mouthful of fries.

'Parker, it's Inspector Honeysett here, I've tried Commander Saxon's mobile but he isn't answering, I've left a message on his voicemail. Do you know about the camera we set up to watch Clarke's house?'

'Go on, what's happened?' said Parker trying to swallow, as fast as possible.

'Well there've been developments. A light has come on in the house – there must be someone home.'

'I'm on my way. Keep trying Commander Saxon's number, He must be in the shower or something.' Parker hung up the phone and gunned the engine. He didn't bother to check the traffic, swinging his car round in a big arc across four lanes; causing at least two fender benders. But he didn't care, he was pleased that the commander was safe in his apartment; he knew that Saxon could take care of himself, but as always, he had more faith in his own physical abilities. He liked Saxon, and viewed him as a bit of a father figure. And as sure as hell, he didn't want any father figure of his getting into potentially dangerous situations. He'd leave Honeysett to keep trying to get through on the phone. Meanwhile, he would get to Clarke's house and sort the bastard out, once and for all.

Saxon was thrown sideways by the first blow, but managed to keep his balance. The pain was intense and he felt his right arm suddenly go limp. Even with the searing pain he was going through, he knew he was lucky that whatever had hit him had missed his head. The second blow was across his back, and he fell forwards onto the floor.

The lights were off, but there was enough ambient light for him to make out the shape of a person standing next to the door. Saxon rolled on his back as he hit the floor, so that at least he could use his legs to defend himself. As he rolled, he felt his gun press against his ribs – if only he could make his right arm respond so he could reach it. *Does he have a knife – what did he hit me with, and why, oh fucking why, can't I reach my fucking gun?*

The figure stood watching him. Saxon could just make out that he was holding what could have been a chair leg, and if that's what it was, then Saxon knew it had to weigh at least four pounds and a blow to his head would finish him. He kept as still as possible. Maybe Clarke thought he was unconscious. Time to play dead. The figure moved slowly across the room and switched on a small table lamp. Saxon immediately closed his eyes, enough so he looked as though he was no longer a threat. He could still see enough to realise that Clarke was naked, but covered with latex. He resembled a burns victim with ridges all over his body, where the latex had solidified before he'd managed to smooth it out properly.

Clarke paced back and forth, sucking and expelling air rapidly through the hole he had left in the latex. As he did so, he held what Saxon could now see was indeed a heavy chair leg. He continually used it to beat the palm of his left hand, making a loud thud, which under normal circumstances would have been painful. After a minute, Clarke started to speak – quietly to begin with, but clearly with barely suppressed rage, occasionally struggling to find the words.

'Why couldn't you just leave me alone – why did you make me do this? I didn't want this, Paul. You are not one of them…this will go against me. You don't understand…' He paused, then continued, whispering, 'I will be made to suffer for this. He will be angry with me. So angry!' he screamed as he started to smash everything near to him, thrashing around wildly with the chair leg.

Saxon decided to use the noise, and the fact that Clarke was no longer looking at him, to move slightly. His left shoulder was partially obscured by his coffee table. Carefully, he started to move his left hand up toward the shoulder holster. Clarke, without warning stopped his destruction spree and walked quickly to Saxon, who instantly froze. *Shit this is it*, as he held his breath – but ready to move if the need arose.

Clarke leant over him, pointing the chair leg at Saxon as if he had no control over it. He screamed down at Saxon. 'You had no fucking idea what you were getting into.'

Clarke turned away for a second, giving Saxon another chance to move his hand closer to his gun. He knew that to try for a sudden grab at the holster, to release the safety strap could fail if he couldn't manoeuvre his left hand up quickly enough. Before Clarke turned, he managed to feel the strap and left his hand there – waiting for the next opportunity. Clarke didn't turn. He stood facing the wall and started to talk again. 'You don't know how lucky you are now…of course you will never see the plague that is going to decimate mankind. I've saved you from that pain. Millions of innocent people are going to die because a few selfish sexual deviants pursue pleasure at any cost.'

Saxon saw his chance and took it. He flicked open the stud and released the strap. With one swift movement, he pulled his gun from the holster. The coffee table moved and Clarke turned, raising the chair leg over his head. His eyes blazed with surprise and he lunged forward. Saxon sat forward, pointing the gun at Clarke's chest.

'Don't!' yelled Saxon. 'Don't fucking move, Richard.'

Clarke stopped dead, mid-stride, but still held the chair leg over his head. He seemed to relax for a second, lowering his arm to his side. He dropped the leg to the floor and backed away a step.

'You don't seriously think you can stop me with that, thing, do you? There are forces at work here that you can't possibly comprehend… I can't die, Paul. You won't understand this but I am protected from death – until I've completed my mission… By all means, shoot if you wish, but it will do you no good, because my time has not come yet. I'll know when that time comes – and then I will take care of that little task.'

Saxon hauled himself up. He felt dizzy and lurched sideways to lean on the back of an armchair. The room appeared to be moving in circles. He knew that if Clarke rushed him he wouldn't stand a chance at the moment. *Play for time to get your head clear.* The feeling slowly started to return to his right arm. He kept his gun firmly pointed at Clarke, who walked over to one of the windows. He looked out over the square towards the sea.

He looked back at Saxon. 'I suppose that idiot lackey of yours, Detective Sergeant Parker, is out there somewhere waiting for you to call for help. But that's going to be difficult, as I've disconnected your telephone – and when I decide to kill you, there will be no time for you to use your mobile phone.' Saxon thought he saw Clarke smiling – he couldn't be sure because of the latex distorting his face.

Saxon felt his pockets for his mobile, realising swiftly that it was not there. A quick look around the floor told him that it must be either in the car or that he'd left it his office. What was he to do? His possible options raced through his mind. He had an injured right arm, no means of communication with Parker, or anyone in fact, and he was faced with a man who was physically fit and four inches taller than he.

If only he'd kept a pair of handcuffs in his apartment. He looked around with the chance that he may have something he could tie Clarke up with, but there was nothing. He'd just have to hope Clarke would see reason and just give up. Though, he knew that wouldn't happen.

Unknown to Saxon, Clarke had taken a carving knife from the kitchen while he lay in wait for Saxon to return. That knife was hidden behind the curtain a few inches from his hand, which was slowly but surely, moving towards it.

Suddenly, Clarke went for it. Saxon, in his concussed state was taken by surprise and was slow to respond. It was an automatic reflex that fired the gun causing his aim to go off centre. The bullet entered Clarke's right chest just below his collarbone. For a moment he stood, his eyes staring with disbelief as the blood travelled over his skin, but under the latex. As it spread down towards his waist, he quickly took the knife in his left hand and threw it at Saxon who dived out of the way. In the second it took Saxon to get to his feet, Clarke had disappeared through the door.

Saxon ran after him as fast as the pain in his back would permit. Considering he was running at one speed and Brighton at that moment was moving at a completely different one, he didn't do too badly, but Clarke was too fast for him. When Saxon burst through the front door and then down the steps and into the square he caught a glimpse of Clarke aggressively pushing some people out of his way. He then climbed into a large estate car and reversed out of the square into the main flow of traffic on the seafront. The wheels screamed – sending clouds of smoke into the air as a van careered into the back of Clarke's car.

Saxon hesitated to be sure of Clarke's direction of travel. Then he rushed to his Land Rover and found his mobile.

Parker drove past the entrance to Clarke's house. He continued along the lane until he found Honeysett's van. It had to be the right one. It could be a very small hippy commune, or it could be a police surveillance vehicle in disguise. Whoever was inside, Parker needed to know quickly, so he banged his hand on the side. Honeysett poked his head out through the window looking just a bit annoyed.

'Sergeant, next time please take the time to phone me – rather than give me a sodding heart attack. Now, get your arse in here and take a look at the screen.'

'Sorry, Inspector,' he said peering at the monitor. 'I can see that there is a light on – have you actually seen anyone moving about in the house, or is that it…just a light?'

'That's it, but it stands to reason there must be someone in there,' said Honeysett as if it were the most obvious thing in the world.

'Not necessarily,' muttered Parker. 'But I'd better take a look.' Honeysett gave him a pair of night-vision goggles and slipped his own on. 'Follow me,' he said, after he locked the van and started to jog off down the lane. He took the same route as on his last visit, with Parker following behind. Soon they were at the side of the house.

The room with the light was the one where Saxon had broken a small pane to let him in. Parker removed his goggles and carefully looked in. When he was satisfied that there was nobody home, he quietly opened the window for a better look. Then he saw what he had suspected. A standard lamp in the far corner – it was the only light burning, and was plugged into a timer switch.

'Shit,' said Parker. 'I had a funny feeling things weren't going to go smoothly tonight. Did you manage to get Commander Saxon on the phone?'

'No, I didn't. All I got was voicemail, and his landline just kept ringing.'

Parker raised his voice. 'With respect, sir, why the fuck didn't you call me? And how long, and how many times did you ring him?'

'Don't use that tone with me, Sergeant – just remember your rank,' he said sternly.

'Fuck my rank – just tell me for Christ's sake,' Parker shot back.

'Well, if you must know, I rang six or seven times over a period of about forty minutes.'

Parker looked up to the stars. 'And you didn't think that maybe that's rather a long time for anyone to take a shower?' he shouted back as he ran off to his car.

Parker was speeding along the coast road, back to Brighton, with his lights flashing but no siren, when he noticed the car travelling in the opposite direction. The driver had switched his lights to full-beam and as far as Parker could tell, was veering from one lane to another. He could identify some cars at night by their headlights, and he was sure that it was a Volvo. Traffic could sort that one out. Then he noticed another car close behind it, and he recognised the way the lights were flashing, alternating with the sidelights.

The pit of his stomach churned…could it be… Then his mobile rang.

'Parker, at last – where are you?'

Relief. Saxon was okay. 'I'm on the coast road heading back to Brighton.' He could hear the sound of Saxon's car in the background. 'Is that you going the other way – chasing what I thought was a Volvo?'

'Yes, it's Clarke – he must have hired it and dumped his own car somewhere. I don't think there's much chance of him stopping for us – so let's stick with him… I think he's going home.'

Parker found a gap in the central reservation and swung onto the opposite carriageway. Saxon filled him in on the events of the evening as they sped along. Saxon called the control room and asked for backup. He told them not to try to stop the suspect – at least if they let him get to his house, he would have nowhere else to go.

Clarke didn't stop to open his gates – he crashed through them, sending them flying along the gravel drive. He drove on, too fast for the bends up to the house, ending up skidding across the grass sideways and eventually slowing to a halt at the foot of the steps by the main door.

He fell out of the car – weakened by the loss of blood. Almost every part of his skin underneath the latex was now covered in it. The only place it hadn't seeped was his left arm. He had no key because they were in his clothes, which he'd left in Saxon's apartment.

In his rage, he felt no pain; taking a few steps back from the door, he launched himself at it with all his strength. It took two attempts before the door surrendered with a loud cracking sound and he fell into the hallway. The pain from the gunshot made itself known, causing him to wince as he half crawled across the floor. The hall was big – the door he wanted to get to appeared to move further and further out of reach. He knew he would make it, though…he had to.

Saxon didn't bother to use the driveway. As his Land Rover was designed to go off-road occasionally, why not make the most of it?

Inspector Honeysett appeared out of nowhere…an action, which could have caused his head to be blown off, if Saxon and Parker had drawn their guns at that moment.

'Sorry, Commander, I heard what was going on via the radio but by the time I managed to get up here he'd already managed to get inside the house – otherwise I'd have grabbed him.'

They all turned and looked back towards Brighton. From where they stood, they could just make out the flashing blue lights in the distance.

'Backup's a good few minutes away yet – it could be too late if we wait for them – let's go and get him. Believe me, he won't negotiate,' said Saxon.

Guns drawn, they walked in through the door. The lights in the hall were off. The only light source available was coming from the headlights of their cars shining through the doorway. To their right, a closed door showed light creeping underneath.

'That's the room with the timer switch,' whispered Honeysett, 'but that one over there wasn't lit earlier.'

Straight ahead was the door to the piano room. Saxon and Parker ran forward and stopped either side of the doorway. Honeysett moved forward and gently turned the crystal handle – moving out of the way as the door was allowed to swing open. Saxon cautiously looked into the room, which was dimly lit by a small table lamp on the piano.

The first thing that struck all three of them, as the door opened, was the smell. The smell that greets you every time you stop at a garage for a top-up. Petrol. The floor was flooded with it.

Clarke sat at the piano. He was dripping with petrol. In his hand, he held a lighter, and with his other hand, he was turning all the photographs of his late wife towards the three policemen. He lifted his head slowly and looked at them, barely able to speak through the massive loss of blood. His voice rasped. 'This is why I did it – to get Helen back... He promised I would have her back, if I sent him enough dirty souls. Do you think I sent enough, Paul?'

Saxon started to move Parker and Honeysett back through the door, and shouted, 'Down on the floor!'

Clarke flicked the lighter and turned the room into hell – the flash blowing out the windows and a pall of flame shooting through the door and into the hallway. Fortunately, Saxon and his colleagues were well out of the line of fire. When the initial blast had subsided sufficiently, Saxon took a brief look into the room before following the other two out of the house. He couldn't be sure, but it appeared that Clarke was still sitting at the piano. He appeared to be melting.

Saxon waited around until daylight, as did Parker. The fire brigade did a good job of controlling the fire in time to save vital evidence. Not that there was anyone to arrest. The forensics people started digging up the bodies from the cellar – there were five. They were all identified eventually. All of them were intravenous drug users, who lived rough on the streets of London. All of them were HIV positive – two girls, and three young men.

Parker drove home to his wife and children with a story that he wouldn't be able to tell the kids, until they were a lot older.

Saxon went home to clean himself up and then dropped into the police station to see Francesca. He woke her up with a cup of tea and a bowl of porridge, causing a great deal of laughter from the custody sergeant.

She looked up at him, still drowsy, but very pleased to see him.

'You have a bruise on the side of your face,' she said, touching his face gently. 'Have you had an interesting night?'

Saxon smiled. 'You could say that.'

Emma still hadn't bothered to phone... But what the hell.

A Taste of the next book

GONE

A small crowd had gathered on the beach. They couldn't see a thing from where they stood. Commander Paul Saxon couldn't help but wonder why they would want to be there in the first place. Why force yourself to gaze at something so gruesome? It didn't seem to matter how many policemen over the years repeated the words, "Move along, there's nothing to see." They always did want to see. No matter how awful the sight was, they always had to try and see.

Maybe these people had the kind of vision that vultures had – the dead-flesh-seeking kind. Maybe they saw a plume in the sky from miles away, which made them want to circle the prey and then with a bit of luck, maybe even get a peck at it.

The people stood in a tight huddle, like sheep that had been rounded up by dogs. None of them able to think for themselves, just a quick dash forward periodically for a quick peek, a visual peck, because they were nervous of being barked at and sent back behind the invisible line marked out by the policeman's arms.

Saxon had parked his Land Rover on the boat slipway of Downderry Village, on the south coast of Cornwall, and was more than halfway through the long walk along the beach. It was high tide, which made walking tiresome; at least he would have had some hard sand to walk on if the tide had been out, instead of one-step-forward, half-a-step-back shingle.

Black Headed Gulls screamed overhead as if trying to frighten the people below away, so they could hack away at the corpse. After all, they probably saw it first – and anything washed up on the beach was lunch as far as they were concerned.

It took almost ten minutes to reach Bass Rock, but there was not much point in complaining – the sea isn't fussy where she gives up her dead and certainly not helpful to policemen. Saxon had to climb over Bass Rock and down the other side into a deceptively large bay. From his vantage point on the rock, the bay appeared small but that was an illusion caused by the vast cliffs towering over the beach. Two hundred yards further on stood the two small crowds of people. One crowd standing around a body, and the other crowd trying to get closer to the body.

Saxon approached the person who seemed to be in charge and started to take out his warrant card. The man didn't give him a chance to speak.

'Please, sir, just go away and stand over there with the other ghouls. We are a bit busy in case you hadn't noticed.' The man turned to one of the uniforms and told him to get rid of the intruder. Saxon held his ID in the face of the constable, who stopped dead. 'Inspector Warrender, I think you had better take a look at this gentleman's, I mean, commander's warrant card.'

The magic words "warrant card" and "commander" had the usual effect. Warrender turned abruptly. 'Who are you then?' he said as he read the card. 'Oh, sorry, Commander, I didn't realise – my superintendent never told me you'd be coming.'

Saxon smiled, 'Superintendents can be a pain sometimes.'

He took a closer look at Saxon's ID, as he shook hands with him. 'I've heard of the Serial Crimes Unit. I guess the name speaks for itself.'

'Yes, we're based in New Scotland Yard; we keep our eyes peeled for any suspicious deaths nationwide that could be linked. Most of our time is spent looking at computer screens – until we find a case that interests us of course.' Saxon paused to take in the scenery, then he continued, 'I understand that this is the fourth body you've had washed up around here in the last two months. You could say, that whoever's doing it, could be developing a taste for his hobby – wouldn't you agree, Inspector?'

'I have to agree, it's starting to look that way. But I have a question for you, Commander…why can't they leave it to us to sort out? It's a bit demeaning to have you people appearing out of nowhere to give us a hand – with respect, sir, I think we can cope quite well on our own… No offence intended,' he added nervously.

'None taken, Inspector. Tell me – how many serial killers have you or your squad traced, or even come into contact with in the last ten years?'

Warrender hesitated, and raised his eyebrows. 'Well, none actually.'

'Okay, case rested – can we take a look at the body now?'

Inspector Charles Warrender was a tall, dark-haired man, in his mid-thirties with a wind-dried face and a year-round tan. He wore a tweed jacket and corduroy trousers, which gave him more the appearance of a schoolmaster rather than a police inspector.

He led the way to the body, which had been dragged a short distance up the beach and covered with plastic. He nodded to one of the uniforms to pull back the sheet.

'Brace yourself, Commander – he's not very pretty.'

Saxon put on a pair of rubber gloves and knelt down beside the body. Warrender was right. The man was bloated and wouldn't have been recognisable to his own mother. His mouth was open, making it obvious that his teeth had been pulled out. A patch of skin had been neatly cut from his right forearm. His hands were missing. He was trussed up like a pig for the BBQ, but his ties had come loose and he had popped to the surface.

Warrender crouched down next to Saxon. 'The others were in the same sort of condition. We've still got the bodies in the morgue, and if you think he looks bad – wait until you see the others. All of them have a severe wound to the back of the head.'

'Shot?'

'No, the pathologist reckons...'

About the Author

Stuart Davies has already been in print in Geographical magazine, as the bug man in Costa Rica – a memorable experience both for Stuart and for the insects he encountered.

Well and truly bitten by the writing bug as a result, Stuart has now ventured into the world of crime with his first novel, *Saxon*. Crime detection has always been a passion of his, but as an interested observer rather than a participant, you understand. Before granting himself some time in order to pursue a literary career, Stuart worked for umpteen years in the publishing world, as Design Editor at *Country Life*, and most recently as Art Director at *Geographical*.

Stuart now lives in France designing books, painting landscapes and working on the *Saxon Chronicles*, which will pit Paul Saxon and his colleagues against a number of villains.

At Roundfire we publish great stories. We lean towards the spiritual and thought-provoking. But whether it's literary or popular, a gentle tale or a pulsating thriller, the connecting theme in all Roundfire fiction titles is that once you pick them up you won't want to put them down.